IN
THE
HANDS
OF
WOMEN

IN
THE
HANDS
OF
WOMEN

A NOVEL

JANE LOEB RUBIN

ISBN: 978-1-68512-346-8

Cover art by Level Best Designs

This book was professionally typeset on Reedsy.
Find out more at reedsy.com

To my family, writing partners, and all those who inspire hope.

Praise for In the Hands of Women

"Rubin has written a fascinating novel, well-paced and brimming with historical detail. It's 1905 in New York City, a time and place of dramatic social changes. Hannah Isaacson has graduated from a major university with an MD in obstetrics but faces widespread discrimination as a professional woman. She encounters chronic antisemitism, realistically depicted. One can't help cheering her on as she fights for decent health care for women, for equality within the medical profession, and for respect in her own personal relationships. Ultimately, *In the Hands of Women* is a compelling and heartwarming historical novel."—Libby H. O'Connell, Chief Historian Emeritus, History Channel, and author, *The American Plate*

"Vividly written and meticulously researched, *In the Hands of Women* is a gripping story of female friendship, the challenges women doctors faced in the early 1900s, and the noxious impact of antisemitism. Young obstetrician Hannah Isaacson returns home to her beloved sister and to a job at New York City's Mount Sinai Hospital in 1905 after becoming one of the first female graduates of the Johns Hopkins Medical School. But Hannah's passion for helping pregnant women–at a time when birth control and abortion were illegal–puts her life at risk and leads to high-stake confrontations with her fiancé and some of New York's most powerful men. I lost myself in this novel as I followed Hannah from high-society restaurants and lower East Side tenements to New York City's hospitals and jails ... And I cheered for her every step of the way. I'm crossing my fingers Jane Rubin is working on her next tale starring Hannah, her family, and friends."—Mally Becker, Agatha Award-nominated author of *The Turncoat's Widow* and *The Counterfeit Wife*

"Jane Rubin's stunning debut, *In The Hands Of Women*, is historical fiction at its best. Hannah Isaacson, a young doctor at Mount Sinai Hospital is a force, fighting for women's healthcare in the early 1900's. She confronts antisemitism and demands equal treatment in her professional and personal life. With empathy, Rubin takes us through the travails of the medical system when poor women had little access to good maternity care. Her impeccable research weaves the subjects of midwifery and abortion within the intricacies of the twentieth century class system in New York. Rubin's characters stay with me. They're compassionate, smart, and strong. Reading this page-turner gave me more than a thrilling read. It gave me a lesson on history and how we can do better. I couldn't put it down."—Julie Maloney, author and director of *Women Reading Aloud*, an international writing organization

"A rallying cry from the past to women of today to defend our rights, especially our medical ones—and a reminder of the horrors that can occur when we don't. An immaculately researched and immersive debut novel."—Michelle Cameron, award-winning author of *Beyond the Ghetto Gates*, https://michelle-cameron.com

———

I

Part 1

1900 – Baltimore

Chapter One

"Push! Stop the damn screaming!" Dr. Adams shouted at Mrs. Everly. He twisted his head to me. "My Pa's dairy cow birthed quieter than her!"

My ears stung from his insult, but I kept my composure. "She's doing her best. It's her first." Clean towels in hand, I waited to receive the newborn. Why did he feel it necessary to degrade her? What did Dr. Adams know about a woman's pain?

Another anguished shriek. "I can't take it any longer."

The nurse mopped her forehead. "You're doing fine, Mrs. Everly. Keep up the good work."

"One last push! Head's out. And for heaven's sake, stop screaming," Dr. Adams admonished, wiping the sweat from his brow. "How am I supposed to concentrate?"

The nurse helped Mrs. Everly lean forward. "Bear down again. Almost there."

"I can't," she cried.

Ignoring her words, Dr. Adams commanded back, "Now! Push harder... shoulders are out...damn it, nurse, keep her legs in the stirrups! Here it comes, and... it's a boy." His face relaxed, visibly relieved the ordeal was over.

The nurse helped our patient lay back in the disheveled bedding, adjusting the damp pillows behind her head. "Very good, dear."

"Isaacson, get over here!" Dr. Adams ordered.

"I'm right next to you," I answered calmly, grasping the squealing, slippery baby from his filmy hands. I wrapped the child in a warm white towel, gently clearing the mucous and blood from his tiny face as his crying quelled.

Stepping to the mother's side, I carefully set the newborn in her eager arms. "Here you go, Mrs. Everly. Meet your little boy." I watched the anxious lines on her forehead melt as she cuddled her infant. "Such a brave job, both of you."

Dr. Adams snorted. Barely taller than my short frame but twice the width, he had a fiery disposition. Balding, with deeply rutted acne scars, his poor looks matched his personality. I was assigned to work with him for the next few weeks; every day was a challenge. I'd yet to encounter him in a pleasant mood.

"Finish up here, Isaacson. Patient will pass the afterbirth. Catch it, no tugging." Dr. Adams stepped to the sink to scrub his hands and arms. "Nurse, take the baby and wipe him clean. I'll tell the father he's got a son. Lucky devil."

Heat rose to my cheeks. Like so many men, Adams was ready to congratulate the father rather than recognize the painful work of the mother. I moved to his chair at the foot of the table and glanced up at Mrs. Everly. She looked from the baby into my eyes, and an exhausted smile crossed her face. She mouthed, *thank you.*

Now in my third year of medical school, I was fully prepared to deliver babies. I'd assisted on dozens of births both with midwives and doctors. And I'd observed that, in more cases than not, a good deal of the screaming came from male physicians made irritable and impatient by the mothers' labors.

Once the delivery room door closed behind Dr. Adams, I was the senior clinician in charge. "Nurse, hold off a few minutes. First, help baby latch onto Mama's breast. That'll make the afterbirth easier to pass."

The nurse nodded and guided the baby onto his mother's nipple. Within moments, the placenta and remaining pregnancy tissue slid from her body, filling the pan propped on the stool in front of me. My dear mentor back home in New York, Dr. Boro, had always cautioned, "Don't tamper with Mother Nature. That's when most trouble begins." One of his earliest lessons had been how effective nursing right after birth helped coax out the afterbirth.

"Good job, Mrs. Everly. I'll clean you up, and you can watch the nurse give your son his first bath."

* * *

Hours later, in the Women's Ward, I checked each of my patients. There were twenty-four iron-framed beds, arranged evenly around the perimeter of the large room. Each was separated by a thin curtain and contained a small table and chair for visitors. New mothers were placed together on the left side of the room, where Mrs. Everly rested in Bed Four, while other ailments were bedded on the right.

"How are you feeling?" I asked the newest of our mothers.

Still fighting her way through the residual anesthesia, she shifted her doe-like eyes my way. "I think I'm fine. Don't remember too much."

"Any pain, discharge? Have you gotten out of bed?" I lifted her chart hanging from the metal frame at the foot of the bed.

"Not yet, but I'd like to use the commode, Nurse."

"I'm a doctor in training, but I'll need a nurse to help me support you, just in case you feel light-headed." I signaled to Nurse Hammond, who sat at the end of the ward, a stout, middle-aged woman with a tight bun scarcely harnessing her grey frizzy hair. I pulled the privacy drapes around the bed and wheeled in a commode.

"A doctor, you say? How unusual." Mrs. Everly twisted into a sitting position, draping her legs over the side of the bed.

Nurse Hammond slipped through the curtain, repositioning her nursing cap, its design unique to Johns Hopkins. "I couldn't help but hear. Dr. Isaacson is heaven-sent. In a million years, men could never understand what women go through. You're lucky she was assigned to you."

I was surprised by Nurse Hammond's support. "Why, thank you." I'd often observed her watching me critically while I worked and assumed she was waiting for me to make a mistake. *Jumping to conclusions again, Hannah.*

Moments later, we helped Mrs. Everly back into bed and sponge-bathed her lower body, replacing her cotton pads.

"Feeling refreshed?" Nurse Hammond asked.

"Much better. I had no idea I'd be so sore afterwards."

So many new mothers were dismally ill-prepared for childbirth. It was a constant challenge, particularly for first-time mothers. Almost without fail, they hadn't been seen by a midwife or doctor until the last weeks of their pregnancies.

"Every day, you'll feel a little more like yourself. Be patient. Have you nursed your baby again?" I asked.

She looked at her chest. "I shouldn't have before. I'll need binding. My husband's forbidden it. He's hiring a wet nurse. Doesn't want my figure ruined."

Was it shame or disappointment on her face?

I stiffened, recalling memories of my older sister, Tillie, singing nursery rhymes to my niece, Miriam, as she nursed her.

Medical students were told, in no uncertain terms, not to interfere or attempt to influence our patients about nursing their infants. Nurse Hammond, who knew my feelings, changed the topic. "Miss Isaacson is one of twenty or so women training to be doctors here at Johns Hopkins. We're proud our medical school joined this modern effort."

"I wasn't aware," the patient said.

Nurse Hammond continued. "It must be getting close to seven or eight years since the program started. I don't recall exactly. What a difference it's made." She pulled the covers up to Mrs. Everly's shoulders, smoothing the top. "They're quite smart doctors, all of them."

"Thank you, Nurse. It's good to hear you say that." I answered gratefully. I knew the decision to accept women had been controversial. For centuries, medicine had been an exclusive men's club. In most places, it still was. For the first time, I noticed warmth in the nurse's grey eyes as she smiled at me.

Nurse Hammond filled the pitcher with fresh water and set it by Mrs. Everly's bed. "Try to relax now. You worked hard today and earned a rest. And don't forget to drink your water."

We left the patient's bay and walked to the end of the ward, where I sat behind a large, worn oak table, laid out my patients' charts, and began writing notes with the ballpoint pen my sister, Tillie, had sent to me as a gift. She had a passion for new inventions, especially those that reduced mess and staining.

Nurse Hammond cleared her throat. "Can I ask why you chose to study medicine?"

I looked at her curious face, framed with creases around her eyes, belying her youthful appearance. Having worked as a nurse for decades, she was the most experienced nurse on the unit. "There were so many reasons. My sister pushed me to study hard and continue my education. And my local doctor, Dr. Boro, held our community together through thick and thin with his fine care. In high school, he took me under his wing and let me follow him on house calls." I silently reflected, recalling how upset I was at my first deathbed, but pulled myself together when I saw Dr. Boro's composure. And the joy of seeing women deliver babies was exhilarating. "He showed me many ways to help patients heal. The entire community depended on him."

Nurse Hammond's smile deepened. "He sounds like a fine inspiration. You have many of those same gifts despite your youth. I'm certain big things are in store for you." She gazed toward the patients' beds. "Time for me to get back to work." Nurse Hammond circled back to her patients, methodically attending to them one by one.

Her encouraging words were energizing, giving me the lift I needed to finish my notes. I carried the stack of completed charts into the patient ward, hanging each on its corresponding bedframe. Waving good night to Nurse Hammond, I gathered my cloak and left the ward. As I descended the steps to the lobby, a nearby church bell chimed nine in the evening. At long last, time to go home.

The hospital was quiet, its daytime commotion evaporating as visitors, doctors, and staff left. Patients settled in for the night. Any overnight emergencies would be handled by medical students and residents.

Walking through the quiet corridor, my footsteps echoing, *rat tap, rat tap,*

I thought of the heart-wrenching reasons I chose medicine that I hadn't shared with Nurse Hammond. I'd lost too many members of my family to disease. My mother died while I was still in diapers, and within the year, Papa married my stepmother, Rebecca. But ever since I could remember, I lived with my sister, Tillie, and her husband, in the Lower East Side of New York City.

Months before I moved in with Tillie, she had given birth to twins, and the smaller, Sarah, perished during a flu epidemic. Although I barely recalled baby Sarah, who shared Mama's name, I absorbed Tillie's grief. As Tillie recovered from her loss, I depended on our neighbors, whose daughter, Eva, quickly became my playmate and dearest friend.

In high school, Eva died from consumption before my eyes, and I slid into a sea of grief. But Dr. Boro helped me channel that anguish into the study of medicine. A giant in my small world, he was brilliant and compassionate. In his customary big-hearted way, he coached me through the most grueling courses in both high school and at Barnard College.

But choosing obstetrics came later, after the delivery of my sister's daughter, Miriam. After a childhood of loss, Miriam's birth restored my belief in the miracle of life. Tillie allowed me to assist, helping our local midwife. When I wrapped the infant in her first blanket and met those searching eyes, I knew my destiny was in obstetrics.

I was one of a handful of women attending Johns Hopkins Medical School in Baltimore, and always under scrutiny. Those of us who made it through the rigorous admissions process were treated as an experiment. Most men doctors expected us to fail, viewing us with doubt, believing we lacked their sturdy disposition. Sadly, some of the nursing staff agreed. I spent every minute of every day in the hospital, proving them wrong. Determined to rise above their expectations, my dream was to return home and find an obstetrical post at Mount Sinai Hospital in New York City.

Chapter Two

The gas lamps glowed, casting their light through the mist, dimly illuminating the sidewalk. Within a few blocks, I arrived at my rooming house on Madison Street. The home, an older three-story Victorian, was a replica of others on the block. Stacked like doll houses, they had gabled roofs, rounded towers, and large windows—charming, but eerie for anyone with an active imagination. The brick and wood exterior were in dire need of repair, while the trim was shattered to pieces, a haven for nesting squirrels.

Mine was the only women's boarding house I could locate close to the medical school that had streetlamps nearby. Tillie had insisted on a house with outdoor lighting, knowing I'd be walking home from the hospital alone at night.

Rotten floorboards creaked as I stepped onto the once ornate wrap-around porch, the gingerbread latticework absent slats here and there. I slid my key in the rusty knob, knowing Mrs. Collins would call to me any moment. My landlady had the ears of a hound.

I removed my shoes on the threadbare runner by the door and carried them, dripping, to the fireplace to dry. The hand-knotted carpets and interior were a vestige of the original European furnishings from the home's early days of splendor. Hanging my blue wool cloak on the mahogany rack above my shoes, I walked through the parlor into the dining room. A long oak table with ten chairs filled the space. Seven other boarders, not counting Mrs. Collins, lived and ate breakfast and dinner in the house. It was a snug fit when we were all at home, but the dining room, designed for a large family seemed to inhale, making room for everyone at mealtime.

Stained damask fleur-de-lis wallpaper in light blues and greens covered the parlor and dining room walls, adding a hit of past refinement. Sadly, the furniture suggested the opposite. The torn and lumpy chairs and sofa were in sore need of reupholstering, and the dining room table was deeply scratched from years of serving as both a meal and sewing table.

Mrs. Collins swept into the dining room from the kitchen. "'Tis you, Hannah? Have you had your supper?" she asked in her heavy brogue.

"Not yet, but shouldn't you be asleep? It's almost ten."

"I can't fall asleep till you're home. Now that my children are grown, I need to worry after someone."

I swung my arm around Mrs. Collins's stout body and squeezed. "That's fine with me." Although I sometimes found Mrs. Collins overbearing, I appreciated her sincere interest and protectiveness toward all the girls in her boarding house.

She was a window in her early fifties, having lost her husband to a heart attack years earlier. Left with the house and her husband's gambling debts, she barely got by. Following a year of mourning and with no romantic prospects in sight, she decided to convert her aging home to living quarters for female students at Johns Hopkins.

In true form, she repeated, "Are you hungry? I kept a pot of soup on the stove for you."

"A bowl of soup would be perfect. It's been a long day."

"Of course. It's only a simple potato vegetable soup, nothing to keep you from a sound sleep." She studied my face. "You look tired, dear. I'll sit and keep you company."

Moments later, Mrs. Collins waddled into the dining room, holding a steaming bowl of soup. The aroma immediately triggered my stomach. She scurried back to the kitchen to retrieve warm soda bread and her cup of tea, sitting across the table from me. "Eat while it's hot."

I smiled at her cheerful face. "This is heavenly. Exactly what I need."

Her bright blue eyes and high cheekbones suggested a long-gone beauty. Cooking for her boarders, I imagined she'd grown heavy with constant sampling, adding an additional chin to her round face and flesh to her underarms and belly. That ivory skin, probably flawless in her youth, was now heavily lined, paper thin. Despite her heft, it was common knowledge among the girls that she spent considerable time every morning applying her special creams, arranging a tight bun, and ironing her dress to appear presentable to her boarders, as well as any friends who might happen to visit. Mrs. Collins set a clear example of how a lady should comport herself. Of course, she ultimately wanted us to set the correct impression to snare a smart, wealthy husband.

"I knew you'd be hungry," she said, satisfied at my obvious enjoyment of the simple meal. "How was your day at the hospital? Anything interesting?"

"We delivered a beautiful little boy this afternoon, but the father forbade his wife to nurse. I can't imagine why."

She tsked, "I hear that's the new fashion for the wealthy. The up-and-coming men want their women sent right back into society and their marital bed, just like royalty. A shame."

I filled my spoon with soup, holding it up to cool. "I hope it goes out of favor soon. It's sad. Nursing helps new mamas grow close to their babies, and being expected to instantly regain their shapes is far too much pressure for them. It takes months, nursing or not. Not to mention, nursing delays the next pregnancy."

Mrs. Collins became uncharacteristically silent, her eyes drifting to the crucifix on the wall. She crossed herself and continued. "If they don't nurse and get with child, they end up going to the midwives to take care of things." She shuddered, quickly genuflecting.

"What do you mean?" I set down my spoon, mystified.

She pursed her lips. "You're studying medicine, and ye don't know?"

I shook my head, peering into her eyes.

"Before quickening, these ladies see the midwives to end their pregnancies. Since they haven't felt the baby move yet, they believe there's no life, so no one minds if they rid themselves of the child. They call it 'relieving the female complaint' or 'loosening the obstruction.'" Mrs. Collins, flustered, set her teacup down with a clatter. "It's disgraceful! God will punish them, believe me."

"How do they know there's no life? I've heard heartbeats a full month before mamas feel movement." I thought about the mothers in the Maternity Clinic. Of course, I'd heard of abortion. Everyone in medical school knew about it. But I'd never seen it performed or treated a patient afterward. If it was as common as Mrs. Collins seemed to suggest, I wondered why.

"Those midwives will burn in hell for slaughtering those innocent lambs. I don't know how they live with themselves. The subject always spoils my day." Her jowls quivered.

"I know it's illegal, but perhaps the women have good reasons."

Mrs. Collins raised her voice. "It's against the law and immoral, but no one cares so long as the mother isn't injured. Too many mouths to feed in the city, and those fancy gadgets for blocking pregnancy are illegal. Those girls, hussies all of them, should learn to keep their legs crossed! That would put those evil midwives out of business for good." Mrs. Collins rose from the table and stormed into the kitchen, muttering, "Don't let me disturb your meal with such a terrible subject."

Disturbing or not, Mrs. Collins had given me a lot to think about. She was a reservoir of information when it came to the day-to-day lives of ordinary people. But I wondered why Marta, Dr. Boro's midwife, had never talked to me about abortions. Did she perform them too? Would I see them on my current obstetrics rotation?

Moments later, appearing calmer, Mrs. Collins returned, shifting the conversation to a different topic. "How did you come to live with your sister?"

Too exhausted for a long conversation, I shared a quick version. "Tillie was fourteen when my mother died after breast cancer surgery. Mama developed a fatal infection. I was still a tot and don't remember a thing about her, only the stories Tillie shared. My Papa remarried soon after, but my stepmother couldn't manage all his children. Tillie moved out and married at sixteen, and within a year, I moved in with her. She had just given birth to twins." I'd finished my soup and mopped the last of the broth with soda bread. Now, with a full stomach, fatigue engulfed me. I yawned.

"I'm so sorry, the soup was delicious. Let's talk more another night." I stood, reaching to clear my bowl and spoon.

"Oh no, I'll manage those. Tillie is a remarkable sister, an amazing story." Mrs. Collins jumped from her seat. "You go on up to your room and get a sound sleep. I'll have breakfast ready for you before seven."

I smiled. "You're a dear, but I'll be deep into patient rounding by then. Please don't wake early on my account."

"Then I'll leave you a sandwich in the icebox to take on your way out the door."

* * *

My room was on the second floor, two doors from the lavatory and wash basin. Four students rented small private rooms on my level, the other four on the third floor. At some point, Mrs. Collins had built walls within the original bedrooms, doubling the house's occupancy. While two of us were studying to be doctors, the other boarders were undergraduates. Elspeth Fletcher, my Scottish neighbor, was in her final year of medical school, a year ahead of me. Her room was adjacent to mine. As I reached the first landing, we bumped into each other.

"You're getting in late," Elspeth said, looking at her watch. "Not much time for a full night's rest."

I nodded. "There's endless work on the ward. I had a late delivery and wanted to make sure the mother was properly settled." I entered the lavatory and turned on the hot water.

Elspeth followed me, dropping her voice. "A few of us are meeting this weekend at a pub in Fells Point, you know, by the harbor. You're welcome to come. I hear the oysters are delicious." An impish smile grew on her face.

"Sure, but why the mischievous look? What are you up to?" I squinted my eyes at her reflection in the mirror above the sink.

"Some men in my class are coming, including a secret admirer of yours and my friend, Dr. Frank, whom I adore." She lifted her brows suggestively.

"That's ridiculous. None of the men are interested in me. I'm Jewish." I shrugged. "And right now, I'm too exhausted to care. Let's talk tomorrow."

Elspeth acknowledged my fatigue with a knowing nod. She knew exhaustion came with our lengthy shifts.

Lying in bed, feeling the full weight of the day, I thought about having a boyfriend. I came close in college, but each time, my ambition to study medicine got in the way. I was either in the library reviewing my textbooks rather than attending social events with the boys from Columbia University, or the men I met thought my choice of career unseemly for a woman. Despite being hurt by their attitudes, I'd forged forward, toiling too hard to allow narrow-minded men to stand in my way. Three years later, as a Jewish female medical student, there were few men at Hopkins suitable for courting.

But I imagined it would be pleasant having a husband. Working, living, loving, eventually making a family. Although I'd been kissed once in college, I wondered about those mysterious sensations beyond.

Chapter Three

Friday evening finally arrived, the end of my work week. Elspeth and I walked home from the hospital together and agreed it was high time for a night on the town. Happy to have a sympathetic ear, I recounted my hectic week with Dr. Adams.

"Every day, we had more births, a total of thirteen in just five days. They were non-stop. By this morning, I was ready to strangle him with my bare hands. He's rude to patients, unless, of course, the husband's around. Then he's sweet as honey." I huffed. "If the man hates birthing babies, he should find something else to do."

Elspeth's face took on a knowing turn. "I heard he needs the extra money to support a nurse who had his child. It's the worst-kept secret in the hospital. Maybe that's why…"

I pinched my face. "Ugh! I can't imagine anyone finding him attractive."

Elspeth threw her head back and laughed. "Love, the mystery of the ages."

I wasn't finished sharing my frustration. "We had a difficult breach birth on Thursday, and at the end, he said, 'That was the most challenge I've had on this miserable service all month. At least the kid was fine. Lucky it wasn't stuck in there any longer.' And he said it right in front of the mother. Can you imagine?"

"What did you do?"

"I changed the subject, and once the mother was taken to her room. I asked him what he enjoyed most in medicine."

Elspeth scoffed. "I'll bet he said *nothing*. I think he hates it all."

"No, listen to this. He said, 'Bones, broken bones. The more, the better.

Now, that makes the time pass fast.' His mood lifted, telling me a gory story about a boating collision in the harbor. Nine men were brought to the hospital with severe injuries. Then he said, 'The best was the femur fracture. The lower part of the bone stuck straight through the skin and pointed to the ceiling. The pain knocked the young man out cold.'"

"Was he able to set the bone?" Elspeth asked, her brows raised with curiosity. *Was she also excited by gore?*

"It was too far gone. He amputated and took the leg to the laboratory to practice reducing the fracture. He was so excited about it. No compassion for the patient whatsoever!"

"The man's crazy." Elspeth laughed. "He loves the blood. A few of the old-timers do."

I agreed. "Adams told me his old senior attending got his training in the Civil War, and that's how they treated compound fractures. The race was to get the leg off before infection set in. When I asked more about infection, he told me, 'Whoever solves that one will be set for life.' Then the bonehead said, "Any other brilliant ideas in that pretty, little Jew head of yours?" I rolled my eyes upward.

"Shake it off, Hannah. I hate to admit it, but I've been dealt with just as bad. It's tough being a woman here. They love to call me a 'doaty mick.' They've no idea how hard my family's worked to rise from poverty. And those dopes don't know the difference between Scots and Irish." She kicked a chunk of ice out of her way. "They don't take women seriously, think we're only here to get married to doctors, nothing more. But, you'll see, there are a few good men too."

I thought about Dr. Boro. *Of course, there must be more doctors like him.*

I began kicking chunks of ice too. Before long, we were playing like children, seeing who could kick the ice farthest, and as we did, my anger evaporated. "Who else are we meeting tomorrow night?"

I invited Julia and Penelope and four men from my class. I think they'll come, but you can't make a reservation at a pub, and who knows what the weather will be. So, we'll have to see tomorrow."

I was confused. "No reservations at a restaurant?"

She winked intriguingly. "It's an old pub called the Oyster House at Fells Point, not exactly a restaurant like you're used to. Lots of us go there for a good time. Just don't mention it at the house."

I hoped the restaurant served more than oysters. I'd never eaten one.

Mrs. Collins, who believed our characters and reputations were her responsibility, would have forbidden the outing. Meeting men for dinner unchaperoned in the dark of night was stepping far over the line of dignified lady-like behavior, at least in her eyes.

Elspeth was twenty-six, and although she was a top notch medical student, she was still pining for a husband. By far the smartest of her seven brothers and sisters in a working-class Scottish family from Pittsburgh, she was the only unmarried sibling. Her parents, pressured by one of Elspeth's teachers, grudgingly allowed her to attend college after she was awarded a full scholarship. She met her next mentor while an undergraduate in Philadelphia. Elspeth scored at the top of her college class four years in a row. Her mentor was so impressed that she introduced Elspeth to the female trustees at Johns Hopkins. They offered her another scholarship for the duration of medical school. None of her education had cost her family a cent.

As we approached the boarding house, Elspeth said, "Next week, I have my monthly dinner with the women trustees. They like to see I'm keeping my grades steady."

"What are the trustees like?"

"Intimidating!" Elspeth exhaled loudly. "I think they expect me to discover a cure for tuberculosis. It's a lot of pressure trying to deliver on their scholarship."

Elspeth piqued my curiosity. "What would you like to do when you finish?" My dream job was an appointment to the medical staff at Mount Sinai, working beside the esteemed physicians of New York City.

"Of course, I want to practice medicine, but truth be told, I'd also like to find myself a husband. I'll be done with school this spring and am tired of my family heckling me as the 'ole maid.'" She curled her lip. "Don't *you* worry about that?"

"Sometimes I'm lonely, but they run us so ragged, I barely have the energy to worry about men. I suppose I'll deal with it when I finish." Studying, along with overcoming the insidious assumptions about being a woman student, was my top priority.

She giggled. "Not me. Finding a man will be my next accomplishment. And it will be amusing sizing up the men tomorrow tonight. I'm sure they're getting randy with spring around the corner, just like bulls on the farm!"

"I'm a big fan of spring, but my Papa had a chicken farm. I know nothing about bulls," I laughed. "But Elspeth, you're taking things too far from my end. The plan is dinner, a drink, then back home, right?"

"We'll see," she said with a teasing smile, skipping ahead.

I ran to catch up with her. "I need the full day Sunday for studying."

* * *

Saturday evening Elspeth and I dressed together for the outing. Standing in front of the bathroom mirror, we each dipped a finger in her rouge pot, spreading the sticky paste on our lips. Looking at our reflections, we laughed at how different we looked. Elspeth, with her tall curvy figure, had the classic beauty of a traditional Scottish lass—long auburn hair, freckles peppering her pale skin, and delicate, pink cupid lips. One could imagine her dancing amidst the spring flowers along the ragged cliffs that dropped to the rough sea. And if her appearance didn't give away her Scottish background, all she needed to do was open her mouth, her thick working-class accent with its rolling "r's" and long vowels, always turned heads.

Far shorter and skinny as a rake, I had my family's fair coloring and small features, at least compared to most of our Jewish community in New York. People always asked where the green eyes and blond wavy hair came from, my neighbors telling me I could pass for practically any European from England to Poland. Was there a little Cossack blood thrown in? From what we studied in genetics, I assumed my appearance came from my Mama's German line. No one was certain of Papa's roots. My name, Isaacson, typically answered any question about my ethnicity.

Just as we applied our finishing touches, Mrs. Collins called upstairs, "Girls, the carriage is here to take you to dinner. Dress warmly and bring your mufflers."

We scrambled down the steps, snatching our hats, cloaks, and mufflers off the coat pegs, slipping by Mrs. Collins so she didn't spot the rouge. I climbed into the frigid coach while Elspeth gave the driver directions. Relieved there was a coal foot warmer and carriage blankets to cover our laps, we bundled up, and the driver snapped his whip. While we rode on the icy surface, Elspeth shared information on the men.

"They come from more wealth than either of us could imagine. Mr. Frank and Mr. Slater's families are from industry, although I can't remember what kind. And Mr. Holloway owns the largest brewery in Manhattan. That must have been entertaining, all the beer they could drink."

"Are they good students?" I wondered why they didn't work in their family businesses.

"Yes, but their lives are so exciting I don't know why they bothered with medical school."

"I was wondering the same thing."

Elspeth rested her head on the bench back, speaking in a dreamy tone, "Their summers are filled with glorious travel and grand balls. Mr. Frank's family summers on the Gold Coast of Long Island with New York's elite. And Mr. Slater takes steamer trips abroad to famous European cities. He's seen the world. They all go to grand balls. Can you imagine?"

The biggest outing of my life was to the Chicago World's Columbian Exposition seven years ago. My stomach knotted. How little we shared with them. What could they possibly want with us? I eyed my companion with doubt. And didn't their social circles match them for marriage, like European royalty? *Was Elspeth only looking for money? Was she setting herself up for heartbreak?* "No, Elspeth, I can't."

* * *

The freezing winds howled off the Chesapeake Bay, driving straight through the fabric of my wool coat and scarf. I clutched Elspeth's arm, pulling her close, and shouted over the wind, "Elspeth, is this the right place? The building looks about to collapse."

"It's fine. I've come here with my brothers. Let's get inside and see who's arrived." She hooked her arm through mine. "Don't worry, it'll be fun." Her hair whipped about her face.

A patrol wagon passed by with two police scanning the alleys, holding lanterns. Where on earth did she bring us?

The wooden door, thick and heavy, resisted our efforts. While we pulled, someone inside pushed in our direction, forcing it open. The man rushed past me, shouting, "I'm gonna puke."

I stepped backward in disgust.

Elspeth yanked me inside before I could object. "Come on, Hannah, let's grab that table by the fire before someone snaps it up."

Just as we crossed the clamorous room, a tall man threw his hat on the table and sat.

My stomach dropped. "He took our table!" Annoyed, I was ready to return home.

"That's Roger Holloway, one of my classmates. Incidentally...the blue-eyed crush I told you about? That's him."

Mr. Holloway was handsome indeed. Tall, well-dressed with a matching waistcoat and jacket, he stood in stark contrast to the dingy atmosphere. *Perhaps the night holds promise after all.*

He looked about until he spotted us, rising from his chair. "Good evening, ladies. I'm so glad you made it. I'm the first one here and was afraid the cold might chase you off."

"We've been dying to do something fun. It's been such a busy week." Elspeth shouted into the din.

While we waited for the others, I took a seat in front of the enormous stone fireplace facing the room. A fish out of water, I'd never visited a pub and could understand why my sister had never brought me. Unwashed dock workers filled the crowded tables in the shadowed corners of the room. Heavily painted women sat on their laps, crowing in shrill, drunken laughter. Mrs. Collins was right. *Saloons are not places for respectable young women.* Suddenly, I recognized a lady from the Clinic. She'd come to the hospital badly beaten.

Miss Doyle, or Dillon, or some such name, stared at me. I saw the tell-tale yellow on her skin from her healing bruises. She shot a haughty smirk my way, as if I had no business in her world. She was right.

I looked away just in time to greet Mr. Frank and Mr. Slater, both wearing playful smiles.

Mr. Frank, a tall man with short cropped blond hair, full moustache, and deep brown eyes, reached out his hand, "So glad you made it. I'm Ethan Frank. You must be Miss Isaacson, Elspeth's friend." He wiggled into the chair beside Elspeth, obviously happy to see her.

I knew Elspeth frequently studied with the men. Did this explain his familiarity?

A jovial voice slipped into the fray. "Don't forget me. I'm Henry, Henry Slater. Good evening, Miss Isaacson." Mr. Slater, inches shorter than his companion, shared the same broad smile on his confident face. His thinning brown hair made him appear older than his age, but his skin was as smooth as a child's face, and his brown eyes held a delightful twinkle.

Elspeth came alive with small talk, giggling and touching Mr. Frank's arm. She seemed to know so much about the three men and reveled in their attention. Whereas, in the shadow of these well-bred, confident men, I was a misfit, a year younger and a full step behind—nowhere near as worldly. But, despite my discomfort, I wanted them to like me.

"Do you think we should wait to order until the others come?" I asked, hoping the other women were en route.

Mr. Slater shook his head. "Nah, they probably chose to stay home."

The waiter arrived with mugs of stout and an enormous platter of oysters, pried open.

"Who ordered?" Elspeth asked.

"We did before sitting down. I'm thirsty." Mr. Frank lifted his brows at Elspeth as he took a swig.

I studied the platter. "Are these oysters? Shellfish? I've never had one." I was curious about the strange-looking creatures. Were some still moving? I froze.

Mr. Slater answered. "First time? You're in for a treat. This is how to eat them." He put a dash of red sauce atop the creature and held the half shell to his mouth. With a noisy slurp, it slid down his throat whole. "Delicious. Try one."

Even coming from a liberal Jewish family, we had clear boundaries around certain food, and shellfish, a bottom-feeding sea creature, was well over the line. *How am I going to handle this?*

"I...I don't think I can. Shellfish don't agree with me." I stumbled, revolted by the prospect of slurping one down my throat.

"Oh, come on. Try one!" urged Mr. Frank.

Mr. Holloway studied my face. "No, don't make her sick. I'll order some fish and chips. That goes well with stout."

I answered with a hesitant smile. "Good idea. Thank you, Mr. Holloway." Frankly, I'd never tasted stout either but didn't want to seem prudish. I'd drunk holiday wines and an occasional schnapps with my sister and brother-in-law before bed. Stout was a new experience—thick, briny, but thirst-quenching. Before I knew it, my head grew pleasantly light, and I relaxed in the atmosphere of these spirited men.

I summoned the courage to ask the group, "What made you men decide to study medicine?"

Mr. Slater jumped in. "A fascination with science. My parents, despite their wealth, also expected their children to spend time helping the unfortunate. My sisters are involved in raising funds for the poor in one way or another, usually exciting events, designed to also snare a man." He winked at Mr. Frank.

I nodded, confused at the signal passing between them.

Mr. Slater continued, "To my mother's keen displeasure, I decided to study medicine because I find diseases fascinating. Mother thinks I've taken things to the extreme, that I'll catch an unseemly ailment and bring it home to the family, like what happened with typhus at Bellevue."

Sounds like the boys from college. They thought I'd bring home a horrible disease. I was impressed that despite his mother, he followed his dream.

Mr. Frank interrupted. "My father's hoping I'll invent some new thing-a-ma-jig he can take to market and make another fortune. I think there's a goldmine in surgical tools, especially for bones. I already have a few ideas with clamps and screws. If all goes well, I'll only practice a few years."

Shocked, I'd never imagined such a self-serving reason for the vocation. *That's the type of man Elspeth desires?*

"How about you, Mr. Holloway?" I looked into his pale blue eyes, partly obscured by his mop of brown curls.

"Call me Roger." He set his mug on the dirty table. "Honestly, I was a bit unsure when I started medical school. Mostly, I was just happy to be far from my family. But, over the last few years, I've grown concerned for the poor immigrants. I may go back to New York and set up a clinic when I'm done. I'm hoping my parents will help fund it."

The two other men laughed. Mr. Slater said, "That's the first time you've ever mentioned that."

What was so amusing? I felt a sparkle of kinship with Roger and glanced at Elspeth to see her reaction, but she was preoccupied, flirting with Mr. Frank. His arm was hidden beneath the roughened table. Elspeth was giggling like a schoolgirl. Was it the stout making her silly, or was something else going on? *It's going to take an army to unbolt that girl from him!*

Close to two hours of drinking and eating had passed when Mr. Frank, quite inebriated, stood and began singing "An Ode to Charlie Mops."

Mr. Slater and Holloway jumped up to join him,

I glanced across the table at Elspeth. Her eyes feasted on Mr. Frank. Finally, I reached over his empty seat and shook her arm.

"Time to go home," I mouthed. "I want to go, now."

Her shoulders dropped, returning a sour face. "Just a little longer." she insisted.

I shook my head, worried we wouldn't be able to hail a carriage and make our midnight curfew. What driver in his right mind would want to wait around this part of the city on a dark, cold night?

The song finally ended, all six verses, and I touched Mr. Holloway's arm.

"Would you be so kind as to help Elspeth and I hail a carriage? We must get back by curfew."

He pouted. "Really, so soon? The party's just starting."

I nodded firmly. "Sorry."

"Very well. Henry, grab your coat. We're getting the ladies a carriage. Time to go."

Elspeth glared at me, her voice tight as a fist. "I told you I wasn't ready."

"I am." I insisted, feeling like her chaperone.

A wave of concern shot through me. *What were they up to?*

Mr. Frank, again sitting between us, held Elspeth's chin in his fingers. "It's all right, Elspeth. Same place, Monday?"

"All right then. We'll leave some money." Elspeth said.

"Absolutely not. The evening is on the men," Mr. Slater said firmly.

Not a single word was spoken the entire trip home. Instead, Elspeth dropped her head back, fell asleep, her snoring only interrupted by the pits in the road. Although I enjoyed meeting Mr. Holloway, I was annoyed at Elspeth, bamboozling me into a bawdy night, her heavy drinking, and her public behavior with Mr. Frank. For now, it was a blessing to hear the clip-clopping of the horses pulling the carriage back home. I'd talk to her later.

Chapter Four

Early the next morning, pounding on my bedroom door woke me. My eyes were crusted, mouth parched. "Who is it?" I croaked.

"Elspeth, get up for church!"

"It's Hannah. Elspeth is next door." I lay under the warm covers, too tired to move; my hot water bottle cool at my feet.

"Sorry." I heard footsteps move down the hall. The banging resumed.

Unable to drift back to sleep, with a full day of studying ahead, I threw back the quilt and sat. As I poured a cup of water from the bone china pitcher by my bed, last night's altercation with Elspeth resurfaced. *I must speak to her before she leaves.* With our busy clinical schedules, there might not be another moment for days. I slipped on my robe, cinching it tightly around my waist, and walked into the hallway.

The house was freezing cold. I hoped Mrs. Collins had put coal in the furnace.

"Elspeth, can I come in?" I called through her door. "We need to talk."

She groaned. "What is it, Hannah?"

Elspeth was still under her blankets, her clothing from last night strewn about the floor, half-hanging from her desk chair.

"Are you going to church?"

"In a few minutes. I'll catch up. My head's killing me." She dug her face into her soft pillow.

"Can we talk?" I poured a glass of water from her pitcher and handed it to her.

Elspeth reluctantly sat up. "Now? I feel like hell and must hurry."

25

I could smell her sour breath across the room. "I know, but when else?" I insisted.

Elspeth scowled as she rose from bed. "If you're looking for an apology, I'm not giving one. I'm still angry we didn't stay on." She swept her wild hair off her face.

I dragged her desk chair to the bed and sat. "Honestly, Elspeth, if I'd know *that* was your intention, I never would have gone. It's beneath us, and far too dangerous. Those pub people were scary. And the harbor was a dive. Didn't you see the police wagon?"

"It was innocent fun," she said, waving a dismissive hand. "I suppose I'm more accustomed to pubs than you. I told you I used to go with my brothers."

"It's still wrong." I insisted, "And, dangerous."

Elspeth was unfazed. "I didn't notice anything dangerous. Certainly nothing more than we've seen at the hospital."

I thought through the events of the evening and grudgingly had to agree. "I suppose that's true, but why look for trouble? And drink so much?"

"We all do from time to time. Stop being a killjoy. What's the harm in blowing off a little steam?" She stood and picked up her clothing, shaking out the garments, then hanging them in her tiny closet.

Her words contradicted everything my family expected of me and my own expectations for myself. "I don't want to end up getting hurt or *in trouble.*"

Elspeth cocked her head to the side, her tired eyes now twinkling with curiosity. "Have you never been intimate?"

Surprised, I hesitated before answering. "No…. I mean, I've kissed boys, but not *that.*" The question disturbed me. Maybe I shouldn't share anything more with Elspeth.

"You're kidding!" Elspeth's face broke into a grin. "Young lady, you have some happy evenings heading your way."

I was stunned. Who was this reckless woman? Since I'd moved to the rooming house, I'd held her in the highest esteem. Elspeth was brilliant, academically competitive with any man, always at the top of the class. But this? What an enigma!

"Elspeth, you may be right, but you better be careful, or your dream of marrying a wealthy husband will be just that—a dream." I looked at her smug face and shifted into doctor mode, far more comfortable asking personal questions with my 'white coat' on. "Are you intimate now? With Ethan?"

She hesitated, but her coy smile told me the truth. "He said he wants to marry when we graduate." She walked to her closet and pulled out a fresh dress and hat.

I pressed further. "Are you using anything to block his seed?"

Elspeth laughed, turning to me. "Hannah, it's not your concern."

"I'm worried about you. All these years of hard work could come crashing down." I cast about for another line of reason. "Have you met his parents?"

"No, but you needn't worry. We're adults and just a few months shy of graduating. Besides, if I get pregnant, we'll marry sooner." Elspeth climbed into her dress, buttoning the bodice. In her haste, she pinned her hair into a disheveled chignon at her neck. "No more prying, Hannah. I mean it. I must wash my face and leave for church."

I reopened the door and looked back as she continued to speak.

"Worry about yourself and start living a little."

I waited in my room for Elspeth to leave. I knew she'd be out the door in a flash. Like clockwork, seconds later, I heard her light footsteps bouncing down the stairs and the front door slamming. Still wrapped in my warm robe, I gathered my textbooks and followed her echo downstairs. Mrs. Collins had turned up the radiator in the parlor, and the house was warming, but I still set a small fire in the stone fireplace to make the room cozier. I could barely feel my fingertips. Once the logs began to catch and crackle, I walked into the kitchen to prepare a cup of tea and toast with cheese.

I sat at the dining room table and fanned out my textbooks. This morning, I planned to review puerperal fever, otherwise known to patients as childbed fever. Although less frequent since we understood the role of invisible germs, the fever continued to plague us, as it struck terrible fear in our mothers and their families. Despite our aggressive washing, we still encountered heartbreaking cases.

I relished Sunday mornings when I could study in complete quiet. In a few short hours, the house would be abuzz with my housemates and Mrs. Collins, who took great pleasure in preparing a large Sunday mid-afternoon dinner. Somehow, attending church injected renewed energy and appetite into the house. Today, troubled by my conversation with Elspeth, I needed this window of silence to take stock.

Why would a group of wealthy boys choose a pub when they could have eaten anywhere in the city? Had they planned all along to get drunk and boisterous? What was Elspeth up to with Mr. Frank?

Having grown up in New York City, I thought I had a good grip on city life, but I was wrong. Most likely, spending my years in college studying in the library had removed me from normal social activities. But truth be told, I had no interest in consorting further with Elspeth's friends.

Nonetheless, I was uncomfortable on my lonesome path, never aspiring to be a spinster. Did anyone? There must be a way to succeed in medicine and still find love. By the end of college at Barnard, I watched my girlfriends, one after another, accept engagements and head off to charmed married lives. I attended lavish weddings, each couple stomping on the glass under an elegant chuppah, lonely without a beloved by my side. By the end of June that year, I grew despondent.

My career choice offered little substitution for the excitement around me. Seeing my friends marry, wearing radiant smiles, made me question why I chose such a difficult path. Love was a steep price to pay, and my desires painfully difficult to shut off. Was I only infatuated with the idea of love?

Pull yourself together, Hannah. You have studying to do.

Like clockwork, two hours later, my housemates' return interrupted my concentration. As Mrs. Collins opened the door, a strong waft of cold air blew in. Behind her, five girls and Elspeth all wore their Sunday finest, chirping about the sermon, upcoming classes, and young men. Emily and Sarah were in their first year of nursing school, and Margaret and Victoria, their second. Mary, who was an undergraduate student, was in her final year of college. They pulled off their brown high-button boots, lining them against the hearth to dry, and quickly replaced them with fur-lined slippers kept warm by the hearth. Despite their tall boots, the lower foot of their overcoats and dresses held crusted patches of snow.

"Girls, shake off that snow outside! We'll have puddles everywhere. Take this hat brush." Mrs. Collins scurried to the door, leading them onto the porch like a sheepdog, slippers, and all. "Out you go. Help each other, why don't you!"

Elspeth returned inside. As our eyes met, she mouthed *sorry*. I gathered my books and followed her to the stairs, stopping on my way to greet everyone and admire their Sunday attire. Mary, short in stance like me, wore a full deep blue velvet skirt offset by a long crimson wool jacket trimmed in gold braid and nipped at the waist with a handsome leather belt. Her long blond waves created a stunning contrast to the deep jewel colors of her garments. It must have cost a fortune, but I knew she came from old Boston money and was accustomed to finer things.

"Is that a new suit?" I asked. "It's very flattering." Her profile was narrow and appeared elongated by the effect of the overlaying jacket. "I should try that design. It makes you look tall." I would shop with Tillie during my next school break. Having worked in the garment business, she knew all the best clothing stores in New York.

"Why, yes, thank you. It's extra warm under my cape and very comfortable." She beamed. "I wasn't one bit cold in that drafty church."

* * *

Beef stew was a new delight for me; the aroma made me dizzy with anticipation. Served on a wide platter soaking in its sumptuous cooking gravy, Mrs. Collins dressed the edges of the plate with roasted carrots and turnips. This, all accompanied by bowls of mashed potatoes and home-baked Parker House rolls, made a delicious, comforting, and filling meal on this cold winter day.

The girls bowed their heads while Mrs. Collins recited grace. "Lord God, Heavenly Father, bless us and keep us safe…"

For me, dinner prayers were also a new custom. Except for the *Motzi*, a prayer for breaking the braided challah bread on Shabbos and holidays, when the entire meal was interlaced with symbolic prayer and discussion, most prayers in my home took place inside the synagogue, not at the table.

I awkwardly waited, rolling and rerolling the cloth napkin on my lap until they finished praying. A second later, all eyes connected, smiles emerged, and loud clamor replaced the quiet reflection. Everyone served themselves hearty helpings, talking over one other and complimenting Mrs. Collins, who sat with a gratified smile, filling her plate last.

No longer able to eat another bite, we all helped clear, scrape, and stack the dishes in the kitchen. Mrs. Collins kept the scraps for her mice-chasing cats. She handed us a small stack of clean cups, saucers, and a tray of cookies for dessert. As we reassembled in our seats, she announced from the kitchen, "I've made something new I found in my Fanny Farmer cookbook. It's called a brownie."

I exclaimed, "I know what that is! I ate one at the Chicago World's Columbian Exposition a few years ago. It was divine!"

Mrs. Collins stood at the door frame with a porcelain plate piled high with squares of dense chocolate cake. A loud knock at the door interrupted our clapping.

"I wonder who that could be?" Mrs. Collins asked. "Was anyone expecting a visitor?"

Elspeth jumped up from the table, hurrying to answer the door.

Was she expecting Mr. Frank for a social visit?

As she led the guest into the house, every girl at the table twisted toward the door, curious to see who'd come to visit. It was Mr. Holloway.

Elspeth greeted him flirtatiously. "Well, good afternoon, Mr. Holloway. What brings you here today?"

He took the black felt Derby off his head and bowed to the group, obviously delighted by all the smiling girls at the table. "I apologize. It seems I disturbed your Sunday dinner. I came to speak to Miss Isaacson. We're schoolmates."

I nodded, offering a weak smile, glancing at the ring of girls tittering

30

coquettishly, surprised he'd shown up at the house without an invitation.

"Have you had your supper?" Mrs. Collins asked, delighted by a prospective suitor.

Mr. Holloway shook his head. "No, ma'am."

"Come right in, and I'll fix a plate for you." She rose from the table, gesturing to her chair. "Sit here."

Mr. Holloway removed his boots by the fireplace, then ambled to the table wearing his winning smile and sat beside me. "This is a rare treat. I typically go out for my Sunday meal. There's not much cooking where I live."

Mrs. Collins called to him from the kitchen. "You go to school with Miss Fletcher and Miss Isaacson?"

He settled into Mrs. Collin's empty chair and winked at my curious housemates. "Yes, I'm in Miss Fletcher's class."

Mrs. Collins carried Mr. Holloway's plate into the dining room, setting it in front of him. "Have some dinner, then you two can visit in the parlor."

My housemates all sat, their eyes glued to his every move.

Chapter Five

The small hospital lobby, located precisely beneath the imposing roof spire, was a hive of activity at 6:30 in the morning. Nurses, doctors, and attendants filled the space, darting about, preparing for the day. Although family and visitors were not permitted until mid-morning, the lobby sounded like a train station with loud voices and clamor, everyone purposefully on the move, aides pushing supply carts, students carrying stacks of patient charts, and day shift nurses racing to relieve the night staff.

My workday began with patient rounds at 7:00 am, leaving me thirty precious minutes to scout overnight issues ahead of my senior physician and, if I was lucky, enjoy a hot coffee. I hurried up the rear staircase to the Women's Ward on the fourth floor.

The day's first light filtered through the tall windows on the ward. With most patients still sleeping, it was the perfect time to catch up with the night nurse before she left. Scanning the room, I spotted Nurse Hammond assisting a patient in Bed Five.

"Good morning, Nurse. Do you have a moment?"

"Certainly. Just finishing here with Mrs. Johnston. She had a beautiful set of delicate twin boys last night." She adjusted the patient's pillows and filled the water pitcher.

"Twins. Oh, my, who handled the delivery?" I asked as we walked to the hallway outside the ward.

She whispered, "Dr. Adams, and he was none too pleased. The first baby was difficult to birth, and his little brother was in there far too long. We're watching them carefully in the nursery." She glanced back at the mother, whose eyes were closed, exhausted from the ordeal.

"Any other problems on the floor? How's the mother who had the breach delivery on Friday?"

"Fine. We're mainly concerned with Mrs. Johnston's twins. Otherwise, all's right as rain."

"I'll review her chart and check the infants before rounds."

"Can I get you a coffee?"

"That would be lovely." I caught her gaze and smiled appreciatively. Lifting the chart from the hook at the foot of Bed Five, I walked to the charting table at the opposite end of the ward.

I flipped through the handwritten pages. As expected, the nursing notes were a quick read, while Dr. Adam's scribbles were near impossible to decipher. What caught my eye was the large volume of ether used to sedate the mother. Long labor, excessive anesthesia, babies both fragile, *Why he didn't use chloroform like the newer doctors?*

Before I knew it, my half hour of grace vanished, and I was trailing behind the pack of students and resident doctors, walking from one patient bed to the next, answering Dr. Adam as he fired questions at us.

His pace was fast and impatient, not always greeting his patients, stridently barking out the daily orders as well as posing obscure questions to the residents, hoping to trip them up. When we reached Bed Five, he stopped. "Twins last night. Isaacson, what's the most common birth complication?"

"Preterm labor. But weren't these babies thirty-five weeks, almost full-term?"

He shot me an angry glare. "Indeed, but the first was almost full-sized, and the second hadn't moved into an optimal birthing position," Dr. Adams spit back. "Was taking too long, so we used forceps on both. We'll check them next."

We? The decision was his, alone.

The infants were sleeping when I'd peeked in earlier, the larger baby with bruises on his face and shoulders. The smaller infant's skin had a subtle blue cast. Was he breathing normally?

I glanced at Nurse Hammond. Her head was bent to the wood floor, hands squeezed so tightly, I could see the white in her knuckles. The navy muslin dress worn beneath her white apron matched the dark circles under her eyes. I held back from the pack of students as they left the ward. Nurse Hammond was at the end of her night shift, little time left to hear the full story.

"Nurse, were you in delivery during the twins' births?" I whispered.

"I was." She straightened her back, darting her eyes to the nursery.

I took a step closer to her. "Did anything unusual happen?"

After a lengthy pause, she rubbed her fingers, eyes downcast.

"Nurse Hammond, what happened?" I persisted.

"You know Adams, always impatient." She turned her eyes from the floor, then to mine. "He couldn't stand the mother's screaming and knocked her out cold with ether. Then he went in deep with the forceps, taking forever. I think he would have had more luck if he'd kept her awake and changed her position." She took in a sharp breath. "But who am I to say? You can't utter a word. I need my job. I've four children at home."

I nodded, understanding. "You can trust me. Go home and get some rest." I scurried down the hall to the nursery.

"Where've you been, Isaacson?" Dr. Adams barked as I walked through the doorway.

"My apology, Doctor, lavatory."

Dr. Adams crossed his arms on his chest, haughtily shaking his head at the ring of men standing around the twins' bassinets. "See there, gentlemen? That's what happens when women are allowed into the profession. Always needing to fix their hair."

Blood shot to my face. *How long would he get away with his negligence?* I stifled my annoyance while studying the infants. The smaller baby's hand began to tremor.

"Doctor, he's having a seizure!" I called out, my voice slicing through their laughter, reaching to pick up the baby. The tremor traveled up his arm, unfurling into all his tiny limbs, erupting into a grand mal seizure.

"God dammit! He was in there too long without air," Dr. Adams thundered.

The first baby jolted awake, wailing as if sensing his younger brother was not long for this world.

"If the mothers aren't screaming in labor, their babies are howling in the nursery! I can't stand this loathsome ward any longer." Dr. Adam's face contorted with anger as his eyes fixed on the dying baby.

The rest of us stood silently, surrounding the bassinet. The infant in my arms stopped shaking, stopped breathing, and lay still. A grey cast swept across his skin. I sniffled, a tear escaping the corner of my eye.

"Are *you* going to cry now?" Dr. Adams sneered.

I stared back, pouring hate into his eyes.

"You don't like the way I handle things?" he challenged me. "Then, *you* go tell the mother!"

I took the blanket from the bassinet, gently wrapped the newborn, and turned toward the exit.

"Leave the body here, Isaacson," he demanded.

I twisted my shoulders, baby in arms, and said, with the calmest voice I could muster, "I will bring him back after the mother properly says her goodbye."

The men stood in shock as I walked into the women's ward with the dead infant. When I turned to look back moments later, they were gone.

I stood over the dozing mother holding the swaddled infant, only his tiny grey face visible. She opened her eyes and immediately understood. I lowered him into her outstretched arms. No words were needed. In the Clinic, she had been advised of the risks, delivering twins, but nonetheless, her sobs came from deep in her heart, not her brain.

Through jagged breaths, she spoke softly to her tiny son, comforting him on his journey to the spiritual world. "I'm so sorry I couldn't do better, sweetness. I'll always miss you."

I sat beside her, gently sweeping the tangled hair off her forehead, knowing she needed this time before letting go of his body.

"God will watch over you, my little angel," she murmured. "I'll carry you in my heart till my very last breath."

* * *

I had fifteen minutes to squeeze in a quick lunch at the coffee shop before my afternoon shift in the Women's Clinic. Halfway there, I approached the Doctor's Lounge, a privileged location where students were admitted only with a personal invitation. The door was open, angry conversation spilling out. Dr. Adam's abrasive voice was impossible to miss. I slowed when I heard my name.

"Isaacson should be thrown out for insubordination! She's a damn *know-it-all* and isn't competent to practice medicine. Never will be."

"It can't be all that bad, Adams. She was a big help when she worked with me. I could finally turn the patients over to someone trustworthy," a second doctor answered in a reassuring tone. "Give her a chance. She'll either hang herself or shape up."

"I suppose, but she can't continue to contradict me on rounds. I'm going to take this up with the President of the Medical School," Adams insisted.

The other voice shifted to a cautionary tone. "Do as you must, but the trustees are fiercely protective of their female students. Be careful opening that can of worms. Once you do, you'll lose control."

My God, Adams is on the warpath! A knot grew in my empty stomach. *Could he get me expelled?*

Realizing I hadn't anything to eat since morning coffee, I turned on my heel and walked the long way around the building's perimeter to the hospital cafe. Rounding the final corner, I saw Elspeth sitting alone, reading. Perfect. I needed her advice.

I approached her table. "Hi, Elspeth. Can I interrupt you?"

The edges of her mouth curled upward. "So, we're friends now?"

I rolled my eyes, frustrated. "I never stopped being your friend."

"Well then, what's going on?"

I sat at her table, placed an order for a toasted cheese sandwich and coffee, and shared what I just heard Dr. Adams say. "I think he wants to bring me

36

in front of the Disciplinary Board."

Elspeth scoffed. "Ridiculous. Adams is a poor excuse for a doctor, much less a man. He hates the women students and looks for every chance to trip us up." She lifted her brows. "Did you know that this isn't the first time he's accused one of us?"

"What do you mean?" I stirred milk in my cup.

Elspeth began. "Remember Sally Manning? She was a fourth year when you started and dropped out before graduating."

"I think so. Tall, glasses, dark hair?"

"Yes, that was her. Adams got her expelled for immoral behavior."

"No." I set down my spoon, aghast. *How could someone so incompetent have so much power?*

"Turns out one of the young doctors broke off an engagement to Adam's niece. A few months later, the same doctor began courting Sally. Adams found out and accused her of lascivious behavior, of interfering with the engagement, even though it had been called off months before." Elspeth took a long sip of her tea.

I set my cup in its saucer with a clunk. "That's horrible. They let an innocent student come so close to graduating and then expelled her on his word?"

"Later, when the Board learned the truth about Adam's family story and wanted to bring her back, it was too late. Sally had gone home to Chicago and was never heard from again. The trustees were outraged. I suspect the Chief of Medicine will be more careful believing him after the mess that caused." Elspeth swirled the remaining tea in the bottom of her cup.

"But still. He's the one who practices sloppy medicine and loses his composure every time things get difficult." I took a bite of my sandwich. "I don't know how he gets away with it."

"I have an idea," Elspeth said, a sneaky grin growing across her face. "Next week, I have one of my Trustee dinners. How about I ask if you can join us? That way, they can meet another talented medical student?"

"That would be wonderful. I'm flattered." I beamed, feeling both complimented and reassured.

"It's good for both of us. It gives you protection, and frankly, I'm tired of the high expectations they have for me. It would be nice to share the pressure with someone else." She laughed conspiratorially. "Besides, next year, I'll be off to New York with Ethan, and they'll need someone new to dote on."

Feeling far more relieved, I gobbled my sandwich, aware of the minutes ticking. My clinic started in five minutes. "Thanks, Elspeth. I'm glad we're friends again."

Nurse O'Neal ran, breathless, into the hospital cafe just as we were paying our tab at the register. "Oh, girls. Thank goodness you're here. We have a woman in Emergency—she's hemorrhaging."

We dropped our money on the counter and flew to Emergency at the nurse's heels, weaving through the linen and supply carts strewn about the corridor.

As we neared the hospital's rear entrance, Nurse O'Neal said in a hushed tone. "I think it was an abortion. I tried to find a senior doctor."

* * *

The Emergency Department was divided into two large bays, left for trauma, right for cuts and bruises. Beds separated by curtains gave patients a semblance of privacy. A cluster of anxious nurses surrounded our patient on the trauma side.

"Here, over here!" A nurse called to us. "We've been packing her with towels."

I hurried to the sink and washed my hands, Elspeth close behind, then entered the patient bay. "I'm covering emergencies. Let me examine her." I removed the blood-soaked towels between the woman's legs, setting them in a large basin. A fresh burst of blood squirted from her body. Pulling up my sleeves, I inserted my hand. "Light, Nurses, shine the lamp right here and call the operating theater. We may need to take her upstairs. What else do you know about her?"

A nurse stepped forward. "The ambulance driver told me he picked her up by the wharves, not too far from one of those midwife clinics. She was bent over, bleeding. A tavern owner put her in a livery and sent her here."

"Have you gotten a name?"

"Afraid not, a Jane Doe."

While I pressed on her abdomen with my left hand, I explored the inside of her body. Large clumps of tissue separated from the uterus, spilling by my hand into the basin. Behind was a trickle of blood. The heavy bleeding had stopped.

"Oh, good Lord!" a nurse screamed. "A tiny hand."

The staff circled the basin, curious to examine the macabre sight.

"Call the police!" a nurse demanded. "Things have gotten out of hand with the midwives in this city. This is murder!"

I continued the internal exam, my fingers searching for additional tissue or lacerations, fixing my eyes on her abdomen, determined not to look inside the basin. My stomach was in knots. I wanted to know how far along she was and why she would end a pregnancy at this late stage? What was the midwife thinking?

The nurses' nonstop railing lit my anger. I shouted, "Quiet! Nurses, we're not done yet. How are her breathing and pulse?"

I heard from the head of the table, "She's starting to level off, but her pulse is still high, one hundred twenty beats a minute. Respiration is eighteen."

I shifted my gaze to the patient's unconscious face and exhaled. We would save this woman, but by a hair. Had she been left on the street, she would have bled to death. I glanced at her hand. No wedding ring. Her young face was white as a ghost, her lips absent any color. Unlike most of our indigent patients, her smooth hair and clean nails were characteristic of a well-cared-for debutante. Her parents must be frantic about her whereabouts.

"Cancel the operating room and clean her carefully. She'll need a bed on Four. I'll talk to her later when she's awake. In the meantime, send the content of the basin to Pathology. I want to know how far along she was." I glared at the gaggle of nurses, their eyes fixed on me, awaiting further instructions. "And no police yet. Let's find out more first."

I walked to the sink to clean my hands, arms, and dress. Elspeth stood by the faucet, white as a sheet.

"I forgot you were here," I said.

"You had it under control. I didn't think you needed my help," Elspeth said softly.

I studied her face. "Why are you so pale?"

"I—I don't know. Usually, blood doesn't bother me, but that little hand...." She broke off. "Made me ill."

I dried my hands, shaking my head furiously. "I must expose the quacks doing this butchery and end it. This girl practically died." I turned back to the nurses. "Good job today. You helped save her." I paused. "I meant what I said about notifying the police. I'll contact them after I speak to the patient tonight."

* * *

By the time I finished in Emergency and reached the Maternity Clinic, it was close to dinner. My Clinic patients, the poorest in Baltimore, often didn't show up for appointments but other times, they arrived in droves. We never knew how busy we'd be.

Nurse O'Neal approached me. "I sent the first group home and told them to come back later in the week, that you were running late. A couple of late arrivals chose to stay. Shouldn't take you too long."

"Thank you."

She hung to my side, eager to learn more. "Did the woman in Emergency survive? I thought she didn't stand a chance without a doctor to help her through." She shook her head sadly.

I stopped in my tracks, glaring at her. "What were you thinking? I'm covering Emergency. You should have gotten me first. She was bleeding to death," I snapped.

Nurse O'Neal looked at the floor and mumbled, "I was told not to trust you. I—I apologize."

"Did Adams tell you that?" I demanded, not expecting her to answer. "You've known me for the last three years. How could you possibly believe such a thing?" I shook my head, disgusted. "As it turns out, I saved her. She's headed to the Women's Ward right now instead of the morgue."

"That's a relief." She wrung her hands, finally looking up at me. "I apologize."

The knot of insult didn't loosen. "Nurse, always put the patient's welfare first. Waiting could have cost her life." My energy was depleted. I was in no condition to argue and softened my tone. "What do you know about the midwives in town?"

Nurse O'Neal was visibly relieved to shift the subject. "They're getting hungry for work now that more women are birthing at the hospital. They need to make up the lost income. I hear they're now doing second-trimester unblocking. We didn't see many girls here when they did them early on with the herbals."

"You mean abortions," I corrected, annoyed at her euphemism.

"Err, yes, ma'am. They're scattered throughout the city, and it's not just the poor who use them. Many a married woman and socialite has found herself in trouble or with too many children already at home and resort to a midwife." She exhaled, "And you know, of course, the mothers are terrified of childbed fever."

My first and only true concern was safety. Midwives had no oversight, no formal training, and the anti-abortion laws were difficult to enforce. This practice of later-term abortions was a disaster already happening. I had to learn more. The issue stretched far beyond the moral issues Mrs. Collins professed; it was a matter of mothers' lives.

* * *

I finished my Clinic patients and headed to the fourth floor. The afternoon light had dissolved, replaced by the new electric ceiling lights, washing out all color, making the reclined patients appear mummy-like. I checked the time. Nurse Hammond wouldn't arrive for another hour. A new nurse bent over a patient across the room.

I approached the nurse. "Good evening. I'm the third-year doctor in training, Hannah Isaacson, covering the floor."

"I was hoping to see you. I'm Nurse Bell." She finished pouring a cup of water for her patient. "Jane Doc from Emergency is waking up. I thought you should speak to her." She led me to Bed Ten.

I lifted a gas lantern and walked to Ben Ten, setting the light on her nightstand. I studied the patient's pallid face. "Hello. I took care of you today in Emergency. How are you feeling?"

Her eyelids fluttered. A tear escaped.

I stroked her arm. "You're all right now. Can you tell me your name?"

She hesitated. "Catherine."

Nurse Bell brought a water pitcher to the side table and handed Catherine a starched white handkerchief. She placed an extra pillow behind Catherine's head, helping her sit upright, then handed her a cup of water. "Please drink all of this. You need fluids every hour."

Blood loss had left her face terribly pale. It would take days to recover her strength. Wavy, honey-colored hair draped over her quivering shoulders.

"Are you cold?" Without waiting for an answer, the nurse reached into the linen cart and wrapped Catherine in a thick white blanket. "Better now?"

Catherine nodded, wiping her tears, blowing her nose softly into the handkerchief.

"Ready to talk?" I nodded to the nurse.

Nurse Bell backed out of the bay and closed the drapes around Catherine and me.

"I'd like you to tell me what happened. I need to know the truth. Let's start with your whole name."

"My parents will disown me." Large tears fell from her dewy young eyes. "I can't talk about it."

"Catherine, if that is your real name, your midwife nearly killed you. Thanks to a Good Samaritan, we were able to save you here, at the hospital—but only by a thread." I looked hard into her eyes.

She continued to cry.

I knew we'd go nowhere if I wasn't stern. "Stop crying and look at me." I waited until her tears stopped. "Your condition was critical when you arrived at the hospital. At first, you were bleeding so heavily we weren't sure we could save you." I gave the message a moment to sink in. "I understand you're feeling miserable right now, but you have to trust me."

She lifted her head, her sad eyes peering into mine. Then, the slightest nod.

I softened my tone. "Let's start with your real name and age."

Her jagged breathing slowed as she composed herself. Her eyes were puffy, full of regret. "It's Mary."

"Mary what?" I said gently.

She looked at her lap. "Fitzsimmons."

"That's a good start, Mary. Are you sure about the name? This is the second one in five minutes." I smiled. "And that's not including the name, Jane Doe, we gave you when you arrived."

She nodded, clearly appreciating the absurdity, the corners of her mouth slowly curling upward. "I'm sorry. I'm seventeen; my birthday is this summer, July 7th."

I leaned closer to her face. "Mary, tell me what happened."

"I thought he'd marry me. He promised and then left to visit his uncle and wouldn't answer my letters." Mary sniffled.

"Who did you see to end your pregnancy?"

Mary drew a deep breath. "I'd heard there were midwives who could fix such things. They do it all the time. Miss Haggarty's name kept coming up as the best place to go. So, I went to her Clinic near the wharves." She studied my eyes. "Will I get better? You know, to have a baby someday, when I'm older?"

I nodded, reassuring her. "Other than blood loss, I believe you're out of the woods. But a terrible crime was committed on your body. Right now, we must address it."

Mary exhaled deeply, visibly relieved.

"I'm giving Miss Haggarty's name to the police. She must be stopped." I reached for her hand, giving it a reassuring squeeze. "Mary, before you went to Miss Haggarty, were you able to feel any fluttering in your belly? Like butterflies?"

She dropped her head and nodded. "I don't want my parents to know! I've committed a terrible sin," Mary whispered. The sniffling resumed.

"Mary, they must know. You're young and will require care when you go home. Since you're not yet eighteen, the police won't release your name to the newspaper, and all this can remain a private family matter." I gave her a moment to digest my words. "Do you have a telephone at home? Would you like me to speak with your parents before they see you?"

"You can't tell them!" she cried out. "I mean it. They'll send me away."

I waited for this fresh round of sobbing to end. Mary had little energy left. Depleted of blood, she quickly tired.

"Mary, you're right. Your parents will be angry—as they should be—but you're their precious child, and they'll want to care for you. You need to remember, your decisions come with consequences." I checked to make sure the drape was closed. "I suggest you keep your voice down."

"I can't face them. Would you really tell them for me?" Mary pleaded.

"Yes, of course, I'll help. I know it's been an ordeal, and I want you to rest and feel better again. Your body's working hard to heal."

Mary's face contorted with fear as she dictated her telephone number. "Thank you. I can't possibly look them in the face and see their shame."

The nurse immediately called the Fitzsimmons' home. Within the hour, I was sitting with Mary's parents in a small conference room beside the ward.

Mrs. Fitzsimmons was frantic, crying, mopping her eyes with a dainty lace handkerchief. "I'm so glad you called. I was beside myself with worry. Mary was supposed to be visiting her friend, Alice, but when she didn't return home, I rang their house. Mary hadn't been there at all!"

"I want to know what's going on," Mr. Fitzsimmons demanded. "Why is she here?"

The nurse and I locked eyes. I carefully unfolded the harsh truth. "Mary is resting and out of physical danger." I paused. "Nurse Hammond will take you to her in a moment. From what we've pieced together, she was impregnated by a boyfriend who later wouldn't take responsibility. So, Mary became desperate and went to a midwife she'd heard about for a termination."

Mr. Fitzsimmons bolted from his chair. "What? Impossible! You're lying to us," he stormed. "I want to speak to a real doctor."

Keeping my voice even, I continued. "The police have been notified about the midwife and will bring her to the station for questioning. Mr. Fitzsimmons, this is serious. Your daughter almost bled to death."

"I must see her." Mrs. Fitzsimmons shouted in panic. "We need to see she's alive." She stood, pulling her husband's arm.

He shook her off. "No, she shamed us. Mary's our only child, our pride and joy, and look what happened!" He looked accusingly at his wife. "It's your fault, allowing her to court so young. Too loose on the reins. Now she's committed a mortal sin." He charged out of the room.

Silence descended upon us. Over the past year, I'd learned to hold back and remain silent. It was during these periods of quiet that distraught families collected themselves, found their footing, and thought more clearly. I waited patiently. Moments later, Mr. Fitzsimmons walked back into the room, head down, defeated.

Mrs. Fitzsimmons broke the stillness. "Oh darling, remember with us...?"

Mr. Fitzsimmons squirmed, shaking off her words.

"Please sit down, sir. I know it's a lot to hear, but Mary almost lost her life trying to protect you from her shame." I stood, facing him. "Nurse, could you take Mrs. Fitzsimmons to see Mary for a brief visit and then bring her back? I'll see which doctors are still at the hospital and ask one of them to speak to you, Mr. Fitzsimmons."

I felt his anguish as he dropped into his chair, buried his face in his hands, and wept. "No, don't do that. This is lady business. Just promise we won't lose our little lamb."

Chapter Six

It was past nine when I slipped out of the Women's Ward to head home. Entering the lobby, I noticed Mr. Holloway standing near the coffee shop, holding his coat and hat. "Hello, Mr. Holloway. Heading in for house call tonight?" I couldn't help but admire his chiseled features, straight off a Roman sculpture.

"No, just leaving. Thought I'd wait for you," he said. "I was hoping to escort you home. Heard you had a tough day." His inscrutable smile heightened the twinkle in his eyes.

"That's thoughtful, but don't you live in the other direction?" Drained from the day, I tried to discourage him. I was looking forward to a quiet walk home by myself, listening only to the crunch of snow beneath my boots.

"Hannah, it's my pleasure. I insist." His confidence was hard to dismiss.

We walked out the hospital door onto its massive marble steps. Flurries swirled around us as if cleansing the air of its evils, dragging them to the gutters below where they belonged. It was an impossibly sad day. The pathology report had come back after dinner. Mary's fetus was five months—far beyond a safe termination. She'd postponed her decision too long, and the midwife was incompetent. I was silent, still struggling to digest the horrific reality.

"A penny for your thoughts," said Mr. Holloway.

Still overwhelmed, I wasn't ready to discuss the complexity of my thoughts. I simplified. "It was a miserable day. One infant died this morning and another later in the day. The deaths were avoidable." My lips drew tight. "Both due to sloppy medicine."

He patted my shoulder reassuringly. "That's rough."

The gaslights spilled their light onto the street and sidewalk. I hoped I'd lessened my patients' suffering, but I'd had my fill for one day. I wanted to free my mind.

The crisp air cleared my head. I was determined to change the subject, lighten the evening, and enjoy this handsome man. "What a beautiful night."

"It certainly is, and you make it more so."

I ignored his compliment. "Mr. Holloway, tell me about yourself. We didn't have a minute to talk yesterday when you stopped by. My housemates swarmed around you like a flutter of butterflies." It was a ridiculous sight, all those young women in their Sunday finest vying for his attention.

"Call me Roger, please. I won't lie, the attention was fun, and the dinner delicious!" He patted his belly. "I don't eat that well at my boarding house."

My spirits began to lift, both from my favorite deep purple scarf warming my neck, but more so by having a new friend by my side. "I want to hear about your family and the brewery. That's a different kind of business than I'm used to."

Roger snickered. "In some ways, my family is fairly run of the mill, and in other ways, demonic." He gazed into the distance, knitting his brows. "I grew up with both my parents, two younger sisters, and an older brother who's being groomed to take Father's place in the business."

"What do you mean, demonic? Sounds normal to me."

"Let's just say there was too much product sampling." He took my elbow to edge me around a patch of black ice. "And it brought out the worst."

"You mean, drinking?" My curiosity grew.

"All day, every day. My father and brother have wooden legs, but my uncles were another story, always drunk. I'm surprised they haven't run the brewery into the ground. The four of them were always drunk and fighting over money."

"I'm sorry. You alluded to some reason you chose medical school that involved your family. Was that why?" More curious than cautious, I wanted to know more about this mysterious man.

Roger was silent.

I instantly regretted pushing so hard. "I apologize. I'm overstepping."

"It's all right. I was a misfit, and medical school got me out of town. Leaving was liberating." Roger stopped and reached for my hand. "You're easy to talk to. Do people tell you that?"

"Sometimes." I pulled my hand back, uncomfortable at his forwardness.

Roger's crystalline eyes flashed at me. "Would you like to join me for dinner this weekend?" he asked eagerly. "I know a much nicer restaurant near town."

"I suppose, but...." Maybe courting wasn't wise given our different religions.

"No buts." That infectious confidence again.

He reached again for my hand and pulled me into a hug. The intoxication of a man's embrace was impossible to resist. But still, it was far too soon for this level of intimacy. I pulled back awkwardly.

Roger, sensing my reluctance, said in a soft, reassuring voice, "Just dinner. I like being with you."

I nodded, still hesitant. "Dinner would be lovely."

* * *

Why did I have the jitters? Banter with Roger came easily, and I looked forward to a relaxing meal together. Although he hadn't fully explained the circumstances with his family, I couldn't imagine it was overly important. And Elspeth hadn't sent any cautionary signals my way. So, what was it? The hug?

My sister, Tillie, believed I took life too seriously, prone to clinging to people I knew and trusted, not welcoming newcomers. She thought the trauma of losing Mama as a baby had scarred me permanently. That my reaction to that loss was to control my world and relationships, unwilling to take personal risks. The publication of Freud's books made everyone an armchair doctor of the mind. *Was this romantic temptation undermining my confidence?*

Roger and I walked home from the hospital together every day that week. He kept a careful distance. Companionship with someone who understood the strange world of medicine came as a welcome relief. We discovered a treasure of common ground despite our different faiths. Both families were from Lower Manhattan and enjoyed museums and theater. Roger had attended Columbia University, and we were certain we had crossed paths a few times.

* * *

Saturday night was glorious, a clear sky lit by a full winter moon. Roger arrived with his coach at seven sharp, ready to travel to a charming restaurant a half hour west. Helping me into the carriage, I noticed the smell of whiskey on his breath. *How odd.*

The Baltimore, an established restaurant in the city, was on the street level of its companion hotel. The intimate dining room held twelve tables, each adorned with fresh flowers, a lace tablecloth, and fine china. I couldn't recall when I'd last dined in such high style. We nestled into the comfortable chairs, swapping stories of our years at Hopkins. Roger did near-perfect impersonations of our professors, keeping me in stitches. We placed our orders while our waiter refilled our goblets. Roger finished off the first bottle of wine just as our entrees were served. I hungrily dove into a plate of succulent leg of lamb with homemade mint jelly, roasted beets, and potatoes. The red wine made me tipsy, but Roger's behavior didn't change. Midway through the main course, he ordered a second bottle.

"Don't order more on my account. I've had quite enough; I've barely started my second glass." I pointed to my full goblet. Although fortunate to come from a home where money wasn't a struggle, we were never allowed to be wasteful. Tillie frequently reminded us of our hungry neighbors in the Lower East Side. Besides, alcohol wasn't a part of our normal day-to-day lives.

"It's fine, Hannah. I've been wanting to try the local red."

By the time dessert arrived, Roger was still drinking, growing sloppier by the minute. His transformation was shocking. In place of twinkling blue eyes was a hangdog, flaccid face. His voice grew loud and garbled, disturbing the other diners. As he spoke, he clumsily swung his hands about, precariously close to the glassware. I sat poised to catch a goblet or vase. Finally, in a slurred voice, he began professing his feelings for me. "Hannah, my darling, I'm infatuated with you."

I noticed the second bottle was empty. Roger drank more at a simple dinner than my entire family consumed at a wedding or holiday meal. His vulgar voice and manners continued to worsen, eating more like an animal than a refined gentleman.

I was flushed with humiliation, my dinner churning in my stomach. I thought about sneaking out, finding a coach, and riding home in peace. I had ample money with me, but what would he say to Elspeth? That I left him at the restaurant because he drank a bit too much wine? That, once again, I was a killjoy? *I can surely put up with him until the end of dinner.*

"Roger, since you live in the opposite direction, how about I take a separate carriage home? I have money with me."

"No, I'm a gentleman. Can't allow that." he slurred. "Would you like a cordial to complete the meal?"

"No. I'd like to go home now." I said firmly, my anger growing. "Let's settle the bill."

"Not much for imbibing, are you?" he scoffed.

I tried a different approach. "Roger, I'm happy to take my own carriage if you'd like to stay longer."

Diners turned to stare as his voice rose. "I said no. I'll take you home."

I sighed. *What's the harm? I'll be back at the boarding house soon enough.*

Roger tugged at his jacket pocket, pulling out his billfold. Fumbling, he dropped bills and coins on the floor, some rolling out of reach. As he leaned down to recover his cash, he lost his balance, tipping the chair and collapsing on the floor with an earsplitting crash. Time froze. I looked from him to the other dinner guests. All eyes were on him, watching as he crawled across the floor, gathering his coins. The waiter righted his chair. Women averted their faces, embarrassed for me.

I grew more impatient to leave. "Do you need help?"

"I have it handled," he answered gruffly.

Moments later, we were on the sidewalk, hailing a coach. The air was cold and dry, stars twinkling overhead exactly as they had earlier in the evening. The ingredients for romance were still there, but he was plainly the wrong man.

Roger stopped a coach and opened the door. As I settled onto the bench, he lingered outside, gesturing to the driver, finally handing something to him. I slid to the opposite side of the carriage bench, hoping to leave space between us, fixated on getting home. But as Roger stepped inside, he shifted himself tightly against my body, grabbing the coach blanket, and draped it across our laps.

"Hannah, you are everything I've ever wanted." He placed his right arm around my neck, yanking my face to his. He kissed me roughly, his tongue filling my mouth with the acrid taste of wine and saliva.

I pushed him away, wiping my mouth on my sleeve. "Stop, Roger. You're crushing me."

Deaf to my protest, he slid his hand under the blanket, lifting my skirt with his left hand, pulling at my undergarments.

"Stop it!" I shouted. I prayed the driver would hear me and pull over.

Roger taunted me. "He won't be stopping. I gave him the *special* tip."

He continued groping under the blanket.

Panic coursed through me. I struggled, scratching his face, slapping his cheeks, desperate to make him stop. Finally, I reached through the folds of my skirt for my pocket purse, squeezing the coins in a tight ball, and pulled it through the skirt opening. As he leaned away from my face, I hit him hard on the nose.

"Ouch! Damn it, woman." He released me and grabbed his nose. Quickly regaining his composure, he jumped on me again, teasing, "Oh, you like to play rough, you little vixen."

By this point, he'd torn my undergarments. Undeterred, he fumbled with his pants.

I clawed at him. "You dare touch me again, and I'll report you to the Dean of the Medical School!" I screamed. "You're assaulting me. This is rape."

He stopped abruptly, pulling back, his face astonished. "You'd have me thrown out? I thought you liked me."

"You've done this to others, haven't you?" I accused him with fury. "I'll wager this isn't the first time you've forced yourself on a woman." Then it finally occurred to me, "They already know about you, don't they?"

Roger dragged himself to the other side of the coach, growling, "You girls are all teases. I know you want it. Eventually, you'll beg me for it."

Stop talking, Hannah. Don't incite him further.

Now I knew why he was banished from home. What was wrong with this man? A fine gentleman by day, a rapist by night? I straightened my outfit and angrily threw the blanket his way. Keeping my pocket purse clenched in my fist, I trembled, counting the seconds until we pulled up to my boarding house.

Chapter Seven

The following morning, after a fitful night's sleep, I sat at the dining room table with my tea, thankful for a quiet Sunday morning and the chance to hide alone in the boarding house. I was outraged by Roger's attack, and at myself for playing into his hands. How could I have been so naïve? Trusting a man I'd known less than a month was reckless. Still shaky, I thought of the irony; Roger, insisting on walking me home to *protect* me all those nights after work when in fact, he was fattening the kill. Would anyone besides Tillie believe my story and not blame me? And even she would certainly remind me that she'd taught me better. That I should have invited a chaperone.

To make matters worse, I needed a way to handle Dr. Adams. I was scheduled to work with him for the next two weeks. Would he carry out his vicious threat and report me to the President of the Medical Staff or was he simply blowing hot air? How could I shield myself from his vindictiveness? Was there another way besides sidling up to the Trustees and taking him head-on?

Winter recess was scheduled in two weeks at the end of this obstetrics rotation. I'd never needed a break this badly. Up to now, I'd considered staying in Baltimore over the holiday break, studying, and keeping Mrs. Collins company at the boarding house through the holidays. But the last few months had left me unmoored. Constant haranguing from Dr. Adams affected my nerves, always dreading his next assault. I wasn't close to anyone except Elspeth, and now I questioned the wisdom of that friendship. After Roger's attack, I needed my family's reassurance more than ever.

One and a half more years remained in medical school. Instead of worrying about deranged men, this was the time I should be weighing career options, considering what I'd choose next. Was my dream of obstetrics still best suited for me? Could I take on the aftermath of dangerous abortions and offer the women in my community a measure of protection? I prayed that my meeting with the trustees might provide needed guidance.

At times like these, I missed the close companionship of my sister, Tillie, always my sounding board and anchor. She'd guided me through the many challenges I faced working in a man's occupation. Clever and bold, Tillie had grown a thriving garment business in an industry dominated by men who resented her success. But despite her ambitious plans for me, and for herself, she was always most concerned with my happiness.

Tillie, at times, was more like a mother, and knew me better than anyone, both my talents and the fragile vessel of sadness I kept hidden. It began in early childhood after the loss of my mother and feeling abandoned by my father. Back then, I developed nervous behaviors, pulling at my eyelashes and eyebrows until they disappeared, later picking at my fingernails. When Tillie took me in, I enjoyed a few years respite and happiness, and the vile habits fell by the wayside. But then I lost my dearest childhood friend to consumption and fell into a deep well of sadness. Over time, with help from family and friends, I channeled that despair into my ambition, excelling in school, trailing Dr. Boro on house calls in the Lower East Side.

The summer after college, before moving to Baltimore, I attended many glorious weddings, watching my girlfriends' lives tuck neatly into the fancy pleats of their futures. Although I was eager to start medical school, I was lonely, sitting for hours in Tillie's parlor on her soft Queen Anne chair.

Tillie and Abe began their adult lives poor as mice. It took years of hard work to buy furnishings, and when they did, Tillie embraced the warmth and detail of Victorian design. Walls covered in calming botanical wallpaper and fanciful moldings along the ceiling and floor seams created a cozy wrapping around her family. The parlor was decorated with paintings depicting bucolic life, evoking childhood memories on Papa's farm. Glass-enclosed shelving displayed fascinating photographs and objects from her limited travels. Tillie's plush cherry furniture all had cabriole legs, a Queen Anne trademark.

I occupied that same Queen Anne chair for hours on end, reading or staring at the Brooklyn Bridge construction postcards, family photos from the Chicago World's Columbian Exposition, and treasured porcelain pieces that filled the glass shelves in her curio cabinet. The chair eventually held the imprint of my derriere.

She'd say, "Hannah, if you don't get out of that chair, I'll need to dust you off too. And will you stop picking your nails? No patients will want to put their care in mutilated hands."

Often in the afternoon, we'd head uptown with her children for museum trips, theater, and picnics in Central Park. Tillie insisted the world was vibrant, offering effervescence and hope. "Open your eyes and pay attention. Your life is ahead of you."

Medical school kept me busy and content for two years. But since early autumn, when I began clinical work, I had bouts of exhaustion and anxiety, my warning signs. The episode with Roger exacerbated everything. I hoped if I shared his attack later in the day with Elspeth, my symptoms would subside. But my decision had been made. I'd return to New York for the holiday break and recover.

With my immediate dilemma resolved, I needed to study. My flock of giddy housemates were stowed quietly at church for the next two hours, and I'd no time to waste. I forced myself to concentrate on childbed fever, a devastating condition that worried all mothers.

* * *

"Oh, it's you, Isaacson. What do you want?" Dr. Adams asked imperiously. "I thought I might enjoy an Isaacson-free day for a change."

Like a dagger, his words deflated my resolve. It was only six-thirty Monday morning, and he'd already pierced me. Despite my hurt, I smiled, pretending it was a joke.

"Doctor Adams, I was wondering if you could spare a moment to offer advice. Have you had coffee? My treat."

He grimaced. "Of course I have. It's free for the senior medical staff in our lounge."

Was I supposed to know that? "Then perhaps we can sit and talk. It's important."

"Very well." He led me to the fourth-floor conference room where I'd met with the Fitzsimmons the week before. Entering that room, still echoing with their grief, galvanized my courage.

"We had a close call last week with a midwife in town. I'm sure you've heard." My strategy was to turn the tables and have the idea come from him.

"Of course I have," he barked. "Get to the point."

Another arrow. *Calm down, Hannah. Don't be so frail.*

"The nurses are telling me that abortions are on the rise." I pointed to the window and the buildings beyond. "We may see more in the future, especially mid-pregnancy, like last week's case. With women choosing to deliver their babies at the hospital, midwives are hungry for work."

He was quiet, his forehead furrowed in concentration.

Was it possible I'd snared his attention? "I was hoping you could lend your expertise. Is there anything we can do to stop them?"

I waited. Would he leave me be if I helped improve his standing at the hospital? An important cause with favorable press might do the trick.

He huffed. "I was hoping to finally finish with obstetrics for good. Too much yelling and screaming. I would stay home if I wanted all that commotion." He paused. "And those gullible girls should stop teasing the men. Then none of this would happen."

His poor wife, having to live with that man.

My stomach dropped. He wasn't taking the bait. Of course, he blamed it on the girls. I searched for another tactic. "I know they're illegal, but after seeing more than a couple a week in Emergency, it's clear no one pays any attention to the law."

He eyed me suspiciously. "What are you getting at?"

"This may be an opportunity for you and the hospital to protect the public, educate them about the dangers of mid-term abortions." I opened my hands to him, aiming my comment carefully, using my most convincing voice. "After all, you're the foremost expert in Baltimore."

A quick shift in his eyes to mine. His right brow raised almost imperceptibly. Was it suspicion? Self-importance? Would he bite?

"Let me think about it." He rose and ambled out of the room.

Was his step lighter?

* * *

"I'm glad I found you." I'd been on the watch for Elspeth all day. I finally saw her sitting with a cup of coffee in the café just as I was leaving the hospital. "Any chance you're heading home soon? I need to talk."

"No, I have more patients to see, and I'm not feeling well. Can it wait until tomorrow?"

I cocked my head to the side, studying her. "Of course. Anything I can do?"

Elspeth shook her head, then glanced at me self-consciously. "Can I trust you? Can you keep a secret?"

"You know I can. What's wrong?" I pulled out a chair and sat beside her.

She leaned into my ear, whispering, "I've missed two monthlies, and I have all the symptoms. And what's worse, Ethan's avoiding me." She hugged her chest. It was the first time I'd ever witnessed Elspeth nervous.

I scanned the lobby to ensure no one could eavesdrop. "When are you going to tell him?" I thought about their plan to marry. "Perhaps you can join him on the holiday break and meet his family," I whispered back.

Her eyes held a new determination. "I'm going to hunt him down before he goes home. Wish me luck."

My dilemma with Roger shrank in size. After all, it was only a scare. Telling Elspeth about Roger Holloway could wait.

I called after her. "Are we still on for Wednesday with the trustees?"

"Oh yes, I almost forgot. I'll get the details to you later."

* * *

My eyes burned from reading the small print in my textbook. I turned off my lamp, relishing the wave of relaxation sweeping through my body. A soft knock at the bedroom door interrupted my calm.

"Hannah, are you still up?" Elspeth called hesitantly in a panic-filled voice.

"Come in." I sat up as she entered.

Her eyes were red and puffy.

I knew right away. "Oh, Elspeth. Tell me. What happened?"

She dropped on my quilt and sobbed, shoulders shaking, gulping for air.

My heart broke for us both. *Why are women so vulnerable, such easy targets?* I sat beside her, pulling her sturdy frame to me, hugging her until she settled. After her sniffling subsided, she recounted her conversation with Ethan.

"He won't marry me. He told his parents about me weeks ago, and they won't allow him to court a low-class Scot, especially with my thick accent." Elspeth blew her nose and scoffed, "As if they know anything about me or my family." She caught her breath. "And they've never heard me talk!"

My sense of indignation flamed. "That's so unfair. The old New York families think they're superior to everyone else. You'll see, while they play ostrich, the world will pass them right by."

She exhaled a deep shuddering breath. "I've never felt so weak."

"It's his child. What did he suggest you do?" I was furious at Ethan, kowtowing to his parents. Perhaps if they knew she was pregnant, they'd change their minds.

"Get rid of it. Ethan offered to pay. And to top that, he admitted meeting Mr. Slater's sister at one of those fancy balls of hers. It turns out he's planning to officially court her this summer." She wiped her face on her sleeve.

"God almighty, no! What a miserable swine." My head was about to explode.

"I know, I should have guessed. Ethan and Slater are thick as thieves." She lay back, eyes fixed on the ceiling, "Entitled bastards."

"Elspeth, you were with me last week and saw the abortion disaster with your own eyes. You can't trust the midwives. They're not properly trained." I stood, my hands quivering. "Honestly, Elspeth, you have to promise you won't go to one of those butchers."

She looked at me with desperation, her eyes again brimming with tears. "Hannah, would you do it?"

I clutched the back of my desk chair, upset she'd asked me to do something illegal. "Absolutely not. We'd get caught and expelled. We've both worked too hard." I inhaled deeply, hoping to calm down. "We'll come up with a plan, without damaging your body or our futures. Let me think." I dropped into my desk chair, sinking my chin in my hand.

Elspeth lay back on my bed sniffling, her indomitable spirit crushed. Meanwhile, I closed my eyes, trying to make room in my head for one more problem.

Alternatives slowly crystallized. "It sounds like you're not far along." She nodded.

I calculated. "It's already late December, and you graduate in May. Maybe you can request the next semester off, say you've caught a malady you can't shake. Then ask to return in the fall to finish. Lots of men students have done it."

"I don't know." She hesitated a moment. "I wanted to graduate on time."

"Can you make arrangements with your mother or one of your aunts to help you with the baby when it's born?" I thought aloud. "You can set things in place, return and graduate next December. No one will ever know."

"That would destroy my mam and pa. I'm their bragging rights." She pointed her nose upward and sniffed haughtily. "Elspeth earned this award, that scholarship, and so on. I can't do that to them." She rolled to face the wall, looking absently at the floral wallpaper. "They were never convinced I could pull medical school off."

"Oh, Elspeth, I'm sure they'd understand. These things happen to women all the time." I said gently.

Her shoulders quivered. "I know, but not to me. No one else will want me after this."

"Try to keep calm and think about it." I offered, "Don't forget, the churches make provisions for unwed mothers who want to give up their infants. You could make up a story and disappear for a few months."

"I thought of that, but I was looking forward to going to New York with Ethan and practicing medicine there." She hugged her stomach. "How could he do this to me? Maybe he'll change his mind."

I sat beside her, rubbing her back until her tears dried. *What was it about love? It was supposed to be so wonderful.*

Elspeth turned her head to mine. "I can still practice in New York or stay here. Can't I?"

"Of course, you can. We'll find a way."

Minutes later, composure restored, Elspeth rose from my bed. She gazed down at me. "Hannah, you've been a true friend. Let me give it some thought."

I was troubled by her rapid recovery. "Please don't do anything rash. Promise me." I begged.

"I promise."

Chapter Eight

"Hannah, you're spending too much time fussing with your hair for a bunch of 'ole biddies." Elspeth mocked my reflection. "These women care far less about your coif and clothing than what you will do for their cause. They want to show the men they've been right all along, you know, in accepting women."

I pursed my lips and nodded. "Good for them. I've had about enough of men."

Her eyebrows arched. "Did something else happen with Dr. Adams? And you never said anything about your dinner with Roger."

I changed the subject, not in the mood to relive my nightmare with Roger. "Elspeth, are you sure you're feeling up to eating a rich dinner out?" Overnight, Elspeth had begun behaving indifferently to her condition, as if it weren't a real new chapter of her life.

"I'm starving, can't wait," she quipped. "Nothing's getting in my way."

My head was full of topics I hoped we'd discuss over dinner. "Do you suppose it would be appropriate to bring up the committee idea?"

"What committee?"

"You know, about educating the community... on mid-term abortions? Today, Dr. Adams shocked me. He asked if I'd work on it with him." I shook my head in disbelief. "And, predictably, he's acting as if it was his idea in the first place."

"I'll bet. Just like a man to have the memory of an ant and no soul," Elspeth scoffed.

"My plan worked, though." I twisted my brows slyly. "Dr. Adams is off my back. Besides, we get more done if we stop caring about who gets credit. The committee work will save lives." I'd kept my eye on the greater good despite knowing I'd only be remembered as Dr. Adam's little helper.

Elspeth sighed. "It's been the curse of women since Adam and Eve. We'll always be the temptress, and men get credit for populating the world—after we pushed out millions of babies."

"Elspeth, is that how Ethan's making you feel? As if you tempted him, and he's not equally responsible?" I placed my hand on her shoulder.

She sighed. "Not exactly. We haven't spoken since I told him."

I squeezed her into a hug. It did seem women were always gathering the shattered pieces of life. "Things will sort themselves out."

Elspeth pulled back, shaking me off. "I'm done thinking about it. We'd better go. It'll take a half hour to cross town."

Had Elspeth made her decision? Would she keep her promise to me?

Mrs. Collin's shrill voice cut through my thoughts. "Girls, girls, I hailed a coach. Come quickly before he leaves."

We scrambled down the stairs, pulling on our outerwear, running to the porch. I stopped briefly to give Mrs. Collins a hug. "Thank you. Don't stay up."

"I'm so proud of you, Hannah," she beamed. "Can't wait to hear about dinner. I'll want to know every word."

* * *

This looks familiar. The row houses on the wealthier west side of town were more elaborate and expensive than our neighborhood, each adorned with tooth and groove concrete molding along the roof lines and accented with curlicue corbels. Every house had three tall windows across the front, some with arched lids that looked out on snow-covered patches of garden. *Could it be?* Minutes later, the coach pulled up before The Baltimore, the same hotel where Roger and I had dined a week earlier. *Good God, what a horrible coincidence.*

I squeezed my eyes shut, forcing the memory to the back of my mind.

I couldn't spoil this important opportunity. Roger didn't deserve to hold such sway over me. I exhaled deeply, steadying my nerves. I straightened my hat and climbed from the coach.

Elspeth studied my face. "Nervous, Hannah?"

"A little." I took a long step out of the coach onto the sidewalk. "Let's go in."

She led the way, clearly more skilled than I at concealing her personal concerns.

Elspeth led me into the tiny lobby, where an attendant took our coats and led us into the dining room, where Mrs. Martha Thomas and Mrs. Mary Garrett were already engaged in an animated discussion, each sipping from a goblet of wine. Elspeth introduced me, and we took our seats. I was surprised by how ordinary they looked—no fancy clothing or jewels hinting at their pedigree. Instead, each wore a serviceable dark wool suit, crisp white cotton blouse, and simple cameo brooch.

"Your brooches are so unusual," I commented.

Mrs. Thomas looked down at hers. "Thank you, Miss Isaacson. We picked these up in England last year when we visited the Wedgwood factory. They're nice day pieces."

"I much prefer their modern look, not too lacy or ornate," Mrs. Garrett added. "Do you girls mind if we order?"

Once our order was placed, they resumed their conversation. While listening closely, I relinquished every preconception I had of the wealthy.

"Can you believe Congress approved a million-dollar expansion to the White House? With taxpayer money? The nerve!" Mrs. Garrett set down her wine goblet with a thud.

Mrs. Thomas shook her head. "They better allow the public into the building for tours so people can see what they paid for."

I was spellbound. These were two of the four legendary trustees' daughters who strong-armed Johns Hopkins into accepting women. Strong-armed, that is, in exchange for a tidy sum of money to help build the hospital-medical school complex. Mrs. Garrett was the unyielding mastermind who, at the same time, founded the Bryn Mawr School for Girls in downtown

Baltimore. All raised in highly restrictive homes, once their parents were gone, these women became resolute in their commitment to the suffragist movement while advancing educational opportunities for women. It was no wonder the medical staff didn't want to offend them.

The engaging company, together with the velvety red wine, dissolved any remaining trepidation I'd felt upon arrival. I sank back against the soft cushion on my chair, absorbed in their banter.

The owner approached our table, smirking at me. "Welcome back. I'm pleased to see you again so soon. Saturday night was certainly exciting."

"You were here recently?" Mrs. Thomas tilted her head, eyeing me curiously.

I squirmed. *How dare he.* "Yes, this past weekend, I came with a classmate for dinner. My companion was a bit of a character. But the food was lovely." I hoped my vague description would quell her curiosity. I did not want to recount my embarrassment with Roger. To my relief, Mrs. Garrett changed the topic entirely.

"Tell me, Hannah, as a female student, what do you see as your most pressing issue at school today?"

I sat up straight, choosing my words carefully. "As Elspeth mentioned, I plan to become an obstetrician. It's a new specialty, growing quickly as more women schedule hospital births. As you can imagine, they prefer receiving pain relief during labor and hope to reduce their risk of childbed fever." I stopped and studied their attentive faces before continuing. "But it appears to be taking routine work away from the midwives in town. Unfortunately, they're backfilling that work with more terminations, including late-term pregnancies, presenting a very dangerous risk to their patients."

My words were met with wide-eyed stares and silence. Had I taken things too far? *Hannah, you should have known the subject was indelicate for a dinner table conversation.* "I apologize for my poor manners or if I have offended either of you."

They both shook their head vigorously. "No need. I want to hear more," Mrs. Garrett said. "I'm shocked. I thought abortions were illegal."

"They are. But as I'm sure you know, in the past, almost all infants were delivered at home by midwives, except for the very poor. Back then, they were the only women who came to the hospital because they couldn't afford to pay a midwife. The midwives had always performed very early-term abortions, mostly with herbals, despite the newer law. But they avoided midterm ones. Now we're seeing too many damaged women in Emergency."

An irritated cough came from the woman seated behind us. I turned my head and was met with a fiery glare. I nodded at the woman politely.

Mrs. Garrett whispered loudly, "Do go on."

I lowered my voice. "It's been commonplace for many years. There are numerous unplanned pregnancies, rich and poor. Far too many mouths to feed for the parents, parishes, or the city, and a silent understanding that the law looks the other way so long as the termination is early in the pregnancy, before 'quickening.' I watched their confused expressions.

"Quickening is when the mother feels movement," Elspeth clarified.

A loud bang on the table behind us. A gentleman shouted, "Enough of that talk! You're upsetting my wife."

The waiter approached, glaring at me. "Ladies, please keep your voices down. You're creating a scene." He turned to face me. "Again."

Mrs. Garrett scoffed. "Ignorance is bliss." Turning to the waiter, she continued. "Please offer the couple a bottle of your best red wine for any offense taken—on my tab, of course."

Surprised by her bravado, I nodded to the waiter contritely.

I whispered to the trustees. "Perhaps I can share more another time."

Mrs. Thomas ignored me, pushing harder for more. "I had no idea. When I was much younger, we thanked the Lord for every pregnancy. Trust me, we had lots of surprises."

I listened silently.

She continued, "My Nathan was completely unexpected, years after the rest of my brood. I'll admit only to you that he's my favorite. I wouldn't trade that 'surprise' for the world."

I couldn't help glancing at Elspeth.

She was looking at her lap, rubbing her knuckles.

Mrs. Garrett broke the silence. "What are their qualifications? The midwives, I mean."

These women had all the right questions. They were a marvel.

I was more at ease now, moving away from the socially offensive topic. "That strikes at the heart of the issue. For the most part, midwifery has been taught through apprenticeship, much like doctors a half-century ago. But today, midwives are a mix of nurses who've chosen to work in childbirth, the apprenticeship model, and I understand there are a few midwifery schools. But by far, most are still trained by older midwives."

"No oversight like students at the hospital?" Mrs. Thomas pursued the issue.

Elspeth chimed in. "No, but bad results get around. The good ones are known and charge more."

How does she know that?

"So, help me understand the bigger picture. Tell me how the pieces fit," asked Mrs. Garrett.

I took a deep breath, searching for the best way to describe how the war between doctors and midwives was taking its toll. "Today, doctors consider childbirth a legitimate part of their practice and view midwives as inadequately trained and undisciplined. The midwives see the doctors as interlopers, forcing them to seek ways to replace lost income. They need to find a way to work together."

"Yes, indeed," said Mrs. Thomas.

"In the meantime, the unscrupulous have extended the window for terminations into the second trimester." I checked the table behind us. They were enjoying their new bottle of red. The gentleman lifted his glass to me with a smile.

Mrs. Garrett leaned forward with interest in her eyes.

I continued. "Not only do many mothers feel movement in the fourth and early fifth months, but the procedure becomes far more dangerous at the mid-point of a pregnancy. There's much more tissue and blood supporting the growing baby. Frankly, it's even dangerous when performed in our clean operating theater at the hospital." I glanced about the room. No one was paying attention. I whispered, "Last week, a young society girl was brought in off the street, practically bleeding to death."

Mrs. Thomas grabbed the brooch pinned on her chest. "Good Lord, no!"

"What can be done?" Mrs. Garrett's forehead was deeply creased with concern.

I sighed. "It has everyone on edge, both doctors and nurses."

Elspeth kicked me under the table. She pointed her chin at the waiter, who stared at us from the doorway.

I lowered my voice further. "Earlier today, I approached my senior physician, Dr. Adams, to discuss the matter. We agreed to form a hospital committee to provide education to the community about these dangers. And we must insist on more education for midwives, a new modernized midwife."

"Oh my, you're ambitious. I like that about you, Miss Isaacson." Mrs. Garrett scrutinized me, then looked at Mrs. Thomas. "Martha, isn't Adams the one with the niece? You remember. The engagement gone bad?"

"I believe so. This is an about-face." Mrs. Thomas shrugged her shoulders.

"Personally, I don't trust Dr. Adams either," Elspeth added. "But Hannah's not quite a doctor and can't do a thing without support from a senior physician."

Mrs. Garrett's eyebrows shot up. "What did I tell you, Martha? Women's health needs are entirely different from men's. We need to pay more attention to this." She shifted her eyes to me. "Miss Isaacson, once you're ready, we'll help get the good word out."

Mrs. Thomas nodded. "I know the Abells of the *Baltimore Sun*. Let me know when you're ready, and I'll speak to one of the sons. They're helping their father with the business, and this would be a good story for them."

Chapter Nine

Elspeth left the house before I opened my eyes. Disappointed to miss her, I threw on my clothes and headed out, hoping to catch up. I was eager to discuss last evening's dinner with the trustees. It was the first time since my tangle with Roger that I felt optimistic about my future at Johns Hopkins.

Even at my fast pace, I couldn't catch up to her. Once at the hospital, I was swept into the hectic pace of the Clinic. At two in the afternoon, I was interrupted in the middle of a patient examination. I realized immediately something was amiss.

Nurse O'Neal knocked hard at the exam room door. "Come immediately. You're needed in Emergency."

Leaving my patient half-dressed, I flew out the exam room door, a sense of foreboding creeping through me.

Nurse O'Neal grabbed my arm and ran to the stairwell at the rear of the building.

"What is it?" I demanded.

"Another bloody miscarriage! The patient insisted, only you." Nurse O'Neal was breathless as we raced down the floors, taking steps two at a time, finally opening the ground-level door directly into Emergency. "She's one of us."

"Who?" I demanded, my stomach in knots. But I knew. Elspeth would never allow something as ordinary as a pregnancy to crush her dreams.

Nurse O'Neil squeezed my arm tighter as we tore into the trauma bay. She pulled the curtain open.

I gasped, "Oh, sweet Lord, no!" She lay unconscious, her body splayed across the bed, half-naked with blood oozing into the towels between her legs. Quickly washing my hands, I cleared the towels away to examine her. There was so much blood, soaking the sheets and mattress, spilling onto the floor. *What were you thinking, Elspeth?* The pregnancy tissue had been expelled, and I could see the spongy placenta on the sheets. I felt tears in the lining of her uterus. The bungling midwife must have pierced the uterus and hit a major blood vessel. *Could she survive?*

"Get word upstairs immediately! She'll need a hysterectomy. Call the elevator." I packed her with fresh towels and rolled the stretcher to the lift. *Come on, come on, damn it.* It took an eternity for the grated door to unfold. My body pulsed with impatience.

I clutched Elspeth's hand. It was growing cold. Her face, so pale. With every second, more blood was lost. I wished I could lift her into my arms like an angel and fly to the operating theater.

"I'm sorry, Hannah." A weak voice whispered from beneath me.

My eyes shot to hers. "Elspeth, you're awake?" I leaned over her face, marshaling my most reassuring voice. "We need to operate."

Elspeth's eyes fluttered, her voice barely audible. "I should've listened. Call the pastor."

"No! You're going to be fine. Stay with me!" Panicked tears rolled down my cheeks as I stroked her forehead, unwilling, unable to accept what I already knew.

The nurse to my left scrambled away. "I'll get him."

Silence.

"Elspeth, Elspeth!" My voice rose in pitch. "Stay with me!"

Nothing.

"No…please don't die," I shouted desperately.

"I can't find a pulse," Nurse O'Neal cried. "Good Lord in Heaven!"

I held Elspeth's shoulders, leaning over her beautiful face. Her wayward hair was spread over the pillow. I helplessly watched her rosy freckles fade, crying onto her body. "No, Elspeth, don't leave me."

I was devastated, holding her body to me, sobbing. I finally caught my breath and stood upright. The nurses were clustered together several feet away, waiting to cover her body and take it to the morgue. She was an unfortunate casualty on an otherwise busy day, another body for the ice chest.

A rush of fury raced through me. This was not over. "Get Ethan Frank *immediately!*" I screamed. "We're not moving her an inch until he sees what he's done."

Chapter Ten

I charged into the hospital's telephone room and pleaded for permission to make a long-distance call. My body was shaking with panic while I waited for Tillie to pick up. Four rings later, she was accosted by my gut-wrenching sobs.

"I'm on my way." Her voice coursed back through the telephone wires. "Go to the boarding house and wait for me."

As Tillie later recounted, she scribbled a note to her husband, Abe, and bolted for Grand Central Station with only her coat and purse, leaving my nephew in charge of his younger sister, Miriam. Hours later, Mrs. Collins, bleary-eyed from crying, greeted Tillie at the boarding house door.

Distraught weeping from my housemates and Mrs. Collins snaked up the stairs into my room, shaking the bones of our row house. Mrs. Collins attempted to retell the story to Tillie between her bouts of tears. "Hannah won't come out and refuses to speak to anyone. All the girls are devastated. This has been a terrible, terrible day. Miss Elspeth's parents are coming later for the body. I don't know how I'll console them."

Tillie didn't wait for Mrs. Collins to finish. She raced up the stairs and burst through my door. The sight of her face broke me again as I collapsed in her arms, still barely believing my only friend was gone forever.

"There's no God." I sobbed. "I can't do this anymore."

I clutched Tillie's strong frame, inhaling the soothing fragrance of her favorite lavender soap through my stuffed nose. She hugged me until I could cry no longer.

Loosening her grip, she held me at arm's length, forcing me to look into

71

her eyes. "You're coming home with me tomorrow. If need be, I will personally speak to the Dean. They can survive without you for a few weeks."

Her words were a salve on my broken spirit. There was no way I could pull myself together and return to work right away. All I wanted was to burrow away and hide. *Would I ever be able to return?*

Mrs. Collins' shrill voice called from downstairs. "Hannah, please come down. Mrs. Thomas and Mrs. Garrett are here to speak with you."

"Are they the trustees you wrote about?" Tillie asked. "Who else would come here so soon after...?" Her voice trailed off.

"Yes, they're the women I described in my last letter. The Hospital must have notified them." I touched my disheveled hair. "I have to go downstairs and speak to them, but I'm a mess."

Tillie led me to the lavatory. "Let's get a cool cloth for your face and fix your hair. Then we'll see what they have to say."

By the time we made our entrance, Mrs. Collins, now filled with purpose—bless her sweet soul—had the women seated on the threadbare couches serving tea and biscuits as if her house had been restored to its former Victorian glory. Self-conscious of my swollen eyes, I nodded a greeting while dragging two dining room chairs close to the couch. "I'd like to introduce Mrs. Tillie Levine, my sister. She just arrived by train from New York. If you don't mind, I've asked her to join us."

Both women stood.

Mrs. Garrett, tall, full-bodied, and fair like Tillie, was first to introduce herself. "Welcome to Baltimore, although under unthinkable circumstances."

Mrs. Thomas was a hair shorter than me and twice my girth. "We are enamored by your sister. But to lose a dear friend and talent this way is a terrible blow."

As Tillie and I sat, the ladies followed.

I continued to sniffle, unable to hold back tears. Tillie handed her lace handkerchief to me.

"We heard the devastating news about Elspeth from the Hospital President." Mrs. Garrett spoke softly, reaching to take my hand. "There are simply no words that could make things better. Death is the final blow."

I nodded, drawing a jagged breath. She was right. No one could bring Elspeth back.

Mrs. Thomas's face collapsed. "I simply don't understand. I've been racking my brain since we were informed. Our discussion at last Thursday night's dinner keeps nagging at me. I can't believe Elspeth would put her life in the hands of an incompetent."

I looked from one to the other. "Elspeth didn't believe anything terrible could happen to her. She was early, not yet nine weeks. Besides, she was convinced from the start that he'd marry her if she became pregnant. Everything always snapped into place for Elspeth."

"Who knew about her condition?" Mrs. Garrett asked.

I drew a shaky breath. "Only her boyfriend, Ethan Frank, and me. And when she spoke to him a few days ago, he told her he would not marry her, that she should destroy the pregnancy. He said his parents would never accept a Scot in their family." My voice now steadier, I recounted the evening when Elspeth shared their conversation. "She was a force of nature and didn't want to ever disappoint her parents or either of you." I paused. "But she promised me that she wouldn't go to a midwife."

"Did she realize her other options?" Mrs. Thomas handed me a handkerchief.

"I tried to convince her to have the child through the church or ask for her family's help, but in the end, she listened to Mr. Frank." I stared at the useless hands on my lap, the very hands unable to save her. "She still had dreams of marrying him and working in New York. She was in love. She would have done anything he asked."

Mrs. Garrett smacked her hands on her thighs, rising from the couch. "I've heard enough. The lout must be punished! How dare he push her to hurt herself? Who the Devil does he think he is?" she growled. "Those damn uppity New Yorkers thinking their stinking money is better than everyone else's. They're amnesic, forgetting their own dirty antics, the laws their grandfathers broke to get rich. And on top of it all, they probably bought his spot in college and medical school."

Mrs. Thomas cast a knowing look at Mrs. Garrett. "Mary, calm down. You and I can discuss that later. I was told he cried like a baby when he saw her in Emergency. Right now, let's see how we can help Hannah through this."

I whispered, "I completely misread her. I should have known. I was the only friend she trusted. At one point, she asked me to do it. I know she was scared, but I couldn't chance getting caught and losing my career."

Tillie, who'd been listening to the women, interrupted. "That's rubbish, Hannah. You know better. She was an adult, almost a fully trained doctor. Elspeth may have lost her head in love, but she was no one's fool. It was her decision. You handled the situation exactly as a responsible doctor should."

Mrs. Garrett sat down again and sighed. "Your sister's right, Hannah. You can't control others. And she had no right to ask you to break the law."

I nodded, still staring at my lap. "The laws are wrong. They put too many women in harm's way. Desperation drives them to take terrible risks."

Mrs. Thomas's voice softened. "I heard that Elspeth's last words were that she was sorry. She knew it was her responsibility." She paused, exhaling a chest full of air. "Look at me, Hannah."

I turned my eyes to hers.

"Mrs. Garrett and I spoke in the carriage on our way here. We agreed you should go home until the end of the holiday break. That gives you four weeks to settle down and pull yourself together. Then we want...no, need you back here. You're irreplaceable."

Mrs. Garrett inched closer, taking my hand. "This school needs you here more than ever. We promise to devote our time and influence to support you. Together, we'll put an end to these dangerous procedures and see you through the rest of medical school."

"And we know the right people to make it happen," said Mrs. Thomas, turning to her companion. "Step one, that Frank boy has to take responsibility!"

Chapter Eleven

At long last, my Queen Anne wing chair. What a relief to sink into those puffy cushions far from the turmoil in Baltimore. My heart was awash with remorse, numbness overtaking my fragile spirit, silence replacing tears. I berated myself for not recognizing Elspeth's deception. I was her truest friend and should have saved her. After all, she exemplified the very issue I was fighting for—safer care for women.

"Hannah, stop blaming yourself," Tillie admonished. "Enough is enough. People make their own choices and live or die with the consequences. Elspeth wasn't a child."

I peered back at her.

"Talk to me," Tillie said. "Tell me what's tearing at you."

I lamented. "She was still naive, at least inside. All she wanted was Ethan's love."

Tillie countered, "And she made a deadly choice, but it was her choice. She was a doctor, highly educated. She had seen terminations gone wrong at the hospital."

Could Tillie understand how complex it was? She'd been happily married for so long. "She wasn't thinking like a doctor."

"I'm giving you a couple of days to wallow, then you must pull yourself together." She stood frustrated, holding clenched hands on her hips. "Speaking of which, are you going to her funeral?"

"I don't know," I said meekly. I'd received a note that morning from Elspeth's parents asking me to say a few words on her behalf.

A rap at the door interrupted our conversation.

Tillie headed into the bathroom. "Would you please answer that? I need to freshen up."

I sighed deeply and lifted myself from my perch.

Another rap.

"Coming." I opened the door to a familiar face, one I'd known my whole life. "Doctor Boro, how nice to see you. Please come in. Are you here to see Tillie?"

"It's lovely to see you, Hannah. I'm here to speak with you."

My stomach hitched. That sister of mine. How dare she!

"I'm fine, really. Let me get tea. Come, sit."

"That would be grand. I've only a few minutes and heard you were home."

Nestled by the fireplace, the glowing embers littered the hearth. "I'm sure Tillie asked you to speak with me. She didn't need to do that."

Dr. Boro cocked his head, looking at me, "And why not? Have you departed our human race? No feelings left in that big heart of yours?"

I sighed. "It's just that there's nothing I can do now. She's gone."

Dr. Boro sat beside me, staring at the embers. "You have forgotten how grief can affect you. Remember our precious Eva?"

The memory of my paralysis after Eva, my childhood friend who died from consumption, returned to me like an electric shock. I wiggled uncomfortably in my chair. "Maybe I have. Things have been difficult, but losing Elspeth hit me so unexpectedly. I thought I had convinced her not to do it." My eyes welled with tears.

"I know, dear. You tried your best. You always do. As doctors, we're often surprised when our patients don't listen. Then grief hits us, and we don't recognize it. We see it in others and convince ourselves we're immune. But we're not. Doctors break too, just like other mortals."

I wiped my tears. He was right.

"When my Elsie passed two years ago, I was unable to speak for a week. Then Rabbi came and dragged me out of the apartment. He pulled me from my chair as if I was stuck. He said, 'Our community depends on you, with or without your dear Elsie.'" Dr. Boro looked down. "Elsie left a hole in my heart. Only our wonderful memories of marriage can fill it now."

I exhaled deeply. "I'm so sorry. I can't even imagine." My voice trailed off. "Elspeth's family wants me to speak at the funeral. I don't know if I can. I feel too responsible."

Tillie carried a tray of cookies into the parlor. "Hannah, I can ask Abe to watch Miriam so I can accompany you."

Dr. Boro admired the tray, reaching for a sugar cookie. "That's a generous offer. Hannah, I was also hoping you could find time to lend a hand at the Clinic before you head back to Baltimore. It's never been so busy."

He's dragging me out of my chair, crafty old doctor. "You know I can't refuse you." The corners of my mouth curled. How strange, feeling a smile on my face.

"Wonderful. Immigrants keep coming, and so many need medical care. Very bad things are happening in Europe. I don't see an end to it. I'm thinking of hiring one or two doctors this summer. Any chance...?"

I interrupted him. "I'm sorry. I hate to disappoint you, but I was hoping to practice obstetrics at a medical school. To stay in academics after my last year."

"Ah, very well. But can I borrow you while you are home?"

"Of course. I'd love to help." I reached for Dr. Boro's hand, squeezing it warmly.

* * *

A month later, back in Baltimore, no longer as fragile, I kept to myself, spending the hours working, studying, and sharing dinners with house-mates. My Baltimore mother, dear Mrs. Collins, and the trustees were true to their word, fussing over me at home and increasing their involvement at both the school and with me personally.

Across campus, a palpable intolerance for unapproved socializing reset the tone between men and women. News in the hospital traveled briskly. Within days after Elspeth's death, Dr. Frank's public dishonor reverberated through the hospital, sending a severe warning to anyone tempted to test the boundaries. Social trips to Fells Point were curtailed, and a distance between the genders was boldly marked.

In March, Roger was expelled after arriving at the patient clinic soused.

* * *

We settled in our regular seats at the Baltimore. Mrs. Garrett fumed. "The stories we heard about that Roger Holloway were galling—arriving at the hospital first thing in the morning drunk from the evening before, stumbling about, knocking over linen carts with soiled sheets, towels, and breaking expensive medicines. Who on God's green earth did he think he was?"

Mrs. Thomas's lips were set in a tight line. "Thank heavens it happened during the day shift. The nurse on duty had the good sense to call the Chief of Medicine. Did you know they had to drag the man out of there?"

"And taking advantage of all those women." Mrs. Garrett scoffed. "It was shocking how many shy nurses and hospital workers came forward after he was banned from the premises. He cornered them in closets, forcing himself on staff in empty beds at night. I feel terrible knowing how unsafe they felt in a place of healing."

I listened, not sure if the anxiety fluttering in my stomach came from reliving my own trauma or from the plight of my colleagues. Or was it an unraveling of relief that Roger had finally been caught? But I knew, with his artful duplicity, he might find somewhere else where he wasn't known to finish his degree and set up a practice. He possessed the right amount of chutzpah and charm to bury his failure in Baltimore. My suspicion was confirmed when I had the misfortune to pass Roger holding an armful of boxes in the hospital lobby the morning he was expelled.

He stopped in his tracks, glowering at me.

My breath caught.

Roger snarled, "I know you were behind this. You think you and your precious trustees can get me thrown out? I'm not done—with my medical career or you!"

I inhaled sharply. "You brought this on yourself, Roger."

He shouted back at me as he stormed out the hospital doors, "You haven't seen the last of me."

I was shaken, knowing I would never feel entirely safe. Casting the thought from my mind, I returned my attention to the dinner at hand.

Mrs. Thomas, noticing my distraction, interrupted my thoughts. "Hannah, did you know this man?"

I paused, deciding to share my truth. "I did. Do you remember our first dinner together with Elspeth here at the Baltimore? When the waiter recognized me?" I twisted the napkin on my lap.

"Of course," Mrs. Thomas said.

"I was at the Baltimore with Mr. Holloway the Saturday before, and he drank far too much. In the carriage ride home, he became unleashed, ripping at my dress and underthings, trying to force himself on me. I was terrified." I exhaled, relieved to shed a painful weight. I smoothed the napkin across my legs.

Mrs. Garrett's mouth dropped open. "Why on earth didn't you speak up?"

Shame coursed through me. I might have saved the other women if I'd spoken up sooner. "I wish I had, but Elspeth died the next day, and all I could think of was going home." I took out my handkerchief and dabbed my eyes.

"Mother of God. Now I'm more certain than ever that my vote to expel him was correct. His family had some nerve. They threatened to pull a sizable gift to the school if he wasn't issued a diploma." Mrs. Garrett sat tall. Angry bullets of saliva flew from her mouth. "I informed his pompous father that if he acted on his threat, we would prosecute his disgraceful son." She paused, "That was the end of that."

Agreeing, Mrs. Thomas added, "That ne'er-do-well has no right practicing medicine. He can't be trusted around vulnerable patients. He got what he deserved." She reached for my arm, squeezing it gently. "You are a strong woman, Hannah. I know you'll put it behind you.

I knew I could, but would Roger?

* * *

By mid-winter break, my future fell into place when a letter arrived from Mount Sinai Hospital in New York City.

"What does it say?" Mrs. Collins hung over me, panting with excitement.

My hands shook as I tore open the envelope. I read the first paragraph and jumped up and down, clapping like a child. "They offered me a residency in obstetrics!"

Mrs. Collins cheered with me, running to her newly installed telephone. "You jolly well must call your sister." Her eyes sparkled. "Well deserved, my girl!"

Tillie was thrilled, but when I hung up, Mrs. Collin's face had turned damp with tears. I pulled out my handkerchief. "What's wrong?"

"I hoped you'd stay on and work in Baltimore." Mrs. Collins sniffled. "I love you like you were mine. The girls all leave in the end."

My heart dropped. Mrs. Collins put every shred of herself into caring for her flock of boarders. I would miss her too. "I'll visit, I promise." I hugged her full frame. "And you must believe that I'll carry you in my heart until the end of my days."

At the hospital, when news spread of my obstetrics residency, even Dr. Adams beamed, all part of his new public persona. He boasted to anyone who'd listen. "Hannah has been my protege. I've taught her everything she knows."

Predictably, his conduct had changed for the better once the committee to improve health education in the community was formed and press coverage increased. He reveled in the limelight, claiming full credit for himself. It came as no surprise to me that when it was time to say goodbye, Dr. Adams was nowhere to be found. He had no further use for me.

II

Part 2

New York City – September 1905

Chapter Twelve

Happiness—finally. I was brimming with anticipation of the future. In a flash, five years had shot by. I'd completed my residency at Mount Sinai, then was invited to join the faculty. My dream of becoming a women's physician had come true. In no time, my clinic and private appointments were filled with patients seeking a female doctor. Hospital leadership had begun discussing expanding my practice with the addition of another female physician.

During that time, I moved in with my stepmother, Rebecca, and her new husband, Leo. They lived uptown on the seventh floor of a plush apartment across from Central Park—only a brisk ten-block walk to the hospital. Over the years since I moved out of Papa's farmhouse as a small child, our relationship had softened.

While at Barnard College, my Papa died. His death had been especially hard on Rebecca. Early in their marriage, with the city expanding northward, he moved the family chicken farm from Harlem to Sullivan County. When he passed, Rebecca and their daughter, Abby, were left isolated in the country with only my eldest brother's family nearby. Tillie convinced Rebecca to bring Abby back to the city where Rebecca could start her life anew, launching a career as a dress designer in a fashion house. The farm was left in the hands of my oldest brother, Nathan, the only sibling who enjoyed the livestock business.

As things turned out, Tillie and Abe's dear friend Leo, the lead designer at Bloomingdale's, was on the lookout for talent, particularly with a rising demand for premade garments. *Off the Rack* was the newest trend for women and men. Leo was thrilled to add Rebecca to his burgeoning design team and kept a careful eye on her, eventually developing a personal friendship. His proposal came as no surprise.

I was delighted when Rebecca and Leo invited me to move into their lavish Upper East Side apartment. My half-sister, Abby, married in 1898, the year I left for Baltimore. Her room sat empty for four years as if patiently waiting for me. The arrangement was ideal—Rebecca kept a nutritious dinner for me in the icebox no matter what time I got home, they were good-spirited company, and I had a spectacular view of Central Park right from my bedroom window.

As if that wasn't enough, I met Joseph. He was racing down the hospital corridor as I left the library; both of us lost in our own worlds. We collided, falling to the floor, books, pens, and paper flying in every direction. We later described it to our families as "love at first collision." Sitting on the wood floor among our scattered belongings, I studied his face. Something about him reminded me of my arch high school competitor, a boy with whom I fought tooth and nail for the coveted spot of valedictorian.

He broke the spell. "Let me introduce myself." His broad smile revealed uncommonly straight white teeth. "I'm Joseph Kaufman, Doctor of Medicine, although interested primarily in the heart." He kneeled, gathering his books, gallantly placing mine in a neat pile, finally standing. He was almost a full head taller than me with cleanly cut brown hair, an aquiline nose, and wire-rimmed spectacles.

All I could muster was a head nod. No words came out. *What's the matter with you, Hannah?*

Joseph offered his hand. "Are you hurt? I should have checked." He prompted me further. "May I assist you?"

"Thank you. I'm fine. Startled, that's all." I drew in a quick breath, surprised at the electricity passing into my hand. He seemed familiar, as if small pieces of him were already woven into my life.

"Hannah, gynecology."

That spectacular smile again. "It's a pleasure to bump into you, Hannah Gynecology!

* * *

Since that fateful collision, a day didn't pass without seeing Joseph. Within weeks of meeting, we were spending all our free time together. He had a marvelous sense of humor and generously shared it with colleagues and patients. I glued myself to him, always craving more, seduced by the tonic of happiness.

Joseph had suffered a broken engagement. But instead of retreating after that disappointment, he poured his energy into his profession, brushing off his misfortune. I could learn a great deal about resiliency from him.

Rebecca cautioned me. "So many couples grow to love one other slowly, like your father and me. This romance is very fast. Be careful, Hannah. You've been through a lot of heartbreak."

"I will, but it's wonderful to be happy."

* * *

Months later, as another summer ended, fresh-faced medical students moved into campus apartments. Riding along Central Park downtown to 33rd Street in our carriage, Joseph and I marveled at the trees lining Fifth Avenue, bursting with the first hints of color. Falling acorns littered the sidewalks we often walked together. Carriage horses trotted down the avenue with an energetic hike to their step, enjoying the cool spark in the air and relieved to shake off the suffocating summer humidity.

Passing Central Park, I told Joseph, "Olmsted was building this park when my parents arrived in New York. There were farms then, sheep and other animals roaming the streets."

"And before that, the farms extended to midtown. And before that, the natives lived here trading pelts and beavers with the Dutch settlers." He laughed, enjoying the history. "The city has invaded the island."

"And it all happened in only two hundred years." I thought about the rapid pace of time and how modern Manhattan had become. "I wonder how the city will look one hundred years from now. Perhaps all illnesses will be cured, and there'll be no need for doctors?"

Joseph patted my hand. "Don't you worry, darling. That will never happen. And besides, what's important now is that there's more than enough disease around today for us to make our fortunes."

I was struck by how odd his remark was for a physician. We were both making plenty of money, but it certainly wasn't why I chose the profession. Was Joseph's only motivation money?

The coach slowed to a halt before the arched marble entryway of the Waldorf Hotel. Taken aback by the building's majesty, conjuring images of European structures, I couldn't help but notice how the city scenery had suddenly changed. First, neighborhoods scarred by the rickety buildings peppered the city blocks, and then, voila, this wonder. The Metropolitan Museum of Art, the most ornate building I'd ever seen, paled in comparison to the Waldorf, dubbed by the Times "a resplendent palace." I gazed out the carriage window in a delighted trance, knowing Joseph had planned something extraordinary for the evening. Perhaps he was right after all; it was fun to have money.

"Is there a special occasion you haven't shared?" I gathered my crepe shawl and clutch as we stepped from the carriage onto the cobblestone sidewalk. "I feel like a princess." I straightened my pale green chiffon dress, throwing my shoulders back and standing as tall as my short frame would permit.

"You are my princess." Joseph pulled me into a hug. "Let's have a look inside. I understand it's magnificent."

I gazed upward at the Waldorf's artful lettering engraved on the facade. Standing beside Joseph, I felt deeply grateful. Through so many twists and turns, I'd finally found a good man.

"Would you like to hear more about the hotel? I would be honored to serve as your tour guide," he said.

I reached for the crook of his arm, eager to hear his newly discovered trivia. "I'd be delighted."

Joseph bent his head to mine and said in his deep baritone voice, "It all started with a farmer who sold his land to John Astor in the early part of the

1800s. Remember what I just said about the farms where we now stand? Old Astor owned one that he split up for his children, each of whom later built mansions for their families. The old man expected them to get along. Good thing he passed away before witnessing their backbiting and just how wrong he was."

I thought wistfully of my childhood bedtime stories about Papa's chicken farm in Harlem. The farm had been leveled to build city blocks in the 1880s. I wished I remembered living there.

Joseph looked at me curiously. "Did I lose you already?" He studied my face as if I held the answer to a final exam.

Immediately brought back to the conversation, I shook my head. "I'm listening. Just thinking about my years on the farm when I was young."

He continued, unfettered. "As I was saying, the Astor children and their cousins fought like cats and dogs. William at this end of the block and John at the other were sworn enemies. John's mother, Caroline, was beside herself when William decided to raze his family's mansion and build the Waldorf in its place."

I rolled my eyes. "Tsk, tsk." *The problems of the rich.*

"Caroline pestered John incessantly about the noise and disruption. Finally, he concocted a plan to get his comeuppance. You see, most of the wealthy were moving uptown along Central Park just then. So, he threatened to tear down Caroline's mansion and build horse stables in its place, assuring her that the smell would drive off William's hotel guests."

"What a waste when half the city's starving. They hadn't a clue what real problems were." I looked at the uniformed staff, standing stoically as if guarding their castle. A well-dressed doorman with a top hat snapped his fingers, and a younger man in a cap hopped, opening the door for us. Amid all this splendor, I couldn't help but wonder: *Do they bring home enough to properly care for their families?*

"The threat was short-lived," Joseph continued. "Once John got a whiff of William's hotel profits, he decided money smelled better than revenge and jumped into the hotel business too, building a bigger, grander hotel next door. The Astoria is a few stories taller than the Waldorf; his way of outshining his cousin."

"That's childish, and an absurd amount of money to throw around while others struggle. They play with money like it's a game."

Joseph ignored me. "Listen, the story gets better. When they realized there was an even greater fortune to be gained by combining businesses—especially with their spectacular guest lists, the wealthiest Americans and, of course, European dignitaries—they joined the two hotels through the marble alleyway out front." Joseph pointed to the entryway in the lobby. "They call it 'Peacock Ally' so guests can display their finery while strolling back and forth."

I shook my head in disbelief. "Charming, but how do they keep it going, disliking each other as much as they do?"

Joseph laughed loudly. "My practical princess. Always seeking solutions to problems."

I looked about to see if we were drawing attention. "What do you mean?" I didn't care for the way he was patronizing me. *Don't ruin things, Hannah. He's worked hard to make a special evening. It's just his way.*

"My dear Hannah, you're so innocent, such a caring soul. Don't you know these boys would never dirty their hands running a hotel? That's work for commoners. The Astors and their kind don't work the same way we do. They simply invest and count their money. The cousins hired someone outside their families to run the entire block. They leased it to a Prussian, George Boldt, a hotel genius."

We drifted inside. I was immediately distracted by the ornate lobby, filled with precious antique furniture: Asian vases, marble columns, and enormously high ceilings opulently decorated, all fit with electric chandeliers.

Joseph followed my gaze. "The entire hotel runs on electricity. Every guest room has a light and a private lavatory." He squeezed my hand, whispering in my ear. "Maybe we can book a room here someday, for a honeymoon, perhaps?"

I turned, and my eyes met his. *What was he up to?*

"Come, let me show you the garden court." Joseph led me into a botanical room overflowing with full-grown palm trees and vibrant purple, pink, and yellow tropical flowering plants. "They keep plants in bloom year-round."

I stopped walking and took his hand. "Joseph, this is the most spectacular building I've ever seen. I don't deserve such a treat."

Joseph's smile stretched from ear to ear. "Of course, you do. We both work so hard." He pulled me in for a quick hug, looking about to ensure no one was watching. "Now darling, let me lead you into the Palm Room. I've planned a special dinner."

Seated in an intimate corner of the dining room, we gazed at the ornate European décor, with pale palm-themed silk wall coverings and detailed moldings. Our table and chairs, plush in a darker, coordinated silk fabric, enveloped us as we settled in for the feast of a lifetime. Musicians entered the room holding their instruments. Moments later, the string orchestra began playing Tchaikovsky's "Swan Lake Waltz." Two couples floated about on the dance floor, the women's pastel chiffon dresses billowing and swaying as their partners swung them as gracefully as the composer's musical swans, gliding through deep crystal blue water.

Joseph ordered for both of us, starting the meal with a crisp French champagne. The heavenly liquid sparkled in my mouth from the moment it touched my lips. Our first course consisted of spiced beets for me and turtle soup for Joseph. Although Joseph was eager to taste mine, I had no interest in turtle soup, which wouldn't suit my quasi-Jewish diet.

While waiting for our entree, we joined other finely dressed couples on the dance floor. Unlike the work week, when dining was a necessary interruption in a busy schedule or a plate from Rebecca's icebox, these guests dressed to the nines for dinner and made an entire evening of the meal. What a divine way to live.

At the end of the string selection, Joseph led me back to the table.

Still considering the speed of growth in the city and great wealth that fueled it, I said, "This morning, I read in *The Times* that it only took New York City the last fifty years to rival any European city in wealth and industry."

Joseph raised his bushy brows and smirked. "That's because so many of our grandparents left those cities. The great European cities drove out a generation of smart, hard-working Jews because of hate." He shook his head with disgust. "Lucky, America. Now we have the best of Europe right here."

I extended my hands. "But so much of this wealth is held by earlier families like the Astors and Carnegies, not the new immigrants. Walk a few blocks in any direction, and you're surrounded by terrible poverty. None of the day laborers, sweatshop workers, or children work within sight of the mansions on Fifth Avenue."

"It's true. But they're the muscle of the city. And things are changing fast as they build businesses. Just look at the money in the garment industry." Joseph sighed. "Besides, the old money built our hospital uptown." He sat back thoughtfully.

I interjected, "Perhaps to assuage their guilt."

"Maybe, but up on the east side, the banking is largely run by the German Jews who've been here since the early 1800s." Joseph said, "They helped build our part of the city."

Our part of the city? What was he suggesting? I took a tactful turn. "I imagine in a few years, the wealth will even out through the city, especially with a new generation of talent. Look at Tillie and Abe. They came from nothing. Abe started out with a handful of buttons." I looked about. "And Leo and Rebecca too. Neither had anything more than raw talent when they arrived. And now they live comfortably up and downtown."

Joseph leaned forward and kissed my cheek. "Indeed, you are my bleeding heart. I suggest though, that you and I relax and enjoy every bit of this opulence tonight. We've worked hard to get here too."

And opulent it was! Dinner was a culinary extravaganza. Sole, red snapper, both prepared with rich French sauces I couldn't pronounce, delicious fresh vegetables, and a potato soufflé. Finally, after a leisurely stretch and a second waltz around the dance floor, we returned to our table. It was adorned with splendid desserts. Fresh figs, cheeses, a gooseberry tartlet, and a cherries jubilee, lit by a server at our table. *It will take a week to digest all of this!*

I pointed to the plates of delicacies. "I can't eat another bite, but it pains me to think this will be wasted. Do you think we can bring it home?"

"Don't worry about that right now." Joseph reached into his pocket and pulled out a small black velvet pouch. He knelt to the floor and reached for my hand, stroking it gently with his thumb. "I've searched the four corners of New York for the perfect woman, never expecting to bump into her right outside the hospital library, on the floor no less. Hannah, would you make me the happiest man on earth and be my wife?" He emptied the pouch into his hand and held out a spectacular ring with a large red ruby in the center, surrounded by a halo of small diamonds.

My hands shot to my mouth in disbelief, forgetting the table of wasted desserts. I reached for his hand, kissing his fingers. "Yes, yes, Joseph. I would be thrilled to marry you!"

His smile grew as he placed the ring on my finger. "Ah, it's a bit loose. We'll adjust it. My dear mother's ring was waiting for the perfect finger." He added under his breath, "I had to pry it away from my sister."

The room filled with applause, drowning out his comment. Not only was Joseph's proposal the jubilee of my evening, but we ignited the entire Palm Room.

Moments later, an impeccably dressed, sturdy man in his late thirties approached our table. He had a wide, kind face with large, deep-set eyes. "Good evening. My name is Oscar Tschirky, the maître d' of the Waldorf."

We smiled, both enjoying the attention.

"I'd like to convey my congratulations and that of the entire restaurant staff. I'm delighted for you. May I treat you to a brandy?"

"Thank you, sir." Joseph stood and shook his hand, reveling in the attention.

The waiter filled three cognac glasses.

We raised our glasses together as Mr. Tschirky toasted us with a smile. "May all your years together be filled with the finest of health and fortunes. And perhaps you might consider entertaining the thought of holding your wedding party at the Waldorf!" He looked to the doorway for the cameraman. "Any chance we can capture this happy occasion for the society pages?"

"Now, that's an idea," laughed Joseph. "But first, could you direct me to the men's lavatory?"

Once Joseph left, Mr. Tschirky pulled a chair to the table and sat. "Please excuse my intrusion, but when Doctor Kaufman booked the reservation, he mentioned in passing that you are also a physician, quite a remarkable one I might add."

"Thank you." I beamed back.

He leaned toward me, whispering, "From time to time, a hotel guest calls our reception desk requesting medical assistance. Sometimes with our women guests, the need is of a female nature. Do you understand?"

"I believe so. But surely you can hail one of our ambulances. We have a telephone in our hospital coach station, and they are always ready to hitch the horses and come to your aid."

"Yes, doctor, I realize that. But sometimes our guests prefer the doctor come to the hotel, particularly for smaller, more private issues." Mr. Tschirky cleared his throat.

"I see. How can I help?"

"We are updating our service directory and would like to include a few highly reputable physicians in the city." He explained further, "Not for time-sensitive emergencies, mind you, but a same-day hotel call. A female doctor would add a nice touch."

I nodded, thinking of my busy clinics and responsibilities with the medical students. "How frequent are these requests?"

"Not frequent, perhaps two or three each month. And you will be paid handsomely, of course. It's an excellent way to establish an international name for yourself among an elite clientele." He raised bushy eyebrows and nodded to punctuate his point.

"I suppose I could try it." I worried about the additional patients but was swept in by his gentile manners.

"May I have your card? I'll include your hospital contact information in our next brochure."

"Yes, of course." I reached into my purse, pulling out my office card.

Joseph strode back to the table, glowing. "That was the fanciest men's room I've ever seen." He looked at the two of us. "Has she enchanted you as much as me?"

"Indeed. What a gifted couple. When you're ready, let me know if you'd like to celebrate here, and we'll plan a party you'll never forget." He handed Joseph his card as he stood and bowed. "I'll send a photographer to your table."

He left, and Joseph looked at me quizzically. "You both looked so intent as I crossed the room. What was that all about?"

"Nothing much. He likes the idea of having a female doctor at the beck and call of his fussy hotel guests and wanted me to be that doctor. He made it difficult for me to say 'no.'" I laughed. "Apparently, it pays quite well."

"Let's get the photo and head home. I've been waiting all evening to have you in my arms." Joseph gazed lovingly into my eyes.

As we climbed into the coach, Joseph asked, "Now that we're engaged, would it be wildly impulsive to invite you to my apartment for the night? After all, we're not children."

My body stiffened. I stammered. "Jo...Joseph, I'm not sure."

He smiled sweetly. "Whatever you feel comfortable with, darling. But, in a few months, we'll be married, so who cares?"

He was right. We weren't children. My stomach was in knots remembering the long-ago promise Mr. Frank made to Elspeth. "Joseph, I'm not ready to be with child."

He whispered, "But you will be soon. In the meantime, if it makes you feel more comfortable, I have something in my nightstand to address that concern. It's entirely up to you."

I didn't think twice about the privacy or my calamity years ago with Roger Holloway. I was in love, enraptured, and engaged. I wiggled tighter to his body, feeling warmth between my thighs.

Chapter Thirteen

The sun broke through the grey autumn sky, illuminating the crimson and ginger-colored leaves, transforming their dull, foggy hues to brilliant colors. The temperature warmed, making everyone nostalgic for a summer that ended too quickly. It was a perfect evening for our engagement party. Tillie insisted on hosting, and with the Jewish New Year, Rosh Hashanah, around the corner, chose a delightful holiday menu.

Tillie and I spent the better part of the day working side by side, roasting tender, deep brown briskets and honey-baked carrots while the dough for the challah loaves rose, finally baked to perfection. Oil splattered our aprons as we fried crispy potato latkes to perfection, with a salty outer crunch and a creamy heaven within.

"It's too bad our brothers aren't coming," said Tillie as she flipped the latkes in her cast iron pan. Do you think we still need the table extensions?"

"Let's see. We have Joseph and me, your four, Rebecca and Leo, and Joseph's sister, Ellen. That's nine." I walked to the hall closet. "We should use them so we're not on top of each other."

"I ironed my best linen tablecloth." Tillie pointed to the counter where it sat with matching napkins. "What do you know about Ellen? Have you met her?"

I set the extensions against the parlor wall. "I met her once, and she seemed dour. She's tall like Joseph, about twelve years older than him, and wears her grey hair in a severe bun like the spinster teacher she is." I returned to the kitchen, resuming slicing apples for dessert. "Apparently, she took over with Joseph after their parents died. Ellen was already grown and working as a teacher. Between the little their father left, the money she squirreled away, and scholarships, Ellen managed to put Joseph through college and medical school." I placed a handful of apples in a ceramic bowl. "Even though he's repaid every penny, she still acts like his mother. Worse than that, as if he owes her."

Tillie turned to me. "I understand the mother part. I was only seventeen when you moved in with us. Sometimes you and I are best friends, but other times, I do feel like your mother. It's hard to shake off."

I jumped. "Ouch! Pay attention, Tillie. The oil is spitting all over the kitchen."

"Sorry, I'll turn down the flame."

I asked wistfully, "How was it different when Mama was alive?" Discussing Mama always dredged sad, sometimes resentful emotions. "She only comes alive through your stories and when Papa spoke about her. She's more like a ghost to me."

Tillie reached for my hand and squeezed it gently. "She was crazy about her baby, Hannah'la. She asked me to look after you on her deathbed when I was only fourteen."

I scoffed. "At the farm, after she died, Papa couldn't discuss Mama within earshot of Rebecca. She didn't like sharing Papa, even with a ghost." I shook my head in disbelief. "Rebecca's changed for the better now that she's married to Leo."

Tillie sighed. "It took me a long time to accept Rebecca. But eventually, I understood life from her standpoint. After Mama died, Papa was desperate for help. Can you imagine a man raising four young children and running a chicken farm all by himself? Rebecca was a lamb led to slaughter when she landed in our upside-down house, the boys killing each other, you crying in dirty diapers, and me fighting with her tooth and nail. The only thing that kept her sane was Papa's love and her own child, Abby. Once I became a mother, I understood how overwhelmed she had been back then."

My thoughts flipped back in time. Despite growing up in Tillie's home, Papa had visited us every few months, always providing money for my schooling and clothes. "I'm glad Papa shared a few stories with me about Mama." I continued, "As much as I loved living with you and Abe, I dreamt what our lives would have been like if she had lived. I imagine her a suffragist."

"Funny, I never thought of Mama that way, but you're probably right. She wanted her children, especially her daughters, to receive a good education. After she died, I was heartbroken. I couldn't go on to high school. It took a long time to get over that disappointment." Tillie shook her head, reliving that time. "No sense looking back. I would never trade my life now for all the education in the world." She removed the last latke from her cast iron pan, setting it on the brown-papered counter.

I quickly placed the extensions in the table frame, opened the pads, and smoothed out Tillie's special linen tablecloth. It was beautiful, ivory fabric framed with open crochet work around the edges.

Tillie dragged the step stool across the kitchen to the cupboard, stretching to the top shelf, carefully lifting out her beloved Rosenthal dishes. She handed short stacks to me. I took each into the dining room, gently setting the plates on the sideboard. Over the years, Tillie had built a robust collection of Rosenthal china, some solid white and others with hand-painted delicate flowers. "Mama brought two place settings from Germany when they came in 1866. She saved the dishes for special dinners with Papa. Rebecca gave them to me when I married Abe."

"That was thoughtful of Rebecca," I answered.

"Mama told me any good Jewish cook deserved a set of Rosenthal. I'm not so sure I'm a talent in the kitchen, but over the years, we've collected quite a lot. Abe used to buy two place settings every Chanukah. Now look!" She opened her arms to the piles of creamy plates. "Now that you're engaged, you may want to start collecting. Feel free to take two settings of mine."

"That's very generous, but I don't know. Let me think about it. Mama's things don't carry the same sentimentality for me."

After the food was cooked, plated, and wrapped, and the cooking pans cleaned and stored, Tillie loosened her apron. "Let's set the table later. We still have a few hours. What do you say we get off our feet and relax?"

I kicked my shoes off by the fireplace. "That would be lovely. I forgot how sore my feet get when I'm cooking."

Tillie pulled her two Queen Anne chairs together by the coffee table and set down butter cookies, cups, and the tea cozy. After the tea steeped, she poured it into her chipped hand-painted cups. Tillie studied her cup, lingering over the finely etched cracks. "Do you remember how Sadie and I drank from these cups every morning back in the tenements? I simply can't throw them out."

How could I forget? I spent every day of my childhood with Sadie and Eva. "You and Sadie always had your heads together, concocting new business schemes. Has she written lately? Does she like living in Chicago?" I bit into a butter shortbread cookie. "This is delicious."

"She and Max are happy living there near their grandchildren, but I miss her terribly. Sadie was my dearest friend."

I thought about their business and its extraordinary success. "You two were brilliant businesswomen."

A confident laugh. "We were. Sometimes I regret selling the company. That might have kept her in New York."

"Didn't you say you were ready to try something new? Investing the profit in apartment houses has been far more lucrative, and with supers handling repairs, you have more spare time."

"That's true, but it was never really about the time. Sadie could not get over losing Eva, and when her sons moved to Chicago, she saw an opportunity to get away from the constant reminders. It was difficult for her to shake off the sadness. There's nothing worse in life than losing a child."

The sheer mention of Eva, my dearest childhood friend, sent a spray of goosebumps to my arms. I would never stop missing her, either. "I can't get away from the feeling, no matter where I live," I said. "Sadie sent a sweet note wishing Joseph and me all the best. I hope she comes back for the wedding."

Tillie's eyes slipped into the past. "I don't think we ever entirely put our losses behind us. For me, baby Sarah will always be alive in my heart." Tillie gazed into the empty fireplace. "Do you think I should set up a fire for tonight's dinner? Perhaps it will get cold again."

I barely heard her question. "I still think about Eva. She and Elspeth were my closest friends, and they were gone – both so young."

Tillie cleared her throat. "Let's talk about something else."

"Oh? What's on your mind?" I bid a silent goodbye to Eva and Elspeth.

"I've been thinking about you and your future. Even though we're sisters, we're also good friends, right?"

I nodded. "You're my closest friend."

"It seems the last few years have been kinder to you."

"Yes, they have." Perplexed, I knit my brows. "What are you thinking? Just say it."

Tillie cleared her throat again. "After all you've been through, I hope Joseph loves you as much as you love him. That he'll support you through thick and thin." She paused. "You remember years ago when I had my surgery?"

I nodded, remembering the unforgettable image of Tillie weeping in her hospital bed, holding her remaining breast after surgery.

"Abe stayed with me every moment." Tillie picked at a hangnail. "I don't want to be a wet blanket, but I still worry the disease could rear its ugly head again. Have you told Joseph about my experience?"

A chill swept through me. *Was Tillie sick again? Did she worry I'd get breast cancer too?* That curse was the last thing I wanted to think about. It had stricken so many women in our family and the larger Jewish community too. First, my Bubbe in Germany, then my mother when I was a baby, and then Tillie, the first to survive. But the surgery left her with a brutal disfigurement, and I knew all too well, as a doctor, the looming threat of recurrence.

Tillie studied me. "Hannah, I'm sorry to upset you. But you're both doctors. I'm surprised this hasn't come up before."

"I told him about Mama, but I didn't think it was right to discuss you." I looked at the curio cabinet and our family's framed pictures at the Chicago World's Columbian Exposition. "I prefer to share happier family times."

Tillie nodded. "I understand. But remember, it's easy to be a happy couple when everything is going well. Marriages are tested when the waters get rough." She looked out the window. "I know without a shred of doubt you'd stand by Joseph. I'm only asking if you're confident he'd do the same."

"I believe so." I exhaled, my annoyance growing. *Why is she challenging our commitment?* "I suppose only time will tell, but he's mad about me, always fluttering about, finding gifts and ways to make me happy."

"Good. That's what I hoped to hear. Now, let's freshen up and have a good time tonight." Her frown turned to a smile. "One last thing. Do you need wedding night advice?"

A laugh broke through my irritation. "Always so nosy. You do know what happened to the curious cat?"

Her eyes sparkled. "Indeed."

"No, I don't need marital advice. We're quite good in that department. You know, I'm twenty-eight, not an innocent girl anymore." I rolled my eyes. "Some things can't wait forever."

"Good, I just wanted to be certain. Mama never had a chance to talk with either of us about marriage. I would have loved to hear her version. She was never shy about discussing the body." Tillie giggled as she rose.

"I'm not shy either. I hear crazy questions all the time in my office. When will mothers start telling their daughters the truth about their bodies? Last week a patient told me she was having a boy because her urine was bright yellow. I asked her how much water she was drinking." I laughed. "Only a cup a day! She should be drinking at least four times that. So much misinformation and shame."

* * *

That evening, Tillie's parlor was filled with delicious food and laughter. It was the first opportunity for our families to meet, and I hoped Ellen, Joseph's older sister, would feel at ease. Tillie's husband Abe, a growing connoisseur of wines, had stumbled on the excellent vineyards north of the city when he and Tillie last visited our brother in Sullivan County. Abe kept the glasses full, all but his daughter, Miriam's, who was still quite young.

Smiles sparkled on everyone's faces by the time we sat to eat. I placed Ellen beside Abe and across from Leo. Their good humor always put others at ease, and I had a feeling Ellen might need extra attention.

Abe, the consummate salesman, cast his spell immediately. "Ellen, I hear from Hannah you're one of the city's finest teachers."

Ellen, somewhat intoxicated, reveled in the attention. "I am quite experienced. It was a calling." Her narrow hazel eyes circled the table. "Joseph, it's a shame our parents can't be here to enjoy this lovely event."

Tillie lifted her glass. "Indeed. How about a toast to both sets of our beloved parents?"

Ellen quickly followed. "And to Tillie and Abe for hosting such a beautiful party."

The clinking of crystal filled the room.

Was I the only person who noticed she hadn't toasted Joseph and me? I faced Joseph, who was busy talking to Miriam and didn't see my pointed glance, but Leo did.

Leo stood. "Now, let's not forget what brought us together this fine evening! Two of the most brilliant young adults I have had the good fortune to know. Blessings and congratulations to Hannah and Joseph."

"Hear, hear," Abe called out.

The table was soon noisy with cross-conversation, impatient talkers cutting off each other's sentences, and questions about our wedding plans.

"Will you have a flower girl?" asked Miriam. "Or a matron of honor?"

Tillie interrupted, "Have you given thought to having your wedding in the synagogue?

"I'd like to design your gown as a wedding gift." Rebecca offered.

Joseph waved his hands in the air. "No more wedding questions. We've only been engaged five minutes!"

Leo tapped his glass with a spoon. "I heard a joke the other day."

The room quieted. No one wanted to miss out.

"A minister, a priest, and a rabbi die in a car crash. They go to heaven for orientation and are all asked the same question, "When you were in your casket, and friends, family, and congregants mourned over you, what did you wish they said about you?"

The minister answered, "That I was a wonderful husband, a fine spiritual leader, and a great family man."

The priest said, "That I was a wonderful teacher and a servant of God who made a huge difference in people's lives."

The rabbi replied, "I wanted to hear them say, 'Look! He's moving.'"

Everyone around the table erupted in laughter.

"Oh, Leo, that was a good one!" Tillie hooted.

I noticed Ellen laughing, then a troubled expression crossed her face. Her eyes bulged as her hands shot to her throat.

"Joseph, help Ellen. She's choking!" I shouted.

He jumped from his chair, knocking it backward onto the floor, moved behind Ellen, then hit her back with his open hand. Nothing. Then he hit her harder. A piece of brisket dislodged from her throat and shot across the table, landing on Leo's plate.

Gasping for air, she scolded Leo. "Shame on you! You're lucky you're not one of my students. I would have put you in the corner with a dunce cap for making me laugh with a full mouth of food." She opened her napkin, wiping her mouth.

"Enough with the jokes, Leo!" Rebecca scolded. "We don't want to put our special guest in the hospital."

Ellen settled back in her chair, inhaling deeply. "I'm fine, truly. This is the best time I've had in a long while, but it is a joy to breathe again," she added with relief.

Leo picked up the half-chewed piece of brisket sitting on his plate and held it up for all to see. "It's disgraceful what a man has to do around here to get seconds."

While the table ripped with laughter again, Joseph whispered in my ear, "I haven't seen her laugh this way in years. She made such a fuss about coming down to the tenements, as she calls this part of town, I thought she was going to make me call off the wedding. She's still angry I gave you Mama's ring."

My stomach roiled. This was the first time he shared Ellen's disapproval of our family. *Is she going to be a problem?*

Chapter Fourteen

After debating the merits of winter versus spring nuptials, we decided to hold the wedding in April after Passover when Rabbi was again available. Much to my delight, Joseph met with Oscar from the Waldorf and settled on a Sunday afternoon affair. I was dancing on clouds thinking about their lovely orchestra and our guests basking in our happiness. While Joseph and I planned the details, most of the family signed up for ballroom dancing lessons. We were intent on dazzling our guests with the latest steps.

In the evenings, Rebecca and I spent time together designing my gown, pouring through fashion sketches.

"Remember, I'm no longer a spring chicken," I said. "Keep it simple and sophisticated. Besides, my secretary, Ina, who follows the new fashions, told me frilly is now out of style."

Rebecca opened her worn leather portfolio, where she kept charcoal and pencil drawings, neatly separated with tracing paper to reduce smudges. Leafing through, she pulled out a sketch. The model was long and lean, her right arm resting on the charcoal outline of a chair. "This is what I see for you. A high bodice with soft, slightly puffed short sleeves and a cinched waist to show off your slender figure."

I pointed at her charcoal model. "Pretty. Could you make me look that tall, too? What type of fabric?"

"How about an ivory messaline? The light satin will be comfortable no matter the weather. And, you never know in April. I'd like to add some hand-made lace and pearl buttons, too."

103

I interrupted, "Rebecca, please don't go overboard with the lacy detail. I don't want to look like a child's doll."

"Stop worrying about frills. Let's firm up the design, and then we'll see where touches are needed." Rebecca closed her eyes. "When I picture the gown on you, I see a sheer layer of fine lace over the bodice and a small amount draped along one side of the skirt to carry the eye downward. That's a trick designers use with small women. It makes them appear taller."

I tried to imagine the finished gown. Rebecca's taste was flawless. Why was I getting worked up about the dress? It wasn't like me to care so much about mundane details.

"Trust me, sweetheart," she said. "I'll share the final drawings before we measure and order fabric."

I pulled my stepmother into a hug. "You're wonderful, Rebecca. Thank you for your thoughtful gift."

Joseph convinced the Chief of Medicine at the hospital to approve an extended summer leave for our honeymoon. He was planning a six-week trip to the major European cities, minus the ten days spent on a steamer ship back and forth to Liverpool. If we were lucky, it would be faster. In the calm summer waters, some ships made the Atlantic crossing in as few as five days.

I'd spent uncountable hours in the Metropolitan Museum of Art as a child, in college, and often with Joseph, captivated by the brilliant paintings and relics. Exploring the famous museums in Florence, Rome, and Paris would fulfill a lifelong dream. But as eager as I was to examine the masters, Joseph was equally intent on starting our family.

"We'll have a little addition to the family by the time we return to New York harbor in August. I can hardly wait."

"Let's hope so," I answered carefully. Inwardly I worried my age might be a problem, as I occasionally consoled the older mothers in my Clinic when their efforts resulted in failure. And I was already twenty-eight. Well, I'd cross that bridge when we came to it.

Chapter Fifteen

As my reputation circulated in the community, the list for new patients grew. There was now a four-month wait for an appointment, far too long for newly pregnant women. After multiple meetings with the Chief of Medicine, I finally convinced him to act on his promise and begin recruiting a second female obstetrician, a difficult undertaking with so few of us in the field. I planned to contact Mrs. Thomas and Mrs. Garrett at Johns Hopkins and ask for their help. If Joseph was right, and I did become pregnant, a partner would take pressure off me.

At times, patients still confused me for a nurse or midwife, but I brushed it off. There was little doubt most pregnant women felt more relaxed with a woman at the foot of the bed. Less self-conscious about anatomical issues, odors, or intimate questions, my patients were confident I'd do my job as a doctor without judgment.

"Dr. Isaacson, you have a packed schedule today, four new patients," said my perky assistant, Miss Ina Klein. She leaned over me as I reviewed the appointment book, pointing to an entry. "I noticed you have an appointment with a Mrs. Margaret Sanger. Isn't she the woman in the papers? The suffragette?"

"Hum. We'll see soon enough." I flipped to the prior months and sighed. Four months ago, there were so many more empty appointment slots. Then, I had time to think, chit-chat with patients and husbands, and occasionally slip out for lunch with Joseph. Now I was lucky to squeeze in an afternoon cup of tea and biscuit.

"Ina, would you mind ordering a sandwich for me at noon? Dr. Kaufman wants more meat on my bones before the wedding. He's worried I'm becoming too thin." Although I found Joseph's scrutiny of my weight tiresome, I knew I needed to stay on top of myself. It was too easy to skip meals when the hospital was busy. But did his focus on my body mean he saw me more as a breeder or wife?

"What funny expressions Americans have." Ina laughed. "As if he's taking you to the slaughterhouse."

I was impressed by the rate Ina was picking up the language. "He'd like to start our own family soon and thinks I won't get pregnant if I'm too thin. Dr. Kaufman should see the unhappy pregnant women we see in the Clinic. Many are undernourished, too poor to feed their children, never mind themselves. I'm shocked at the state of their hair and teeth." I shook my head slowly, thinking how, despite their compromised condition, these poor women, thin or heavy, kept becoming pregnant.

"You think he's wrong?" Ina tilted her head to the side, her long blond curls falling in her face.

"Partly. I think he's heard a lot of old wives' tales. But he's right that having a healthy baby requires eating the right foods, lots of milk, meat, and vegetables. If the Mama isn't healthy, the baby can be undersized and fragile."

Ina tilted her neck forward, her fingers combing through her hair, then collected it in a long tail. Swinging her head upright, pins in her mouth, she fastened the tail into a high bun. Securing the final pin, she said, "I think you're lucky you can eat anything without puffing up. Some of our patients are gigantic."

I'd noticed she had been arriving at work increasingly unkempt. *Couldn't she have done her hair at home?*

Ina had worked with me for the better part of a year. Occasionally, we'd have a cup of tea together before my office hours. She enjoyed telling me about her family and their journey to America in 1901. Nineteen, single, and living with her parents and younger siblings in a small walk-up apartment north of Central Park, she contributed to the family till. Having a knack for languages, Ina's English was by far the most advanced in her home. Tall, slim, and eye-catching, she spent most of her leftover earnings on accessories, often arriving at the office with a smart new muffler, purse, or scarf. Her love of fashion was her most visible talent. But Ina was incredibly smart, efficient, and insightful, often spotting problems with patients before me.

"Is something going on at home?" I asked.

She looked down as she smoothed her skirt. "Why do you ask?" she mumbled.

"Just a feeling." I considered her bun with concern.

A deep sigh. "Mama has trouble breathing at night. She's coughing so much it's keeping us all up. I'm worried about her. She's very thin and pale." Ina's eyes filled.

"I see," I said softly. "Perhaps you should bring her back to the Tuberculosis Clinic for a check-up? They may have something new to help her."

I thought about tuberculosis, or consumption as most still called it, and how my family had managed to skirt it, so far. The disease had ravaged the city for decades, with no cure in sight. It subsided over the summer when windows were kept open, and people spent more time outdoors, but come winter, it repeated its tortuous cycle. Now that it was October, the hospital was bracing for another outbreak.

"I know I've said this to you before, but please remember to protect the rest of your family. Open your windows and air out the apartment every day. Never forget to wash your hands after caring for her." I placed my hand on her shoulder. "I don't want you getting ill too."

My tea grew cold by three in the afternoon, the sandwich untouched on its brown wrapping. The bread had turned stale, the turkey a dry copper hue. Into the garbage, it went. "Ina, I finally have a few minutes to write notes. Would you kindly refresh my tea?" I called out from my office.

"In a jiffy, Doctor," she called back, enjoying her new-found slang. "Your next appointment is here."

"Please send her in." I sighed. "I'll have tea later."

Ina led a willowy, sharply dressed, barely pregnant woman to the visitor chair. She had bright red hair and a cocky expression that bespoke trouble. "Mrs. Margaret Sanger, Doctor."

"Good afternoon, Mrs. Sanger. Please have a seat. How can I help you today?" Immediately, I noticed her terribly thin frame and tiny abdominal pouch. I wondered if she was seeking a second opinion. A woman of her stature certainly would already have a doctor.

"Good afternoon, Dr. Isaacson. I've been eager to meet you. My neighbors in Hastings-on-Hudson recommended I make an appointment with you. They hold you in the highest regard." Her eyes studied my face.

Was she interviewing me?

"I thought it might be a pleasant change to have a female obstetrician—and an anesthetic with my delivery." Her green eyes sparkled. "As an almost-nurse and midwife, I'm convinced caring for women is best left in the hands of women. Men are clueless when it comes to the female body and our very personal relationship to it."

I was hit with a wave of satisfaction. "I agree. I've long advocated to my colleagues that they adopt a different approach for women." Aghast at the degree to which women's ailments took second fiddle to men's and the routine overdosing of women because the male body was used to scale anesthesia and pharmaceutical doses, I was steadfast in my opinion that medicine needed to change.

"For some reason, men have a difficult time appreciating female pain. They blame it on our *hysterical nature*," I said sarcastically.

Mrs. Sanger cracked a smile. "I'd love to see Mr. Sanger handle the pain of childbirth. That would shut him up."

After a full examination where she talked non-stop about her career, we settled back in my office. She looked at my hands, my ruby ring reflecting sparkles of light. "You're not married?" she asked.

"Engaged." I hesitated, ill at ease discussing my personal life with a patient.

"I regret marrying. I dropped out of nursing school after meeting Mr. Sanger and got married. Then I became pregnant, and the consumption flared up that I caught from my mother. God rest her soul. Did I mention my Mama was pregnant over fifteen times? Eleven of us lived, but then Mama

108

died, so young." She winced. "It's criminal to make a woman pregnant so often that her body can't keep up. She was in her forties and looked eighty when she died."

I studied Mrs. Sanger. The disease had taken some toll on her as well. Just twenty-six, she appeared tired, puffy-eyed, and thin as a scarecrow. "Do you have help at home?"

"I do. The first time, I spent my pregnancy in Saranac Lake at Dr. Trudeau's sanatorium. I'd never been so bored in my life! Sitting outside breathing cold air in the winter was not for me," she said. "Then the delivery was grueling. This time, I'm having anesthesia. And after that, I'm using a *veil*."

"I see. You and your husband use devices to avoid pregnancy?" I asked.

She looked at me as if I'd grown a second head and whipped back her answer. "Of course I do. Don't you?"

I didn't answer but nearly cracked a smile. It was all I could do to remain professional. "May I inquire where you secure your devices? Patients often ask, and I'd like to be able to offer options. Of course, being illegal, we cannot dispense them here at the hospital."

She began to laugh. "It's all such hogwash. Mail order for the veils, err, diaphragms, and my husband gets condoms from the pharmacy in the rubber goods section." She howled with laughter. "The rubber glove section, along with cleaning items—isn't that a stitch?"

Finally drawn in, I found myself laughing along with her. *What a charismatic character!*

Mrs. Sanger collected herself, growing more serious. "Truly, though, it's not amusing. The laws need to change. As I said, I used to work as a midwife, and trust me, too many women seek to end pregnancies. It's safer to avoid them in the first place."

"My view exactly." My thoughts raced to poor Elspeth, now lying deep under the grass. I reached out my hand to shake hers. "It's been a pleasure meeting you, Mrs. Sanger. Remember to take care of yourself; try to eat a bit more and rest every afternoon. Your pregnancy is normal, and the tuberculosis seems to be in a remissive state. Let's try and keep it that way.

I'll see you in a month."

Chapter Sixteen

The following Monday morning, Ina stood in my office doorway reviewing a list of telephone messages. "Mrs. Sanger called."

"What do you mean?" It had been under a week since her appointment.

"She's coming to the city Wednesday evening for a lecture by Lillie Devereux Blake, the suffragist, and thought you might want to join her. Mrs. Sanger said she'd make a dinner reservation."

Normally I wouldn't socialize with a patient, but curiosity got the better of me. I hadn't attended a suffragist lecture since college at Barnard ten years ago, and Lillie Blake, known for founding Barnard, was a giant in the suffragist community. She'd repeatedly made national newspaper coverage with her clever successes in court, eventually changing estate law. Because of her tireless work, married women could now have their own wills, separate from their spouses. She was a close friend of Susan B. Anthony, another remarkable woman advancing the suffragist movement. Unfortunately, progress was much slower when it came to the vote. *What were men so afraid of?*

Later that evening, Joseph expressed displeasure. "You don't really want to spend Wednesday evening with a group of angry women. You've been working nonstop for the past month. Wouldn't you rather spend a peaceful evening with me? I'll take you to Delmonico's, and we can have a decent dinner and wine."

"Why so fancy? Is it because you're worried about my weight?" I couldn't restrain my annoyance. "I've always been thin, and healthy as a horse.

Besides, Mrs. Sanger and I plan to have dinner before the lecture." I took a deep breath. "I'd like to have a few friends of my own outside of work and home."

Joseph put his arms around me. "I understand, darling. It's just that I miss our time alone. Don't you think those women can handle the vote without you?" He massaged my shoulders, sliding the pins out of my bun, freeing up my waves. "My roommate is sleeping at the hospital tonight, on call. We have the apartment to ourselves."

My resolve melted as quickly as snow in spring. I cast a resigned smile his way and entered the washroom to insert my shield. It was near impossible to resist the pleasure he gave.

He called through the door. "Do you really need that thing?"

"Nice try. It stays in until we're married."

Shortly later, tangled in the covers, still pulsing from pleasure, I stroked his chest hair. "I love you, Joseph. We're so good together."

"How about a little dinner? I'm hungry, and it's almost ten. I'll make eggs and toast." Joseph rose from the bed. "Aren't you glad Ellen taught me how to cook?"

"Mm-hm." I closed my eyes, losing my fight with sleep. He ate alone.

* * *

Early the following morning I was heading to the door when Joseph woke. "Why are you leaving so early?" He sat rubbing his eyes.

"Morning rounds. By the way, I'll sleep at Rebecca's Wednesday after the lecture. I'm not sure when I'll be getting home."

Joseph threw on his robe. "What? I thought we agreed on Delmonico's tomorrow." He followed me to the door.

I tilted my head, gazing at him. I understood his frustration, but I was accustomed to making my own decisions and didn't intend to surrender all my freedom. "Sweetheart, there's plenty of time for everything. Try not to worry." I lifted myself on my toes and planted a soft kiss on his lips. "I'll catch breakfast at the hospital. I love you." I closed the door gently, leaving him standing alone in the apartment.

* * *

In many respects, Mrs. Sanger reminded me of Elspeth but without the academic polish my poor friend had. A true firebrand, she shared precisely what was on her mind, often without considering the consequences. Her instinct was to lead and be heard. So, I was not in the least surprised when she stirred the crowd later in the evening.

My Clinic ran late, and we missed our dinner reservation. Instead, we found a small restaurant located near the lecture hall. As we walked into the empty restaurant, an older bent waitress was cleaning off the tables, closing for the evening. Mrs. Sanger and I walked inside before the waitress could lock the door, hoping to squeeze in a light dinner.

Standing in the entrance, I apologized to Mrs. Sanger for my tardiness. "The patients kept streaming in, even after Clinic hours had officially ended." I sighed, shaking my head. "I didn't have the heart to send them home."

Mrs. Sanger called to the waitress. "Any chance we can order two sandwiches and a couple of coffees?

The waitress brushed her hair away from her tired face. "If you're fast. I need to get home to my family." She turned and walked to the counter, muttering, "I should've locked the door."

"We understand," Mrs. Sanger sang back. "How about a roast beef sandwich with lettuce and mustard?" Margaret called to the waitress's back. "Pickles, too, if you have them," she added, patting her little pouch.

"Make that two," I called out as politely as I could.

Sitting across from Mrs. Sanger, I said, "Again, please accept my apologies for spoiling a leisurely meal." I worried that I'd started out the evening on the wrong foot. She was one of the first adult women I could imagine as a friend.

She wore an amused expression. "It's not a problem. A sandwich is gourmet cooking compared to dinners where I came from—porridge, porridge, and sometimes thin soup for variety." She laughed with gusto. "If the orchards were in season, stolen apples too. By the way, you must call me Margaret."

"Certainly. And I'm Hannah." We sat at a small table in the corner and draped our coats over an empty chair. "Tell me, how did you become so interested in women's causes?" I asked.

"It started when I was a tot. I already told you about my mother. After she died, I was pulled out of school and sent to work, all boring factory jobs. I finally convinced my Pa, a lazy drunk, to let me board at a nursing school. I promised I'd bring home better wages for the family."

"You were only a child."

"I was. But Pa could barely hold a job. He kept getting fired with all his drinking and bluster." She smiled. "I inherited his fresh mouth, I'm afraid."

I shook my head slowly. I had to hand it to her. Margaret's self-effacing nature made her antics even more amusing.

The waitress set the sandwich plates and coffee on the table along with our check, leaving no question she was done for the evening.

I sank my teeth into the roast beef sandwich, realizing how hungry I was. I couldn't recall if I'd eaten lunch. "What about your sisters and brothers?"

"One of my sisters was a secretary, and that helped keep food on the table, but we never owned a home, always moving from here to there." She paused, looking at her food. "This looks good." She took a small bite, wiping off the corners of her mouth with her cloth napkin.

I attempted to steer the conversation back to her. "Tell me about nursing school." Her drunk father, gruel, sick mother, what would she reveal next?

"It was fascinating. I enjoyed studying reproduction, so I dropped out and practiced midwifery. Then I got married, and the rest, as you know, is history."

I took a bite of pickle. "It sounds so easy the way you describe it. Nothing has ever worked that smoothly for me." What an adaptive woman. She could teach me a thing or two.

"Of course, I courted a few young men before marrying Mr. Sanger—if you want to call it that. More like experimentation. I was a bit free." She winked. "But always careful. I had no interest in becoming pregnant. Even after I married, I wasn't terribly keen on the idea."

"Why not?" I wondered aloud.

"Frankly, I had my fill raising a house full of siblings. My poor mother was always sick, so my sister and I did everything. But I promised my William we'd have a family. It's part of our arrangement. It's all a negotiation." She wrinkled her nose. "In return, he agreed to let me keep my suffragist friends and causes. We women have scarcely begun our fight and need every influential woman we can recruit."

I understood, assuming this why she'd invited me. "I haven't seen Mrs. Blake in years. She helped found Barnard and spoke at my graduation. She was an inspiration. We all left that speech ready to conquer the world."

Margaret nodded. "She's like that. I only wish she'd help me with legalizing pregnancy devices. It could finally be a solution for desperate mothers in the city. Now that she's older, Mrs. Blake has begun studying and writing about topics less interesting to me."

"What do you mean?"

"She believes that behavioral differences between girls and boys are taught, that at birth babies are more alike than we realize." Margaret smiled at the waitress, who stood at the soda counter looking from her watch to our table. She picked up her sandwich.

Margaret got me thinking about the trustees and their belief that women were as capable as men. "When I lived in Baltimore, I worked with two inspiring older women connected to the medical school at Johns Hopkins. They pushed the old guard to open the door to women students."

"How'd they wrangle that?"

"The medical school and hospital project needed their money—the money left to them in their fathers' wills. That gave them power."

"Money's the way to stir up change. Wealth creates influence. Unfortunately, I can't bring the money, but I can sway a crowd." She nibbled on her sandwich, looking content.

I looked at my watch. Fifteen minutes remained before the lecture, and the waitress was about to explode. "Finish your sandwich, Margaret. I'll pay."

* * *

The streetlights stood like sentries in the dark when my carriage dropped me back at Rebecca and Leo's. I headed straight to bed but could not settle down. Burrowing into the soft sheets and listening to the hot water swish through the furnace did not induce my typical slumber. It had been the most exhilarating evening I'd experienced in years. These women, entirely opposite from the stodgy doctors and nurses I worked with daily, had astounding energy. Bright, determined to create a better life for all women, they were turning the gears of a powerful movement and awakening a dormant part inside me. I was determined to participate.

As Margaret predicted, Mrs. Blake's presentation centered on her past work concerning estate laws and suffrage. Over the past few years, now absorbed in her recent theories on gender-acquired roles, she'd left her fiery speeches behind. Although her theories piqued my interest as a physician, I knew they wouldn't advance women's causes today.

But Margaret, with her charismatic nature, set the lecture hall on fire, imploring, pleading with the women in the audience to demand control of their bodies and family size. In her passionate style, she moved the spectators through her rationale. All were spellbound. When she was finished, she received a standing ovation, filling a bucket from audience donations. I was convinced Margaret would become a powerful force in this movement, that is if the politicians didn't muzzle her first.

Afterwards, she assembled a dozen women for additional conversation. They spanned two decades in age. Margaret led the group, chattering behind her like hens, down a sleepy, darkened block to a nearby tavern. It was already after ten, and I worried about my early morning clinic.

I leaned into Margaret's ear. "I think I'll hail a carriage and head home."

"No, you can't." She countered. "The best part of the evening is listening to what everyone says afterwards. Besides, they've been wanting to meet you. We don't have a doctor in our group."

As we approached the tavern, thoughts of Fells Point returned. The exterior of the building was in shambles, its sign broken, barely hanging from its hooks, the door shoddy with splinters. I decided then and there to politely introduce myself and leave.

My eyes quickly adjusted to the darkness. There was one customer bent over the bar, his face practically in his stout. Although I expected the unforgettable odors of stale beer and filthy bodies, all I smelled was lingering traces of freshly cooked food.

"Where is everyone?" I asked Margaret.

"In this part of town, probably home. It's late and a work night for most. I know the owner, and he doesn't mind me bringing groups here." Margaret nodded at the bartender and began rearranging tables and chairs to make room for everyone. Three small tables were pushed together while some of the women noisily dragged chairs into the new arrangement.

"What'll it be, ladies?" the bartender shouted over the din. The women called out their orders of wine and ale. I was thirsty for a cup of tea, but hoping to fit in, I ordered a glass of wine instead.

We found our seats, and Margaret immediately stood. "Before we start, I would like to introduce my new friend and obstetrician, Dr. Hannah Isaacson."

The women clapped. Echoes of "welcome" and "nice to meet you" circled the table, instantly followed by a shift back to their prior conversation and debate.

I felt blood rush to my face. *Well, that was fast.* I listened to their intense debate.

"The Southern chapters insist on an educational requirement for the vote," complained an older woman. "You all know who they're trying to keep out!"

"Seems like nothing ever changes for the better," echoed her companion.

Margaret jumped in. "They're just afraid of too many poor folk voting. Whites, Negroes, and don't forget, immigrants. They've tried that tactic before."

"The Constitution says 'We the People, '" called out a young woman as she untied her bonnet.

A shrill voice cut in from the doorway behind us. Mrs. Blake had arrived late. "We the people…we've all heard that bunk. Don't forget, that document was written by a bunch of wealthy, educated men, many of whom were slave owners." She pulled a chair beside Margaret.

The group clapped as she sat.

Margaret chimed in, "I'm sure they never intended 'we' to refer to women, or immigrants or Negroes, for that matter."

"Or maybe they had the foresight to imagine the country continuing to change and intended to leave the door open," I said before realizing I was thinking aloud.

Mrs. Blake locked eyes with me. "And who are you, my dear?"

I stumbled, suddenly self-conscience. "My name is Hannah, Dr. Hannah Isaacson. It's an honor, Mrs. Blake. I first saw you on stage at my commencement from Barnard a decade ago. It's an inspiration to finally meet in person."

"It's a pleasure to meet you too, Dr. Isaacson. I'm pleased and impressed you became a physician."

"Hannah is *my* physician," said Margaret. "An obstetrician, no less. And we're going to get devices legalized."

Before I had a chance to glance at my pocket watch, more than an hour had slipped by. Empty glasses and half-filled baskets of peanuts and shells littered the table. Excitement lit the room as our discussion grew in passion and volume. I sat back in my chair, thinking about our founders and their spirited debates as they imagined a new country. More than ever, I wanted to be a part of this powerful chorus. I knew in my heart these women would drive important change.

But I also knew I'd be sleepwalking the next day if I didn't leave soon. I whispered in Margaret's ear. "I really must leave. I have an early morning. Are you going back to Hastings?"

"No, I'm staying with a friend in the city. I'll take a train home in the morning." She signaled to the bartender. "He'll help you hail a cab."

I put my arm on her shoulder and gave it a light squeeze. "Good. I look forward to seeing you again soon." I rose, waved my goodbyes to the ladies, and placed a few coins on the table to cover my drink.

Chapter Seventeen

There wasn't enough tea in China to give me the lift I needed the next morning. I woke exhausted and knew office hours would be a strain. As I arrived at the hospital, things grew worse, my punishment for enjoying a work night out. Ina informed me that in addition to my dozen private patients, I also had two first-time mothers upstairs in labor. Unlike the Clinic, my private patients had set appointment times, arrived punctually, and expected me to be timely in return. But no one could predict when the laboring mothers would give birth. I hoped the infants would wait until after my morning appointments.

Ina studied me from her perch at the door. Today, she was nicely groomed and ready for a workday, her hair wrapped in a neat chignon at the base of her neck encircled with a smart violet bow. "You look on your last leg," she commented, amused with herself.

"Very funny," I said sarcastically. "It's 'you look like you're on your last leg.' And yes, I just might be."

She offered, "How about I get eggs and toast to go with your tea? It might give you some pep."

I nodded. "Yes, but first take a gander upstairs and check with the nurses about my patients. I need to know how far along they are."

Ina nodded. "Where'd you go last night? Did you have fun?"

I handed her money. "I'll tell you later. In the meantime, please get breakfast for both of us. We can talk when you get back. I'll review the morning charts in the meantime."

"You're going to eat while you work? Kill two birds with one stone, yes?'"

She glanced toward me, checking to see if she had the expression correct.

I smiled, lifted from my sleepy fog. At the least, Ina's efforts at English were entertaining.

Half-way through the charts, the telephone rang on Ina's desk. She had not yet returned. By the third ring, I rose to answer it, hoping for a cancellation. I closed the *Ladies Home Journal* Ina had left open on her desk. "Hello, this is Dr. Isaacson speaking."

The hospital operator said, "Sorry to disturb you, Doctor, but I have a call from the Waldorf Hotel. The woman said it's important."

Bewildered at first, I realized my contact information must now be available in the guest rooms. It had been well over a month since I'd spoken with Mr. Tschirky. I'd practically forgotten about giving permission to add my name to their physician list. "Oh yes, please put her through."

A woman's voice crackled through the line. She had a heavy British accent. I listened closely.

"Hello, this is Mrs. Graham. I'm a guest at the Waldorf. Am I speaking to Dr. Isaacson?"

"Yes, this is Dr. Isaacson. How can I help you?"

The woman paused. "I'm sorry to interrupt your morning, but I'm quite worried. Frankly, it's very embarrassing, but it's been close to a week since I've, um, eliminated. I'm uncomfortable and getting concerned."

Relief rushed through me. I'd been braced for a serious problem. This was her idea of important? Were the British particularly preoccupied with bowel movements? "Try not to worry. Constipation is common when one travels. Do you have a paper to write down my instructions?" I asked.

"Just a moment." A loud clunk in my ear as she dropped the telephone on a hard surface. A minute slipped by. "I'm ready."

"First, drink lots of water. A glass every hour or two. Do you have that?"

"Yes, doctor. Is the water safe to drink? I hear typhus is particularly problematic in New York."

"You can definitely trust the water at the Waldorf." How could she possibly think our water was more dangerous than London's? "Second, I'd like you to have porridge for breakfast every day and then take a nice long morning walk. That will help wake up your system."

"I can do that. I imagine the porridge here will do. It's probably not quite up to snuff, but I can put cream and sugar on it," she said dismissively.

Good Lord, is this typical of the type of patient Mr. Tschirky was planning to send to me? "Mrs. Graham, you may be the first person in the history of the Waldorf Hotel to complain about the food. New York isn't the Wild West; they imported a European chef."

"My, I had no idea."

I continued with my list. "Please avoid using potions. We have no idea what they contain, and they can upset your system. If you're still uncomfortable in two days, call my office, and I'll leave instructions with my secretary." I thought for a moment. "Oh, one more thing, no corsets until you're regular again."

She drew in a quick breath. "But...but doctor, I can't go out in society without one." Her voice was desperate.

I wondered how much flesh her corset was holding in and up. "Of course, you can, for the morning at least. You'll be surprised at the freedom you'll feel, and I promise it will help set you straight."

"If you say so. It's lovely speaking to a woman doctor."

"Thank you. One final thing—have a grand time visiting our city across the pond."

"Marvelous. Thank you again, Doctor."

That was easy. I pulled a fresh journal from Ina's credenza and labeled it *Waldorf -. Patients.* I made my first chart entry, noting the date and patient's name. At some point in the future, I'd use the journal to generate a bill for Mr. Tschirky, hoping all my calls from the Waldorf would be this easy.

* * *

I finished my morning patients by twelve thirty and left my office. Joseph sat in the waiting room, bouncing his crossed leg, impatiently tapping his other shoe on the floor.

"You're a sight for sore eyes," I said cautiously.

"Sore eyes, right. What time did you get home?" he demanded. "You look like you were up all night."

Stunned, I did not expect his attack. "It's nice to see you too, Joseph." My eyes narrowed, studying him.

He huffed so loudly that Ina looked up from her desk.

I pointed to the door. "Let's walk. I have two patients in labor waiting for me. If they're holding steady, can we get lunch?"

"I have an hour before my afternoon rounds with the medical students."

"Then, let's not waste any more time." I opened the door to the hallway and pecked him on the cheek as he brushed past me, not slowing in the least. Ina and I shrugged at each other.

Without a word, Joseph and I climbed the stairs to the Labor Unit.

My first patient was a new mother who'd arrived at the hospital early that morning. Her labor was dragging.

"Doctor, I'm in so much pain. When can I get the medicine?" She panted, desperately searching my eyes.

I examined her and then sat beside the bed, lightly rubbing her arm. "Not quite yet. Your labor needs to move further along. Try to breath in and out during contractions. It will help you get through the pain."

Her face crumbled as she began crying. "I came here to avoid pain. Now you're keeping the medicine from me." Suddenly her eyes bulged with panic as another contraction took hold. "Make it stop. Make it stop." She begged as she rolled on her side.

I leaned over the bed, placing my arms over her, putting pressure on her lower back. "That's it, breathe in slowly, breathe out slowly. Nurse, can you please come here? Help her with the next contraction. Just copy what I'm doing."

The contraction ebbed.

"Now, a long inhale and slow exhale through your mouth. That's a girl. Did that help?"

Her face showed relief. "It still hurt, but not as bad."

"Good. I'll be back in an hour to check again. With the nurse helping, I'm sure you can manage that long. Agree?"

She searched my face, absorbing my words.

"You're very brave. I'll get your anesthesia when you're a tiny bit further. I promise." Too many women expected to be knocked out when they walked through the door. I'd have to do a better job counseling them beforehand.

A resigned sigh came seconds before her next contraction took hold. "Oh my God, another one."

"Nurse, please help her.

The second patient was an unwed woman who had missed all of her prenatal Clinic visits. Instead, she came to the hospital through Emergency earlier that morning in active labor. The nurses had time to sponge bathe her lower parts, but from her smell, I knew it had to have been weeks since her last head-to-toe bath. Her frightened glare swung in my direction as she opened her mouth to talk. Half her teeth were missing.

I stepped back, shocked by the vision of this pitiful woman about to become a mother. She couldn't even take care of herself. "Nurse, come with me."

We walked to the opposite end of the ward. "What do you know about her?" I asked.

"She didn't give her name, Doctor. Said she was twenty and has no address. She doesn't want the baby."

"Does she know the father?"

"Wouldn't tell me. Just wants us to take the poor thing and put it in a better home."

I returned to her labor bed, where I watched her face transform as she slid from rest into the agonizing grip of a contraction. I rubbed her arm, guiding her through with the same breathing instructions I gave everyone. At its end, I said. "Miss, please take a deep breath and blow it out slowly. I'm Dr. Isaacson. I'm here to help deliver your baby."

She grunted.

Looking softly in her eyes, I asked, "Can you tell me about yourself? Your name and who the father is?"

"No," she snapped. "Just give it a home. I don't want it. Didn't have the boodle for the midwife to end it."

A thread of hopelessness ran through me. This woman, like so many others, had no means of preventing pregnancy, no money for a termination, and no home. Even if she had the money, the risk of butchery was high. She knew her child was headed for a life of destitution. And all I could do was nod my head in empathy. *How in God's name can we fix this utter mess?*

"Very well. I will return soon to check on you. Please try your best to cooperate with the nurse. She knows how to help you along." *Margaret is right. It's time we overturn the antiquated laws.*

Minutes later, I met Joseph back in the corridor. He was leaning his shoulder against the wall, reading his notes. "That took long enough."

My defenses mounted. "I needed to check my patients. Neither is ready for anesthesia, and they were both miserable." My face flushed with anger.

"Why didn't you just start the anesthesia? That's why they come here, isn't it?"

I stopped in my tracks. How dare he criticize my care. For that matter, he'd no clue about the personal circumstances these women faced. At that moment, I had no desire to enlighten him. "What's bothering you, Joseph?"

He stomped ahead.

"Talk to me. What's wrong?" I stood rooted in place. I would not chase after him as if we were an insolent child.

He stepped back to me, his anger palpable. "Do you even want to get married? It doesn't seem like it. You've pushed me aside since you've started consorting with that Mrs. Sanger."

My stomach clenched. "What? How could you ask that? Of course, I want to marry you."

He reached for my shoulders. "Hannah, you always have an excuse not to see me, late patients, new friends. What will it be next? Ellen says this isn't normal."

I placed my hands on his strong arms and pulled him to me. "I'm tired, but I haven't stopped loving you. We both work hard and don't have much time. Once we're married and have our own apartment, we'll see each other every day." I paused. "Please don't start taking marriage advice from your sister. How could she possibly know what's normal?"

"I suppose. But I want you to slow down once you're pregnant and begin acting more like a wife and mother. I want a real home for our children. One I never had." His eyes glistened.

I felt it too. Tired and emotionally wrought, I didn't want anything to go wrong with our plans. "You know my upbringing wasn't typical either. But there will be nothing more important than keeping our children safe from loss and harm."

He drew me into his strong arms, hugging me tightly. "We still have a few minutes. Let's grab a sandwich. I'm on hospital call tonight, so we'll see each other Saturday for dinner? I'll get reservations at Delmonico's, and we can have that steak dinner after all."

"Let's plan on it. I know just the dress to wear."

Later that afternoon, with one healthy infant born to a delighted, mildly anesthetized mother, and the other child undersized, in the nursery destined for the church orphanage, my body was charged with anxious energy. I decided to take a carriage downtown to Tillie's, hoping to learn how she managed during my childhood years, keeping a home while running a business.

Tillie opened the door, surprise registering on her face. "Hannah, what brings you here?"

"I'm sorry I didn't call first. I decided to take a gamble you'd be home, and I could join you for dinner."

"There's always room for you," Tillie said, studying my face.

I hung my coat on the same peg I'd used each day as a child. The apartment encircled me like a warm embrace—the smell of roasting chicken, the comfortable furniture, the melody of Tillie's voice.

"We'll be eating soon. Why don't you help me set the table? Miriam's at her friend's apartment down the hall and will be back by seven. Abe's lying down."

I felt better already. How did she manage to handle so many people at the same time? "You must tell me your secret to holding it together, the business, children, a happy husband," I begged. "Joseph already feels neglected, and there's only the two of us."

"Did something happen?" Tillie asked as she walked back into the kitchen.

I sighed. "He was furious with me today. I went out last night with a group of women to a suffragist lecture instead of having dinner with him. Now he thinks I won't have time for a family or him. He's already issuing pronouncements about changing my schedule when I get pregnant."

"I see." Tillie pulled the dinner plates off the shelf and handed them to me. "What do you think?"

I began to melt, tears filling my eyes. "He has a good heart, but he's so controlling. I'm exhausted trying to convince him to understand my other needs. I had such a stimulating time meeting these intelligent women at the lecture, so different from anyone else I know. Not that there's anything wrong with my friends, but the women last night were so purposeful in their views. I'd love to remain involved with the suffragists, but I'm afraid it will threaten Joseph." I dabbed my eyes on a table napkin and set it at my place. "Is it possible to have both worlds?"

She searched my face. "If you love and respect one other, you'll work it out."

"I'm not sure why he suddenly has so many concerns—my free time, my weight, everything about me. Do you think it could be Ellen's influence?"

"I don't know. Think about his circumstances. Has he ever seen how a typical, happy family functions? We both know it's full of pushes and tugs, laughing and crying. For someone like Joseph who lost both parents young, his expectations may be distorted."

Maybe she was right. "He compares us to his colleagues. Most have wives at home who handle all the domestic matters. Some are quite bright, but they don't get out much. They spend their spare time reading and playing bridge during the day. They don't have vocations and are definitely not suffragists."

Tillie pulled out two chairs and sat on one. I sat on the other. "It wasn't always easy. You know Abe and I had a few rough patches. But most of the time, we tried to work together on business and at home with you children. Like you, I was often tired, but, deep down, very happy. It's gratifying to have something special of your own. If he loves you, he'll try to understand

126

your needs, not compare you to some vision of perfection." She paused, letting her message sink in.

It made sense. "I suppose we should try to talk. I hope he'll listen."

"Find the right time. It's as important as the conversation. You both need to pay attention to one other." She patted my hand. "Let's have dinner and then get you home. I have a feeling you could use a full night's sleep."

Chapter Eighteen

The dining room at Delmonico's was magnificent. Every detail was perfect, from the heavy wood molding on the soaring ceilings to the silk wallpaper. The fine china was light and delicate, as was the Irish Waterford crystal, both imported from Europe. I began my meal with a recommendation from Joseph, Delmonico's famous split pea soup, perfect for the chilly night.

"This is delicious! But it tastes different from the pea soup Rebecca makes." I tried not to slurp. I found it difficult to slow down and remember my manners after so many rushed hospital meals.

Joseph laughed heartily for the first time in ages. "That's because it's cooked with pork. You have no idea what you've been missing all this time. Delicious, isn't it?" He sat back in his chair with a satisfied smirk.

My stomach lurched. "You know I don't eat pork. Why did you order it?" My skin prickled with anger.

"You German Jews are such hypocrites with your self-made Jewish rules. And now there's this ridiculous Reformed Movement? You either commit to being kosher, or you don't." His triumphant expression unnerved me further.

I set my spoon down and frowned. "Joseph, we need to talk. Your prank was cruel, especially after your promise to be more understanding the other day."

He looked at his plate and shook his head. "It was only a joke."

"But why pick now to have a debate about keeping kosher? You know many people with different personal relationships to our religion. Besides, we were supposed to relax tonight."

He looked at me as if I spoke another language. "Since when are you so sensitive?"

I would not be placated that easily. "We're not only arguing every time we get together, but I'm getting the sense you view me with contempt. Why would you play a mean-spirited trick like that? It was disrespectful." I wiped my mouth with the soft white napkin. *Would I regret taking this argument further?*

Joseph, unfazed, continued eating his oysters. He may have been Jewish by birth, but there wasn't a thread of observance in him. After fleeing the Cossacks in Belarus, his father distanced himself from the Jewish community, viewing his Eastern European clan as weak. There was no synagogue or Jewish tradition during Joseph's formative years. Instead, the family struggled to blend into the Christian world. Perhaps Tillie was right when she suggested I delve deeper into his childhood.

"Did you hear me? Why would you invite me to a romantic restaurant only to taunt me?" I demanded.

He pinched his face with incredulity. "You're making a fuss over nothing." He tipped the last oyster into his mouth and set the shell on his plate. "Are you planning to eat that soup? If not, I will."

I pushed my bowl to him. "Can we talk about us?"

He answered gruffly. "Let me eat in peace."

I saw fire. "I've lost my appetite. Excuse me." I pushed my chair back, gathering my damask skirt and jacket, and stood, shoulders squared.

"Where are you going?" For the first time that evening, his mirth dissolved, replaced by worry. He glanced at the nearby tables, checking to see if other guests were watching us.

"Home," I said softly, walking to the lobby.

"Wait, Hannah. Don't go." Joseph called from his seat.

I didn't turn back. My soup churned in my belly as I left the restaurant and boarded a coach back to Rebecca's.

* * *

Sunday morning, I slept past dawn for the first time in weeks. The exhaustion from attending laboring women, excitement over my new-found friends, and Joseph's persistent testing had taken its toll. I lay under my soft quilt, preferring its relaxing warmth to the uncertainty of a new day.

"Hannah, is that you I'm hearing?" Rebecca asked through my closed door.

So much for hiding. "Yes, I'm awake. I'll be out in a moment."

I wrapped myself in the beautiful rose flannel robe Rebecca had sewn for my birthday earlier in the year. Warm and soft. Yes, I would hold onto comfort a few moments longer.

Rebecca called from the kitchen. "Tea or coffee? What's your preference this sunny morning?"

"Tea, please."

I heard her rattling the pot and cups, knowing she was chomping at the bit to hear why I'd come home early. Rebecca was the last of our family to keep a kosher home, and I was curious to hear her reaction.

There was a fresh log on the fire, crackling as it caught, spitting heat into the parlor. Seated in a plush cushioned chair covered with a heavy silk green brocade, I watched the flames lick the dry logs, constantly moving. Nothing stays the same for long in this life.

Rebecca pulled me out of my trance as she set a tray with tea, lemon slices, and buttered toast on the table between our chairs. "Would it feel better to talk?" she asked. "We heard you came home early, and he already called this morning while you were asleep."

"What did he say?" I twisted my engagement ring around my finger.

Rebecca sighed. "That you'd had an argument and to let you know he's coming at noon to talk to you. I didn't want to interfere."

I dropped my head, resigned and frustrated. "I'm worried Joseph may not be the right man for me after all. Since we've been engaged, I'm seeing a whole new side of him. Maybe it was there all along, and I was blinded by love." I proceeded to share the events of the past several weeks and Tillie's advice. "How would you feel if Leo tricked you that way?"

Rebecca tilted her head, her eyes full of empathy.

130

"Of course, I'd be furious, but you're not me, and Joseph isn't Leo. Every match is different. I think Tillie's right about getting to the bottom of his problem."

I sniffled. "I don't want to go through life alone, but I don't want to be trapped in an unhappy marriage either. I see so many women in my practice who are miserable and imprisoned by their marriages. Besides, Joseph and I have been very close, you know, behaving as if married." I paused. *Had I shared too much?*

Rebecca sat quietly, studying me with the eye of a designer. "When I met your Papa, Sam, his needs were bottomless, and I knew he still loved your dear departed mother. But I married him anyway for two reasons."

My ears perked. Rebecca rarely shared her private thoughts, especially when it involved my parents.

"You know that my first marriage had hardly begun when my husband died of consumption. I was lonely and frightened about my future and didn't want to spend my life childless as a spinster. Even though I knew your Papa and I were still strangers, I saw something in his eyes that told me he was capable of great love. I hoped Sam would open his heart again and one day feel that same way toward me." Rebecca reached for her napkin and blotted the corners of her eyes. "Eventually, he did. We shared many lovely years together."

I softened my shoulders. "You took excellent care of Papa at the end. It made me more certain than ever to apply to medical school. You knew how to make him comfortable and peaceful at every turn. And he trusted you with his care. It *was* a great love."

Rebecca nodded slowly as she collected her thoughts. "There's something I've needed to say to you for a long time."

My brow creased, wondering what secret she might share.

"I owe you an apology." She sighed deeply. "I should have been a better mother to you during those early years. There's no excuse for how shamefully I treated you. I don't know what was wrong with me, but after Abby was born, I felt a deep sadness when I should have been delighted to be a mother. Instead of sharing my love, I wanted to climb inside a shell and never come out. I thank God for your kind sister."

I felt goosebumps rise on my arms, barely remembering those long-ago years. What I could recall was Tillie's relief when I stopped nervously picking at my eyebrows and lashes, and they grew back. She'd say, 'Now my little birdie looks like a happy little girly.' I'd all but forgotten about my first few years on the farm and had no recollection of Mama at all.

Rebecca wiped the tears from her cheeks. "Your sister had her hands full with the twins, Sarah especially, such a frail child. It was selfish leaving you there. Tillie was so young, not much more than a child herself. Please believe me when I say you were a beautiful, sweet child."

My childhood was a strange blur. I switched my thoughts to Rebecca as a young mother. "That sadness after birth sometimes happens to my patients. I don't think they can control it."

"Really? I thought there was something dreadfully wrong inside me. I was so ashamed."

I struggled to recall a kernel of memory from my earliest years and could not. "I don't remember much from my childhood on the farm, but I do appreciate your kindness since I've been back in the city. You're a loving stepmother to me now. You and Leo made the last few years in New York warm and welcoming."

Rebecca nodded, her mind still in the past. "Your sister, clever as the dickens, knew I'd need a job after your Papa passed. So, she introduced me to Leo at Bloomingdale's. I was thrilled to work in the city as a dress designer, a new life for me, and for Abby too. She loved high school downtown."

My mouth curled up. Such a relief from the frown I'd been wearing.

"You see, Hannah, you never know what's in store for you around the next corner. Just try to make your best decision and let God lead you through your life."

I sat quietly, sipping my tea, detecting a bright citrus flavor. "Rebecca, where did you find lemons this time of the year?"

Rebecca laughed. "I was wondering if you'd notice. My grocer hid one under the counter for me. He'd gotten a few by train from California. Can you imagine? Lemons in November?" She studied me. "Are you ready to find out what's ahead with Joseph?"

"Yes, I am. You've been wonderful." A hint of laughter escaped. "But don't give out my room too fast. I may need it a while longer."

* * *

I considered my upcoming discussion with Joseph as I stood gazing at Central Park through my bedroom window. The trees were bare, skeletons compared to the glorious foliage they wore a few weeks earlier. Was our relationship also past its bloom? Had I missed something important in his character? Dirty brown leaves blanketed the footpaths lacing through the grounds. A wave of irritation ran through me. I'd hoped to walk through the park and talk. But the autumn debris would soil my boots in minutes. Perhaps we were better off heading to the Metropolitan Museum, a ten-block walk north. The quiet of the museum would ensure we kept our voices civil.

I slipped into a warm woolen dress, suitable for an outdoor walk. It was a lovely heather blend, mixing shades of grey and blue, offsetting my eyes to their best advantage. Arranging my hair carefully, I pulled two teasing tendrils from my chignon. If Joseph was planning to ruin our engagement, I wanted him to realize what he'd be sacrificing.

Moments later, he knocked at the door. I walked to the parlor as Rebecca and Leo slipped into their bedroom, gently closing their door behind them.

"Hello, Joseph. Let me get my coat." I avoided his eyes.

He stepped into the apartment. "No tea? I'd hoped you'd made lunch."

Ignoring his comment, I said. "Don't take off your coat. I'd like to speak in private and it's a beautiful day for a walk." I pinned my felt hat to my bun.

"I'm sorry. I realize last night wasn't kind of me." Studying my face for a reaction, he continued, "I honestly thought you'd find it funny."

We walked past the doorman into the brisk air.

I stopped in my tracks, scowling. "Don't take me for a fool. You knew exactly what you were doing. I thought we'd been together long enough to understand one another. But now I'm starting to think you don't know me at all, or perhaps you do, and detest me."

"Hannah, you're taking things too far. It wasn't as bad as you're making it out to be," he pleaded.

"No, I'm not! Don't make light of your bad behavior. Margaret was just telling me the other night…."

He interrupted me mid-sentence. "Margaret again? I'm beginning to think she's a bad influence."

I fumed. "Do not insult her. She's made me more aware than ever of the importance of my work as a doctor." I felt a surge of confidence, realizing I now had the upper hand.

Joseph stopped walking. "Hannah, you know I adore you. I…I just worry that you won't always love me back. You have so many other passions in your life." He lifted his top hat, holding it to his chest. "Please accept my apology. I was a cad last night and am sorry. I'd be crushed to lose you."

I studied his face, searching his eyes for sincerity. What I saw was fear, not regret. "Joseph, I need to know this side of you better and why you'd play such an ugly trick. Frankly, it made me uncomfortable and fearful of marriage. Please help me understand."

As we walked along the park, I hoped he would dig into his past for a plausible explanation.

Joseph cleared his throat. "I'm not entirely sure. I look around and see most happy families living a certain way and would like that for us, too."

I sighed. "I understand, but you picked a woman who doesn't fit that mold. I'm a doctor like you and don't intend to walk away from my career."

"But, what about children?" he stammered. "Won't you stop then?"

"Of course, I want children with you. Remember, I grew up in a home where Tillie and Abe both worked, and they're still crazy about each other. Tillie had help in our home while she was at work. Abe pitched in by reading to us when we were little and, later, helping us with schoolwork. They were partners." I paused a moment. "Couldn't we do that too?"

He looped his arm through mine. "Uncharted territory, like Lewis and Clark."

"I suppose. You had an unusual childhood, with Ellen working while taking your parents' places. What was it like for you?"

He expelled an audible exhale. "Lonely, terribly lonely. I spent most days by myself, with only a book for companionship. I don't want that for my children," he said softly, barely loud enough for me to hear.

"I'm so sorry, Joseph. I would never want our children to feel lonely, or you either." My anger melted, my heart aching for the sad child within him. I knew it took a great deal of courage to admit what he felt. "I want them to have happy childhoods and fulfilled parents."

We'd arrived at the museum. I gazed at the Corinthian columns guarding the building. "I'm a strong person, but I'm human and vulnerable too. I need to know that you'll see me for who I am and care about my happiness. Right now, I doubt I can trust you'll do that."

He stood two steps lower than me on the grand staircase. We were eye to eye. "Darling Hannah, you will never doubt me again. Please accept my apology and give me another chance. I beg you."

I reached my arms around his neck and drew him into an embrace, then a kiss, hoping with all my strength he could honor his promise.

Chapter Nineteen

This time, Joseph took our conversation seriously. He silently accepted my evenings with Margaret as I attended suffragist events, admitting that the fear of losing a second engagement rattled him, and was reassured to learn that several other doctors' wives occasionally attended the same meetings. As we approached Thanksgiving, the rhythm of our lives took a tender turn, much like our early courtship. Sharing our fears broke through a layer of doubt and mistrust, forging a pathway to a deeper, fuller understanding of each other.

I received calls from patrons at the Waldorf once or twice each week. Their complaints typically ranged from headaches and head colds to constipation. Although I was pleased to have my name bantered among the wealthy, the calls often came at the most inopportune times.

The more I was drawn into the suffragist causes—legal rights, employment, education, health—the more I saw opportunities for reform. Margaret and I shared the same philosophy toward pregnancy planning and prevention, both determined to reverse the puritanical Comstock Laws that outlawed education or the dispensing of devices. Just the other night, she surprised me with a list she'd made.

"I went in and out of every apothecary and hardware store near your office to see where your patients could pick up a veil or condoms. Here's a list you can give patients who ask."

"Terrific, Margaret. I know they'll appreciate your effort. The women especially like to use diaphragms. I measure them first, so they know the correct size to order." I gave her forearm an appreciative squeeze. "It's the only way to reduce undesired pregnancies and abortions."

We spent hours exploring strategies to publicize and garner support for our stance, knowing we must convince politicians and legislators to listen. When it came to strategy, the Hopkins trustees immediately came to mind. After dinner with Margaret one evening, I pulled out a clean sheet of stationery and wrote to Mrs. Garrett at Johns Hopkins.

November 5, 1906

Dear Mrs. Garrett,

I hope this letter finds you in good health as we head into the holiday season. I miss our dinners and your wise counsel, always the finest course at every meal. Recently, I began an exciting project I'd like to discuss with you and Mrs. Thomas in greater detail.

But first, please accept my appreciation for the obstetrical candidate you sent to Mount Sinai. She's an exceptional young woman, and I'm delighted to invite her to join our residents next year.

In the meantime, I've become active with the New York suffragist movement. Together with Margaret Sanger, whom you've undoubtedly heard of, we are gathering support to overturn the Comstock Laws. You and Mrs. Thomas guided us in Baltimore with tremendous insight, and I hoped once again I could seek your sage advice.

Sadly, I see many women in the hospital Clinic who face unplanned, undesired pregnancies. Without the financial means to properly care for either an infant or a large household, they resort to abortion. Even sadder, the number of butchered abortions in New York has not ebbed. We continue to lose too many otherwise healthy women from bleeding and infection. While we forge ahead with our efforts to overturn Comstock, we must demand a more formal education of midwives to mitigate these maternal casualties.

I'd like to visit Baltimore before the Thanksgiving holiday. Not only would I appreciate your wisdom, but would cherish a visit with both of you over dinner. This time, I insist I treat.

Please suggest a weekend that works with your schedule.

With affection,
Hannah Isaacson, MD

I examined the letter, checking for spelling errors. Throughout my school years, teachers were always surprised at my abysmal spelling, considering my near-perfect grades in every other subject. The brain, the final frontier of medicine, remains a mystery.

Next, I checked Joseph's call schedule, intending to plan the trip on a weekend he was occupied at the hospital. Once I settled on a date, I would send a note to Mrs. Collins announcing my visit and drop off an early Christmas gift.

When I visited two years ago, she was so excited I thought she'd faint. "Oh, my beautiful Hannah!" She waved from the front porch, jumping up and down as my carriage pulled up.

I was welcomed with an embrace so strong; it practically knocked me backward. Mrs. Collins insisted on cooking every meal, regaling me with my favorite recipes—chicken pudding with gravy, ambrosia, and my favorite, the newfangled lemon Jell-O. For Christmas that year, I sent her the newly published Settlement Cookbook, all the rage in New York. Since then, I have sent a different cookbook every Christmas along with extra money for a new dress and hat.

Within nine days, I had my answer from Mrs. Garrett. The trustees offered two-weekend dates between Thanksgiving and Christmas. My next dinner with Margaret was later in the week. I wondered if I should invite her to join me. Normally, I wouldn't hesitate, but a shred of concern gnawed at me. Would an out-of-town trip with Margaret push Joseph too far?

* * *

"Last patient for the morning," Ina announced. "I'll bring her back to the exam room. Also, you have a swarm up in labor. Do you want me to call for help?"

A laugh escaped my lips. "A swarm?"

138

"A lot, more than three." Ina played along.

"Ina, swarm is a word for bees or mosquitoes, not people. But let me finish my appointments and check. I may need a hand, so don't go far."

It was mayhem upstairs with five women in different stages of labor. Mrs. Roth, a six-time mother of boys, was furthest along, and I headed straight to the sink to scrub my hands, placing my white apron over my head on the way.

"Doctor, she arrived at the hospital fifteen minutes ago, fully dilated," the nurse said.

Mrs. Roth screamed hysterically. "I want the medicine. I can't take it any longer!"

I walked to the foot of her bed. "Let me look and see how you're doing," I said calmly, gently sliding my fingers inside her body. I felt a furry head, fully crowned. "You're ready to push. I want you to bear down with your next contraction. Nurse, are you ready for the baby?"

"Yes, doctor, all set."

A powerful contraction and the patient screamed, "Medicine, now! You promised!"

"Push!" the nurse, and I shouted in unison.

The baby's head was visible. Birth was another push or two away.

"Damn you, doctor. You promised."

"Mrs. Roth, you're almost there. There's no time for anesthesia." My job now was to deliver a healthy baby.

Another contraction. "Dear Lord, take me now!" she howled, squeezing her eyes shut.

"Push," the nurse, and I shouted in unison.

A chubby baby girl slid into my hands, face down, in perfect position. I carefully turned her body and cradled her, locking eyes with Mrs. Roth. "You've done it. You've gotten your little girl."

Mrs. Roth's eyes watered, tears dripping down her cheeks. She whimpered, "I can't believe it. Let me see my sweet angel."

She studied the infant in my hands, watching me lift her tiny body, tilting her head upward so there was a full view.

"Finally." She dropped her head back on the damp pillow, her face illuminated by the ceiling lights. "Thank you, Lord. You answered my prayers." The nurse and I smiled, knowing her plea for anesthesia was already ancient history. We wiped and swaddled her precious child.

I set the baby in her outstretched arms. "Do you have a name for her?"

"This time, only a boy name. I thought it would bring bad luck to dare imagine a girl. We were going to name the baby Samuel, after my Zadie. Maybe now we'll name her Samantha." A halted breath. "I was crazy about my old grandpa."

I smiled at her, thinking about the joy I'd feel someday using my parents' names. Papa was the only Sam in our family, and if Joseph and I had a son, he'd be given Papa's name.

"That's a special name for me, too. Good choice." The baby was rooting in her swaddle. "Nurse, please put baby on mama's breast."

I waited patiently for the afterbirth. "Nurse, when we're done here, I'll check the next patient."

Ina's head popped through the door, breaking the spell. "Doctor, there's a call from the Waldorf. A woman on the line asked for you."

"See if she can call another doctor. Things are too busy here." I thought a moment. "If it's not urgent, I can call back later. Get the room number." It was ridiculous to interrupt a string of laboring women with another congested or constipated patient.

I turned my attention back to my mothers, lined up in the delivery unit, metal beds separated by white drapes. Half had received anesthesia and were laboring comfortably; the other half were not far enough along for the medication. Over the next five hours, I checked one after another, helping them deliver their babies—boy, girl, girl, girl. Thank God, they were all healthy, both infants and mothers.

I said a silent prayer of thanks as I walked to the charting desk and sat, meticulously recording the labor and birth information for each patient, not skipping a detail. Halfway through, Ina rushed back into the room, highly agitated.

"Doctor, the same woman from the Waldorf is on the line. She wants you to go down there now. She's in room 642. There was something in her voice…. I think you'd better go."

I lifted my head, sharpening my attention, pushing aside my exhaustion. I never second-guessed Ina. "Did you offer the emergency livery?"

"I did, but she wanted to wait for you. Said she preferred privacy." Ina knitted her brow, trying to remember every word. "But there was something odd…."

Chapter Twenty

I t was only five, but autumn darkness had fully descended when I stepped out of the hospital. It had been raining on and off all afternoon. The air, thick with dampness, seeped through my clothes, leaving me chilled. I was grateful the coach had waited for me. This time of day, they were at their busiest and wouldn't waste a moment idling. Leave it to Ina, stalling the driver with her unabashed flirting.

"Doctor, want me to come?" She held her unopened umbrella in her hand.

"You're a peach, Ina, but no, I'll handle it. Can I borrow your umbrella?"

"Step in, madam. We best get started, the streets are crowded, and there's more rain comin' in," called the coachman.

I peered out the coach window, looking down Fifth Avenue, crammed with traffic as offices closed for the day. Sidewalks and crosswalks were packed with pedestrians holding open umbrellas, a sea of dark coats swimming through the city's sidewalks, the streets filled with shiny black coaches wet from the rain. I settled on the bench, resenting the inconvenience. It would take forever to drive forty blocks to the Waldorf. Just as I banged on the ceiling, alerting the driver that I was ready to go, a flash of lightning streaked through the sky. I sunk further into my seat.

To kill time, I opened my physician bag and inspected the instruments, all clean and polished. If I were lucky, I wouldn't need them, but Ina's ominous tone made me grab the bag on my way out. Fortunately, Joseph was working late at the hospital and didn't expect me. But still, I would have savored putting up my feet by the fire at Rebecca and Leo's, sharing a drink and a hot dinner. Anything was preferable to traipsing downtown. Fielding telephone complaints was one thing, but jumping at the beck and call of fussy hotel guests was another matter altogether. Enough was enough. Mr. Tschirky would receive my resignation later this week.

I handed the driver a large tip with my fare. It had taken over forty minutes to travel under two miles in the rain. I could have walked faster. More determined than ever to end the obligation, I hurried into the hotel, nodding at the doormen, rushing through the crowded lobby to the elevator. Contrary to my earlier impressions, tonight, the hotel's celestial qualities, suggesting romance, wealth, and beauty, irritated me. I suppressed my annoyance at the patrons' sense of entitlement and stepped inside the lift, an over-decorated jewel box, politely requesting the sixth floor. The elevator filled with cigar smoke as a man in an overcoat and top hat strode inside on floor two. He was followed by a parade of passengers wearing their finest apparel, stepping on and off as we stopped at every floor, swatting the smoke.

I finally exited, followed by a trail of woodsy cigar smoke. A distasteful habit. Brass sconces cast scalloped patterns of light along the walls. Beneath, a plush carpet runner zig-zagged over the darkly stained floor. I twisted to the right: 601, 602, reaching the end of the corridor. 624. Annoyed, I retraced my steps, passing the elevator again, increasing my gait in the opposite direction, 625...630...640. There it was, 642, the last room on the right. The door was ajar.

"Hello," I called from the hall.

No answer.

I waited a few seconds and called again, "Hello."

Nothing.

I opened the door further, peering into a white marble foyer, joining the parlor. Stepping through the entrance, I called louder, "Hello, this is Dr. Isaacson from Mount Sinai Hospital."

Still no sound. Was the guest sleeping? Had she stepped out? I stood quietly, listening. "Hello!" I shouted again.

A barely audible cough came from the adjacent bedroom. The door was closed.

My eyes were drawn to the carpet. I detected a trail of crimson droplets, still bubbling on the wool surface. My coat and umbrella fell from my arms. I tightened my grip on the instrument bag and charged into the bedroom.

The scene was all too familiar.

Dear God, no!

Pale, drained of blood, she lay half-dead on a sheet covering the bed. Her legs were open, a viscous pool of blood between them, old, coagulated puddles coated by a clearer liquid, all soaking through the linens and bedspread.

My hand rushed to her neck to feel for a pulse. A faint beat, alive. *Thank God.* If I could only keep her that way. I screamed for help while laying out my instruments, forceps, curettes, sutures, launching into the well-rehearsed steps, examine, search for tears, stem the bleeding. Minutes ticked by.

A porter ran in. He gasped loudly, eyes bulging with shock.

I shouted, "Run! Get help *now*! Call the livery for an ambulance!"

Working furiously, I tried every technique I knew to save the poor woman. As I worked, one by one, people entered the bedroom. First, Mr. Tschirky, then a policeman, and finally, the ambulance transporters. By that point, it was over; blood and fetal tissue covered the bed. I pronounced her time of death, 6:15 pm. Exhausted, I dropped into a side chair by the bed.

"What have you done?" shouted Mr. Tschirky, his face lit with anger. "How dare you!"

His words stung. "What are you talking about? I just got here." I began shaking, confused.

"You're a quack!" he shouted. "You killed her!"

Fury raced through me. "How dare you! I did nothing of the sort. You said the calls would be minor. This woman should have come to the hospital. We might have saved her there. Too much time was lost."

"Who is she?" the policeman demanded.

I looked at him, astonished. "I have absolutely no idea. There was a call from a woman in room 642; that's all I knew. I hurried here after the second call, later in the day."

"You're lying! A sordid business, right under our very noses—in *my* hotel, no less." Mr. Tschirky's eyes scrutinized my body, running from my head to shoes and back. "You'll pay for this."

The policeman, a portly middle-aged man, grabbed my arm, wrenching me from the chair with such force I thought he'd dislocated my shoulder. He shouted in my ear. "You're under arrest for murder. We caught you red-handed."

Astonished, my jaw dropped as realization set in. A cold panic ran through my blood. I struggled to keep my voice steady while his scream reverberated in my ear. "You're wrong! The hotel called for help."

"Convenient story," shouted the cop as he dragged me out of the bedroom, reaching for his handcuffs, roughly latching them around my wrists in front of me.

Mr. Tschirky's eyes scanned the bedroom. "You made a disgusting mess of this room."

I beseeched them, crying with frustration. "She was half-dead and abandoned when I arrived. Your culprit fled, leaving this poor woman hemorrhaging. I don't even know her name!"

The policeman scoffed. "Save it for the judge. You're goin' downtown."

III

Part 3

Chapter Twenty-One

My body would not stop shaking. Hour after hour, I sat waiting on a metal bench in the holding cell, overcome with disbelief and humiliation. Afraid to sleep, afraid to talk, I waited for someone to come to end the nightmare, tell me it was a false arrest made in haste without the benefit of a proper investigation. I waited alone with my fear, scarcely conscious of the snoring, cackling, and coughing of the other women in the cell.

"Lunch!" A heavy guard hit the bars with a metal spoon, sliding a tray of tin cups filled with tepid soup and a mound of torn bread through a wide slot in the door. Hands shot to the tray, grabbing the food. I hadn't eaten since lunch the day before, but one whiff of the rancid soup turned my stomach. What in God's name was in it? My eyes traveled up the brick wall to the narrow opening, passing for a window, and realized it was already midday. How long had I been here? A day or more?

My dress was still soiled from the woman's blood, hair undone, body unclean from using the single chamber pot in the corner. The room reeked from the filthy women, an odor beyond description. I pondered how little time it took for the body to decline.

Another clanking. The guard's spoon strumming the bars, our meal bell, and a tray of cups passed through the same opening. "Water!"

Again, a bundle of hands flew in desperation for the tin cups of water, for anything to quench thirst. This time my hand joined the fray, but it was too late. The last cup, knocked on its side, spilled dirty water over the tin tray, puddling on the filthy floor, reflecting a filmy rainbow of scum.

The guard sneered, "That's what you get, baby killer—nothing! Just what you deserve."

"You're da murderin' midwife from da Waldorf," a toothless woman across from me mocked. "Girls, we got ourselves a real society lady."

A chorus of raucous laughter broke out.

I knew their type from the clinics at Johns Hopkins and Mount Sinai. I made my feeble medical contribution to help these women. But it was a hopeless struggle. They were the basest, most disreputable women living in the city, their lives reduced to basic survival.

In a little over a day, I'd gone from hero to villain, deliverer of babies to a murderess. That morning, the guards had paraded each newspaper on the other side of the cell bars with hideous glee as the allegations hit the front pages with forceful, sensational headlines, *The Jewish Murderess from the Mount, Murdering Midwife from the Waldorf, Doctor, or Murderer?* and more, too awful to repeat. New York, with its unquenchable thirst for scandal, pounced, my hard-earned reputation poisoned in their feeding frenzy. In just one day, the calamity bore down upon me with herculean force, leaving me shaken and empty.

Tillie had hurried to the precinct an hour after my arrest. Outraged, she assured me she'd hire a lawyer and have me released immediately, promising to alert Rebecca and Joseph. I waited all night, expecting, hoping. No one returned.

Instead, early the following morning, I was paraded into a packed courtroom filled with the press and jeering onlookers for my arraignment. My attorney, a Mr. Clemson, whom Tillie had retained, had barely enough time to review the background facts or prepare a bail application. But to the court, it didn't matter. It was an open-and-shut case lasting under five minutes.

The prosecutor sneered at me as he presented the police report. I sat in my crusted, blood-stained dress, listening in disbelief to the charge—*murder in the first degree!*

The judge shook his head in disgust. "Mr. Clemson, what have you to say for the defendant?"

Mr. Clemson cleared his throat, shuffling his notes, standing slowly. "Your Honor, Dr. Isaacson is a prestigious physician at Mount Sinai Hospital and was called to the Waldorf Hotel to save a helpless woman in need, the victim of an illegal procedure that Dr. Isaacson did not perform. We will prove there is absolutely no way she could have murdered the victim. She poses no flight risk."

The judge stared at me, my disarray contrary to my lawyer's every word. "Rarely do we find the perpetrator so openly caught in the act of malfeasance. This felony charge is of the highest magnitude and leaves no room for leniency. There will be no bail. Suspect will be held in the Workhouse at Blackwell's Island until her trial." The gavel hit its platform with ringing finality.

I turned to face the courtroom. Tillie, Abe, Ina, and Rebecca were sitting together rows behind me, Tillie's face frozen in shock, Rebecca and Ina weeping. Abe's nostrils flared in anger. I scanned the room for Joseph, finally spotting him in the rear by the door. I willed him to meet my eyes to calm my fear, but instead, he exited without eye contact.

How was that possible? He must have known how frightened and desperate I was. My eyes filled as I tried to settle myself. Perhaps he was seeking more help. Yes, that must be where he was heading.

Now, back in my cell, I awaited transfer to the Workhouse on Blackwell's, the same island Nellie Bly infiltrated undercover two decades before. Her explosive expose of the atrocities committed in the Insane Asylum had left the world in shock. The sheer mention of Blackwell's Island drove terror through me. How would I survive?

Startled out of my thoughts, I heard my name. "Isaacson, someone to see you." The guard peered at me through narrow eyes, picking at the heavy metal keys tied to her waist. Finally, she found the key to the holding cell and slid it into the hole of the iron grate. "Come with me, and don't try anything."

I followed her through a heavy door, down a long stone corridor into a small conference room. Tillie was pacing like a caged animal. She leapt toward me with her arms extended for an embrace.

"No touching the prisoner!" the guard screamed. "Sit at the table. You have five minutes."

Tillie and I jumped apart and sat obediently. She handed me a sandwich and a jar of water. "Eat this quickly. I have much to tell you. Listen carefully."

I nodded, stuffing my mouth with bread and chicken, devouring the sandwich like the starving animal I'd become, afraid someone would take it from me.

"We can't free you yet. The judge wasn't willing to hear any additional evidence, but Mr. Clemson is determined to get you out. He requested you write a full accounting of everything that happened yesterday afternoon and evening; every person you passed at the hotel, looked at, or spoke to; anyone who might recognize you. We're going to find every one of them and show your picture. We'll prove you arrived at the Waldorf too close to the woman's death and didn't have time to commit the crime."

She reached into her purse and pulled out my engagement photo. "We'll use this to ask around."

That picture. A joyful time already buried in the brief history of my engagement. But I pushed my sadness aside, knowing there wasn't time for it. "Have the police spoken to Ina? What about Joseph? What did the hospital say? Will you be able to come see me?"

"Ina has been a tremendous help and will review your list to ensure nothing important is forgotten. She's already hunting down the carriage driver, but it hasn't been easy." Tillie reached back into her bag and pulled out another sandwich wrapped in paper and a small pad with pencil. "Here, hide these in your pockets and work on the list."

I whispered. "And Joseph?" Where was he, and why did he leave the courtroom?

Tillie cast her eyes downward and shrugged. "I couldn't reach him." Her words fell on my heart. She must have realized how devastating they were. "Look at me, Hannah." She reached toward my shoulders, then withdrew her hands, remembering the guard. "Our first order of business is getting you out of here. We'll worry about Joseph later."

I began to cry. "Will you visit me...there?"

"I'll find a way. Maybe I can slip in as Mr. Clemson's secretary when he visits. They don't permit family. Let's pray it works."

The door opened abruptly. The guard snapped, "Time's up. Your ferry leaves in ten minutes."

I grabbed Tillie's hands and squeezed them so quickly, the guard didn't have time to intervene. "I love you."

"Godspeed. Remember what you need to do." Her face was creased with worry.

I spun around and walked through the door, attempting to keep my balance as the guard shoved me ahead of her.

Chapter Twenty-Two

The freezing wind blew in gusts across the East River as the ferry made the quick crossing to Blackwell's Island. Longing for my warm woolen coat, I realized most of my fellow prisoners probably never owned one, always dreading the cold of winter, shivering, and dying from the harsh elements. I drew the thin wrap issued to each of us upon boarding, tightly around my upper body and hair.

"Stand closer, fancy girl," said a voice nearby. "There's nothing left to steal on ya, and we'll both be warmer. I'm Erma. What's yer name?"

She looked harmless, a mousy face with small features surrounded by a blowing mop of tangled hair, short in stature like me. I stepped closer. "I'm Hannah."

She closed the gap separating us. "Ya headin' for the Workhouse or prison?"

I studied her bloodshot eyes, squinting from the wind blowing off the starboard side of the ferry. "Workhouse until my trial."

"Prison. Got me again for hookin'. Sorta glad. Could use the break. Hate the winter and sleepin' outside. Whatcha in fer?"

A break? Unthinkable. I faced my choice. Do I cozy up or stay distant? What was the lesser of evils? I thought of Nellie Bly, the reporter who chose to blend in. I chose the truth. "I'm a doctor and was called to help a woman left bleeding from a botched abortion. They thought I did it."

Erma opened her small mouth, revealing brown-stained teeth, her front incisors both chipped. She forced a disbelieving laugh. "Sure. Dat's what we all say."

I looked down and closed my eyes. *No one is going to believe me. No more conversations.* My decision became clear. Take her body warmth. Shut up and survive.

Stepping onto the pier at Blackwell's, we were separated into three groups. The first consisted of eight scrawny women, Erma among them. Two husky guards dressed in ill-fitting coats led them down a path to the right, presumably to the prison. The second group of women was visibly ill, some stumbling, coughing, barely able to stand. They were taken by cart, the last two practically thrown on top of others, to the Charity Hospital at the southernmost tip.

I'd heard about Charity Hospital while practicing at Mount Sinai. Built for the sick and dying, it was intended as a sanctuary for the poor. But those who spent time tending the patients came back to Manhattan with horrific reports of experimentation and abuse. It might be better to die on the streets.

Another two guards approached the remaining six of us. "Don't just stand there! Follow us."

The Workhouse was situated in the upper center of the two-mile narrow island, just south of the insane asylum. The exterior appeared innocent enough, factory-like, a wide rectangular box with hundreds of symmetrical windows. We approached its central steps.

Once inside, we were taken to the baths, told to undress, and leave our clothing for delousing. My list for Tillie was in my skirt pocket. I knew I wouldn't keep it long, so I committed it to memory. After delousing, we'd be issued prison wear sewn by the inmates. A bath, how wonderful. My scalp itched, and I knew my body reeked. I'd started menstruating in the holding cell, and all the guard would give me were filthy rags. What a relief to have clean undergarments again.

I stood shivering in the dressing area, naked with the other five women, covering my private parts with my hands and arms. As we waited to be called one by one to the bath, it occurred to me that there was one tub. We'd take turns using the same bath in the same dirty water. The first woman was called. "Prisoner Sullivan, get in here!"

The door to the bath opened. I watched Sullivan walk into the room and swing a leg into the tub. She screamed when her leg hit the water. "It's freezing!"

"Get in," the first guard ordered, pushing her into the icy water. "Wash the lice from yer hair, or we'll cut it off."

Miss Sullivan hurried through the most rudimentary motions of a bath, jumping out of the tub, unceremoniously slipping on the wet tiled floor, finally wrapping herself in a threadbare towel. She was led to an adjoining room, shivering and cursing the entire way.

The guard cackled. "Isaacson. Your turn. Come get your bubble bath. No pissing in the water." The guards' raucous laughter stung my ears.

I cautiously entered the bathroom and glanced at the water. Islands of hair floated on the surface, already filthy from Sullivan. I knew I had no choice, so I closed my eyes and stepped over the edge of the tub, imagining the first swim of spring on Papa's farm, the pond water always bracing. I dipped my head back, held my breath, and scrubbed my body and hair without soap, knowing the grime had to be removed.

"Well, wasn't that lady-like. I expected more screaming outta ya." The first guard chortled. Her two front teeth were missing, and a pea-sized black mole beside her nostril seemed to stare right at me.

The second guard, tall and thin with stringy black hair escaping her head cap, chortled. "She's cold-blooded; must be the baby killer." She bore her eyes into mine. "You the midwife?"

I shivered in my thin towel and nodded.

"Should've made you go last!" the toothless guard scoffed. "Next time, you will."

Chapter Twenty-Three

I knew how to navigate the academic world, the back-stabbing nature of many medical students and doctors, but I was entirely out of my depth in prison. From a distance, the rigid structure of each day—mutely standing in straight lines, obeying the guards' commands, and eating silently, all appeared orderly. However, up close, it was replete with riptides of powerful forces amongst inmates that lurked beneath the thin veneer of prison civility. The surface, at times so porous, simmered with tension.

The prison had a hierarchy, unwritten rules, and most inmates from the streets were well-versed. I, on the other hand, far from my natural element, was at a distinct disadvantage. I fixed my eyes on everyone and every interaction, attempting to unravel the clues, marking who had influence, who could make my life more hellish than it already was. It was clear my best opportunity for safety came from using my single asset, medical knowledge. What I couldn't discern was how to make it work in my favor.

The first evening, after my cold-water cleansing, I was taken to my new home, a tiny cinder block cell with a barred window. I had three cellmates who shared two bunk beds with an arm's length between them. A scratchy straw mattress sat on each metal bedframe, topped with a parchment-thin sheet and blanket, woefully inadequate for the winter temperatures ahead. A chamber pot and bucket of water for washing sat in the corner of the cell, their proximity a recipe for typhus. We were squeezed so tightly together I could smell my cellmates' fetid breath. The odors alone would make sleep impossible. Caged animals were treated better than this.

That evening, after a dinner of baked beans, no doubt laced with pork fat, and mashed potatoes in the Mess Hall, I returned to the cell and greeted the women.

"What's yer name?" a petite, curly hair girl asked, eyes wide with curiosity. "I'm Daisy."

"Hannah." I studied the young woman, barely a girl, as she sat opposite me on the other lower bunk. "What did you do to get yourself in here?"

Daisy giggled. "Oldest profession in da world. Been here a month's time. Should be out soon." Her estimate of time was confirmed by the half-inch growth of dark brown roots that stood in striking contrast to her flaming red hair straight out of a cheap bottle of dye.

"Shannon," came a voice above Daisy. A thin woman rolled to face me. "Pickpocket. Best in Gotham." She grinned, revealing two neat rows of brown chipped teeth. Shannon, with her straight brown hair and slender build, was nondescript, perfect for a thief, able to weave through a crowd undetected.

I twisted around to see who slept in the bunk above me. Another small woman was napping fitfully.

"She's Martha," said Daisy. "Came here yesterday drunk as a skunk. Still sleepin' it off."

"Whatcha in for?" Shannon asked from the opposite top bunk.

I twisted back. "Nothing. They think I hurt a woman, but I didn't." I answered.

Shannon sat up, eyeing me more closely. "Whadda, you mean hurt?"

I glared back. "I'm a doctor. I was called to a hotel to help a bleeding woman, and she died. No one else was there to witness."

Shannon snickered. "Oh, yer the one. The midwife. Figures."

A streak of anger whipped through me. "I'm a doctor. There's a big difference." I wasn't going to let any of them intimidate me.

"Yeah, right." Shannon continued to laugh.

Chapter Twenty-Four

After my first week of incarceration, bored out of my skull in the women's Sewing and Knitting Halls, I wondered how the masses in the sweatshops across the East River withstood the monotony day after day. Finally, the Head Warden, Beatrice, beckoned me into her office. She was a middle-aged, portly woman with thin grey hair partially covered with a prison cap. Her name, Beatrice, was given to infants as an omen of happiness, but her tone and dour looks portended the opposite. Her dress was a formless muslin, brown and loose, with a grease-stained white half-apron tied around her waist. Her face unsettled me. Slit eyes, sallow and pockmarked skin, she was the meanest-looking woman I'd ever met.

"I see you're still a doctor." Her eyes flew back and forth between my prison file and face. "They haven't pulled your license...yet." Her voice, deep like a man's, sent ominous reverberations through me.

"That's correct, an obstetrician," I was afraid to remind her that I had not yet been convicted of a single crime. Such was the harsh reality of the accused, guilty once cuffed.

"We need you in the Clinic. Tomorrow, you'll be taken to the upper floor sick room during work hours and tend to women until lunch." She scrutinized me. "After lunch, you return to the Clinic until dinner. That's where you'll be reassigned every day for your daily work duty."

"Yes, Warden." I kept my face expressionless, scarcely able to contain my joy at this good fortune. "Who else works there?"

"Sometimes another nurse like you. It's well-supervised, so don't think about trying anything stupid. You'll be watched the whole time." She studied me, the creases across her forehead deepening.

"Yes, Warden." I looked at the floor. She'd already forgotten I was a fully trained doctor.

"You'll be called for emergencies around the clock," she said firmly.

My head shot up. "What? What kind of emergencies?"

The Warden cocked her head to the side. "Are you daft? Emergencies. We never know ahead of time."

My mouth went dry. Could this be a set-up? I didn't trust her. "But that's what got me here in the first place. I'll need an assistant to witness...."

She cut me off in mid-sentence. "You're a prisoner, girlie. You get what we give you."

* * *

A metal exam table, glass medicine cabinet, and sink; I was finally on familiar ground. Even though I lacked the polished tools and medications of Mount Sinai, this was my world. Once in the exam room, the familiarity calmed my nerves. I emptied the cabinet drawers and spread the instruments on the table to inspect them. They'd suffice, but each one needed a careful scrubbing. Traces of dried blood were caked on the forceps and scalpels. I turned on the faucet at the basin and grimaced—freezing cold water, a recipe for infection. My shoulders shrunk in frustration.

A guard sat half-asleep on a chair, blocking the door.

I cleared my throat.

She didn't budge.

I spoke loudly. "Guard, where do I get hot water to clean the instruments?"

She opened her eyes and snapped, "What is it?"

"I need hot water, soap, and a scrub brush. The instruments are filthy."

"No hot water," she mumbled, twisting her body sideways into a more comfortable position. She closed her eyes again, placing her hand on an area above her collar with great care.

I persisted. "What about fetching some from the kitchen? We can't use dirty instruments on patients. And we need matches to sterilize. Otherwise, we'll give everyone infections."

"No one cares," she murmured, closing her eyes again.

"What if it were you?" I walked toward her. My eye caught a large purple boil partially hidden under her hand and collar. "What's that on your neck?"

The guard shirked away. "Don't know. It's been killing me for days."

"Would you like me to check?"

She hesitantly unbuttoned the top two buttons of her white blouse and pulled the collar open.

"Tilt your head to the side, and let me examine it." I touched the surface of her deep red skin. Burning hot. It needed to be lanced and drained.

"Ouch, damn it. Can you do something to make it go away? It's keeping me up at night."

I met her eyes. "Without a problem. But I won't lance it with a filthy scalpel. You'll be jumping from the frying pan into the fire and could die from infection." I paused, hoping she got the point. "What's your name?"

The guard rose from her chair. "Guard Olga." She stood. "Come with me. We'll take a pail to the kitchen. And no tricks."

Returning to the Clinic a half hour later with hot water, a brush, and soap, I set the pail on the counter and dropped the instruments in the scalding water to soak. After a few moments, I scrubbed the scalpel clean and wiped it with a towel. Then I lit a match and held it under the pointed tip, hoping to destroy any germs I could not see. "Time to climb up on the table."

She looked nervously at me, then the sharp instrument. "I'm fetching another guard. I don't trust you with that sharp thing."

"That's fine. Whatever makes you comfortable." While I waited, I prepared a basin for the drainage and laid out a clean wrapping. I smiled inside, knowing there was a fair chance her boil might erupt and drain on its own. In only one week, I'd begun thinking like a criminal, seizing opportunities, just like the hardened prisoners. I'd make this gesture work in my favor.

The guard returned moments later with Warden Beatrice. "What's going on in here?" she barked. "I'm too busy for this kind of nonsense."

"I've offered to drain her boil." I pointed to the guard's neck. "Before it grows further into a carbuncle."

The Warden huffed, annoyed. "Carbun…? Oh, never mind, get to it."

Guard Olga tentatively climbed on the table and lay on her side as I spread a towel around the infected area. "This will prick and hurt a moment. Don't move. As soon as the boil drains, you'll feel better."

"Be careful with that sharp thing!" the Warden scolded me, leaning over the other side of the table, thirsty with curiosity.

I punctured the edge of the boil. Hot white puss held back under pressure squirted out across the head of the table onto my apron.

"That hurt like Hell!" Guard Olga cried. "Are you done?"

The Warden craned her neck to watch more closely. "That's disgusting," she said with an edge of glee.

"Stay still. That's one angry boil. It needs more time to drain," I replied with a practiced calm.

Guard Olga moaned. "Can you do something for the pain?"

"No, I'm sorry. There's no anesthesia here. I would have used some if I could've," I said gently. "It's draining well. Pain starting to let up?"

She released a deep breath. "Holy Mother of God, yes."

"Very well," I answered confidently. "Now relax while I finish."

After ten minutes of draining more than a tablespoon of white puss from the boil, the guard lay holding a hot cloth to her neck. "I can't believe how much better it feels. The pain's practically gone."

I lifted the cloth and inspected the wound. Emptied, the skin lay flat on her body. I set about bandaging the wound. "We'll use a clean hot compress every morning when we change the dressing. It should heal in a few days. Leave it covered, and don't touch it," I instructed her. "You're lucky you didn't wait longer. It could've become much more serious."

I placed the scalpel in the tray of hot water I'd set on the counter.

The Warden looked hard at me. "If you can do that, you can take care of my staff, too. It'll keep them here at work instead of staying home like babies when they're sick. Anything else you need?"

Relieved to have the Warden's attention, I rattled, "For now, fresh pails of hot water three times a day to keep wounds and instruments clean. I'd like to prepare a list once I inspect all the cabinets. Definitely, anesthetics." I said, momentarily forgetting where I was.

"You'll get hot water." With that, the Warden spun around and left the Clinic.

* * *

"Crazy, they turned ya loose in there," said Daisy. "Ain't there sharp things?"

I rolled my eyes, reminded again no one believed my story.

Shannon, the pickpocket, asked, "Whatcha see?"

"Not much today. Lanced a boil."

Daisy's eyes widened. "We're all scared of that place. I hear they experiment on us, and they cut the men's balls off in the nut house."

I sat straighter, shocked. "What are you talking about?"

"That's the word," said Daisy. "I heard it at breakfast. You don't return the same after goin' there."

"Well, I certainly won't partake in experiments or neuter men." Were they telling tales? Did the guards frighten the prisoners to keep them in line? No wonder the prisoners would rather suffer from illness than take a chance on a cure.

I pounced, "Change the word around here. I've built my career taking the best care of women I can, and they all come back and trust me. I wouldn't hurt a fly." I lay on my cot, satisfied. I knew I'd done my share of good that day.

Martha rose, shaky from her detoxification stupor, and stuttered, "That's not what the guards say!"

Annoyance shot through me. I sat back up. "Believe what you want. The story was a lie. I was trying to save the poor woman's life, but the midwife did too much damage. The woman's condition was beyond my abilities."

Delirious laughter erupted from Martha in the upper bunk.

Stop caring what anyone thinks. Only I knew the truth.

Daisy and Shannon studied me.

"What kind of doctor are ya? Daisy asked.

I faced her. "A woman's doctor. I deliver babies and take care of other female problems."

Silence.

"Daisy, have you ever gone to a doctor? Or a midwife?" I asked.

"My fancy man took me to a midwife for a veil so I wouldn't get knocked up."

My eyes traveled from one woman to the next. "If any of you ever need help, I'll be in the Clinic. You can trust that I won't harm you." I lay back and pulled my thin blanket up to my neck.

Shannon muttered, "Like the dead lady trusted you?"

"Then don't trust me, Shannon. It's up to you." I rolled toward the wall.

Furious, I pretended to sleep, forcing my thoughts to Joseph. The noose of my new life began to loosen as I imagined us lying together in bed. I ached for his strong body but was worried he had walked out of my life and would end our engagement.

* * *

Finally, after two weeks in the Workhouse, I received a letter from Joseph, his first communication since my arrest.

> *November 19, 1906*
>
> *My dearest Hannah,*
>
> *I can't begin to express how distraught I've been. I miss you so much, holding you in bed and sharing the events of our day over dinner. I've been sleepless every night.*
>
> *There is troubling talk around the hospital. Did you notify the Chief of Staff that you were working for the Waldorf? The word is you took on the assignment without approval, and as you can imagine, they're highly disturbed over the headlines, terribly unfavorable to Mount Sinai. I've tried to assure them you meant well and would never initiate an abortion, in a hotel no less. I hope they believe me.*

In the beginning, I contemplated letting go of everything we had and regret my cowardice. Ellen thinks if you get off, it will take years to repair your reputation and could damage mine in the process. She's putting pressure on me to end our engagement, but doesn't realize how it would destroy my happiness, just when we were getting on so well.

I'll write again soon.

With love,

Joseph

I read the letter several times, searching for a sliver of concern about my well-being. Each time, the same uneasy feeling passed through my heart. Although happy he was missing me, why didn't he ask how I was faring? How I was managing in this hellhole? My anger mounted. How dare his sister wipe me off like a spot of tarnish!

I reminded myself to keep my attention on the trial, as Tillie advised. Dealing with Joseph could wait. But my job? All those years of studying and work…. Was that in jeopardy too? I'd been a fool to believe Mr. Tschirky. He deceived me into thinking I'd only deal with small health matters. How could I be so naïve?

My thoughts bounced from one concern to the next like a string of discordant chords on the piano until my brain was so fatigued, I fell asleep without realizing it. Moments later, the guards clanked the cell bars to wake us for the next monotonous day.

Chapter Twenty-Five

Thanks to Daisy, the most trusting of my cellmates, good word about me spread among the Workhouse inmates. One by one, they made their way to the Clinic with ailments. The most common complaint, toothaches, was postponed for the prison dentist, who made irregular stops with his students, always greeted by an overflowing room of miserable prisoners. The number of tooth extractions was jaw-dropping. Gradually, the averted eyes at mealtime were replaced with head nods and an occasional smile.

In the Clinic, I saw practically every disease I'd studied in my textbooks—pregnancies, skin conditions, coughing, and influenza, plus an endless stream of syphilis and gonorrhea. Although close to twenty percent of the inmates were pregnant, not one was pleased with her condition. But without ready access to blocking devices, they had little control. For the rest, with my limited medications, the most I could prescribe was greater cleanliness and delousing. Then, there were the dreadfully sick.

In my second week, a guard dragged a forty-one-year-old woman to the Clinic, bent forward like a fishhook. She looked years older than her age.

The guard practically threw her at me. "Here's Elsie. She won't knit anymore. Fix her."

I turned my back to the guard. "What seems to be the problem, Elsie?"

Holding up her shaky left hand, she motioned to her right shoulder. "My side's on fire."

I bent to look at her face. "Did you have a fall?"

Elsie shook her head, holding back tears.

I motioned for the guard to step away toward the door.

I said softly, "Let's slip off your blouse so I can take a look."

Helping her onto the table, I couldn't help but notice how little she weighed. Elsie struggled to unbutton the front of her blouse.

"Would you like my help? I asked.

She nodded.

I loosened the flat metal buttons. A foul odor escaped. Decay. Holding my breath, I tried to ignore the putrid smell, gently edging the garment down her arms, freeing her hands. She wore no undergarment. I lowered her onto her back.

Elsie's breath caught. "Christ, that hurts."

My eyes inspected her deformed chest. "My dear woman. You've been suffering with this for quite some time, haven't you?"

The guard leaned in our direction to look.

"Get back," I ordered. "Give the woman privacy."

Silent rivulets of tears ran down Elsie's pale cheeks into her ears and hair.

"What's the matter with her?" demanded Guard Olga.

Ignoring the guard, I began to examine Elsie's breasts, armpits, and neck. They were full of tumors. One, the size of a walnut on her right breast, had broken through the skin, the source of the rancid odor. I pushed gently on her right nipple, and fluid seeped out. She had advanced breast cancer and must have been in terrible pain for weeks, perhaps months, forcing herself not to complain, not to appear weak in the eyes of the other inmates. Crying, a sign of vulnerability, could be fatal among prisoners.

I stood erect, addressing the guard. "Elsie cannot return to work. She must be taken to Charity Hospital. A surgeon needs to address her condition."

Elsie's sniffles turned to sobs. "Am I goin' die, doctor? You can't send me there. I hear they're butchers."

I took her hand in mine. "Someday you will, Elsie, like all of us. But not today. Today, you're going to the hospital to control the pain. The nurses and doctors will give you proper medicine there." I prayed my promise would be kept.

The guards looked at the floor, ill-prepared for this sight of advanced disease.

"We must get Elsie a bed today. Please ask the Warden to call." I stroked Elsie's arm. "How about a warm sponge bath while we wait? I'll bet that will make you feel fresher."

* * *

Thanks to wealthy Jewish matrons uptown, Mount Sinai's Clinic patients were treated to a warm shower, delousing, and clean clothing before their physical exams. By the time my patients arrived in the exam room, they were reasonably presentable. I'd never witnessed the extent of their filth beforehand. Their benefactors hosted a string of annual charity events to raise money for the Clinic, both to solidify their social standing and to feel sincerely useful, convincing themselves that cleanliness for the unfortunate could make a difference. I barely took notice, figuring a shower was a meaningless drop in the bucket compared to their bigger plight. Now that I'd crossed into the world of dirt and misery, I came to appreciate the deep comfort of a warm shower with soap, an extravagance I hadn't seen since my arrest. I pondered, how could these uptown women comprehend this basic need while I hadn't?

Blackwell's inmates were raised from infancy under the cruelest conditions, starved of maternal protection, so unlike the attentive parenting Tillie and Abe gave me as a child. I took for granted my nutritious meals, proper clothing, and education. But for most of the prisoners, deprivation was constant. Their deficiencies, so deeply rooted, drove them to reckless decisions, hurting themselves and others. They were like the poison ivy plants that once tormented my Papa on his farm every summer, infecting anyone who crossed their path.

Tillie, a fan of Shakespeare, used to tell me, "Always look people in the eye. Eyes are the window to the soul." If she was right, then the dark vacant looks surrounding me told me everything I needed to know.

I could lance a boil or prescribe hot tea with honey for persistent coughing,

168

but there was little I could do to improve their lot in life. The city officials had surrendered, finding it simpler to keep the poor under lock and key. With each new patient at Blackwell's, I began to grasp the vastness of their plight.

So, when the prisoners saw me in the Clinic, I respected the complexity of their lives, soothing them as one would a terrified child. While I treated their ailments, I calmed their fears, hoping to forge a foundation of trust. I hummed childhood lullabies while I dressed wounds, rubbed their backs and shoulders when they had coughing fits and placed warm towels on their abdomens for stomach cramps, anything that might strike a light within.

Chapter Twenty-Six

My mood sank as my third week of imprisonment drew near. I prayed for more support from Joseph but heard nothing further. Tillie wrote, informing me she'd be visiting with my attorney, Mr. Clemson, who I'd briefly met during my arraignment, to give me an update. I feared she would not be permitted to enter the Workhouse, even with her ruse.

Thanksgiving, my favorite holiday, came and went, the prison staff serving thin turkey soup as a meager substitute for the bounty my family normally enjoyed. My melancholy inched back as I realized I'd be living at Blackwell's indefinitely. Any ember of hope I'd kindled grew cold.

By the end of November, winter fell upon us harshly, blanketing the ground with ice and snow. Within the walls of the faintly heated Workhouse, we heard howling winds blowing off the East River. Without proper clothing for the bitter season ahead, the threat of tuberculosis and pneumonia was a constant worry, both for my patients and for myself. Would I be freed before it was too late?

* * *

Guard Olga stomped into the Clinic just as I completed the morning lineup of patients. "You have visitors. Come."

I set my instruments in the soapy pail and followed her down a narrow hall to a small conference room. With each step, my hope and apprehension grew. Would it be good news or bad?

Approaching the closed door, I heard women's voices. The guard pulled the heavy door open. I drew a quick breath when I saw both Tillie and Ina seated resolutely at the diminutive table with Mr. Clemson, my attorney.

Guard Olga surveyed the group. "You have thirty minutes, no longer."

Both Tillie and Ina sat facing forward, looking terribly serious. As the door latched, they both leaped atop me, hugging and kissing my cheeks.

Tillie was ecstatic. "The plan worked. They think we're legal secretaries."

Ina's head nodded furiously; her eyes glazed with tears. She grabbed my hand. "Oh, Doctor, this place is horrid!"

I reached for Tillie's cheek, cupping my palm on the side of her face. Her skin brimmed with warmth and love. I could barely hold back my tears.

Mr. Clemson cleared his throat. "We have work to do, ladies. Thirty minutes isn't long. Please sit."

Tillie reached into her bag and handed me a thick sandwich wrapped in paper and a strange-looking jar. "Eat this while we fill you in. You look white as milk. Do they feed you in this awful place?"

"I'm fine, really. What's happening out there?" I held up the jar. "And, what's this?"

"It's called a thermos. It keeps soup and coffee hot for hours. I found it at the provisions store last week."

I unscrewed the top, a cup, and then a smaller top. An aromatic bouquet of nutty steam almost knocked me over, happiness in a thermos. "Oh, Tillie, how extraordinary. I've been dreaming of fresh coffee almost as much as a nice bar of soap."

Tillie winked. "I'll be sure to bring soap next time. Keep the thermos."

"Oh no, it'll get lifted. Take it home with you." I had so many questions. "Have you heard from Joseph? I only got one letter."

Tillie shook her head.

Mr. Clemson interrupted. "Ladies, please. We must get started. There's a great deal to cover. As you recall, Doctor, I'm Mr. Clemson. Your sister retained me from my firm, Andrews, Sullivan, and Clemson, specialists in criminal law."

Criminal? The word offended me, but I was more hungry and happy to see Tillie. I unwrapped my sandwich and took a bite. Crusty bread, moist turkey, and cranberry sauce rolled around my mouth with such insane glory that my jaw hurt. Each mouthful released happy memories, transporting me to our noisy, festive Thanksgiving table, laden with platters of roasted vegetables, tart cranberry sauce, laughter, and love. The ember within me flickered with hope.

I struggled to concentrate on Mr. Clemson. My immediate impression was that he was average in practically every regard. His face, punctuated by a full mustache and bushy eyebrows, perfectly matched his unkempt, brown frizzy hair, balding crown, and rumpled suit. I figured he was around forty-five and hoped he was proficient in criminal matters.

He cleared his throat loudly and summarized. "Let me begin by saying, even though you were at the scene of the crime, that's all the prosecutor has. My job is to introduce reasonable doubt by showing the court you weren't in the hotel room long enough to commit a murder, nor that you had any previous knowledge of or contact with the victim."

Tillie reached out her hand. "Did you bring the list? In the meantime, we've been working on our own accounting of the day."

I shook my head. "They took it along with my clothes, but I memorized the information."

Mr. Clemson knit his bushy brows, glaring at Tillie. "Please let me continue. We'll discuss the list later." His eyes darted to his notes. "Where was I?"

I raised my brows at Tillie. Did this man know what he was doing?

She nodded quickly, confidently, signaling me to give him a chance.

"Let's go through the timeline." Mr. Clemson referred to his papers. "The hospital switchboard had a record of both calls coming in from the Waldorf. The first was at 1 pm, the second at 4:45. We have witnesses, including the nurses and Miss Ina Klein here, who can testify you were in the Labor and Delivery suite throughout that period. We estimate you caught the coach at 5:00, but we're still searching for the coachman, a needle in a haystack if you ask me. Though it would be helpful to establish with certainty the pick-up and drop-off times."

I turned to Ina. "Go ahead and hire a detective to find him." I didn't care what it cost.

Ina nodded eagerly. "Yes, as soon as we get home."

My breath caught. That word, *home*, drove an arrow through my heart. I forced myself back to the discussion. "Mr. Clemson, do we have enough proof without the coachman?" I picked at the sandwich wishing it could last forever, crumbs scattering on the stained brown paper.

"I'm not sure yet. We must establish exactly when you arrived at the Waldorf to show there wasn't ample time between the start of the procedure and when the victim passed at 6:15."

"But—" I started.

He interrupted. "Let me continue." Frowning, Mr. Clemson referred again to his notes. "At that time of day, with the heavy traffic and pouring rain, the coach ride must have taken a half hour at minimum, placing your arrival at the Waldorf at approximately 5:30 pm. If we figure you entered the victim's room by 5:40, that leaves only thirty-five minutes for the crime—very tight. We'll need the coroner's report to know more. The critical question a jury must decide is whether this type of murder could occur in such a brief time."

I began to see Mr. Clemson's argument. Not a bad defense. I swallowed my last mouthful of sandwich and interrupted. "Who was the woman? Has she been identified?"

"No, not yet. She's still a Jane Doe." Mr. Clemson rubbed the back of his neck, his annoyance mounting. "Please, ladies, we won't get through this if you keep interrupting."

I took a sip of Tillie's roasted coffee, wondering why Mr. Clemson appeared ill at ease with our questions. They were all sensible. Did he dislike working with women? Or did he not believe my innocence?

He continued. "There are potential witnesses at the Waldorf whose job is to monitor those entering and leaving the hotel. But with the bad weather, most patrons were wearing the same dark, wet overcoats, hats, or were beneath black umbrellas. When we asked around, not one was one hundred percent certain they could identify you from your picture."

"Did you find the elevator operator? Or the man with the cigar?" I was growing ever more concerned. *Could he get the job done?*

Mr. Clemson let out an exasperated huff. "Not yet."

"What about the coroner? When will you have his report? When is the trial?" My nerves were frayed, and I no longer cared about breaking his concentration or what he thought about women.

Ina, who'd been sitting patiently up to that point, interrupted in a whisper. "I just thought of something."

We all turned to her.

"What is it?" I asked.

"No one found any money. Midwives are paid before they provide service. That means the real killer fled with her payment."

We sat stunned. How could we all miss such an obvious, critical detail? Bless that girl! "Ina's right. The midwife must have been paid before she started the procedure. I had little cash with me, and unless they found money in the room or on the victim, it disappeared with the murderess."

Mr. Clemson made a note on his pad. The right corner of his mouth turned down ever so slightly. "I'll verify with the police. It wasn't in the report."

"You didn't believe us, did you?" I demanded. "You thought I did it?"

Mr. Clemson cleared his throat. "It isn't necessary for me to believe in your innocence. My job is to determine reasonable doubt." He squirmed in his chair. "This would go more smoothly if you women let me do my job." His eyes darted to Tillie as he said gruffly. "I knew it was a bad idea to let ladies come."

I shot back. "Well, sir, if I were you, I'd be thanking your lucky stars. Ina just made your job easier. Thanks to her, you've got your reasonable doubt, the most important lack of evidence. I didn't kill a flea!" I threw my head back, my dislike for him intensifying. What were we paying him for anyway?

The half-hour vanished. We agreed to meet again after Mr. Clemson received the coroner's report. Tillie would hire a detective to help Ina find the driver and identify the victim. Finally, Mr. Clemson would verify

174

there was no cash in either the hotel room or in police storage with my possessions.

Mr. Clemson gathered his notes and pen, stuffing them into his briefcase.

"You haven't told me when the trial is," I said.

He put on his overcoat. "I don't know for certain, but it's unlikely before early spring. There'll be a new Governor in January, and he'll appoint a separate staff. Count on delays.

With that sobering news, my bravado broke, in its place, a fountain of tears.

Tillie pulled me into a hug. "Hannah, we're going to beat this. Trust us. You must stay strong."

"I didn't hurt anyone. Why can't they believe me?" I sniffled. "You have no idea...people die in here."

Tillie handed me an old lace handkerchief, her eyes also full. "Here, use this. Keep it." She reached back into her satchel. "I brought a book for you. It will take your thoughts to a better place, far from this dreadful prison."

She handed me *The Gift of the Magi and Other Short Stories* by O'Henry, a new book I hadn't read. Simply holding it in my hands snapped me out of my self-pity. Reading had always provided me with escape and solace.

I blew my nose into the timeworn handkerchief. "I almost forgot to ask. I need so many things for the Clinic. Ina, can you see if the hospital will donate medicines, blankets, and anything else you can get your hands on? The conditions are pitiful, bare bones."

Ina studied me dubiously. "I don't know if they'll agree. They haven't been terribly happy about all this." She motioned at the room. "But if you don't mind, I'll ask Mrs. Sanger. She calls every day checking for more information, wanting to find a way to help."

"She does?" A shot of hope.

Ina winked. "She's like a dog with a bone."

There must be some, like Margaret, who believed me. But I was furious with Mount Sinai. After offering indisputably fine medical services and giving them the bragging rights of having a female doctor on their medical staff, I was indignant they would brush me off so easily.

"Hannah, what do you need for yourself?" Tillie asked. "Can I bring a warm coat or sweaters for the winter?"

"We don't get outside much, but it is getting colder in the Workhouse." I thought hard for a moment. An idea sprung. "Could you bring five warm sweaters, gloves, and socks?"

"Five?" Tillie's brows lifted with amusement, her eyes twinkling.

I nodded. "One very large one for the guard, the rest, my size for my cellmates. If they all have sweaters, they won't steal mine."

Chapter Twenty-Seven

Hearing little from the world outside of Blackwell's was infuriating. I had no clue if the prison guards were destroying my mail or if I'd been forgotten. I swung from anger at Joseph and my family for not writing more to despair as the remnants of my optimism melted.

In the meanwhile, my popularity in the Clinic grew faster than summer garden weeds on Papa's farm. In my first week, I had only a pittance of patients, most eyeing me dubiously, distrusting my qualifications. Now, weeks later, a long line snaked from the Clinic door through the hallway. Most women were willing to stand for hours with fevers, coughing, and sneezing. Finally, I asked for a meeting with the Warden.

As Guard Olga escorted me to the Warden's office at the opposite end of my hallway, I wondered if I could make a dent in her iron-clad armor. Guard Olga knocked tentatively at the door. Everyone was afraid of the woman.

"Come in," she shouted in her baritone voice.

Guard Olga smirked. "Don't expect miracles."

I stood before the desk, Guard Olga hanging back at the doorway, allowing herself a safe distance. *Did Warden throw things?* I saw no guest chairs, suggesting the Warden didn't have patience for long meetings.

"Well, what is it?" her voice, abrasive as sandpaper, made my hair sting.

"Warden, I'm seeing close to ten patients an hour, most with influenza. The illness has spread through the entire women's section of the Workhouse."

She smiled, rocking her head on her thick neck, amused by the misery of her inmates. "And?"

The brute doesn't care in the least—we're vermin to her. I'll have to give her something she wants.

"I'm growing concerned about several things. First, the illness will infect all the inmates, guards, and other workers here. Second, we'll need to move many patients to Charity Hospital for care. Finally, the fever with this influenza runs high, and you may lose your staff to sick beds while they battle it." I kept my tone even. I knew she'd ignore pleading. My request must serve the Warden's needs, or it would not be answered. I thought back to Dr. Adams at Johns Hopkins and my efforts to gain his cooperation. I hoped that giving her credit for the initiative, as I had with Dr. Adams, would gain her cooperation—despite how much more vicious the Warden was.

Her brow twitched, now curious. "Go on."

Prepared, I handed a paper to her. "I've written a list of our basic needs, mostly warm blankets, clean nose rags, and fever medication. But if we don't keep the prison cleaner and give inmates warm water and soap for bathing, the illness will spread until everyone's caught it. Germs spread through the air, and from contaminated surfaces, you know."

The Warden straightened her back, searching my face. "We don't have the money for luxuries, but I'll assign inmates to wash the joint. You're dismissed."

I locked eyes with her. "I may have another way to get provisions, particularly medicines."

She waved her hand dismissively. "I said I'm done with you. Be off."

I persisted. "It could make for a great newspaper story about you and your ingenuity running the Workhouse."

"My what?" She shot me a sour expression. "Speak plainly, girl."

"I know someone, a suffragette, who'd like to help." I nervously rolled the list in my hands.

"Why would she do that?" The Warden sneered.

I tilted my head to the side, searching for a morsel of compassion. "For one thing, she cares about women and our difficult plight in a men's world."

A gruff laugh. "What use has that ever served? Nothin' ever changes."

I continued. "My contact believes otherwise. She's tied in with powerful people in New York and can raise money and stir up publicity."

The Warden eyed me carefully, then shifted to Guard Olga. "Guard, leave us. Close the door behind you."

Guard Olga quietly exited the office; her lips pressed downward in a disapproving scowl.

"Explain."

"I would like to send this list to my contact and see if she can help us out before the weather turns even colder. When she has the provisions, she'll contact a reporter and have a photographer come when she makes the delivery. Of course, you'll be front and center."

The Warden sat quietly, thinking. A chuckle finally escaped her mouth. "Why not? Seems there's no harm if she fails. And it's free, right?"

"Yes, Warden."

Her smirk turned to an ominous scowl. "Maybe she could simply send money, and I'll buy the provisions."

I could imagine her silently calculating her take. "Of course, you're right, but we've always found that the wealthy donors enjoy giving things. It helps them feel more charitable, and they like receiving publicity, too."

The Warden looked to the ceiling. "Of course, the rich—holier than thou. Well, what are you waiting for?" she demanded.

"I'll get on it right away." I turned to leave the office.

"Wait, inmate." The Warden barked.

I twisted about, facing her, interested to hear her next question.

"How do I keep from getting it? What did you call it, *influ* something or other?"

Of course, she'd worry about herself first. "Clean your hands with soap, ventilate the rooms you inhabit, and teach the inmates and guards to cover their mouths when they cough and sneeze. There's no magic. Simple, good hygiene is the key."

"You make it sound easier than it is," she mocked.

I smiled. "It's not as hard as you might think. Maybe it's time to teach the women a cleaner way of living. But, of course, that's your decision to make."

Having secured the Warden's permission, I rewrote the list for Margaret, copied it, and sent one to Ina, then drafted a short letter explaining my plans.

December 6, 1906

Dear Margaret,

As I find myself in this terrible dilemma at Blackwell's, I call on your offer to help. I've been assigned to run the Workhouse Clinic as I await trial or, God willing, dismissal of charges. Sadly, conditions haven't improved much for the inmates since Nellie Bly's expose.

In the meanwhile, I believe there is more I can do. These women are the saddest of our gender, most with little knowledge of self-care. If we are working so hard to improve women's lives, shouldn't we embrace all levels of society, starting with the most hopeless? For the first time in my life, I see desperation close-up and how it erodes the soul.

I know my list may distract you from your main purpose, but I'm hopeful the women in our cause will find it in their hearts to help the downtrodden through a long, cold winter. Can you believe some inmates find their way here on purpose, to escape life on the streets! It's unimaginable.

I await your reply and look forward to hearing about your latest efforts for the greater cause.

With warmth and my highest regards,

Hannah

P.S. Tillie and Ina are hard at work gathering proof of my innocence. We are also hiring a detective. First, we must discover who the victim was. My guess is someone in the upper class. Her family must be frantic.

* * *

CHAPTER TWENTY-SEVEN

Ten days after Tillie's last visit, Guard Olga led me to the empty conference room. I sat on a stiff-backed oak chair, tapping my foot in time to the passing seconds, growing more nervous by the moment.

Finally, the door flew open. Mr. Clemson and Tillie walked in, both wearing grey business suits, Tillie's a smart tweed with traces of blue and crimson, Mr. Clemson's unremarkable. *What I'd give for a warm woolen suit.* Tillie held a package under one arm, playing her part as secretary, greeting me with a cursory glance, nodding in detachment, acting as if it were just another day of work.

Guard Olga stared at the package. "What's in there? I must inspect it."

I answered, "Guard, you know it's getting cold in the Workhouse, so I asked my attorney to bring warm clothing for my cellmates and myself."

She began shaking her head vigorously, her heavy jowls shuddering with anger. "You can't bring that in here. You'll create too much ruckus."

I opened the side of the package, peaking in. "These are beautiful." I looked up at Guard Olga. "Want to see?"

She rose her voice, "You'll get in trouble with the Warden."

In my most intriguing voice, I added, "They brought a warm sweater and soft wool socks for you, too. I think you should at least have a look."

Guard Olga stood agog, rocking her head slowly. *Had anyone ever given this poor woman a gift?* I unwrapped the large package and separated five shallow piles, each tied with a broad red grosgrain ribbon. Spotting the large navy-blue sweater, socks, and hat, I lifted Guard Olga's bundle, handing it to her. "Thank you for your kindness, Guard. I wanted to give you something special as a holiday gift."

She said nothing, her eyes open in wonder as she took her bundle of warmth and held it gently to her cheek, turning to the exit. She called back in a quiet voice as she shut the door, "I'll be back in an hour."

Tillie sprang from her seat and pulled me into a tight embrace. "You're one clever girl." She stepped back, examining me from head to toe. "Oh dear, you're getting thinner by the week. I can feel your bones. How are you holding up, darling?"

I smiled weakly, eyeing Tillie's satchel. "Don't worry, I'm fine. Did you bring a sandwich? I've dreamt about the last one for days." I'd never known food deprivation before. As a physician, it was common to skip a meal while caring for patients; but I'd never experienced the intense, prolonged hunger I now lived with day and night. I subsisted on two substandard meals: brown gruel in the morning and stale bread with soup or beans for dinner. Lying in bed at night, I could work myself into a frenzy thinking about a ripe apple from Papa's orchard or a simple cheese sandwich.

Tillie reached into her bag, pulled out two thermoses and a thick sandwich wrapped in brown butcher paper. "Brisket today on challah with vegetable soup and coffee – an extra sandwich and cookies to take back." She opened her bag wider, rummaging with her hand. "I have a spoon and napkin in here somewhere."

I barely heard her. I'd already unwrapped the sandwich and dug my teeth into the moist, tender beef. Saliva pooled in my mouth as I grabbed the napkin Tillie placed on the table, hoping to prevent drool from spilling onto my work dress. Is this what starvation does to the body? Directing my attention to Mr. Clemson with a nod, I forced myself to listen.

"First, the big news. The victim was identified as a Miss Dorothy Sinclair, of Albany, New York. After missing for a week, her family engaged the police and a detective agency to determine her whereabouts. They suspected she'd run off to elope," Mr. Clemson reported dryly.

"Unfortunately, they were half-right," Tillie interjected with a dismal edge to her voice. She watched me intently. "A beautiful young woman like that, such a sad loss."

Mr. Clemson exhaled deeply. "Dr. Isaacson, please allow me to finish."

Tillie winked at me, already finding his tetchiness amusing. "Of course."

"The detective's report is due within the week. He's searching for Miss Sinclair's girlfriends to see if we can learn more. You know, about her trip to New York and who her lover was." Mr. Clemson rifled through his notes.

Tillie interjected. "We think the boyfriend had a lot of money. It must have cost a small fortune to set her up at the Waldorf. He wanted her far from home but in a luxurious place to heal."

Mr. Clemson cleared his throat. "By the by, your secretary was right.

There was no trail of money left behind. Someone had been paid."

Tillie laughed lightly. "What would you do without our help, Mr. Clemson? By the end of this ordeal, you'll want to hire us."

Mr. Clemson knit his brows so tightly they merged into one wide bushy eyebrow. "So far, it's been more annoyance than help, but I'll admit, you are a clever group."

A streak of dread ran through me. "I wonder if the boyfriend wanted her dead. She was terribly damaged inside." I flipped from that thought into another. "What about the coroner's report? Did he send it yet?"

"I have it here." He handed the report to me.

I read it quickly, lifting my head, locking my shocked eyes with Tillie's.

* * *

A firm knock at the door. Without waiting for a reply, Guard Olga entered, wearing her new navy cardigan and a cautious smile. She stroked the round metal buttons inscribed with bucolic scenes.

"Fit all right?" I answered her smile. "The buttons are beautiful."

Another wordless nod.

I thanked Mr. Clemson and Tillie for their time and followed Guard Olga back into the hallway. A chorus of hacking, spitting, and sneezing accosted my ears. Keeping pace with Guard Olga's fast gait, I said, "We must do something to keep the inmates healthier or it's going to be a hellacious winter. Any way they can get warm baths and soap?"

Guard Olga looked down. "I'll try, but the Warden never goes soft."

My frustration simmered. "Your job will be far easier if we avoid an epidemic."

Guard Olga huffed back. "Yours too, I'd guess."

I smiled, knowing that sweater or not, there was a line I couldn't cross, at least not while I was an inmate. In my mind, I was back at Johns Hopkins, dealing with the older male physicians. They resented women taking positions from men and expressed their indignation when we aired our opinions, always watching us closely, desperate to find cracks in our judgment or patient care. I imagined that Warden Beatrice was equally tough on the guards, many of whom could have been wasting away on my side of the bars. I'd have to outfox them all.

It was well after sunset when I finished with my last patient, yet another case of influenza. Irritated by the lack of medicine, the best I could offer was bed rest, more water, and a lesson in basic hygiene. I imagined she would return to her bunk that evening, shivering under the thin blanket, slowly developing pneumonia. Her next stop would be Charity Hospital, if she lasted that long. Deaths were mounting among both men and women at Blackwell's. At week's end, at least one or two were found dead in their bunks from pneumonia. For me, it was unspeakably sad to be in the center of all this illness without any effective means to help.

I pulled a clean sheet of paper from the narrow drawer of my charting table and began formulating an idea.

December 13, 1906

Dear Ina,

As the sun sets in the early winter sky, I find myself increasingly worried about the conditions in the Workhouse. With little heat circulating, the inmates are constantly cold, sleeping in their work clothes under thin blankets at night. The Warden claims the cold keeps us awake while we perform our daily jobs in the Sewing and Knitting Halls. But, like a slow drain, I notice the workrooms emptying as patients sicken and die. One by one, pneumonia sets in, sending more inmates to Charity Hospital for care. But alas, it's often too late to save them. By week's end, additional sacks of bodies are piled onto the barge for the Potter's Field on Hart Island.

As you know, I've asked Margaret to find medications and blankets for the Clinic, but I'm hoping you'll embrace an additional idea. The Temple Emanuel Sisterhood, who hosted our fund-raising galas at Mount Sinai, has been seeking new causes. With the holidays approaching, warm sweaters and socks would be a blessing, either second-hand or newly knit. Most women here are of average or small size from undernourishment, but the guards are generally larger, and they need them too. Let me know if the Sisterhood is interested. Who knows, if the indefatigable Mrs. Lowenstein is still in charge, she may reach out to Saint Patrick's for help since many of the inmates are of Irish Catholic heritage. It may boost your efforts to persuade them, if they know that close to twenty percent of the young women are with child.

I've always believed in God and that he's given each of us a purpose on our sacred Earth. I must have been placed in prison for a reason, and while I'm here, I plan to do my small bit. No human, even law-breaking, should be forced to suffer such unending punishment.

Thank you in advance for your generous help with these efforts.

With love and admiration,

Hannah

I set my pen on the small writing table, folded the letter, and wrote Ina's address on the back. I asked Guard Olga, who was sitting in her usual place by the door, "Could you kindly mail this out tomorrow?"

She reached for the letter and stuffed it into her bodice. "Ready to go back to your cell, Doctor? I'll bet those gals in there are goin' love their new duds."

* * *

"Holy Mary, you're an angel," screeched Daisy, pulling on her violet sweater, examining each button before closing it around her body. "Fit's perfect. Socks and a hat, too? For each of us?"

Shannon narrowed her eyes. "Where'd ya lift them?" She pushed her arm into the sleeve of her green sweater, inspecting it carefully.

I heard a laugh behind me. Quickly twisting toward the bars, I saw Guard Olga. I'd never heard her laugh. I smiled back, sharing her amusement at my cellmates' reactions.

"Oh, Shannon. Not everything nice is stolen." I laughed generously. "But the source is my secret. Merry early Christmas!"

Martha was lying still on the top bunk. "Aren't you opening yours, Martha?" I asked.

"Don't feel so good—think I'm goin' puke."

After three weeks, it couldn't still be from the drink. "Martha, when's the last time you had your monthly?" I stood beside her bunk and handed a small towel to her. "Use this."

She sat up and retched into the towel, unceremoniously handing it back, then plopped her head back down on the bed. "Ugh, I don't remember, a couple of months? Maybe more."

I looked at the damp towel with pity. The answer was obvious. So many of the young female inmates arrived at Blackwell's pregnant. Pregnancy and birth were the most heart-wrenching parts of my routine. The saving grace for most Workhouse inmates was that their sentences were relatively short, a few months at most, so they were discharged before giving birth. For those who birthed in prison, their babies were taken away.

I remained by her side, placing my hand on her shoulder. "Try to think back, Martha. When's the last time you bled?"

Shannon laughed. "Oh, leave her be. Ain't goin' remember, especially if she were drinkin', and most likely, she was."

"I dunno." Martha moaned and let out a string of cuss words that could make the dockworkers blush.

"See there, told ya," scoffed Shannon.

* * *

It was lovely to finally have a full night of sleep, my stomach content as I digested my sandwich. I'd shared the cookies and second sandwich with Daisy and Shannon, who both nibbled at them with fastidious care, not daring to lose a crumb. Martha was far too queasy to eat.

The warmth of the sweater took the chill out of my body, lulling me into the deepest slumber I'd had in days. I was greeted by an image taking me back to the family farm in Harlem before I moved downtown to live with

Tillie at five years old. My brothers, Tillie, and I were running through Papa's apple orchard, picking fruit from the trees, gathering as many as I could hold in my apron to make applesauce later in the day. Was it before Mama died? I couldn't recall.

I woke to the sound of the bell and banging at the bars.

"Wake up. Breakfast in ten minutes," called Olga.

I wiggled into my work dress and threw the pale blue sweater back around my shoulders. Addressing my cellmates, I said. "Try to keep warm today, and remember to wash your hands. So far, we've been staying healthier than most here."

Guard Olga arrived at our cell promptly at six thirty to open the door and lead us downstairs to the Mess Hall. From there, I'd go to the Clinic for the day. As she unlocked the door, she handed me a letter. "This came for you yesterday."

I turned the envelope over to read the return address. It was from Margaret, *finally!* "Thank you." I slipped it into my apron pocket and followed the silent line of women into the Mess Hall for breakfast, the predictable lukewarm porridge and stale bread.

Chapter Twenty-Eight

I couldn't reach the privacy of the Clinic fast enough. The letter burned in my pocket while I ate breakfast, forcing down the hideous gruel. Once ensconced at my charting table, I opened Margaret's letter.

December 17, 2006

My dearest Hannah,

You are a brave woman! A warrior, my hero. Instead of self-pity, you have risen from the ashes like a phoenix.

I can barely wait to see you next week and share important news about your Jane Doe. Your old Trustee friends at Hopkins and I have been in constant communication, and oh, what we've learned! But alas, the secrets are far too sensitive for a letter and must wait until I make the delivery and speak to you face-to-face.

Now to your requests. Ina, my new suffragist recruit, and I have created a whirlwind of attention to the abysmal state for women at Blackwell's. Practically every group of charitable women we've approached has joined the cause. For the hesitant, we shared the names of prominent supporters and, lo and behold, their resistance evaporated. Christmas Eve morning, we plan a gargantuan delivery, enough to sink a barge! Although the Hospital, too preoccupied with their standing in the city and concerned about their image, has withheld donations, their Women's Auxiliary raised considerable funds for medicines, stethoscopes, tongue depressors, blankets, and so forth. We found a wholesaler in the city who gave us a reasonable price, and then he threw in a contribution of his own. His wife, who'd been involved in the transaction, admitted she had a relative held in Blackwell's not too long ago, so she pressured him to come up with extra provisions. We'll need three carts just to bring the goods to the steam barge! You will need to ensure it all gets into the right hands if you catch my drift. I'll have an inventory to share with the press.

Ina has punctured the hearts of the local congregations, especially with news of the staggering number of women in the pudding club (don't women just melt when there are babies in the picture?) and has too many sweaters to count. They even knit baby blankets. You were right about Mrs. Lowenstein. She is an unstoppable force!

We're firming up delivery for the 24th with Warden Beatrice. I've already lined up the press and a photographer. What a fabulous Christmas story for the papers. And, by the way, did you know the Warden was appointed by Governor Higgins? You'll have to wait to understand how important that little tidbit is.

Can you request private time to catch up while we're together there?

I hate to switch topics to sobering news, and know how loyal you've been to Joseph, but as your good friend, I must share an observation from Ina. She tells me she's seen Joseph firsthand with several unwed nurses in the cafeteria engaged in flirtatious conversations. She's concerned he might not be quite the dutiful man you've been counting on. I know it's difficult to hear, even under the best of circumstances, but I don't think he deserves you, nor has he the confidence to stand in the shadow of a great woman such as yourself. So, think about it while you are separated. In the meantime, take courage from your steadfast allies who surround you.

I'm counting the hours until we meet. I miss you terribly.

Your devoted friend,

Margaret

I sat stunned, not knowing whether to laugh or cry, thrilled about the whirlwind of action Margaret and Ina stirred, but also bitterly disappointed by Joseph. While reading the letter, a line of inmates had grown at the Clinic door.

Guard Olga cleared her throat, cocking her head to the women.

I sighed. Margaret was right. He'd moved on with his life. For now, I would let nothing spoil my excitement.

* * *

Midway through the morning, a guard muscled her way through the line. "Make way everyone, inmate's water broke in the Knitting Hall. It's her time."

I called back to her, "Wait in the hallway. I don't want a laboring mother in a dirty room. We've had a parade of influenza through here. Let me wash the table and chair. Guard Olga, please help me out here."

Guard Olga shot me a concerned look. "This is gonna be bad. Babies make the prisoners crazy."

We quickly scrubbed the table and chair with soapy water. "I want to check her first to see how far along she is, and then we'll talk about what to do with the other patients. Can you fetch two buckets of hot water and clean towels?"

The Knitting Hall guard led the crying woman into the room as Guard Olga scrambled out the door with empty buckets.

I gestured to the chair. "Please take a seat. What's your name?" I asked the disheveled woman, more girl than adult.

"Nellie's me name. Is it gonna hurt bad?" She brushed her tangled chestnut hair away from her face, revealing luminous light blue eyes framed with the longest black lashes I'd ever seen, a perfect tiny nose, and red cupid lips. A spray of freckles dotted her nose and cheekbones.

"Nellie, how old are you? Is this your first child?" I asked, distracted by her beautiful features.

She winced, bending forward over her belly, gripping the chair tightly. "Christ, it hurts."

I crouched low so my face was even with hers, speaking softly in her ear.

"Breathe with me. Slowly in and slowly out. Good. Again, in and out." I guided her through the time-worn exercise of birthing. "Starting to ease now?"

Nellie nodded, exhaling deeply. "That helped a little." She looked into my eyes. "You gonna help me?"

"Yes, I am. Can you tell me how old you are? First baby?" I asked again. She nodded. "Sixteen and me first."

"Do you have family in New York?" I hoped to heaven she was not alone. For those women who birthed at Blackwell's with no family or spouse on the outside, it meant facing the unfathomable anguish of surrendering the baby. Those infants were whisked away to church orphanages and placed for adoption, often outside the state.

"Me family's all dead." Her eyes watered. "I want my mama." She sniffled, just a child herself.

Before the tears could begin, I pulled her chin upward. "I'm not your Mama, but I'm here for you today and won't let anything bad happen. Having a baby is as normal as the sun rising."

She nodded as another contraction began to squeeze down. "Not another one! Stop them!" she screamed.

As soon as the contraction eased, I guided her onto the table. "Let me check and see how far along you are." I washed her bottom with a soapy cloth, then inserted my fingers, palpating her belly. The baby was in a perfect birthing position, but felt small, probably from the prison food. "Do you remember when you became pregnant?"

"No, but way before here." She moaned as another contraction ripped through her body.

"Breathe in and out slowly, Nellie." I felt for her cervix. Practically ready for birth. Fast for a first baby. Premature? I prayed not.

"Guard Olga," I said, "please have the patients come back tomorrow. I expect Nellie will deliver soon. We'll need the Clinic."

Guard Olga dispersed the crowd.

I gathered scraps of Nellie's story between her intensifying contractions. Her parents and younger brother, all living in the city slum of Five Corners, had died from typhoid fever two years earlier. At fourteen, without anyone to look after Nellie, she was swept into the gangs, committing petty crimes and delivering goods and money to the senior gang leaders. By her fifteenth birthday, her uncommon beauty had attracted the attention of one lieutenant, presumably the infant's father. Although she professed her love for him, it was difficult to imagine she had any clue what mature love was. What she recognized was survival—someone strong to protect her, offer a roof, and provide food. Such was the hard life in the Five Corners slum.

Guard Olga sat near the door, watching spellbound as Nellie's labor progressed. At one point between contractions, she signaled for me to follow her to the far corner of the room, whispering, not wanting Nellie to overhear. "Do you think she knows?"

"Knows what?"

"That Warden will take her baby?" Guard Olga looked at the floor. "I had to tell the Warden there was a baby coming so she could call the church."

My chest tightened. "I don't know. But she needs all her strength to get through this ordeal. Don't frighten her."

We resumed our positions just as a stronger contraction gripped. Nellie cried out. "Mama! Mama, I need you."

"I'm right here. Breathe like I showed you." I stroked her arm. "Let's take another look." I slid my fingers into her and felt the infant's head. "We're ready for those big, hard pushes now."

After the next few contractions, I placed Guard Olga at the head of the bed. "Hold her in a sitting position and support her back." I then arranged two towels and a slop pail at the foot of the table, taking an inventory of everything I did not have. I'd never delivered an infant without a soft, warm wrap for the new child, my trusty bulb syringe, or forceps nearby for emergencies. I prayed the delivery would be uneventful.

"Nellie, catch your breath. When the cramps start again, I want you to push down as hard as you can. Baby's ready to come." I patiently waited, my hand resting on her lower belly until I felt the muscles pulling tightly into her next contraction. I concentrated on the birth, forcing back thoughts of babies torn from mothers' arms, and focused on guiding this infant into the world safely. "Here we go, Nellie. Push with everything you've got."

The baby's head appeared between Nellie's legs, the face blue. "Catch your breath and then another big push. Baby's almost out." I placed my hand on her belly while supporting the infant's head. "One, two, three, push hard!"

The infant's body slid out. The Clinic grew still, silent.

Nellie's panicked screams filled the air. "What's wrong! Where's my baby?"

I barely heard her pleas as I fought to save the infant boy, undersized, not breathing. I cleared his mouth with my pinkie and patted his back, attempting to open his airway. Nothing. *Damn! And no suction bulb.* I shot into action, gently placing my mouth over his tiny face, blowing into his chest. Nothing. My panic grew. *Stay calm. Try again, Hannah.* I wiped out his mouth again and blew with more force. A hesitant cough, then a tiny mew. A breath, the most elemental human connection to life. The blue cast in his skin gradually dissolved, slowly shifting to pink.

Guard Olga was shouting with Nellie. "Is it alive? Can you save it?"

The little cry grew in strength, turning into a gut-wrenching squeal. Guard Olga clapped her hands, and Nellie cried aloud. I laughed with relief, inwardly thanking God for his mercy. The baby shivered, objecting to the cold air outside his Mama's body. I would have traded my right arm for a clean, warm wrap.

I sighed deeply, trying to steady myself. I said aloud as if dictating to my nurse at Mount Sinai. "A small male child, anoxic at birth, revived, likely premature." I wrapped him tightly in a small sheet and tilted my head upward, the filthy prison coming back into focus. "Nellie, you have a little boy. Would you like to hold him?"

Guard Olga shook her head vigorously. "No, we don't do things that way."

I stood, holding the tiny, trembling bundle in my arms. "Move aside, Guard Olga. It's her child."

Guard Olga stepped in my path. "Isaacson, I said, no!"

I raised my voice. "This is my Clinic, and in here, I'm in charge. Step aside."

Nellie lay crying, eyes flaring in desperation, stretching out her arms. She frantically took the baby and drew him close to her thin chest, burying her face in his tiny body, smelling, kissing. "My boy, my boy, my boy," she cried.

I drew the threadbare blanket up to Nellie's chin, attempting to warm the two of them. "Don't hold him too tightly, Nellie. Give him space to breathe."

Then I faced Guard Olga. "Leave them be. We'll deal with the Warden later. Don't steal this moment from the girl."

Guard Olga stepped away, pressing her back to the door. "Isaacson, you'll be the death of me."

At my tiny charting table, I filled out the birth certificate while Nellie cuddled the baby against her warm body. When I reached the line for the infant's name, I turned to her. "Do you have a name for the baby?"

No answer, only the gentle sound of Nellie singing sad Gaelic songs. I didn't understand the words, but the melancholy chords reminded me of the Mourner's Kaddish at synagogue.

I shot out of my chair to check the baby. "Nellie, let me examine him again. He came a tad early, and I want another look."

Her head rested on the pillow, face void of emotion as she held the infant tightly to her chest, stroking his tiny back, singing.

I pulled the thin blanket away and gasped. The child was grey. I shouted, "Nellie, when did his breathing stop?" I grabbed the infant, again placing my mouth over his face, blowing into the lungs.

She turned her head my way. "He's mine, only mine. Nobody's gonna take him from me."

No breath from the infant. Dead.

I lifted my head, staring deeply into Nellie's eyes.

"What happened? Tell me," I pleaded.

"The angels took him to Mama in heaven." She began to weep. "She'll love him. Someday I'll see him there."

* * *

194

I languished in a fog for days. If it weren't for the strict prison routine, I would have remained in my bunk, feeling hopeless, aching for the suffocated infant. After so many years, the unshakable malaise had returned, my eyes heavy, appetite gone, energy low. Each morning, I struggled to leave my bed. Like clockwork, Guard Olga arrived at the bars at 6:30, commanding us to rise and dress for breakfast. The routine dragged me along, at times shaking me part way out of my fugue state.

"Isaacson, isn't today when your people come with the sweaters?" Guard Olga prodded me on our way to the Mess Hall. "And you got a letter." She handed it to me through the bars. Indifferent, I slid it into my pocket.

"Guard Olga, you're right." I'd stopped counting the days as my melancholy grew as thick as our morning porridge.

Nellie had fallen into a deeper depression than me, so bottomless that she was soiling herself in bed, reverting to an infant version of herself. Her bunk-mates complained about the foul smell until, in the dead of night, with no opportunity for fanfare or objection, the Warden moved her to the Insane Asylum.

That blow took me to my knees. Nothing Nellie had done in her short life deserved such profound punishment. The poor girl, barely a child herself, had received one cruel blow after another. I lost all emotional distance, taking her burden as my own, carrying the crippling load as if the infant had been mine.

When not in the Clinic, I lay in bed, my fingers tracing the carvings of names and dates scraped into the concrete wall beside me. I contemplated the power of hope. Caged in like animals at the Workhouse, how many others lay innocent and trapped like me? How many women were willing to rebel by killing their infants? I listened to the mindless chatter coming from my cellmates, wondering if they'd ever soften.

Almost at the Mess Hall, Guard Olga brought me back to my senses. "Isaacson, did you hear me? You're getting your goods today. Gonna see your people. It's Christmas Eve! What's the matter with you? Get movin'." She pointed down the hall at the noisy prisoners. "If they don't settle down, Warden's gonna explode."

Before Nellie's disaster, I'd been counting the hours until the barge arrived. Christmas exuded magic for the Christian inmates, a contagion of happiness imbued with good deeds big and small. Slowly, I pried my senses open to the excitement and let a trace seep into my troubled soul.

I shook my head, her words barely penetrating. "Yes, Guard Olga." I followed her into the Mess Hall where the Warden stood, shaking with fury.

"This prison is for punishment. It's no joy garden," The Warden admonished the women. "Get those ridiculous smiles off your faces."

* * *

Before long, the prisoners were chanting Warden's new nickname, *Heart of Stone*. At times so loudly it echoed in the hallway, *Heart of Stone, Heart of Stone*. Now that Guard Olga had reminded me of the coming gifts, I cringed, worried that their small revolt could backfire, that Warden would refuse to allow the delivery.

As Shannon, Daisy, and Margaret dressed for breakfast, I studied the three of them, standing in a knot. "Get the word out to quit chanting. The inmates have nice things coming their way, but the Warden will spoil everything if they keep it up."

Shannon snapped. "They think she'll keep the goods anyway, sell them, and pocket the money. Warden's sly like a rattlesnake, waiting under a rock for the right moment to strike."

Daisy nodded affirmatively. "Wouldn't put it past her."

Anger shot through me. "Don't think that hasn't crossed my mind. Stop the rumor now! I'll see that the photographers insist on taking pictures of her handing out the goods."

They both shrugged and joined the Mess Hall line, Martha lingering behind.

"Martha, are you all right?" I asked.

She held her belly. "Damn cramps, feels like my bleeding's coming."

I stood beside her, rubbing her back. "How painful are they?"

Martha released a loud breath. "Not too bad. Let's go. Maybe breakfast

196

'ill help."

Could an emergency miscarriage derail my plan to see Margaret? I sighed with worry.

* * *

The morning flew by, packed with patients. Guard Olga was on edge, snapping at inmates over the smallest infraction, but word got around, and the chanting stopped. I prayed the exchange of gifts would go smoothly.

"Guard Olga, did the Warden speak to you about distributing the sweaters and blankets?" I asked.

She shook her head. "Nope. I figure she's goin' steal the show with that Sanger lady and then put them in storage."

I simmered with anger. The inmates were spot on all along. The Warden had no clue she'd fashioned a powder keg. Somehow, I must get word to Margaret.

"Since this was my idea, I'd like to go to the dock when Mrs. Sanger arrives. She's a close friend. I must personally thank her for her generous favor." I said sweetly.

Guard Olga twisted the metal buttons on her navy sweater, her bucolic scenes turning every which way. "I can try, but the Warden said no prisoners."

"Guard Olga, just try."

Ten minutes later, I heard the blast of a loud horn reverberating over the East River. It must be the barge.

"Let's clear the Clinic and head to the dock," I said to Guard Olga. "I can be ready in five minutes."

Guard Olga nervously dispersed the line at my door. "Come back later, will you?" She reached into her bodice, pulling out a letter. "By the way, this came for you."

It was from Joseph. Maddened, I shoved it into my apron pocket. I'd get to it later.

* * *

Stepping from the building, we were greeted by a luminous December day, a mild break in the weather. In the distance, I could barely make out Margaret and Ina on the barge. Walking closer to the dock, the shallow snow puddling under our feet, Ina caught my eye. She began to hop up and down, gesticulating wildly.

Warden Beatrice, waiting on the pier, turned to check what the fuss was about. She bellowed, "Guard, I said no prisoners! Take her back in, now."

Guard Olga grumbled. "You heard her. I'll have hell to pay for not listening."

Keeping Ina in view, I threw my hands in the air with despair, twisted about, and walked back toward the building. My apprehension grew with every step. "Guard Olga, if she doesn't keep her end of the deal, the inmates will go crazy. Who knows what they'll do?"

Guard Olga shook her head. "There's no tellin' her anything."

I studied the building, wondering where she planned to hide the supplies and sweaters. There must be a basement storage area somewhere in that dungeon. Glancing up, I saw faces. Good Lord, the women were crowded like canned sardines at all the windows, watching. The closer I stepped to the staircase, the more faces I saw, all wearing hopeful expressions wishing, longing for a Christmas extravagance to carry them through the frigid winter ahead. I heard a faint rhythm of chanting through the glass. *Heart of Stone, Heart of Stone.* The intoning grew louder. What had I begun?

As we reached the front door, a piercing whistle split through the air. Both Guard Olga and I turned and saw the Warden signaling us to return. We hurried back to the water's edge. As we walked toward the dock, I could faintly hear the inmates clapping and cheering behind us.

The Warden straightened her shoulders, narrowing her eyes into slits. "Mrs. Sanger wants prisoners in the photograph wearing sweaters."

I snuck a look at Margaret and, without tipping my hand, gave her a slight nod. "She knows the press and that the public will eat it up," I said.

"Well, I don't like it, not one bit." The Warden's eyes snaked from mine to

Guard Olga's and ordered, "Get twenty reliable girls and two more guards and come back right away."

Margaret, who'd been standing on the pier, asked loudly, "How many women inmates are inside altogether?"

"Over five hundred. You can't seriously be thinking of...."

Margaret interrupted. "We need one hundred fifty for the photo. The guards can bring sweaters back for the remaining prisoners. After that, I'd like to personally deliver the medical supplies to the Clinic and get photos inside with the doctor."

The Warden stared with contempt at Margaret. I wagered she'd never tangled with the likes of Mrs. Margaret Sanger. I bit the insides of my cheeks. This was the most entertainment I'd had in weeks.

"I refuse." Warden Beatrice was apoplectic, beet red, body shaking with fury. "That will not do!"

Margaret pasted on her most charming smile, answering in a superior voice, "Do you have any idea how many high-class women in the city made this happen?" She pointed to the barge, piled high with crates. "Knitting in their parlors for hours on end? Names you'd only read about in the society pages—"

Ina cut in. "They want pictures to be satisfied their sweaters were delivered into the hands of the needy."

Margaret stared down the Warden, twice her size, and spoke in a slow, even voice. "Now, let's get this show on the road. Time's a-wasting."

Warden Beatrice blew her whistle, and over the next hour and a half, one hundred fifty prisoners and guards tugged on colorful sweaters. The inmates formed five rows of thirty prisoners, each wearing bright red, green, blue, and yellow sweaters over their dingy brown muslin work dresses. Ina and Margaret were positioned in front of the inmates handing additional piles of sweaters to the Warden and her ten guards. The photographer perched his tripod and black drape high on the barge, adjusting his camera to capture the full splendor of the event.

"One, two, three, hold still! Don't move." The camera made a loud *poof* as the most iconic shot of the holiday season was taken. It would be seen

Christmas morning, the following day, spread over the front pages of more than five major city newspapers with headlines ranging from *Christmas Miracle Across the River, Bringing Light to Blackwell's,* to *The Unforgotten.*

Finally, the guards, each carrying stacks of extra sweaters, herded the overjoyed inmates back into the Workhouse to resume their duties. I stood beaming at Margaret and Ina. "You're miracle workers."

The Warden, not missing a beat, said, "That's it now. We'll take the rest into the Workhouse and the Clinic."

Margaret laughed. "Warden, perhaps you misheard. We're not leaving without a tour of the Women's Clinic and seeing to that delivery. As a matter of fact, I'd like to speak to the doctor and assess if there are additional provisions needed for the inmates' future care."

The Warden seethed with anger. "Make it fast!"

* * *

Margaret, Ina, and I carried bundles of blankets, bandages, and medicine upstairs to the Clinic. Realizing it was our only opportunity to speak, Margaret leaned in my ear.

"You're not going to believe this. The detective checked out this Miss Sinclair, the poor thing. It turns out she was having an affair with Governor Higgins's son. You know, the married one with the house full of children. The stinkin' bedswerver."

"You've got to be kidding. You think he arranged the midwife at the Waldorf?" I never considered the crime could reach the pinnacle of state government.

"It seems so. If the scandal leaks, who knows what will happen?" Margaret suddenly stopped and looked fiercely into my eyes. "We're going to use his dirty secret to get you out. We're the only ones who know. But we'll have to act fast. Governor Higgins's term is practically over. January, Governor Hughes takes office."

I was breathless. "Does Tillie know? My attorney?"

"Of course. It was despicable they let the son pin the blame on you, but

200

they're not going to get away with it. It was Ina's choice of a sharp detective who helped us unravel the truth."

I fell silent, struck by my bizarre predicament.

"Tillie's coming here the day after Christmas to talk to you, but your Baltimore friends and I already have a plan."

The Warden burst into the Clinic. "That's enough prattling. Prisoner, you, and the guard finish here. I'm escorting your visitors out, finally."

Margaret answered sweetly. "No pictures?"

The Warden scowled. "No!"

I was dying to know what Margaret was up to with Mrs. Garrett and Mrs. Thomas, but there was no more discussion, and I didn't intend to upset the Warden further. Busy unloading and arranging the new supplies in empty cabinets, I inventoried the medications and dressings, planning to lock them securely. Searching through the drugs, I saw a small supply of pain medicines that I set far back, behind more ordinary tinctures. After locking the cabinet, I joined Guard Olga on the walk back to my cell, my malaise practically gone.

Guard Olga laughed lightly. "That was some haul today. You've got smart-ass friends out there."

She was a different Guard Olga with her smile. Was that also a twinkle in her eye?

"I'm praying the influenza settles and we have a healthy winter." It was a great day—warm sweaters on all the inmates and guards, my Clinic prepared for most ailments.

Clanging of bars and shouting filled the air as we entered my cell block.

Guard Olga shouted, "What the hell's going on in here?"

"*Heart of Stone*," cried out an angry voice from a cell deep in the hallway, her words echoing throughout the corridor. Within moments, another voice joined in, then another, until the walls pulsed with the chant. "*Heart of Stone, Heart of Stone.*"

"Warden's takin' our sweaters!" screamed the inmates.

I couldn't believe it. *What on earth?*

The Warden strutted down the corridor blowing her whistle, shrieking,

"Shut up, fools. No supper for any of ya! And no sweaters from the lousy suffra-bitches either." She looked directly at me, her face contorted, purple with anger. "See what you started, you stupid bitch! Get in your cell!"

The shouting ebbed, except for an isolated voice refusing to quit. As more women realized they had forfeited their meager dinner, they fell into bed, hoping to silence their empty bellies through sleep. Soon, we could only hear the rats scratching for a few scattered crumbs.

I fell into my bunk, too, sinking into the prickly straw mattress, slipping back into despair. Could I sleep through the nightmare I'd created? I looked across at Daisy and Shannon's faces, both wrapped with disappointment. "Where's Martha?" I called out, remembering her condition that morning.

"Up here." answered a weak voice.

Martha lay in the bunk over mine, not moving a muscle. In just three short weeks, she'd shrunken to a shadow of her former self.

I placed my hand on her forehead. Cool. "How'd the day go?"

"I lost it. Came out in the john. Been trickling blood all afternoon."

"How heavy was the bleeding?" I stroked her forearm, wondering if she had passed the fetus.

"Not too bad." Martha whimpered. "It passed." She sniffled. "I think it was a girl. Nothin' good ever happens to girls in this life."

* * *

Christmas morning should have begun with a calm sense of goodwill, everyone content in new warm sweaters, but it did not. I lay still in bed, recalling decorated store windows and clever gifts advertised in magazines and newspapers. Even our Jewish family couldn't resist the pull of the holiday every year, happily slipping into joyful celebrations. Tillie would prepare a special family breakfast, and most years my brothers and their children traveled downtown to join us. Naively, I thought all Christians took part in celebrating their blessed day.

It was not the case at Blackwell's. Almost every prisoner, Christian or otherwise, was denied worship, food, and warmth. On the heels of

Thanksgiving, it was a second reminder of our insignificance, the Warden's malice shattering the remaining shred of our spirits. The weight of responsibility, the tease of warmth in the cold season, pushed me deep into my mattress, sinking into the straw until I could no longer move. Meanwhile, New Yorkers all over the city were opening their newspapers to our photos and headlines. The enormity of the lie was outrageous.

Guard Olga's anger shook me from my reverie. "Up, Isaacson. Up I said, now!" She glared at me, her blue sweater gone.

At breakfast, not one woman, prisoner, or guard was wearing a warm sweater. The Warden had hidden them somewhere in the bowels of the building. Unlike the past week, when the Mess Hall air was electrified with excitement and anticipation, the magnitude of silence disturbing. The only sound was the clanking of spoons hitting the bottom of shallow breakfast bowls. Benches screeched against the floor as inmates finished their cold gruel and formed lines heading to the Knitting and Sewing Halls for their dreary workday monotony. As always, Guard Olga signaled for me to join her at the Mess Hall door, then escorted me to the Clinic.

We opened the locked door.

"What the hell!" Guard Olga shouted.

Cabinet doors were ripped from their hinges, my well-stocked shelves emptied, the exam table overturned, and chairs thrown on their sides. The room was entirely ransacked.

After yesterday, the destruction came as no surprise. Too depleted to utter a sound, I collapsed onto the floor, my stomach in knots, my belief in human decency decimated.

"I'm fetching the Warden." Guard Olga stormed out of the room, forgetting I was alone in the middle of the chaos.

I reached for a toppled chair, righting it by the desk, sitting down, straightening my work dress, hoping to restore an increment of order. While smoothing the front of my apron, I heard a crinkle in the pocket and realized I hadn't opened Joseph's letter. Pulling it from my pocket, I unfolded the paper.

December 16, 1906

   My Dear Hannah,

   By the time you receive this, you will have celebrated the arrival of your sweaters and blankets. The scuttlebutt around the hospital is that you've become the Angel of Blackwell's. Isn't that just like you, always rising to the top with your concern for others, a modern-day Joan of Arc.

   I must admit, I don't think I could be so noble if I were in that terrible place. I don't have your confidence and open heart. Sometimes, when I'm with you, I wish that your generous spirit would rub onto me. Instead, I feel more diminished. But I believe knowing you, being together with you, will help make me become better. So, I impatiently wait for your release and happy times together once again.

   With my love,

   Joseph

Stunned, I folded the letter and slid it back into the envelope. The man was an absolute ass, completely self-absorbed. It wasn't my job to make him a better man, and I had no intention of doing so. He was so full of himself; there was no room left for me. How could I be so stupid? *Open heart* be damned! What about Ina's tales of other women? He's the one with the open heart! A shard of hatred tore through me. I dropped my head in my hands, shaking with fury. What else in my life could go wrong?

* * *

Where was Guard Olga? She'd been gone too long. The Clinic clock read one thirty. I opened the door, stepping into the hallway. No one in sight. *How odd.* Venturing quietly down the corridor, I headed to the Warden's office, door open, room empty. The hair on my arms stood on end with dreadful anticipation. Where were they?

   I listened closely. A faint banging at my feet resonated through the floor. What was happening downstairs? It had to be the Knitting Hall. I pulled open the thick stairwell door, and the noises magnified, women's screams, metal crashing. Propelled by panic, I raced down the steps to the workroom, the banging growing louder with each step. *My God, what was going on in there?*

The metal door to the Knitting Hall was heavy, requiring all my strength to pull it open. As I pried it free, a wave of savage screams poured out, drowning me in a din of curses and wailing. The room seemed to swirl, no longer anchored to any fixed structure. Rioting prisoners and frantic guards, hundreds of them with fists flying, clubs swinging, furniture sailing through the air, had taken possession of a once quiet room filled with the rhythmic clicking of knitting needles. I spotted Shannon mid-way in the Knitting Hall, knocking a guard onto the floor, jumping on her back, beating the woman's shoulders, a fistful of hair in her other hand.

I shrieked, "Stop, stop now!" No one turned, my voice lost in a deafening sea of cries. Searching for my other cellmates and Guard Olga, my eye caught Daisy at the edge of the room within a cluster of inmates, too afraid to fight. She hid, curled in a tiny ball behind a yarn table. She spotted me at the exit and slithered along the edge of the room, practically invisible, until she reached me at the door. Meanwhile, I combed the room for Martha, Guard Olga, and the Warden. Where were they? Women were dropping to the floor, some writhing in pain, others immobile. Never in my life had I witnessed such blatant brutality.

I grabbed Daisy's hand and pulled her toward me, through the doorway, into the hall. The metal door crashed closed behind us.

I was dizzy with panic. "Daisy, we must call for help. Someone's going to get killed in there."

She nodded breathlessly, searching the hallway.

Could I trust her to help me, or would she try to escape? There was no way I could manage alone.

"Let's get to the Warden's office. There's a telephone in there." I pulled Daisy's arm, dragging her with me.

"Warden's been stabbed. She was lyin' in the back on the floor. A bunch of them were beating on her with chairs."

Disbelief burned through me. "My God." They'd become bloodthirsty. We had to move fast. "Let's go!"

Within seconds we arrived at the Warden's office. The door was open, the candlestick telephone sat on her desk. I lifted the earpiece from its cradle and held it to my ear, hit the receiver, and dialed "0."

The operator answered in a sweet voice. "Merry Christmas to ya, Warden. What number would you like?"

I yelled into the mouthpiece. "Send for backup! We'll need medical supplies. There's a riot in the Knitting Hall. For God's sake, hurry!"

"Right away, Warden." The line went dead.

My eyes pierced Daisy's. "The Clinic was ransacked. I don't know if I have enough supplies. I can't do it without you."

We hurried down the hall to my clinic and began righting the furniture, grabbing the few supplies the thieves had left scattered on the floor, and began organizing the counters. I handed two empty buckets to Daisy. "Run to the kitchen and get hot water. Can you manage?"

Daisy nodded unevenly, her eyes shifting to the window.

"Fast, Daisy. I need you back here. Can I count on you?" I implored.

Her jaw twisted with indecision, then her face transformed. Her chest puffed out. "Be back in a flash."

While I waited for Daisy and the inevitable onslaught of wounded inmates, I set myself to organizing bandages, iodine, and tape in the order I'd need. Trained long after the Civil War, I knew little about battle trauma. I strained to recall the offhanded lessons from the older doctors, who, from time to time, reminisced about those gruesome battles, hastily erecting hospital tents, triaging patients, reusing instruments. In all my years as a doctor, I'd only experienced emergencies one patient at a time. I'd no first-hand experience delivering mass trauma care.

Hannah, you can do this. I'd follow the logic. Triage in the hallway, use up the cots, then place wounded on clean blankets, treating the most critical first. I'd use Daisy to apply pressure for bleeding and seek more help. I prayed the operator called for backup from Charity Hospital two miles down the island. In the distance, I heard gunshots and bells clanging. I ran to the window. There were four barges coming our way from Manhattan's piers to Blackwell's. *Thank God.*

"Got them!" Daisy burst in, wide-eyed, water splashing from the top of the buckets onto the floor.

I took the buckets and set them in the basin. "See anything?"

"You ain't gonna believe how nuts it is!"

A man's voiced boomed through the corridor. "Make way! Make way. Wounded comin'."

Daisy opened the door, and two male guards, likely from the men's prison, each carrying an end of a stretcher, tore into the room, setting the patient on the exam table.

"Mother of God! It's the Warden." Daisy screamed.

"How many more? Can you get help from Charity Hospital?" I implored.

"Who are you?" demanded one of the guards.

"The doctor. Answer me!" I barked back, looking a full foot upward into his shaken eyes. "Who are you?"

The men straightened. "Guards from the Men's side. Most of us were called over. There's a lot more injured comin'."

"Start bringing them up, bleeders first. Set the injured on clean blankets when the cots are full. For God's sake, call for more help from Charity," I ordered.

The guards stared at me in disbelief, looking at my prison wear, not certain what to make of my command.

"Now!" I screamed in their shocked faces. "We've no time to lose."

They both ran from the room, leaving behind a vacuum of silence.

* * *

A thick wooden knitting needle punctured the Warden's chest, precariously close to her heart. But what concerned me more was the cavernous gash on her head. Was that brain I saw? Her skull was cracked open, and she was rapidly losing blood. I placed a thick towel on her head wound, applying steady pressure while blood continued to leech through the white cotton, spreading crimson across the starched cloth. "Warden, can you hear me?" I spoke in her ear. "Warden, open your eyes."

Nothing. Her breathing was jagged.

I felt her neck for a pulse, weak, barely discernible. The knitting needle must have punctured her lung. I could feel her brain pulsing through the towel and was uncertain which injury to tend first? I bent to her ear again, recalling her name from my first day in prison, reaching deep into her earliest memories. "Beatrice, open your eyes, dear."

Her lids fluttered, and her lips opened. Blood dripped from the corner of her mouth down her cheek, pooling inside her ear.

Struggling to breathe, she focused her fluttering eyes on my face. "Am I gonna die?"

I bent my face close to the Warden's. "Stay calm. I'm going to help you. We'll be taking you to the hospital." I lied, doubting she'd live that long.

"It's torture. Get me something—" a pause—"for the pain," the Warden coughed blood through her teeth.

I caught Daisy's eyes, both of us stunned by the irony, our villain now begging for help.

"Where's the medicine? Do we need a key?" I asked softly.

The Warden sniffed and coughed more blood. "On my belt. Office… closet." She sputtered, spraying blood onto my face.

Daisy loosened the Warden's belt, removing the keys. "Be right back."

As she turned to leave the Clinic, two orderlies and a doctor, presumably from Charity Hospital, charged into the room.

Chapter Twenty-Nine

W e worked into the evening like a smooth-running machine. The doctor from Charity Hospital and I split the patients, the most severe in the Clinic with me, and the majority who were less dire in the hallway with him. Daisy stayed by my side in the exam room, and he commandeered the converted hallway hospital with his orderlies. Cots were lined up on one side of the corridor with a makeshift storage cart filled to the brim with bandages and blankets, the tiny area now transformed into two hospital units.

By evening, four bodies were taken to the morgue, including the Warden, who died before Daisy returned with medication. Her injuries were beyond our abilities; the bleeding from her head and chest wounds too extensive to repair. A pang of resentment passed through my mind as I recorded the time of death—her atrocious behavior would never receive the living punishment she deserved. Death was a coward's escape.

Three inmates had been clubbed to death, their skulls crushed beyond recognition, the savageness appalling. Horse-drawn carts transported many others, both inmates and guards, to Charity Hospital to treat extensive injuries.

Guard Olga and Daisy remained by my side the entire time, helping set broken bones, applying bandages, cleaning instruments, always keeping full buckets of uncontaminated, hot water on hand, with ice in a separate bucket. One after another, patients were stitched, bandaged, and escorted back to their cells.

How would we be punished for the uprising? I was full of regret, knowing

I was culpable, having brought the sweaters to Blackwell's in the first place. Perhaps they'd only punish me.

As we finished treating our last patient, the Manhattan Commissioner of Police, Theodore Bingham, arrived on the island. After interviewing the guards, he made his way to the Clinic. The inmates whispered that he was sent by the Mayor and Governor to get to the bottom of things and straighten the place out.

Entering the temporary hospital ward in the hallway, Commissioner Bingham, armed to the hilt, pushed his way into the Clinic, brushing aside orderlies and the wounded. "Where's Prisoner Isaacson?" he commanded.

"That's me," I called back to him. My body was bent over an inmate's face, concentrating on stitching, keeping my sutures small and even. "I'm finishing up." I sewed my final stitch over an inmate's eyebrow and cut the suture thread. "You shouldn't have much of a scar when this heals. Come back in a week, and I'll remove the stitches."

Daisy edged closer. "Hannah, I can bandage her. I'm ready to do it on my own."

"Very good, Daisy." I stepped back, rotating away from the exam table to wash my hands in the sink. If we ever got out of here, I'd make sure she received real nursing training.

Commissioner Bingham studied our every move. "Follow me. We'll speak in the Warden's office."

I untied my apron and set it on a wall hook, then followed him down the hall.

An older inmate lying on a cot stretched her arm to me. "Doctor Hannah, come back and check me? I don't want no one else."

"Of course, I'll be back soon." I squeezed her hand and nodded to the others.

The Commissioner watched as I released her hand. "Who in tarnation do you think you are?" he demanded as he pulled two chairs into the Warden's office, "Clara Barton?"

I dropped onto one, physically and emotionally drained, my feet aching. "I'm just trying to help."

He sat opposite me, shooting his eyes about the room as if the walls held answers. "Do you have any idea of the mess here? Half the Workhouse was rioting, a handful of guards were injured, the men's side left vulnerable for hours until reinforcements came. What do you have to say about it?" He stared at me for a long moment until a look of recognition transformed his face. "You're the dame we arrested for the murder at the Waldorf. Aren't you?"

I nodded. "Wrongly accused."

"You the one stirring up hellfire here? First the barges yesterday, and now a prison riot?"

My thoughts jumped to the Warden, now dead, unable to take account-ability for her shameful actions. "The delivery of sweaters and medical supplies was an effort by the generous women in New York, the Warden, and me. The purpose, of course, was to help the inmates stay healthier through the winter."

"Then what in God's name happened to cause the ruckus?" He lifted his handcuffs from his belt.

Careful Hannah. He's sending you a warning. His office was responsible for my arrest. They were unlikely to believe anything I said. I cleared my throat. "The Warden had different plans for the supplies and sweaters." I looked for a reaction.

His eyes bore into mine. "What do you mean, different plans?"

"The inmates sensed it all along. She'd no tolerance for their excitement and was threatening them for days. When the barges arrived, she only agreed to bring a few women out of the Workhouse for the newspaper photo. But Mrs. Sanger insisted more inmates pose with their sweaters on. She had promised a sensational Christmas photo for the newspapers. Did you happen to see it?"

Finally, a smirk. "Best thing to come off of this damn island in years."

"Mrs. Sanger wanted to properly thank the women in New York who knit and donated over five hundred warm sweaters."

"So, what went wrong?" The Commissioner seemed absorbed in my accounting, his voice losing its angry edge.

211

"After the photo, the guards brought the inmates back to their cells and began handing out the rest of the sweaters and blankets, including sweaters made for the guards. While that was happening, Mrs. Sanger and I brought the medical supplies to the Clinic." I sighed. "Once Mrs. Sanger left, the Warden began walking the halls with her cruelest guards banging their billy clubs on the bars. She took back everything and announced there'd be no Christmas Eve dinner." I fidgeted in my chair. "We all went hungry, everyone cold. You can't imagine how discouraged and angry the inmates were."

"Jesus Christ Almighty. What the hell is wrong with that woman? She's been getting worse every year."

Was, I thought. "She must have hidden them somewhere in the basement. Anyway, Christmas morning at breakfast, it seemed way too quiet. I've learned since I've been here to get a sense of these things. Something bad was brewing. After breakfast, when I went to the Clinic, I found it rampaged, most all the blankets and medicines stolen. Guard Olga ran to report the break-in to the Warden, who, as it turns out, was caught in the riot in the Knitting Hall. That's all I know."

He shook his head in disbelief. "What did you do when you saw the riot?"

"I grabbed Daisy, one of my cellmates, went to the Warden's office to call for help, and rushed to the Clinic. Daisy helped me get the place organized. Soon after, the wounded and help for Charity Hospital came. She and Guard Olga stayed by my side the entire time, assisting me until you arrived."

Commissioner cleared his throat. "I'll need to make a report to Mayor McClellan and Governor Higgins before all this hits the newspapers. Hearst's already drooling over the bloody story." He stood. "Go back to the Clinic and see to your job."

I rose slowly from my chair, hating to stand on my tired feet, aching from the hours I'd spent on them today. "Yes, sir."

The Commissioner scrutinized me. "Did ya do it?"

"Do what?"

"Kill the lady in the Waldorf."

I shook my head sadly. "I've never performed an abortion in my entire career. I came after the sordid deed and tried to save her. That's my sworn job as a doctor."

Speechless, he watched as I walked back to the Clinic.

Chapter Thirty

I t was December 29th, a date I'd never forget. The prisoners had both won and lost. They reclaimed their colorful sweaters, and if it had been a happier time, one might agree that standing in line after lunch, they looked like holiday trimming. But the murders that stole lives also took away their limited freedoms. The Knitting Hall was closed indefinitely, and any tool deemed dangerous removed. Sewing scissors, knitting needles, and pinking shears were placed in crates and taken into storage, far from their reach.

Instead of working, prisoners returned to their cells following meals; sat, slept, played cards, and for the literate, read, whiling away the hours with no distractions, feeling the full force of their imprisonment. For a half-hour in the middle of the day, groups were taken outdoors in their sweaters and marched around the island for exercise, a line of colors shivering in the freezing air.

Daisy and I were luckier than most. I was immediately sent back to the Clinic and requested Daisy's assistance. She had proven herself useful and had not been present in the Knitting Hall during the worst of the riot. My request was approved.

* * *

Days later, Guard Olga approached me while I stood in the lunch line. "Come with me."

"Where're you takin' her?" Daisy asked. "We're supposed to go work in the Clinic together."

Guard Olga answered. "You go to your cell."

A look of realization crossed Daisy's face. She reached for my hand. "Don't take her from us."

Guard Olga simply said. "Time to come, now."

I knew I'd be leaving. Margaret told me enough to stoke my hopes. But the feeling was surreal, dream-like.

I held Daisy in a deep hug. "Come find me when you get out. I'll have a plan for you."

She nodded, tears filling her eyes.

"I need to collect a few things," I told Guard Olga.

Back in my cell, I was surprised at my conflicted emotions. In only a few weeks, I'd grown to care about the women in my cell. Particularly Daisy, whom I hoped to assist through nursing school. But Martha, with her deep loneliness, and Shannon, who trusted no one, had both found a trail to my heart. I wondered if, given more time, I could have done more for them. But unfortunately, the sad likelihood is that they'd live on the streets for a short time before returning to their home at Blackwell's.

I looked about my cell, the skimpy blankets tucked neatly in the sides of the bunk beds, the picture magazines, brushes, and hair pins. The only personal items I cared to take were from Tillie: *The Gift of the Magi* and her old lace handkerchief.

Guard Olga led me back to the small conference room near the Clinic. My attorney, Mr. Clemson, and Tillie were sitting at the table wearing broad smiles.

Tillie said, "We've come to take you home. The City dropped their charges."

I squelched a scream and turned to Guard Olga.

Her tight-lipped smile spoke volumes. "It won't be the same here without you, Doc."

I reached for her hand and squeezed it. "Thank you, Guard Olga, for trusting me and helping me try to do some good."

She nodded sadly. "I'll leave you to it," Guard Olga said as she gently closed the door.

I searched their faces. "So, tell me. What happened?"

Tillie pulled two newspapers from her satchel. "Have you seen the newspapers?"

"No papers have been allowed on the island since the riot," I replied, now curious.

She set the papers in front of me so I could read the headlines. *Waldorf Doctor Freed from Blackwell's! The Good Doctor Isaacson, Wrongly Accused.*

Despite my innocence, I was stunned to see my name favorably in print. "Well, I'll be. What made them drop the charges?"

Mr. Clemson answered. "It was a perfect storm. Let's leave it at that for now. There's a boat waiting for us, and I'd like to get you out of here."

Tillie reached into her satchel and pulled out a warm wrap. "Put this on; you'll need it. The winds are freezing on the river."

I handed the torn handkerchief back to Tillie. "I wasn't sure you wanted this back."

Tillie's eyes were warm. "Oh, Hannah, that was Mama's. She was squeezing it in her hand years ago when she died. It's been through thick and thin with me." She placed the handkerchief back in my hand, folding my fingers around it. "You keep it now."

* * *

A half-hour later, I stood in the stern of the boat, the cold wind whipping through my hair, winter sun warming my face, watching Blackwell's Island shrink in size. In a few short weeks, my body had acclimated to the cold, and the temperatures no longer bothered me as much. In solidarity with the inmates' hardships, I removed my wrap and braced myself against the wind. Blackwell's had altered me in more ways than I could have imagined. Although I hadn't lived an entire lifetime in the harshness of poverty and deprivation, I possessed a heightened awareness of how real and vivid their plight was. I knew in my heart this knowledge would never stray far from my thoughts.

Chapter Thirty-One

I moved back in with Tillie, spending the days following my release in front of the fire, with my face buried deep in the newspapers. News from Blackwell's Workhouse dominated the headlines all week. New Yorkers couldn't read enough about the prison uprising, the evil Warden, and the theft of donated sweaters. With the Warden settled in her final resting place on Hart Island, in a show of unity, all walks of New York women knit clothing and blankets for the infants and inmates, flooding the prison storage. Some offered to house babies until their mothers were released. Not since Nellie Bly's undercover expose had there been such fascination with the macabre details of Blackwell's.

By the end of Christmas week, every paper reported the same account of my case: "After careful review, the New York City Prosecutor's Office concluded there was lack of evidence to support the charges." The coroner determined it was impossible to have committed the ghastly crime and for Miss Sinclair to hemorrhage to death in only the thirty-five minutes I had been in her room. The physiological evidence cited, one the public could barely comprehend, rested on a recent medical discovery—platelets, a crucial blood component responsible for blood clotting.

The coroner's report attempted to describe the platelet findings in simple terms. Scrapings from Miss Sinclair's thighs showed two layers of dried blood. The bottom-most layer was the oldest, rich with clotted blood and highly opaque. The uppermost layer was thinner, more transparent, with fewer clots as it dried. The reality was that over time, the victim's blood had run thin with platelets, less able to clot. The coroner's observation underscored the fact she had bled for an extended time, far longer than one half-hour. When combined with the two widely spaced telephone calls from the Waldorf to my office on the afternoon of the murder, the coroner declared that all arrows pointed to a procedure that began closer to noon while I was still at Mount Sinai delivering babies. The murder charge was dropped—as if it never happened.

The public was satisfied with my release, although the Letters to the Editor expressed Puritan outrage, fixating on the lengthy story of abortion but, even more so, the detailed discussion of Miss Sinclair's thighs rather than my wrongful time in prison. But I knew there was more to the story. My trusty friends had been busy in the shadows untangling the murderous mess.

* * *

Two evenings after my release, Tillie, Ina, Margaret, Mrs. Garrett, and Mrs. Thomas gathered in Tillie's apartment in New York's Lower East Side for a celebratory dinner. The clinking of goblets echoed a collective relief. Justice had been served for me, even if the murderer was still at large.

"Time to get you fed properly, Hannah." Tillie studied my tea dress hanging loosely off my shoulders. "You're all skin and bones."

I shrugged. "When I got home yesterday, all I could think about was sinking to the bottom of a hot, soapy tub. But before that, I checked every strand of my hair for lice and fleas. For some crazy reason, in prison, I was more preoccupied with bugs than my safety. For good measure, I dumped my filthy clothing directly in the incinerator."

It was easier to share my preoccupation with bugs than my delicate spirit. How I'd sobbed and sobbed into my soapy hands for the longest time, sinking with weightless fragility into the bubbles, indescribably grateful to be back in the shelter of my family's home.

"We did the same thing after we got to America." Ina scrunched her face. "The whole family had fleas from the ocean crossing. And I'll never forget the smell in steerage. Mama still natters about it, and now she's constantly

218

cleaning our bathroom."

I nodded. "I understand. The filth in prison was medieval. The warm water eventually relaxed me. It had been two months since I had privacy or a hot bath." I sighed. "I'll never again take a simple bath with soap for granted."

While the fatigue was overwhelming, I slept fitfully, reliving my fear of the Warden, her smug acceptance of brutality, and finally, how she'd become a helpless thug with a knitting needle protruding from her chest.

Tillie watched me with concern. "Would you like to buy a new dress? It might help you feel better. We can go to Bloomingdale's to shop."

"I don't think a frock will keep me from having nightmares," I answered in a soft voice.

Margaret adjusted a fly-away tendril on my head. "The nightmares will pass, I promise."

Undeterred, Tillie cast me a reassuring look. "Hannah, Margaret's right. Give it some time. In the meanwhile, you look perfect. Freedom is the finest suit on you."

The circle of women nodded as we toasted again and arranged ourselves at the dinner table for a belated Chanukah meal.

Mrs. Garrett dabbed the corners of her mouth. "My goodness, what kind of potato is this? I'd like to give the recipe to our cook. I can't believe I've never had Jewish food before."

"They're called latkes. I grate potatoes with diced onions, eggs, and flour, then fry them. They go nicely with beef brisket, don't you think?" Tillie beamed and pointed to the other dishes. "This sweet noodle pudding is called kugel. I make it with raisins and cinnamon. And, of course, roasted carrots and turnips. It's a typical holiday dinner."

Mrs. Thomas chimed in, "Absolutely luscious! Thank you for inviting us, Tillie."

All this talk about food! I cringed inside, thinking of the women whom I knew were still imprisoned, eating thin soup and gruel. Although it felt callous, I knew it was impossible for Tillie to fully appreciate how fortunate she was. My thoughts drifted to my release. I still had so many unanswered questions. "I never heard all the gritty details and about your meeting with Governor Higgins."

Mrs. Garrett surveyed the table, studying each of us, heightening the anticipation. "What we share must remain a secret. We promised the Governor it would never hit the newspapers. Can I have your word?" She glanced back at Ina. "You too, young lady?"

Ina crossed her heart.

Heads bobbed as a chorus of consensus circled the table.

Mrs. Garrett signaled Mrs. Thomas. "Go ahead, Carey, you tell. After all, you have more history with Higgins than me."

Mrs. Thomas began in a quiet, careful voice. "I'd be remiss if I didn't give the lion's share of credit to Miss Ina. Without her natural intuition and intelligence, we never would have cracked this case."

Ina grinned. *"Lion's share,* I'll remember that one."

Mrs. Thomas drew a deep breath. "Mr. Burns, the detective Tillie and Ina hired, turned out to be a bona fide Sherlock Holmes. He worked ten times faster than the police investigators. First, he identified the victim, Miss Sinclair, and then quickly made his way to Albany to interview the girl's family and friends. That's where we discovered the connection with Governor Higgin's son, whom they call Junior. For the life of me, I simply can't fathom how it became fashionable to give our sons infantile nicknames."

I watched Ina closely. What had I done to deserve such loyalty and doggedness? Margaret had also been quick to realize Ina's keen intelligence and grit, recruiting her to join her posse of suffragists while I was gone.

Mrs. Thomas cleared her throat. "It was the detective's conversation with Junior that became our treasure trove. Junior was a nervous sort, in deep, far over his entitled well-coiffed head, and was desperate to do anything to make the fiasco disappear. It took little arm-twisting from Mr. Burns to get him to confess that he'd set up the poor woman at the Waldorf for the procedure. Such a sordid matter." She shook her head in disgust.

"Did you find out who the midwife was?" I asked, concerned about getting the menace off the street.

Margaret interrupted, "If you don't mind, Mrs. Thomas, I'd like to continue." She turned to address me. "Mr. Burns pried the midwife's name from Junior. He immediately gave it to the police, but she was long gone. She'd been operating her business under a pseudonym, like most do. When they arrived at her Clinic address, the place was empty, a For Rent sign hanging on the door."

I was furious. "She should be warming my old bunk in the Workhouse right now, awaiting her trial."

My friends nodded soberly.

"How about we move to the parlor for tea and dessert?" Tillie suggested. "I'll clear the table later."

"Oh no, Tillie. I'll clean up while you get off your feet." Ina chimed in. "I can listen from the kitchen."

I didn't want Ina cleaning up alone. "I'll help too. It should only take a moment. And I don't mind waiting another few minutes for the rest of the story." I needed time to digest the rich meal, the likes of which I hadn't had recently. The thought of taking in more information on top of a rich dessert was overwhelming.

Within seconds, we all clustered in the small kitchen carrying our plates, scraping, stacking, and setting the dishes in a sink of soapy water. Even the trustees pitched in, wanting to partake in this melodious chemistry of women, bonded together in task. In the meantime, I placed a kettle of water on the stove for tea.

"Come now, everyone, into the parlor by the fire. Hannah and Ina, the rest can wait." Tillie lifted a tray of cookies and pastries from the counter and carried them with her, setting the silver platter on the coffee table, within everyone's reach.

Once settled, Margaret continued recounting. "Hannah, the rest was sheer brilliance, if I must say so myself." She sat back in her chair, resting her tea saucer on her swollen belly, lost in the retelling.

* * *

After our illustrious Mr. Burns spoke to Junior and discovered the truth, Mrs. Garrett and Mrs. Thomas took a train to New York to meet with Tillie, Ina, and me, two days before Christmas. I took them to a private dining room at Delmonico's, reserved for women only. We needed to plan our next move post haste.

Time was ticking fast, and Governor Higgin's term practically over. The deal had to pass from his hands to Governor Hughes in January. Tillie was most concerned with getting Hannah out of prison, but I insisted on recompense for the time she was held there.

We decided the trustees, and I should call on Governor Higgins right away in Albany. They had met him several times over the years at fundraising balls and had business ventures with his family years back. We initially thought it wise to bring Mr. Clemson and have an attorney present, but Mrs. Clemson wouldn't permit it. Apparently, she's quite religious and refused to allow him to travel overnight with women.

The morning of our train ride was cold, but the sky was clear, no snow in sight. The newsboy was yelling from his soapbox, "Read all about it! Prison riot at Blackwell's." Terrified for your safety, we grabbed a paper and read the article right on the train platform. After all our trouble, the Warden taking the sweaters away from those freezing prisoners was the most abominable misuse of power. We knew Hannah was right about her wickedness. But the Warden was another humiliating embarrassment for the Governor. After all, he'd appointed her. The tide was turning in our favor.

Ina conjured her magic once again, securing a meeting with the Governor despite the Christmas holidays. She told his secretary we had damning evidence involving his son in the Waldorf caper, and suddenly, the Governor's calendar broke wide open.

We stayed at a small, comfortable hotel near the Executive Mansion and arrived on time for our one o'clock appointment. The next day we'd ample time to rehearse our parts over breakfast.

We'd heard Governor Higgins was in poor health, but it was worse than reported in the papers. He looked about to keel over. I'll be surprised if he makes it through winter. He can barely walk on his own and was out of breath simply sitting in his chair. We hadn't a moment to lose.

After Mrs. Garrett and Mrs. Thomas warmed him up with their 'who married whom' and 'who's doing what' in their mutual circle of acquaintances, I got down to business.

"It's time we discuss the matter at hand. Governor, the bottom line is we insist you drop all charges against Dr. Isaacson and release her immediately. There is not proper evidence to hold her a moment longer."

At first, he tried to fake his way through it, the wily devil. "Who are you, her attorney? I refuse to discuss the matter with you women."

I was seeing red, speaking through my gritted teeth. "I promise, you do not want to deal with our attorney. But if you insist, we will go public with Junior's scandal and his underhanded dealings. I'll bet Hearst would love to get his hands on your dirty family secret."

The Governor blanched. I didn't think he could get any paler, but he did and then doubled over in a choking fit. His secretary raced to him with a glass of water and patted his back. We waited, all watching while he was revived. A rat in a corner, that's what he was. Stalling for time.

Finally, he put his hands out to stop me from talking and said in a meek voice, "What do you want?"

"Two things. First, Dr. Isaacson's immediate release. We brought a copy of the coroner's report. As I said, there was no way she could have performed the abortion." I handed the file to him.

That word, abortion, unnerved everyone in the room. His secretary gasped, and we thought the Governor would start choking again. Before he could, I added, "Let's call it what it was, an abortion gone haywire and a dead woman. A crime for which Dr. Isaacson was wrongfully accused. Junior is the one who should be in prison."

I'd never seen a grown man shrink, but he did. He dropped his head in his hands and spoke to the floor. "What else do you want?"

"Restitution."

* * *

Mrs. Garrett broke through Margaret's recounting, reaching for a pastry, a gleeful expression on her face. "I wish I were thirty years younger. What fun I'd have with you sharp girls! At your age, I hadn't the nerve to take command that way. It took years and an ungodly inheritance to get that confident."

Mrs. Thomas chimed in, "Margaret, that was an excellent summary! And you didn't confuse Higgins and Hughes, even once. I can't seem to keep their names straight."

Tillie laughed. "You're not the only one."

Still hanging on Margaret's words, I asked, "What do you mean by restitution? Margaret, what mischief have you been up to?"

"Margaret's brilliant," remarked Mrs. Thomas. "She thought of everything. And, by the way, before we left, the Governor admitted you were a hero for the way you saved lives in that Clinic of yours."

Mrs. Garrett added, "With news spilling about the prison riot in the last days of his term, there was no way Governor Higgins wanted to further tarnish his name. The Governor promised to have you released before New Year's rather than handing your case off to his successor, Hughes, in January. But he insisted we keep his son's ordeal quiet and never speak to the papers."

Only the rich get that kind of extraordinary consideration. I felt my anger rising. No one gave me the benefit of the doubt.

Margaret observed my face. "Hannah, you'll feel better when you hear this." A broad smile crept across her face. "After a few well-placed calls, I discovered there was a pile of money left in the state budget and figured Higgins didn't want to leave it behind for Governor Hughes to spend. It got me thinking." Margaret drew a deep breath, clearly enjoying the suspense. "Since you are dedicated to improving medical care for women, I suggested we'd be satisfied if the funds were allocated for an important project."

"What project?" I asked, wondering if I could conjure the energy to commit to anything new.

"Something to get you started after returning to 'polite' society." Margaret stuck her nose in the air. "Higgins agreed to place the money in a project grant to use for poor women needing medical attention, with you in charge."

I studied her face, confused.

Margaret was breathless with excitement. "Hannah, you can build a new hospital with the grant. If you choose, you can partner with Mount Sinai or Bellevue, or you can construct a spanking new building. It's up to you. And he's giving you $150,000 to kick it off!" Margaret screamed with delight.

My mouth dropped open. It was a staggering amount, perhaps enough to make a true difference.

Chapter Thirty-Two

Tillie kept a careful watch as the days passed after our celebratory dinner. With the instincts of a mother bear, she was the first to notice my retreat. I didn't leave the apartment for days, remaining in bed until noon, tossing and turning, finally rousing with bleary eyes, and then disappearing into my books until evening.

This wasn't my first time retreating from the world. I'd had several rounds of despondency in my childhood following traumatic episodes. I was steady through college but had lows afterwards when my friends set off on their happy married lives, and later when Elspeth passed. The melancholy was powerful, and I sought the refuge of Tillie's home and parlor chairs. So, my wily sister, anticipating what was coming after my ordeal in prison, cut me off at the pass. She understood my attachment to the Queen Anne chairs in her apartment. The softness conformed to my body like a kid glove, the old fabric silky to the touch, smelling of the musky fragrance of family. I could sit for hours with my feet resting on the ottoman, languishing, watching the fire spit and crackle, losing myself in a thick novel. It was my favorite place to hide.

Upon Tillie's return from her first visit at Blackwell's, she sprang into action, anticipating another emotional upheaval. Her parlor furniture, sorely in need of a freshening after a decade of family wear, was reupholstered, beginning with my Queen Anne reading chair. But instead of updating the chair to its original softness, she stuffed it with stiff filling and replaced the silky fabric with a scratchy brocade. Somehow the ottoman disappeared altogether.

Early the morning following my release, we lit a fire and carried our tea to the parlor chairs. "What's this all about?" I pointed to the Queen Anne chair. "The new stuffing is hard as a rock. What in God's name did you put in there, gravel? I used to doze in that chair. You know I don't sleep well. And where did the ottoman go?"

Tillie studied me with her all-business look. "You're too old to hide in a chair, Hannah. You have important matters to attend to. You know Joseph's been calling here twice a day. It's time you faced him. Have you decided what you're going to tell him? What about your work? And now the grant?"

"Tillie, the nightmares are non-stop. I wake in a cold sweat—like a lady going through her changes. Every night I have visions of the Warden's hideous face screaming into mine. It echoes in my head after I wake. I can't shake it. I can't face another thing."

She pulled me into a hug. "I know. I hear you at night. Remember, we've been down this road before, and it always passes. Perhaps if you get busier during the day, you'll find better things to dream about."

I sighed loudly, adding an edge of sarcasm. "Poor little Joseph can wait. Just like he made me wait. Can you imagine sending only two short letters to your fiancée under those vile circumstances? Let him squirm." My anger was mounting. I stood and poked at the fire. "And you know, I heard nothing from Sinai while they had me cooped up there. I can only imagine how they'll point and whisper about me after all the healthy babies I delivered in their name."

Tillie lowered herself into her chair, gesturing to me to follow. "Sit. Let's talk about what you're going to do next with Joseph. At the least, you should meet and have an honest conversation. I'm sure once you do, you can get back on track with the work you love. Your patients need you."

I turned my back on her. "I'm not ready."

Tillie fired back. "You best get ready fast. I invited an old friend to visit this afternoon. If I were you, I'd tidy your dress and comb your hair."

I shot around to face her. "Who's coming? You should have asked before inviting anyone."

No longer placating me, Tillie answered evenly, "You won't mind. It's someone who's known you since you were small."

I knit my brows, searching my memory.

A sharp crack at the door made us both jump.

"I've been telling him to stop using his cane for knocking. He's going to chip my paint," said Tillie scolding as she headed to the front door to let the visitor in.

I stared at my oldest, most trusted friend, Dr. Boro. A few long strides, and I was tucked in his arms. We hadn't seen each other in years. The smell of his cinnamon aftershave was so familiar, so comforting. I could barely restrain my tears.

Tillie clasped her hands, her good nature returning. "Dr. Boro, it's wonderful to see you. Please come in and sit with Hannah by the fire. I'll get refreshments."

"Of course, please come in." I echoed. "It's been far too long." I glanced at Tillie, answering her smile with a nod. "Dr. Boro, how is it that you always find me when I'm in a corner?" I helped him remove his jacket and hung it on a coat hook by the door, noticing his sparse grey hair and deeply etched lines.

"Ah, Hannah, what a dull life it'd be without a few tough corners. But tell me, what was it like in that dreadful prison? I was worried for your safety."

"No, first you, Dr. Boro. How are you feeling? What's happened in your life?" I guided him into a chair and placed a fresh log on the fire.

A crusty laugh. "I'm getting old. I suppose, one of the lucky ones. But my body's tired, and the arthritis is acting up." Dr. Boro reached his hands toward the warm flames.

I could see his swollen joints, reddened and gnarled. His back, once straight as a rod, had developed a slight hunch.

He laughed lightly. "I still spend time with patients, but no more house calls. The steep steps are far too treacherous. And I watch my family grow, trying to keep up with the young ones."

"What's happening at the Clinic? And how's Marta?" I asked, taking his hands, and gently massaging his knuckles.

Tillie entered the room, balancing a full tray. She set the tea cozy on the coffee table and poured the steamy brew into her old china cups. Then she placed a sandwich and napkin in front of Dr. Boro.

He tucked the napkin into his collar and reached for the sandwich. I couldn't help but notice his tremor.

"How'd you guess I hadn't had lunch, young lady? You always seem to know when to feed me."

I watched Tillie, an affectionate glow lighting her eyes, enjoying tending to this quiet man who had touched all our lives, always present to guide us through our greatest challenges. She smiled at him, then returned to the kitchen.

"Yes, back to our talk," he said after a hearty bite. "The Clinic is growing. Have you met the new doctors?"

I shook my head. "No, I've barely left the apartment."

"Hum, so I suspected." He raised his right eyebrow knowingly, then returned to his sandwich. "You must meet them. I'm very pleased with both."

"Who are they?" I asked, knowing full well the true purpose of his visit.

"After you turned us down, we hired Ben Kahn and Josh Greenbaum. Josh trained uptown at Sinai, Ben at Bellevue. Josh was fresh out of medical school, and Ben had practiced surgery a few years up at Sinai. Now he's seeing all patients, surgery or not. Did you know him?"

"Yes, but only in passing. He had a fine reputation."

Dr. Boro cleared his throat. "As you know full well, life can be terribly cruel. A year ago, Ben lost his wife in a carriage accident. Thank God the children weren't with her. Such a wretched tragedy."

I heard Tillie stop fussing in the kitchen as she drew a sharp breath.

He sat back. "His parents still live in the neighborhood. So, he decided to come back to get their help with the young ones."

Tillie stood at the kitchen doorway, wiping her hands on her apron. "Did you say Dr. Kahn?"

Dr. Boro nodded.

"That poor young man. Do you remember he cared for me years back when I was in the hospital? Does he still have that flaming red hair?"

"Is that all you can remember about one of the most brilliant surgeons I've ever worked with?" Dr. Boro sighed. The corners of his mouth curled upward. "You ladies…"

Tillie placed her hand on her chest, the side with her missing breast. "Of course not. He was young then, full of compassion and hope, always checking on me. He knew how frightened I was, that I might die from an infection, like Mama."

Dr. Boro gazed at Tillie. "I know. He's one of the best."

The wheels in my head turned as I realized I'd met Dr. Kahn years ago. "That's why he looked familiar. I'd forgotten," I mused.

Tillie said, "You're remarkable, Dr. Boro, setting up the next generation of doctors for the neighborhood."

Dr. Boro studied us. "You both are very special women." He turned to me. "Hannah, you have important things ahead of you. You know, if you don't want to return to Mount Sinai, you can always join our practice."

I looked at him wistfully, working up the courage to face my new life. "I'll think about it."

He reached for my hand. "But we both know that's not why I'm here. Tell me what's troubling you?"

I knew he'd get around to asking, but I'd forgotten how difficult it was to start sharing painful memories. My words were trapped deep inside. My lips quivered.

He saw my hesitancy. "How are you sleeping?"

A sniffle escaped. I looked at my lap. "Poorly. I have nightmares every night. They scare the living daylights out of me."

"Is it the same dream?" Dr. Boro leaned in my direction, coaxing me to share.

"It is," I said, recounting the parts I could remember:

* * *

The prison walls vibrated, coming to life, creaking, and moaning like an injured animal, waking the prisoners from sleep. Daisy and I rose unsteadily from our

230

beds, holding the metal bunk frame tightly for support. The cell door swung open, unlocked.

"Let's get out of here." Daisy grabbed my arm and pulled me into the corridor.

I felt my way down the dimly lit corridor, holding tightly to Daisy, struggling to maintain our balance as the pulsating waves traveled down the walls into the floor. Finally, we reached the Knitting Hall. Screams and wailing poured out of the workroom with such force, we were pushed away from the entrance. Persisting, pushing back, we inched forward through the gale forces of radiating sound, finally entering the room.

Dead bodies were stacked atop each other, piles of corpses scattered throughout the workroom, all waiting to be moved onto the dead inmate barge tied up by the river. Women continued to fight, gut-wrenching screams penetrating the air. Knitting needles protruded from the dead like pin cushions. My feet felt glued to the shaking floor.

Daisy called out, "I heard a voice in the pile of corpses. She pointed. "Listen, Hannah. There's someone in there."

Still alive, a voice pleaded, "Help me. I want my Mama."

Daisy and I scrambled into the carnage, rolling dead bodies off the woman. It was Nellie, shrunken to the size of a child, barefoot, still holding her dead infant. Frail tiny Daisy reached for Nellie's arm, yanking, attempting to pull her from the heap while I looked for more living souls.

Suddenly, Daisy screamed hysterically. Her shrieks fueled the room's vibrations, knocking me onto the floor.

Daisy held Nellie's arm, ripped free from the woman's body. The fingers were still moving, trying to grasp Daisy's arm, searching for her baby. Suddenly, the limb bent, twisting its way out of Daisy's grip, slithering out of her hands like a snake, disappearing back into the pile of carnage.

Terrified, I gasped helplessly, my eyes still searching for life in the once quiet workroom.

"It's all your fault, smartass bitch! 'Tryin' to change things around here," hollered the Warden, charging at us from behind. Knitting needles protruded through her clothing. "You're both going in for a freezing bath in the river!"

* * *

"That's when I wake, every night." I shuddered, my heart pounding. "Then I recite the 23rd: 'Even though I walk through the valley of the shadow of death, I will fear no evil, for thou art with me; your rod and your staff, they comfort me.' But no matter how many times I say it, I still can't fall back asleep.

For a moment, Dr. Boro sat quietly, digesting the dream. "That's terrifying. It would shake me awake, too. And a fine verse, if I must say so myself. Many a surgeon recited it during the Civil War."

I exhaled a deep breath, relieved to recount my nightmare aloud.

Dr. Boro spoke softly, "Hannah, you can't save everyone. And the Warden is dead. She'll never return."

"I know that. But the dream feels so real. What does it mean?"

He lifted his shoulders. "I'd guess that you were scared witless in there. Who wouldn't be?" His eyes caught mine. "But it's only been a week, dear. You're going to need more time."

He was right. Time played strange tricks on the mind. My patients often told me that while they labored, they thought their contractions would never end, as if time was locked, frozen into moments of anguish. Perhaps I was experiencing something similar.

Dr. Boro interrupted my thought. "When you have another nightmare, I want you to get out of bed, make a cup of warm milk and drink it slowly. While you're drinking, consider how much you accomplished for those prisoners. Feel proud of what you did at Blackwell's. Fight back. Simply having you in that prison clinic, taking care of their ailments, and getting those warm sweaters made their winter bearable. And mainly, I want you to remember that the Warden is gone forever and can never hurt you again."

I digested his words, *never hurt you again*, as I looked into his eyes. "I can do that."

"Then, and only after you are fully settled, feeling strong again, are you to return to bed."

I nodded, beginning to feel a new light, hopeful the Warden would release

232

her unyielding grip.

As the afternoon dissolved into early evening, we continued to talk, stirring the embers, adding more logs. I began to feel myself loosen, realizing it was normal to have pitfalls in life from time to time, nothing I couldn't overcome. In the evening, it grew pitch dark. The smell of roasting chicken filled the apartment with its savory fragrance. For the first time since returning home, my stomach rumbled from hunger. Finally, the apartment door opened, and in walked Abe, returning from work.

Dr. Boro gingerly rose from his chair. "So nice to see you, Abraham. The time slipped away from me. I should be heading home myself."

Tillie stepped into the parlor from the kitchen. "Oh no, Doctor. Stay for dinner. It's almost ready. We have plenty."

Dr. Boro laughed. "I wish I could. But I'm following the same advice I give the widows. I've adopted a dog to care for. Not quite a spouse, but he never talks back so long as he gets his walk, a scratch under his chin, and a bite to eat."

Abe stood at the door, amused, still wearing his coat and hat. "Then give me the pleasure of walking with you. We can catch up on the way."

Dr. Boro shook his head. "Young people, all of you looking after me like I'm going to fall flat on the sidewalk. I don't need an escort."

Tillie hurried to the door with two satchels of food. "Here's something for your icebox, and the other bag has leftovers for your pup. Thank you for visiting."

I held his coat, feeling appreciative as he slipped his arms into the sleeves, marveling at his magical way with people.

Abe placed his derby atop his head. "Did I tell you the joke about the priest, the rabbi, and the minister who walk into a bar..." and handed Dr. Boro his cane, clearly not taking no for an answer. They left the apartment, arm in arm, both laughing.

IV

Part 4

Chapter Thirty-Three

I wrapped my wool tweed coat tightly around myself. The fierce winds of early January had passed, leaving behind subzero temperatures that seeped through my outerwear, stinging my skin. I buried my face deep in my scarf, breathing through the wool, steeling my resolve, concentrating on the words I'd need.

After two weeks hiding from Joseph, I finally agreed to meet him in front of the Gotham Hotel on 55th Street and Fifth Avenue. Open only a year, it was known for its lovely conference rooms and numerous seating alcoves, perfect for private conversations between businessmen or lovers. We were neither. I touched the soft jewelry pouch in my coat pocket. His ruby ring, a beautiful family heirloom, was no longer meant for me.

"There you are!" Joseph called from the end of the block, his long legs taking two lengths for every stride of mine. "Let me look at you." He reached for my shoulders, holding me at arm's length. "My beautiful girl. You've come back."

Not expecting his eager reaction, I shuddered, feeling doubt. Could this be the same man who'd abandoned me in prison? My eyes glazed with tears.

Joseph studied my face. "My little bird, you've flown home to me." He drew me into his chest, enclosing me in his arms. "I'm here now."

His warmth was intoxicating, falsely reassuring. A streak of mistrust shot through me. Yes, this is the same man he always was. *Hannah, you've no need for him.*

I firmly pushed Joseph away. "We need to talk. Let's go inside."

"Of course. We must catch up. It's all somewhat overwhelming. Could it be a month and a half already?" He took my arm in the crook of his elbow and guided me through the over-sized brass-trimmed doors into the lobby. Looking about for a place to talk, finally asking the receptionist, "Could you kindly direct us to the Red Room? Is there's a chance they'd fix us each a warm cup of coffee?"

The porter, a young, clean-shaven man wearing a simple dark, fitted suit and red bellboy hat, pointed to the staircase on the left, pulling his pocket watch from his coat. "I believe they're still serving."

I'd no interest in coffee. This ridiculous engagement had to end. Lingering with food or drink served no purpose. I silently rehearsed Tillie's advice: *Keep it quick.* Barely a few weeks out of Blackwell's, I was still shocked by the opulence around me, access to any food or drink I desired. I knew I'd never take a crumb for granted again.

Entering the Red Room, I drank in the atmosphere of the small room, tall ceiling and red velvet arrangements of mahogany trimmed couches and matching chairs. Joseph selected a cluster of seats by the fireplace. "Let's sit over there."

We removed our coats. Joseph sat on the couch while I chose the opposite armchair. An ornate wood table sat between us. I looked at him carefully. Why was his hair disheveled? Had he bothered to brush it? His shirt was askew, buttoned wrong. Had he rushed to arrive on time?

"Have a late night?" I asked, my voice tight.

He ran his fingers through his hair and examined his shirt. "Whoops, I was in a bit of a hurry this morning, slept late." He corrected the buttons.

I wondered where he'd been. Out with the men, courting more nurses? I stuffed a loose curl back into my chignon, my annoyance barely controlled. "I'm disappointed I hardly heard from you while I was in prison. Why was that?"

Joseph reached across the couch for my hands.

I pulled them away and clasped them on my lap. I had no desire to touch him.

He ignored my question. "Tell me, how do you feel?"

I peered into his eyes. "Abandoned by you. I know who my friends are now. You know, the ones who helped me get out of that god-forsaken place. Why didn't you offer to help? Did you think I was guilty?"

He squirmed uneasily. "I never doubted your innocence. It's just that I wasn't needed. Sometimes it's best to lay low and not get in the way. Too many cooks in the kitchen, right?"

"That's nonsense," I shot back through clenched teeth. "You were ready to cut me loose. I know you and your scheming sister too well to believe that rubbish."

"Hannah, you're out now. We can begin again. I still love you with all my heart." Joseph reached again for my hands. "Please don't pull away. I didn't know how to deal with such an awful—"

I cut him off. "Neither did I. But when people are in love, they'll do anything to help save their dearest. I reached into my satchel and pulled out *The Gift of the Magi*, the book my sister brought to me in prison, setting it halfway between us. Then I pulled the engagement ring from the coin purse in my pocket, placing it atop the book.

He shook his head vigorously. "What's this? Oh, come now, Hannah. You're too fast on the trigger. Let's give it some time," he pleaded.

"Like you did? Dating other women? Did you think I wouldn't hear?" I scoffed.

The color drained from his face. "But—"

"You've already moved on," I accused him. "You thought I wouldn't get out and didn't want to waste a second or offer to help. That's not love."

He looked at the table. "I'm so sorry, Hannah. I'll try harder. I promise."

"That's a joke. You throw promises around like holiday candy. The problem is obvious—you don't truly love me." I pointed to the book. "You should read this. Maybe you'll get an inkling of what true love looks like, what people will sacrifice for each other. Maybe someday, you'll understand what I'm talking about."

Joseph shook his head, ignoring the book. "I'm sure we'll get there if you give us more time. Please forgive me."

I was finished. "No, Joseph, it's over. You're not the man for me." I stood tall and reached for my coat, walking out of the Red Room, down the stairs, and through the lobby door while draping my coat around me, not pausing or turning back to see his reaction. Tired of his empty proclamations of love, I was relieved the engagement was over. I wanted to seal that door closed and move forward with my life.

I walked twenty icy blocks north on Fifth Avenue beside Central Park, all the way to Rebecca and Leo's. Fortunately, they'd kept my room and clothing waiting for my return. I'd planned to stay with them tonight before my meeting at Mount Sinai.

I had my handkerchief in my pocket, anticipated a round of crying, but I'd cried my last tear for Joseph back in prison. The realization struck that I'd begun letting go of him for months, and I was ready to move on. Instead of tears, a calm descended over me as a new window in my life opened.

It was impossible to ignore the homeless scattered across the icy street hobbling out of Central Park, where they sheltered for the night. My romantic disappointment paled in comparison to these ragged souls. The grant had given me a vital purpose, an important lease on life.

* * *

In true Isaacson fashion, Rebecca had prepared a lovely afternoon meal, greeting me at the door with a hug that rocked me back on my heels. "Come right in, sweetheart. How about a little wine to warm you?"

"I know it's early, but today I need it." I removed my coat and boots, falling into a soft chair by the fire. I lifted my stocking feet onto an ottoman, luxuriating as the fire's warmth penetrated my body. Here, I felt safe and loved. Exactly the mindset I needed to prepare for the next hurdle, facing the formidable hospital leadership at Mount Sinai.

Rebecca brought two glasses of sherry and a tray of sliced cheese to the coffee table and sat beside me. "Hannah, I can't shake the image of those women locked in that freezing cold prison. Leo was horrified when he heard about the conditions. He convinced Bloomingdale's to donate a large case of sweaters."

"I didn't know." I gazed at her basket of knitting, thinking about the deadly knitting needles and how in just a week since meeting with Dr. Boro, they'd begun to loosen their haunting grip on my dreams. "Rebecca, did you ever wonder if I was really innocent?"

Rebecca drew her head back in shock, her voice rising. "Of course not. You're not capable of committing a crime like that. How could you ask such a thing?"

I sighed. "I just met with Joseph and got the feeling he thought I might not get out. He'd begun flirting at the hospital, looking for a new girl to court."

Rebecca sat back in the chair, her face impassive. "I see. I'm so sorry, Hannah."

I shook my head and took a long sip of the wine. Its bouquet was floral, delicious. The warmth rolled down the back of my throat. "It's over. I wish I'd realized sooner that he wasn't right for me. Such a waste." My eyes glistened with tears. "Do you think I'll ever meet anyone who'll love me? Really love me?"

Rebecca leaned over and held my hand. "Hannah, don't be so rough on yourself. You've just been through a terrible ordeal. Give yourself time to heal. The light will return."

I stared into the flames, melting into the soft cushions. The fire crackled, spitting intense heat in my direction. I welcomed the warmth, summoning it inside my body, my heart. Fire, as timeless and elemental as love. Yes, the light would return.

* * *

I sat alone at eight a.m., waiting in the dark-paneled Board Room of Mount Sinai. Formal portraits of hospital presidents in gilded frames were affixed to a long wall, medical staff presidents on the opposite wall. The men's dueling eyes stared at each other from across the room, engaged in an age-long battle of wills. The mahogany table was polished to a high gloss, fitting for a space weighed down with matters of gravitas. An enormous grandfather clock stood against the wall. Overhead electric lighting cast a dull glow, emitting a soft buzz. By late morning, generous quantities of daylight would pass through the tall windows replacing the artificial light that strained my eyes and set my nerves on fire.

Stop picking at your nails, I scolded myself. Why was I so on edge? I'd done nothing wrong. The meeting should be quick. I planned to start back at the office by the next Monday and spend today discussing ideas for the state grant. My chief concern was rebuilding my practice after the two-month absence.

But I was vexed by my call last week to the President of the Medical Staff's office. I'd expected a warm reception. Instead, over the staticky line, Dr. Lehr's secretary delivered a frosty message. "The Hospital Presidents want to meet with you in the Board Room. They have matters to discuss." It was the first time I considered the possibility that things may not go smoothly. *What could they possibly need to discuss?*

I squirmed in my seat, impatient to get on with the meeting. Finally, the door opened, and two distinguished older gentlemen entered. I recognized them both. Years earlier, when I moved to New York from Baltimore, I interviewed with Dr. Lehr, the Medical Staff President. He wore a tired tweed jacket, his chin cleanly shaven with a grey moustache. A serious man, he was known to be brilliant, and highly private. The second gentleman, Mr. Blum, had been president of the hospital for the last few years. It was our first face-to-face meeting. Having managed various portions of the hospital in the past, he was known as a stickler for detail, and had a mercurial, Napoleonic temper. Short and rotund, he sported a monocle. Beneath it, a scornful frown.

I rose to greet them.

"Good morning, Dr. Isaacson." They said in succession. Dr. Lehr shook my hand warmly. Mr. Blum nodded, avoiding physical contact.

Mr. Blum cleared his throat, briefly glancing at my face. "Dr. Isaacson, I'm Mr. Blum, President of the Hospital."

I attempted to inject a dose of warmth. "I've seen you about the hospital. It's a pleasure to finally meet in person."

"Please have a seat." Dr. Lehr gestured at the matching plush chairs surrounding the table, sat in one, and began the discussion. "First, let me say, we are relieved you were released and back home. I can only imagine what an unspeakably bleak time you encountered."

I nodded, pleased he'd shown concern. "It was, but I'm excited to be here and can't wait to return to my patients."

The room grew silent. The grandfather clock ticked loudly.

I smoothed my skirt, a growing dread in my belly. I added, "It was also an unexpected education. I learned a tremendous amount about the poorest people living in our city."

"Interesting." Dr. Lehr pulled a pipe bag from the pocket of his starched white coat, stuffed a small amount of tobacco in the chamber of his bent billiard, and lit a match. "Do go on." He took a long draw while lighting the bowl.

"Prison corruption aside, I received a comprehensive education on the dismal health of our city's poor, starting with issues of basic hygiene. We have an uphill crusade to create a healthier city. Their prison clinic didn't help matters. It was an unspeakable disgrace. No one cared an iota." I exhaled, more comfortable discussing a topic I knew so intimately.

Mr. Blum added, "We admired your chutzpah, dear, arranging the warm clothing for the prisoners. Bold move."

Why did his tone sound condescending? I looked from Mr. Blum back to Dr. Lehr, wondering whether I should share the Governor's project. Instead, I tried a different tact, "I couldn't help but think our resident physicians would benefit from spending a few weeks working there. It would be an excellent education about the diseases on the street, malnutrition, and the basic health needs in the city."

Dr. Lehr twisted the hairs in his moustache, leaning against the back of his chair. "Interesting thought." He faced Mr. Blum. "How do you think the idea would be received?"

Mr. Blum picked invisible lint off his suit legs. "You and I should discuss it at greater length." He said firmly, "Later."

I was determined to continue. "As you know, our Women's Hospital

Auxiliary came to the rescue, donating medical supplies and a barge filled with sweaters. I understand our mighty Mrs. Lowenstein found her counterpart at Saint Patrick's and rallied the ladies of New York." I smiled, lips pursed, worried and curious to discover the secret concealed behind their dark looks.

Dr. Lehr cleared his throat. "Mr. Blum, perhaps we should step outside a moment and discuss this privately before we continue."

Mr. Blum shot back. "Absolutely not. It's done."

Dr. Lehr squirmed uncomfortably. "This makes the Board's decision more difficult than we intended."

I searched his face. My heart grew heavy as I braced myself for bad news. "How so?"

"I won't beat around the bush, doctor. You are a gifted and energetic physician who clearly advocates for your patients. But unfortunately, we need to remove you from the medical staff, effective immediately. You violated material provisions in your contract, the first requiring written permission from the hospital to accept outside work, such as your agreement with the Waldorf. Unfortunately, you did not have our approval."

I had anticipated hearing this line of argument and was prepared with my answer. "But, doctor, many of the other medical staff hold part-time commitments outside Mount Sinai. Some even have private practices. It's common. Are you saying they have all submitted proper documentation?"

Dr. Lehr set his pipe in the large metal ashtray and gestured at Mr. Blum to continue.

Mr. Blum coughed into his hand. "Dr. Isaacson, as the hospital president, it's my job to safeguard the institute's reputation. You also violated the contract clause prohibiting conduct that could cast the hospital in an unfavorable light. The sensational publicity not only created a horrific backlash for the hospital, but for Jewish doctors as well. Aren't you aware of the antisemitism in this city? How do you reconcile your actions with the responsibility toward your Jewish colleagues?" He sneered, drilling vengeful eyes into mine.

I sat taller, carefully choosing my words, knowing they'd be my final defense. "When I arrived at the hotel, the poor woman, whom I'd never met, had practically bled to death. I did what any responsible physician would do. Try to save her life. Blaming me is terribly unfair because nothing that transpired was my fault. The police and press didn't wait for legitimate evidence before subjecting me and that poor woman's tragedy to the court of public opinion." I breathed deeply, summoning my courage to continue. "Although it may have been unfortunate for the hospital and the Jewish doctors of New York, at its core, I'm guiltless in this fiasco. What you're saying lays an absurd amount of blame on an innocent doctor."

Dr. Lehr lifted his pipe to his lips, applying a newly struck match to the bowl. "Fair point, doctor. And I concede, at the heart of the matter, it is unfair."

Mr. Blum shot a sharp warning glance at his colleague, cutting in. "But such is the vast responsibility of the profession. Mount Sinai experienced a decline in admissions and must work to repair its reputation because of the press picnic. The entire hospital has suffered. This misfortune will hang over us for years. All due to your actions."

I looked at my lap, fighting back a rush of tears. No matter what defense I mounted, they had decided to make me bear the responsibility. I'd have to start a medical practice somewhere else after all my years of hard work. My ears rang with disbelief.

Dr. Lehr puffed on his pipe, finally adding in a calm voice. "That's why we decided you may reapply for privileges in three years once the ashes from this fire have blown into the East River and are forgotten. In the meantime, no one's challenging your competence as a physician, and your license remains intact."

For a moment, I considered taking a last shot and sharing the news of the state grant. Perhaps that would tip the balance and convince them to change their minds. But that notion was interrupted by Mr. Blum.

"Look at it this way, dear. It's a good opportunity to marry that cardiologist you've been pining after. You can finally get your family started." He sat back, hands clasped on his portly belly, looking pleased with himself.

My face burned at this final insult. I said through clenched teeth, "I am not your 'dear' and have no intention of stepping to the sidelines to make babies instead of fulfilling my life's devotion to medicine."

"I, er, didn't mean it in a disparaging way," he answered, floundering for the right words. "As you well know, especially as an obstetrics practitioner, motherhood is also a noble calling."

I stood and took a deep breath. "I'll collect my things." *Hold your head high, Hannah.*

Mr. Blum said evenly. "No need. We have your personal belongings boxed. Just tell the secretary where to send them."

I rose from my chair, reeling with indignation. They had been fully prepared to fire me when I'd called for my appointment. There was no way in hell they would see a nickel of the grant. I wanted to tell them so, but bit back my furious words. *Don't burn bridges*, something inside me said. "Very well, gentlemen." I nodded once, walking stiffly from the room. Once the door latched behind me, I hurried down the hallway into the stairwell, barely able to breathe, and grabbed the banister while thick tears soaked my cheeks.

Chapter Thirty-Four

Early the next morning, after returning to Tillie's apartment, I rummaged through the coat closet for my old muffler. Wrapped snugly in my warm clothes, I stepped outside into the freezing air. Although the sky was clear, the temperature had dipped again after a late-night storm that left the streets and sidewalks covered in a pristine white blanket. I knew its beauty would soon be sullied by carts and horses, but the magic of fresh snow reflecting the brilliant rays of morning sunlight filled me with optimism. I knew I would find a solution for the grant money, as well as where I'd find it. My fury at Mount Sinai had turned to action; the kindling in my spirit ignited into full-blown indignation. I'd show them a thing or two.

As my boots crunched through the snow, I surveyed the rapid changes in the Lower East Side. There was growth everywhere. New apartment buildings, businesses, and markets had sprung out of the ground like spring's new growth. Even at this hour, street vendors erected their movable shops, appearing one after another, popping up out of nowhere. The Lower East Side burst with industry, multitudes of people from all over the world, starting new lives with little more than hope. A Model T zipped through the streets, honking at people meandering in its path, adding a new sound to the discordant symphony of the neighborhood.

My first stop was Moshe's Bakery and Delicatessen. Jostling my way through the packed shop, I ordered a dozen hot bialys for my morning visit. Back on the sidewalk, I held the bag to my nose, inhaling the pungent onion smell. I wanted to bring something warm and delicious, especially for Dr.

Boro, a life-long early riser. Today was my new beginning.

Dr. Boro had successfully piqued my curiosity, describing his Clinic expansion, new procedure room, and additional doctors. According to Tillie, the old Clinic hadn't moved. Could this be the right use for the grant? Trudging through the snow, passing one apartment building after another, I wondered if most women down here still delivered their babies at home. Were any choosing to deliver at Beth Israel? Was it too expensive? And where were the midwives receiving their education and training, if any? It was imperative that midwife training be an integral part of the grant. Could better sanitation help stem the tide of childbed fever? So many thoughts flooded my mind that I lost track of time. Before I realized how far I'd walked, I found myself at the door of the Clinic.

Startled at the renovations, I slowed, taking in all the details. The freshly painted exterior glowed in the sunlight. A large sign hung beside the door, listing the names of physicians and midwives. Inside, beige walls and new, plaid upholstered furniture welcomed me. Educational posters in Yiddish and English lined the walls. Although many newcomers brought poverty with them from the old country, the Clinic sent the message that life would be welcoming, safer, and more hopeful in this new corner of the world. I made a note to myself to stop by the Settlement House after my visit. I hoped Mrs. Simon, one of Tillie's oldest and dearest friends, was still there.

I walked through the empty waiting area toward the rooms in the rear of the Clinic with a new excitement. Conversation spilled out of Dr. Boro's office. Peeking around the door, I saw an office packed with staff, sitting on the arms of chairs, standing, sharing coffee, engaged in lively discussion.

"Why, come in, Hannah." Dr. Boro greeted me and then addressed the group. "I'd like all of you to meet my dear colleague, Dr. Hannah Isaacson." He proceeded to present me to everyone—three physicians, two midwives, and a nurse.

He paused before introducing Dr. Kahn. "I believe you two met years ago at Mount Sinai. Hannah's older sister, Tillie Levine, was a patient of yours, Ben. Have you worked together more recently?"

I looked at his curly ginger hair and watery blue eyes. Yes, there was something familiar, but if Dr. Boro hadn't mentioned Dr. Kahn when at Tillie's, I may not have remembered.

Dr. Kahn cocked his head, an inviting smile on his face. "Of course, I know you, the esteemed obstetrician. And by the way, how is your sister?"

He remembered.

"My sister, Tillie, is fine. No recurrence of her disease, thank God." That old dread roiled in my stomach.

He nodded. "Cancer still eludes us. We were lucky to catch hers early. Weren't you still in high school? Smart as a whip, as I recall."

I blushed. He remembered more than I would have guessed. How was that possible after so many years? I examined his face. His bushy brows softened his aquiline nose, making him appear more gentle than sharp. "How did you remember?"

He studied me, answering in a solemn tone. "I always remember the ones we saved. There were so few."

My stomach dropped. Breast cancer was usually a death sentence. Most cancers were. I'd have to stop taking Tillie's outcome for granted. Who knew where I'd be today without her in my life?

I nodded, considering my good fortune. "We were lucky to have you there, helping. Years earlier, my blessed mother didn't fare so well. Infection."

Dr. Boro, sensing the sober turn in the conversation, jumped in. "I invited Hannah to meet all of you and see how the Clinic has progressed. We're working hard to keep up with the community's needs. There's always so much more to do."

My attention moved to Marta, Dr. Boro's midwife, who permitted me to shadow her while I was in high school. She was waiting patiently to get a word in. "Marta, how are you?"

Her broad smile broke through the deep wrinkles on her face, revealing her bright inner zest. "Still laboring day and night with the mamas. But now, some are saving their pennies to deliver at the hospital. They want the anesthesia. Who can blame them?"

I nodded, understanding the dilemma in ways she might never imagine. I hoped to steal a few minutes in private, eager to discuss how the patient shift to the hospital affected her practice. I also wanted to find out more about how she put devices into her patients' hands and if she had any information about who was performing abortions downtown.

Dr. Kahn waved his hand, drawing my attention back to him. "Have you been following the news of the new maternity hospital on Broadway? It will be named the Jewish Maternity Hospital, and we expect it to open in the next couple of years. I'll wager it'll be bursting at the seams the first month."

My heart raced. "That's extraordinary. The city wants to build again after moving the Jew Hospital uptown to Mount Sinai?" My curiosity was ignited.

Dr. Boro stroked his beard. "It's not the city. It's backed by a synagogue. No one expected the flood of families from Europe. And they're mostly young, all having babies. We desperately need another neighborhood hospital."

I felt Dr. Kahn's eyes boring down on me. Did they know about the state grant? Impossible. Only my closest friends knew, and they'd been sworn to secrecy.

Dr. Kahn cleared his throat. "I've heard through the Sinai grapevine that you may be looking for another position." He lifted his brows invitingly. "There's no doubt we could use a talented obstetrician in our group. These days, Dr. Boro has all of us delivering babies, and as much as I enjoy bringing life into the world, I'd like to get back to the operating theater."

It appeared that news of my expulsion had leaked out before reaching my ears. Despite my annoyance, my spirits were buoyed, knowing they wanted my skills despite my tarnished reputation. "You make the opportunity enticing." I forced a smile as I handed Marta the bakery bag. "Good food for thought. Speaking of food, how about some bialys straight from the bakery."

I longed to share the exciting news of the grant. But until I spoke with officials at Bellevue, the city-funded hospital for the poorest in the city, I knew it best to keep the money a secret. Once disclosed, all future discussions would be tainted by my new worth, even among my closest allies.

Those thoughts evaporated as I relaxed, enjoying the comradery of this extraordinary group of professionals, all deeply tied to the community and its future. Eventually, they shifted from local news to the more mundane, sorting through cases for the day, assigning house visits, and Clinic coverage. I bid my goodbyes, promising to return soon.

Dr. Kahn walked me to the outer door. "Doctor, would you mind if I followed up with you to discuss the position here? I'm quite serious about the offer."

I looked into his eyes. "Of course, I'd like that." I paused. "And Dr. Kahn, I am terribly sorry to hear of your misfortune."

He answered with a faraway expression. "Thank you. It's been more than a year, but sometimes it feels like yesterday."

Behind me, I heard sniffling. An older gentleman in rumbled clothing was seated behind us in the waiting room, leaning on his wooden cane, blowing his nose in his handkerchief. Before I could react, Dr. Kahn was bent beside him, placing his arm around the man's shoulder, speaking softly in Yiddish.

"There, there, Mr. Dvorkin, let me help you back to an exam room where I can look at you. I am sure there's something I can do to help."

A swell of tenderness grew in my chest as I watched Dr. Kahn guide the gentleman past me. On the way, he gave me a tight-lipped nod.

* * *

I crossed Henry Street to visit Mrs. Simon at the Settlement House. In stark contrast to the Clinic, the building looked tired, sorely needing a renovation. But its familiarity evoked a strange nostalgia, one filled with a mixture of joy and sadness. The Settlement House on Henry Street had been part of my life from the day I moved in with Tillie—the Jewish school, the adjacent synagogue, the Clinic. It was the entry point for most Jewish immigrants. As I recalled from an early age, the Settlement House was managed with great effectiveness by Mrs. Simon and her team of enthusiastic volunteers.

The sound of foreign languages flowing through the doorway had changed from German to Polish and Russian, but the tattered clothing was still the same. And the look of want and hope on the faces of the families waiting in the hallways was still heartbreaking. The same frayed tuberculosis posters hung on the walls, reminding me of the persistent, deadly grip the disease held on this vulnerable community. Would it ever end?

I found Mrs. Simon hunched over the table in the tiny kitchen, sipping her tea, deep in thought. The scene reminded me of mornings when I'd accompanied Tillie to the Settlement House and shared an early breakfast while they excitedly sorted through plans for the language school and food pantry. Those days, sitting in my little chair by the stove taught me how dedicated women could face and solve our community's challenges. The grant was desperately needed on the Lower East Side.

Mrs. Simon's low bun, barely held together with straight pins, seemed more unraveled than usual. Tight corkscrew wisps of grey hairs fanned the sides of her face, refusing to be tamed. Despite her frazzled appearance, her dark eyes darted to the doorway when I approached, immediately softening as she recognized me, radiating warmth. "How lovely to see you, Hannah. Tillie mentioned during services that you might be staying with her a while. Make yourself a cup and sit."

Standing at the sink, stirring milk in my tea, I wondered how much I should share. Mrs. Simon seemed more worn than the last time we'd met. I could only imagine the weight she shouldered. But I'd hoped to explore possibilities for Daisy, who was due to leave Blackwell's in the next few weeks. Should I give Mrs. Simon another weight to carry? I lowered myself onto a flattened cushion set atop wooden chair.

Mrs. Simon smiled. "It's been a long time. I can't begin to tell you what a sight you are for sore eyes. It's good to have you back on this side of the river.

I shook my head, tired of reliving my tale. "I was just at the Clinic and can't believe how much it's grown. What's happening here at the Settlement House?"

She brushed back a spray of loose hair, looking resigned. "I'm growing too old for this. It's not the same world it was years back. When I met your sister in 1880, we saw only the start of the exodus. We had no idea it was just a drizzle before the downpour." She sighed. "I never in a million years could have imagined so many frightened people would leave their homelands. If we'd known then how many thousands were coming, we would have planned better."

I was surprised to hear her minimize her efforts. "Mrs. Simon, you've done so much, more than anyone I know. Your generosity with everyone who comes through your doors has saved lives, kept families together. They'd be lost without you. And you've managed to draw in support from all over the city, even from the rich Jews uptown. How could any of us possibly have known immigrants would continue to pour in?"

Her voice was uncommonly sharp-edged. "Honestly, the German Jews, you know, the wealthy ones uptown you're referring to—the Lehmans, Seligmans, and Loebs—look down their noses at the Jews from the east. Their own people, for God's sake. They should donate far more than they do. After all, they're filthy rich from their banking schemes!" Mrs. Simon's dark brows gathered into deeply creased lines. "They give a pittance, guilt money. Most of their big gifts go to the opera and museums so they can impress the Vanderbilts and Carnegies. They conveniently forget they started out peddling rags on the street, just like the rest of us."

I felt her frustration. It wasn't like her to sound jaded, but I could understand her annoyance after all these years. Even at Mount Sinai on the Upper East Side, derogatory comments were made about the Russian Jews—that they were peasants—dirty. At the hospital, there were few Eastern Jews, Ina an exception. It was discouraging watching Jews hold back their own people, perhaps the worst discrimination of all.

Mrs. Simon brightened. "At least now we're getting good donations from the garment factory owners downtown. They're sending steady support and, most important, hiring the immigrants. Jobs are the fastest way out of the tenements." She paused thoughtfully. "By the way, have you heard about the new maternity hospital?"

"Yes." I beamed. "I heard this morning at the Clinic. Very exciting news."

"Dr. Boro will be an honorary Board member. Did you know he started his practice right after the War between the States? He's seen it all." She probed me with searching eyes. "Now, tell me about you."

I grimaced, knowing I couldn't slip one by her. She was going to persuade me to talk one way or another. I took a sip of tea and set the cup on the table, resigned to again relive my distressing tale. "Mrs. Simon, it's difficult to know where to begin. In the last few months, I've learned more about the poor and their plight than I could have ever dreamt." I sighed. "I don't know how you've managed all these years."

Mrs. Simon tilted her cup back and forth, the liquid rolling. "I suppose it was a calling. Otherwise, it's impossible to explain. I came from a wealthy German family uptown. My parents constantly reminded me that I married beneath our family and then moved to the ghetto. That's what they called it here, as if our neighborhood wasn't inhabited with living, breathing people. They all but disowned me. My husband, Saul, died young, and although there've been chances to leave everything behind and move in with my widowed sister uptown, I just can't. Every time I come close, a hungry child holding his mama's hand walks into the building, and my motherly instincts take over. I feed them, and fret where the child will sleep. I can't stop myself."

Her words pulled at my heart. Did I have that depth of calling? Was that my future? Or would I drift back to wealthy uptown patients and plan vacations on steamers to gilded European cities? Torn in two, I wasn't certain what I wanted, which choice would make me happier, more fulfilled.

I considered her sacrifices. "Your work is what keeps us going. It's why I didn't see many Jewish inmates at Blackwell's. It's not the same story for other groups. The churches are overwhelmed with generations of poverty in their parishes. They haven't had your success."

Mrs. Simon shook her head sadly. "The churches lost their opportunity to step in early. They had no idea what they were up against with the number of starving Irish. They were far worse off than our people."

"And the city always turns its back, putting its money elsewhere," I added.

"It's true, but it's the way of the world," she sighed.

I placed my hands on the table. "Mrs. Simon, I want to discuss an idea I had while I was at Blackwell's." I paused. Why did I suddenly find it near impossible to say the name?

"A new idea? You sound just like your sister." She studied me curiously, the corners of her mouth curling up. "And please, call me Judy."

I sat back. "As you know, the Workhouse Warden had me running their Clinic while I was there. There was a young woman, Daisy, who assisted me. She was a natural—smart, organized, with great instincts. I know her life could be so much better if she only had a chance to become a real nurse."

She reminisced, "Your sister gave jobs to so many when she ran her factory."

I'd forgotten how Mrs. Simon read people. "Yes, but I don't want to give her a handout. She should be given the chance for a vocation, so she can build a better life. She's not yet twenty."

"I don't know, Hannah. We have more on our plate than ever before. I'm not sure we can take on another project."

I was determined to convince Mrs. Simon. "We'll need nurses for the new hospital, and if we could find a way to start a nursing school, maybe attached to a hospital, we could also help girls like Daisy." Was I getting ahead of myself? I hadn't spent time thinking the idea through, nor checked out existing schools. "I may be jumping the gun, but we'd reap far more rewards than it would cost. The students would only need a safe place to live and a way to work off their debt. It could mean a new start for so many." I paused then added, "Do you have an assistant who could help you with this?"

Mrs. Simon stirred her tea, humming softly to herself. I waited patiently for her to consider the idea.

Finally, she said, "I heard there's a new nursing school not too far from here at Beth Israel Hospital. It even houses the students." A small smile crept across her face. "Shall I arrange a meeting, see if we can work together? And yes, I know the perfect person to help."

* * *

That evening, sitting uncomfortably beside Tillie in her refurbished Queen Anne chairs by the fire, I recounted the details of my day, my visits to the Clinic and Settlement House. "I had no idea they were building another hospital down here. Had you heard?" I asked. "Dr. Kahn said it was in the paper."

Tillie sat quietly, thinking. "I didn't know. I don't read the papers like I used to, too much bad news. But I should get more involved in the Settlement House again. My nights teaching English helped me understand Mama and Papa's journey to America."

"It makes perfect sense they'd build one," I thought aloud, barely listening to her reminiscing. "It's unfortunate they moved Sinai uptown years back. Apparently, Beth Israel makes almost everyone pay."

Tillie nodded. "No one could have ever guessed so many would leave Europe. Don't forget, the hospital moved before the Civil War, when most German Jews lived further uptown. It was Irish down here, and they had Saint Vincent's and Bellevue."

"It would have taken a mighty good tea reader to know what was coming next," I said. "But it makes for an interesting opportunity. By the way, Tillie, I haven't mentioned the grant money to anyone but you. I'd like to keep it quiet for now."

Dring, rang the telephone in the foyer vestibule.

Tillie jumped up. "I'll get it." She hurried into the foyer. "Hello. Why yes, let me get her." She called to me. "Hannah, it's for you!"

I mouthed, *who is it?*

Tillie shrugged. Why hadn't she asked?

Frowning in my sister's direction, I said, "Hello, this is Hannah Isaacson."

A deep voice vibrated in the earpiece. "Good morning, Dr. Isaacson. It's Dr. Lehr from Mount Sinai. I was hoping you might have time to speak to me again."

My anger returned with a strong jolt. What could he possibly want? I was silent.

"Hello. Dr. Isaacson? Are you still on the line?"

I hesitated. "Yes, yes, I am. I'm just surprised to hear from you."

Dr. Lehr cleared his throat. "Well, yes. I'll get right to the point. Early this week, Mr. Blum and I had an introductory meeting with our new Governor, Hughes. He asked if you had met with us yet, you know, concerning a grant. I'm astonished you hadn't shared the exciting news."

I didn't know quite how to respond, but I appreciated his directness. So, I matched it with my own. "I intended to discuss the grant, but you didn't give me much of a chance. It seemed you, and Mr. Blum were quite determined to get me out the door." I exhaled a slow, quiet breath, calming my nerves.

"Err, yes. That was a grievous error on my part, particularly after you ignited my interest by discussing the health needs of the inmates and opportunities for our residents."

I could hear him puffing his pipe. He *had* been listening that morning.

Dr. Lehr pressed on. "Dr. Isaacson, would you be willing to meet with me again? I'm far less concerned about hospital publicity than Mr. Blum. My utmost concern is the future health needs of the city and the hospital resources required to meet those needs. I state the obvious when I say that such grant opportunities don't come along every day."

I wasn't inclined to respond too effusively. "No, they don't."

"I share your concern about the effect poverty has on those in the city and, at the very least, would be grateful if we could discuss your thoughts regardless which hospital you choose."

I hesitated. I had always held Dr. Lehr in high regard. He had been listening earnestly before Mr. Blum lowered the gavel. What harm could there be in another meeting? "Yes, let's talk, but not in the Board Room or the hospital. I don't want to be seen there, considering how I was treated. At least not yet."

A pause. "I know this is last minute, but is there any chance an early lunch tomorrow could work before your afternoon appointments? You name the place and time, and I'll be there."

Things were beginning to look up. "Very well, do you know Healy's Café? On 18th and Irving near Washington Square Park? Let's meet there at noon."

"Of course. I know the place."

What I didn't need to remind him was that the café was two blocks from Beth Israel Hospital, one of their chief competitors. I glanced up from the telephone and saw Tillie standing with her arms crossed, wearing a smile that matched mine.

Chapter Thirty-Five

I arrived at the cafe a half hour early, hoping to settle myself and collect my thoughts. I couldn't help but replay our last meeting at the hospital when Dr. Lehr terminated my privileges. I was hurt and angry and could not imagine what he could possibly say to change my mind.

In my booth toward the rear of the café, I could feel a blast of cold air each time the door opened. A loud bell hung from a hinge, clanging when a customer entered or exited. By noon, my coffee cup was practically empty, its remnants cold, but my brain was on fire. I was certain his only motivation for meeting was to claim the grant money.

The bell clanged. I glanced at the door, and Dr. Lehr met my gaze with a nod. His cheeks were red from the harsh air, and from my perch, I could see his lips set in a firm line, prepared for a difficult conversation.

Satisfied he was taking me seriously, I adjusted my posture and relaxed my shoulders. For the first time, I viewed myself as his equal. Especially now that he wanted something from me. "Good morning, Doctor. Please sit and warm up."

He hung his overcoat and hat on a coat rack behind our booth and carefully lowered himself into the chair opposite me, rubbing his hands together for warmth. Without his white coat, he appeared far less imposing, simply an aging man, not the giant of academia I knew. "Thank you, Doctor, for making time to meet me," he said. "It's been a while since I've been to this neighborhood. The place has changed."

I couldn't imagine him ever visiting this part of the city. "Did you train at Bellevue?"

He cocked his head, looking into my eyes. "No, this is where I lived as a child."

I was flabbergasted. Was he spinning a tale to soften me up? I'd always assumed he was from the Upper East Side, where most affluent German Jews lived, worked, and attended school. "That's a surprise. I was raised in an apartment practically around the corner."

The waitress approached our table, interrupting the conversation. "What'll it be? Coffee or ale?"

We answered simultaneously, "Coffee," then smiled at each other. For doctors, ale was out of the question until after work hours.

The waitress set gravy-stained menus on the table. "I'll be back in a minute to take your orders."

Dr. Lehr exhaled deeply. "I know you're angry with me, with all of us at the hospital. You have a perfect right to be. But I hope you will hear me out."

Was he foolish enough to think I'd pick up where I left off before my arrest, competing with his staff of ambitious, back-biting doctors? Revoking my medical staff privileges was cruel and undeserved. Even at Blackwell's, my skills were valued. I'd worked for years, studying, competing, tolerating insults to achieve my esteemed position. For openers, I deserved a steamer load of apologies. Forgiveness would not come easily.

He confirmed. "It goes without saying that I, we, owe you an apology. In the first place, your actions were all in the interest of aiding a woman in need, nothing egregious at all. If we began terminating medical staff over negative publicity, as Jewish doctors, fair or unfair, we'd have no one left on staff. It was a wrong decision."

I felt my shoulders tighten as I listened to him claw through an apology. There was once a time, at the beginning of my career at Mount Sinai, that I craved acceptance by the male medical staff. Prestigious names surrounded me everywhere I went, from portraits along the hallways and lecture halls to publications in the heavy textbooks lining my office walls. Finally, in New York, after the punishing years in Baltimore, I imagined my long-gone parents bursting with pride seeing my portrait hung on the Board

Room wall. But at what expense? To become another arrogant, self-serving doctor? I no longer believed that would make them proud.

"I admit, my termination was the last thing I expected that morning. Would you have done the same to a man?"

Dr. Lehr sat quietly, considering his response. "I can't answer that. I honestly don't know. We made a grave error, for which I once again apologize."

I nodded, still feeling manipulated and unsatisfied. "Let me cut to the point. Why do you think Mount Sinai, which has shown itself to be an institution of arrogance and judgment, should receive this extraordinary grant?" I bore my eyes into his. "Presently, I can't think of one reason."

He sat stunned, as if I had poked a sword in his face.

"Dr. Lehr, why do you care so much about this grant, or for the city's poor?" I challenged him further. Did he think it might merely be another notch in Mount Sinai's belt?

His eyes softened as he studied my angry face. "I'm going to share private information about myself that I trust you will keep private. Most of my colleagues don't know much about me, and I'd prefer to keep it that way."

I nodded, wondering what he'd say next.

The waitress interrupted again. "Did you wish to order lunch?"

I glanced at the menu, realizing I hadn't eaten anything that morning. Surprised to be enjoying the confrontation, I wasn't ready to leave. I selected a chicken sandwich and a refill on my coffee. He did the same.

The duel continued. "As I said before, I was born downtown in the tenements. My parents were immigrant tailors from Germany. They perished close to 1850 in a tuberculosis epidemic. My younger brother, Nathan, died with them. At the time, my world felt shattered. I was only ten."

I, too, knew the pain of parental loss, displacement and the determination to rise above life's obstacles. My heart ached for that little boy. I hadn't forgotten my sadness during the first few months at Tillie's, both parents suddenly cut out of my life. My anger began to dissolve.

"I was one of the lucky ones," he continued. It turned out I had distant

261

relatives living in the Upper East Side who had been in New York for close to ten years. "My mother, God rest her sweet soul, had reached out to her cousin Rachel uptown before her condition turned grave, hoping to build a relationship. They scarcely knew each other, but before my mother died, Rachel promised to look after my brother and me in the event something bad happened. Aunt Rachel kept her word, and I moved uptown alone with only the clothes on my back and a few books."

"I'm so sorry to hear about your hardship. Sadly, it's a common story in the tenements, families devastated by disease." I whispered, still not certain of his motivations. "How did you become interested in medicine?"

The waitress approached our table, carrying a full tray of plates. Setting them down at the empty counter across from us, she arranged our lunches and refilled our coffee cups. "Let me know if you'd like anything else. We baked fresh apple strudel this morning."

Dr. Lehr's lips curled up. "If I knew you had strudel, I would have skipped the sandwich." He turned back to me. "The aroma of my aunt's freshly baked strudel was one of her famous ploys to lull me out of my sad little shell." He looked back at the waitress, "Save a piece for me."

I smiled, remembering the many tricks Tillie and her friend Sadie used, helping me recover from my sadness as a child—tea parties with my doll, painting, and reading books. I was such a nervous little girl back in those days, picking at my eyebrows and lashes. They must have been beside themselves with worry.

I surveyed the cafe walls. They were painted a drab brown, but the posters fixed to them told a different story. Menus, daily specials, and many photos of the owner's family covered every surface, creating a wholesomeness, a sense of community not apparent at Mount Sinai. That was how I wanted to be remembered, as part of a neighborhood, like Dr. Boro. He made simple, basic connections with everyone, no matter what fashions they donned or languages they spoke.

Our lunch flashed by. Every moment of Dr. Lehr's story astonished me further. A loner in his youth and college, he ranked at the top of his class. He had few friends growing up, constantly aware how his roots separated him from the wealthy boys at school. It was his love of science and research that propelled him forward, helping him reach the pinnacle of his career at Mount Sinai. My anger was replaced with an odd mix of admiration for the man and all he'd accomplished and sadness for the little boy tucked inside.

I set my sandwich on the plate. "I know what it's like to be the different one. At Hopkins, I was not only a woman, but Jewish. There weren't many like me. It was my love of medicine and caring for my patients that helped me through. And, of course, the trustees who were protective of the female students."

Dr. Lehr interrupted. "Something just occurred to me. Living down here, you must have known Dr. Boro. We trained together at Mount Sinai during the war. We took care of the injured Union soldiers during our training."

I sat stunned, realizing I'd never known more than the tip of the iceberg about Dr. Lehr. I set my fingers at the table's edge. "Dr. Boro is worshiped in these parts. He was my first mentor."

"An astonishing man and doctor." Dr. Lehr agreed. "Over the years, he's tried to convince me to practice with him. But I can't face all the old memories; they still haunt me. Instead, I accept any referral he sends uptown, no questions asked. We find the money when his patients can't pay."

Suddenly New York felt smaller, knit together by old friendships. My brain was abuzz. Perhaps I could build a connection between the Jewish Maternity Hospital and Mount Sinai.

"I understand we lost a fine surgeon to his practice after his wife died in a terrible carriage accident, Dr. Ben Kahn. I wish we could have held onto him longer at Sinai."

Another connection. Sparks flew in my head. I must work this into my plan.

"Dr. Isaacson, would you tell me your thoughts? How do you envision using the grant money?"

I was determined to match his candor with my own, up to a point. "It may seem unlikely, but my brief time in Blackwell's opened my eyes. I always thought reaching the top of my profession would satisfy me, but after tending inmates, I began to appreciate that my medical career might serve a greater purpose. Publications and dusty plaques are no longer enough for me. Besides, the hospital pecking order only infuriates me."

He cleared his throat, pulling his pipe from his waistcoat pocket.

I continued. "There's something extraordinary about the connection a physician makes with his patients, an intimacy based on vulnerability, medical knowledge, and heartfelt decency. I don't think there's another profession quite like it. I learned I can make a much bigger impact among the poor than tending to wealthy women uptown. I intend to use the grant to improve the plight of those who can't afford basic medical care."

He stuffed tobacco into his pipe, lighting a match, and puffed. "I know the extraordinary hardship you faced at Blackwell's, and I recently learned that fool Kaufman, didn't stand up for you while you were incarcerated." He brushed his sandwich crumbs away from the edge of the table. "I imagine everything seems unfair right now. But all you've experienced has touched you in a meaningful way, at a pivotal point in your career and personal life."

I answered slowly, digesting his words. "Yes, Doctor, it has."

"Are you ready for your strudel?" The waitress appeared out of nowhere, reaching for our empty plates and silverware.

He nodded at the waitress and puffed on his pipe, the fragrance filling the air. "I haven't seen your kind of heroism in a very long time." He looked at me with intensity. "You are an extraordinary woman."

His powerful words struck a vulnerable place, filling my need to be appreciated for my talent and dedication. Would I ever have that inexplicable ability to reach deeply into others?

The waitress set the warm strudel between us. "I brought two forks in case you both want a taste. It's exceptionally good today."

Dr. Lehr laughed loudly. "Charming. I'd all but forgotten how food is shared down here. Please feel free." He handed the second fork to me.

I cut off a corner of the strudel, holding it to my nose, inhaling the delicious smell of baked apples and sugar. "Oh my, this smells delicious. Thank you."

He set down his fork, again studying my face. "Doctor Isaacson, our lives shape us into the people we become as adults. The entitled, who've never faced true deprivation, are soft. They don't know hunger. But those of us who confront true hardship can appreciate the suffering of others less fortunate. It makes us better doctors, better human beings."

I answered slowly, feeling the gravity of my impending decision. "Yes, I believe you're right, Dr. Lehr." Where would I put the money—northern or southern New York? One thing I was certain of, there was poverty in every corner of the city.

We sat quietly, sharing the strudel, all my senses heightened. I listened to the clatter of soiled plates being stacked by busboys, the ringing of silverware hitting the sides of the metal basins carried from table to table for clearing, and the lively conversations surrounding us as the coffee and ale took hold.

Dr. Lehr signaled to the waitress for the check. He turned back to me. "Thank you for meeting with me today. Please think hard about the best use for the grant. I want to assure you I'll be there to help you succeed every step of the way. It's not every day we encounter an opportunity on this scale."

I nodded, releasing my breath.

"Please call me if there's anything further I can do." He stood, looked at the bill, and handed money to the waitress. "Keep the change, Miss."

I watched him button his heavy tweed coat, placing his black derby on his head.

"And Dr. Isaacson, I will attempt to reactivate your medical staff privileges. That vindictive fool, Blum, must go. No matter what you decide, I'm proud to call you my colleague and hope to see you at the hospital."

* * *

I was thankful for the long walk uptown to Bellevue. I needed time to digest much more than lunch. My conversation with Dr. Lehr left me baffled and cynical. Having always viewed money as a necessary means to obtain the essentials in life, I now saw its unfettered power firsthand—how it could humble a man as powerful as Dr. Lehr, making him practically grovel. Margaret was brilliant, demanding the massive sum from Governor Higgins. But now that I held the golden egg, I needed to use it scrupulously.

One glance at Bellevue, and I knew the grant would be consumed in restoration projects. The block-wide building complex was crumbling, its mortar chipped, window trim rotted and splintered.

I checked the wall clock as I entered the building and saw I had fifteen minutes to spare until my meeting with the hospital president. Ordinarily, that would be ample time, but I began to worry when I looked for his office, and I couldn't find my way. Before long, I was swallowed up in the massive building, scurrying down hallways that separated patient wards and laboratories, turned in circles. How on earth would patients ever figure out where to go?

I finally stopped a nurse carrying a bundle of folded linens. "Could you kindly direct me to the hospital president's office?"

She answered in a heavy brogue. "Down two floors, make a right, two lefts, and then another right." She nodded, mentally checking her instructions. "That'll get you there."

Off I hurried with five minutes left. I found the nearest stairwell and scurried down one floor before practically bumping into another doctor coming through a doorway.

"Hey there. what's the hurry?" That unforgettable voice, as slippery as a snake's skin.

I gasped, knowing immediately who he was. "Roger?" I could feel my heart pounding in my chest, my throat tightening. "What are you doing here?"

"Surprised, Doctor Isaacson? I warned you we'd meet again. I'll bet you're here to discuss the state money you're giving to Bellevue."

I recoiled, then pushed past him to descend another floor. "I'm going to be late."

His menacing laugh made the intervening years vanish. In my mind, I was back in the carriage. Just like in Baltimore, he closed in on me, attaching himself to my heels. "You are either stupid or naïve. I'm attending the same

266

meeting. We're delighted to have you invest in Bellevue."

Intimidated, I quickened my pace, struggling to remember the directions, right, left, left, right.

"You don't need to run from me, darling. I don't bite." He mocked. "This time, when you fight me with your money bag, I'm going to take it!"

I stopped, overcome with furious determination. If I could survive the Warden, I could handle Roger. "How did you hear about the grant?" I snarled.

He scoffed, ignited by my anger. "Didn't you realize how well-connected my family was?"

"To whom?" I demanded, my indignation replacing the last of my fear.

He looked at me, his condescending eyes traveling from my hair to my shoes. "The Governor's office, you little fool."

He stuck to me the entire way to the meeting. Once there, I chose to listen, exactly as I had in Blackwell's, sizing up my enemy. Roger sat through the entire hour sitting back in his chair with his arms crossed over his chest, wearing a smug expression. The hospital president unrolled page after page of architectural plans on the table before me, indulging me in the wasteful, frivolous curlicue and gargoyle flairs, offering to put my name on a building wing, appealing to my vanity, as if a name on a building could immortalize me.

As the meeting ended, I asked the president how his plan kept with the purpose of the grant, to improve the health of New York City women.

He looked confused. "My dear, we are constructing a fortress to honor each one who passes through our doors. Receiving care from our prestigious physicians in this awe-inspiring setting will inspire a sense of health and hope in their lives." He sat back, appearing quite pleased with his answer.

I stood. "I see. Thank you for meeting with me today." I tipped my head and turned to the door, completely disgusted.

Chapter Thirty-Six

"Tillie, what should I do?" I threw my arms in the air, overwhelmed. She didn't hear me, standing before the sink, washing celery under the running faucet. "Did you see your messages? There's one from Mrs. Sanger. Also, Dr. Kahn called. What do you think he wants?"

"I must have walked past them. I don't know." I said absently, still reeling from my run-in with Roger. I walked into the kitchen, repeating, "They hired that swine, Holloway! I simply can't believe any hospital would run the risk of taking that vulgar man on staff."

Tillie turned off the water. "He's the same man who tried to hurt you?"

"The very same." I was sickened. How could men get away with such atrocious behavior? "Somehow, he managed to wrangle a medical degree in New York. Sounds like his parents' money got him out of the mess at Johns Hopkins after all. I'll bet they contributed to that outrageous building fund at Bellevue. They think they've persuaded the Governor to reassign the grant."

"What? I thought the money was for you to manage."

My voice rose. "Over the years, they've let those buildings run into the ground and now expect me to use my grant to fix them—at the expense of women's care. They've been begging the city and state for an astronomical amount to turn the hospital into an architectural fortress. And they had the audacity to assume they could steal my grant to build a bunch of silly gargoyles. As if trimmings will heal women."

Tillie was barely listening, lost in her own memories. "I haven't been there since Mama died. That place was appalling."

"There are plans to improve it, but the city hired architects from the firm that designed Fifth Avenue mansions, and their budget is outrageous, with brownstone and expensive ornamentation. They're going back and forth making changes, trying to bring the cost down."

Tillie huffed. "You're right. The grant could solve a dilemma for the Governor. He could get Bellevue off his back by reallocating the grant money. But what will happen to all the desperate women down here?"

"I keep thinking about all those ladies at Blackwell's and the abysmal care they received while their doctors learned medicine practicing on the poor at Bellevue—as if their patients' lives had no real value. No one really cared what happens to them."

Tillie brought our lunch to the table and sat, looking at me with an intensity I hadn't seen for a long while. "Hannah, I know you're tired from your ordeal at Blackwell's, but you must fight this with everything ounce of strength you've got. An opportunity this big is rare and won't come along again in your lifetime. Besides, you have the exact women to help you put this grant to its proper use."

Margaret and Mrs. Garrett had already done so much for me. "I had no idea things would get this complicated. I hate leaning on them again."

Tillie retorted without a pause. "Why? You're not in this alone. It's about all women. When you prevail, every poor woman in Lower Manhattan wins. Mrs. Sanger and Mrs. Garrett have spent their lives fighting for these women. You have already won half the battle with the money in your hands. Invite them in to help strengthen your cause."

She was right. I rose from the table, my lunch untouched, and paced the room. I needed a clear argument why Bellevue should not be considered. "Tell me again what happened with Mama at Bellevue."

"Oh, Hannah, that was a lifetime ago. I don't know if it's even the same there now. I was only fourteen when Papa and I took Mama there in the chicken wagon. They barely spoke English, and I had to sort out where to go. We'd never been to a hospital in the city before. Even elevators were new. Mama was afraid to step inside it. We had to coax her in."

"Where was I?" No one had ever shared my part of the story.

Her eyes disappeared again into the past, staring at her pictures in the curio cabinet. "We left you with the Cohens, a farm neighbor, and our brothers went off to school. You were still in diapers. None of us expected we'd stay at the hospital that night or that Mama would die."

I envied Tillie, who had known Mama until her end. I didn't even own a photo. Irritated, I turned the conversation back to the matter at hand. "Your story may be what we need. Most patients arrive at Bellevue by foot and immediately become lost, just like I did today. And many are helping a sick parent while dragging along their children. It must be completely overwhelming. The signs, if you can find any, are impossible to follow. That is, if you can read English. Nothing has changed there for patients in fifteen years."

Tillie's mouth dropped. "They haven't fixed that yet? We were constantly turned around."

I exploded, my voice filled with disgust. "Honestly, they don't care. It's only about the money and its power. As I said, they practice on the poor!"

"I don't think the Governor's going to want to hear that. You'll have to come across with less emotion. What would a man tell him?"

She was right again. Just like practicing medicine, where I reserved my empathy for the patients, I thought aloud how I'd convey this problem to the Governor and his likely reaction. "I know Bellevue's done fine work for the city, and some excellent doctors have trained there. They've seen it all; nothing could shock them. But the place reminds me of the prison—eerie, rats, soulless, like walking through death's door."

"He's going to want far more than that." Tillie grimaced. "Because you're going to have a far bigger dragon to slay."

"What dragon?"

"Oh, please. Do you live in a bubble? You've picked two Jewish hospitals. You think you'll find any sympathizers in Albany?"

* * *

I walked around the block to clear my head before returning Dr. Kahn's call. This grant, vital for thousands of women, was turning into its own dragon. I must approach the Governor with impeccable caution, thinking one step ahead, knowing nothing would come easily. In the meantime, the best way for me to settle my nerves was by taking care of patients. It had been months since I last treated a soul. I knew Dr. Kahn would get me into Dr. Boro's clinic schedule, so I'd call him first. Margaret would come later, after I had a plan.

* * *

"Hello, Dr. Kahn? Dr. Isaacson, returning your call."

The line crackled, and then I heard a tentative voice. "I'm glad to hear back from you. I was hoping to continue our conversation. Any chance you're available for dinner tomorrow night? I've been missing the restaurants uptown and hoped you'd join me."

Such a familiar overture. Was it business or pleasure? I wasn't sure, but the invitation would take me away from my conundrum and help clear my head. "That would be splendid. Dinner at a restaurant." I mused. "It's been a long time."

"I'll pick you up at seven."

"And, by the way, any chance I can start at the Clinic next week?

* * *

"It's wonderful to see you again." Dr. Kahn helped me into the carriage, his voice, friendly and calming.

I still wasn't sure of the true purpose of dinner and inwardly laughed at how out of practice I'd become with men after being surrounded by women in the prison and insulated at home the last few weeks. "Thank you. Where are we going?"

He winked as he settled beside me on the bench. "It's a surprise. I thought you'd enjoy a special meal after that dreadful prison food. And for that matter, so would I, but for a different reason."

I looked at him quizzically, suddenly nervous to be heading away from the familiarity of Tillie and Abe's home. *Relax, Hannah, you couldn't be safer.*

The whip crack cut through the frigid air as the horses edged the coach away from my apartment stoop into the bustle of our neighborhood. I draped the carriage blanket across my lap.

Dr. Kahn explained. "It's a breath of fresh air having a normal dinner with a colleague." He paused, then added, "And a pretty woman."

I couldn't help but smile at the compliment. "I'm probably not the best company right now. My mind's been elsewhere since I was released from Blackwell's. It's taken a while to get my life back in order."

He cleared his throat. "I completely understand. Did Dr. Boro tell you I'm living with my parents now?"

"No, but don't feel too badly; so am I, sort of—my older sister."

"I left my position at Sinai to work downtown with Dr. Boro after the accident. I thought it would be better for the children. My parents have been a blessing, but it's been difficult."

That explained why he lived downtown. "That must have been an abrupt change for your family."

He straightened his hat. "I wasn't planning to discuss it, but we may as well get it out in the open."

"Please tell me if it makes you feel better." My physician's reflexes kicked in. It was my second nature, a state of mind where I was comfortable. And to be completely honest, I was keen to hear more.

He sighed. "As you may imagine, the first months were chaotic, the children missing their mother, moving, and adjusting to new schools, and of course, me at a new practice. I don't know how I would have managed without my parents and Dr. Boro. He's an extraordinary man."

I knew exactly what he meant. "I'm always drawn back to this part of town when things go wrong in my life. Tillie and Dr. Boro have saved me more times than I can count." I continued wistfully, "There's something about the people south of Delancey. They understand tough knocks."

"I never thought of it that way, but it's true. Bear in mind, they have their fair share of problems on the Upper East Side. They're just more skillful at disguising them."

In the dim light of the carriage, I could scarcely make out the outline of his face. He fidgeted on the cushioned bench. It was easier discussing his predicament than reliving mine.

I asked, "How has it been, you know, leaving Mount Sinai?"

He pursed his lips, thinking aloud. "Easier than expected. I'll admit, I was caught up in the Sinai prestige. But since Dr. Boro put me to work, I've been too busy to go backwards." He turned, locking his eyes with mine. "We're all excited to have you join our group."

"As am I." I felt the sparkle of hope, knowing I was welcome and that a doctor of his caliber could move his career forward in a different direction. Perhaps I would adjust too.

"I wouldn't mind more surgery. That, I do miss." He gazed at me sheepishly. "Having you join our group would free up my time to build a surgical practice."

I laughed. "I was wondering what your plan was." So, this was why he asked me to dinner. I relaxed, knowing his true intention.

"It's no secret that I miss the operating theater. Besides, Dr. Boro gave you a glowing review, and as I recall, you were highly regarded at Sinai. I thought breaking bread would be a good way to get better acquainted."

Feeling more comfortable, I wanted to know more about him too. "How are the children now, a year later?"

"Better, thank you for asking. Honestly, the hardest part has been living with my parents." He straightened the front of his overcoat. "I know I've no right to complain. But in a million years, I never would have guessed I'd move back to their apartment in my mid-thirties. For all their love, they're constantly meddling in my life, especially with my childrearing."

I tilted my head toward him. "If you don't mind my asking, what are they worried about?"

He clasped his hands tightly in his lap. "For starters, they're upset the children, and I don't keep kosher. They think I spoil them with my leniency over food and an excessive amount of playtime. Now they're beginning to pressure me to find another wife since it's been over a year. They won't leave me alone."

My stomach tightened. Maybe this *was* a date. I drew a quick breath.

He heard it. "Now I've embarrassed myself. Please don't take my words the wrong way. That was not the purpose of the evening." He exhaled heavily. "Of course, you are quite lovely." He slapped his forehead. "Could I be any more awkward? I'm a pea brain when it comes to talking to women outside of work."

My tension exploded into laughter. His clumsiness was a welcome relief, especially after Joseph's slick manner.

He couldn't help but join my laughter, then cleared his throat. "Let me start again. I do want to become better acquainted. We have much in common, and I thought you might understand my predicament. And, since we share the Sinai connection, I wanted to bend your ear with a few ideas I've had. Ideas concerning the health and sanitation down here."

I found his frankness refreshing, amused by his unique combination of awkwardness and candor. "I'm glad because I wasn't sure why you asked me to dine. To be fair, you should know I'm still shaking off the last few months. Prison left me with frightening nightmares, like something out of Grimms' Fairy Tales. The prison Warden was crueler than Cinderella's stepmother."

His eyes softened. "That might take you a while. I remember replaying the worst in my dreams, too. But eventually, it blew over, like a nasty thunderstorm."

My heart warmed. "That's exactly what Dr. Boro advised. Thank you for the reassurance."

We sat comfortably in silence, listening to the driver call to his horses, the clip-clopping as their hooves hit the stone street. A wave of quietude passed through me. Had I ever felt such ease sitting beside a man?

Dr. Kahn finally broke our silence. "You can talk to me, Dr. Isaacson, anytime."

"Please call me, Hannah."

"Likewise, Ben."

I recognized Delmonico's as the carriage pulled beside its large doors.

Disconcerted by Ben's extravagance and my memories of Joseph, I said, "This *is* a big treat!" I wondered if my brown suit and unadorned hat were adequate attire. "I look frumpy in my simple clothes." New Yorkers were notorious for dressing to the nines at fancy restaurants.

His blue eyes trapped mine. "Hannah, you could put on an old *schmatta* and you'd still be the prettiest woman here."

I offered a thin smile, the joke about wearing rags making me remember Joseph's empty flattery. The soup trickery the last time I came here with that man was still fresh in my thoughts. I reminded myself, *he's not Joseph.*

Moments later, we were seated at a small round table. The enchanting setting was exactly as I remembered—bone china, silver cutlery, and a small cut glass vase of red roses. Elegant living had its merits. Deliciously prepared food and sparkling clean crystal glassware a pleasant indulgence after a tiring day standing on my feet at the hospital. Perhaps there was a way to have both.

The waiter arrived with a bottle of red wine and poured a small amount into Dr. Kahn's goblet. "Is to your liking, sir?"

Ben smiled at me. "I hope you don't mind. I took the liberty of starting our meal with my favorite red." As he sipped, an approving smile crossed his face.

My mood soured, hoping he didn't plan to order my dinner too. "Just so you know, the soup is made with pork. Although I don't keep strictly kosher, I don't eat pork or shellfish."

His eyes squinted in surprise. "I wasn't aware. Why are you telling me that?"

Flushing with embarrassment, I answered. "Something awful happened last time I was here with Joseph, my ex-fiancé. I should have known then that he was wrong for me." I dropped my shoulders, afraid I'd spoiled the evening. "I shouldn't have said anything."

He knit his brows in concern. "Did I choose the wrong restaurant?"

"Oh no, Dr. Kahn. It couldn't be more perfect. It's me, still full of crazy memories. I ended the relationship with Joseph after eating here. I tried to warn you about my state of mind."

Please don't call me doctor. It makes me feel old." He paused, "and it's formal."

"I'm sorry." I adjusted my silverware.

Ben cocked his head. "And please don't apologize. You have nothing to be sorry for." He gently touched my forearm. "I'd like to know more about you—if you're comfortable sharing."

His simple touch set off an effervescence I hadn't felt in months. I slowly pulled my arm away, uncertain what to share or where to begin. "My life hasn't been all that exciting, at least till prison." I laughed, realizing how absurd I sounded. My nervous laughter got away from me, and soon I was hiccupping. "I'm so sorry. I'm making an utter fool of myself."

Ben watched, amused, as I straightened my jacket, pulling myself back together.

A sip of water later, I exhaled and gradually shared my childhood dream to become a doctor, the difficult climate in Baltimore with mid-term abortions, and, more recently, my broken engagement. "Did you know Joseph?"

He nodded. "I did. Seemed like a decent chap. A bit dazzled with himself and his new money, but a reputable physician, particularly with heart disease."

"I'll give him that. But he only knew the heart physiologically, not poetically." I sighed. "Despite his interest in hearts, he managed to break mine. I was a fool to fall for him." Surprised at the ease I felt with Ben. I could have talked all night.

His clear blue eyes filled with compassion. "I'll be candid. For such a fine person, you've had an unfair share of disappointment."

Was this a dream? He was almost too good to be real. "Sometimes, I think it's me. That I fall for selfish men with overbearing mothers." I quickly added. "I don't mean you. We barely know each other, and I've never met your mother."

Ben laughed. "You're sweet, and I take no offense. I must caution you; my parents are good-hearted and well-intentioned but can be overbearing."

Was this how most parents behaved? I had no idea.

"How about we order, then I want to hear your thoughts on a few professional matters." Ben opened his menu, looking up, winking at me.

The next few hours were filled with delicious food and good cheer. Having established the footings of a new friendship, we shared freely, swapping stories of childhood, our years in medical training, and Mount Sinai gossip. Eventually, I discussed my ongoing concern around the dangers of illegal abortion, how it hit too close to home with Elspeth, and again later in New York, landing me at Blackwell's. "Somehow, some way, we must help women gain more control over their bodies. It begins with eliminating those ridiculous laws outlawing pregnancy devices and ensuring the proper training of midwives. Can you imagine, they perform surgical procedures without ever having taken an anatomy class?"

Ben gazed at me thoughtfully. "You're right. Until I moved downtown, I was shut in the operating theater with no clue what went on in your field. Now that my practice includes every condition and ailment under the sun, I'm shocked at the number of children women have. Besides, childbed fever is still on every mother's mind. Caring for two children myself, I can't imagine fathers left with a large brood, trying to do it all alone. Not everyone has parents willing or able to help.

Thrilled to hear Ben's interest and depth of understanding, I continued. "The laws are outdated. Most educated people don't take them seriously."

By the time dessert arrived, I'd decided to share my news of the state grant and the quandary facing me. I laid it out, including my lunch with Dr. Lehr earlier that week. As promised, I kept his personal information to myself. I then told Ben about Bellevue and Roger Holloway's connection to the Governor's mansion.

Ben raised his bushy eyebrows, his forehead folding in lines. "That's a lot to digest, Hannah. Tell me first about Dr. Lehr. He was an enigma; no one knew him well. What's he like?"

I tilted my head and considered, not knowing quite where to start. "He is a puzzle. First, he caved to Mr. Blum's pressure and threw me out. Now I learn he's a person who cares deeply about the health of the poor. Up to this point, it seemed obvious I should direct the grant funds downtown."

"What happened with Bellevue? This Holloway character sounds like he belongs behind bars."

I shrugged my shoulders. "He's a longer story for another day. For now, believe me when I say he's a scoundrel of the worst sort." I studied his face. "You're familiar with both what Sinai could offer and the situation downtown. Any chance you could share an objective opinion?"

His mouth curled into a smirk. "Honestly, I don't think so. My money is on the new Jewish Maternity Hospital. How much is the grant?

"Let's not go into that now. For now, I'll stick with the bigger plan. I only wanted to tell you a little about what I'm working on." I knew in my gut, once the amount was shared, every conversation would become skewed.

"Such suspense." He gestured at our untouched confection, with its peaks of toasted meringue, almost too delicate to disturb. "Since you won't share the amount, let's at least share dessert. The Baked Alaska is their signature confection dating back thirty years to the restaurant's opening. It's an *objet d'art.*"

Objet d'art? I laughed inwardly. Was he trying to impress me with his French?

French or not, I enjoyed the remainder of the evening fully. We conversed nonstop, revealing more obscure corners of our lives, eventually switching to a discussion of the difficulties practicing medicine among the poor. "I've been trying to sort out what each hospital brings to the table. Sinai is easy. They have some of the finest doctors in the world, people who can help write the grant and put it into action. With Dr. Lehr's commitment, they wouldn't waste a penny."

Ben pounced, growing exasperated. "Hannah, don't be blinded by their glitter. The greatest need is downtown among the poor Jews and other immigrant groups. They're desperate for help and birthing hungry children at an alarming rate. You could create the maternity program of your dreams without any challenge from the Board Room, and while you're at it, address other health needs women have, such as a school for midwifery. Besides, you wouldn't be dealing with all the highfalutin' doctors and administrators at Sinai who'll steal your recognition when they're not standing in your way."

"Don't forget, Ben, there's only so much risk I'm willing to take. I'm not like my friend, Margaret Sanger, willing to dispense birth control at the risk of prison. I refuse to be arrested again. Once was enough for me." I winced. Politicians and police didn't care a hoot about women's health, preferring to exert their sense of superiority over women through laws and incarceration.

Ben sat quietly, sipping his coffee, sorting through his thoughts. "I know this shouldn't matter, but did you know Sinai doesn't accept Eastern Jews in their medical school? It's hard to believe they would stick their necks out to build a bigger clinic to care for them. Besides, how would these people get uptown?"

I cringed. "What? I know there weren't Russian doctors on staff, but I didn't think they were excluded from admission. Is that true?"

"Ask your new friend, Dr. Lehr. He knows. The old German Jews can't stand the Russian immigrants. They view us as peasants, low brow. I'm surprised I was accepted. Must have been my German surname, Kahn. They never knew my mother was Romanian. Her people were all from the east."

"I'd no idea," I whispered, considering the names of my colleagues: Jakobs, Zimmerman, Krugmann, Arnold, and so forth. He was right. "Unbelievable."

"Face it, Hannah, the urgency is downtown. More people will benefit if you work with the new maternity hospital. At the end of the day, isn't it about helping the greatest number of people and the neediest?"

"Bellevue claims to help the neediest. How should I get Albany to give them up?" I asked.

"What a wasteful fiasco that's become." He threw his hands in the air. "Exactly what happens when politicians design a building." He huffed. "Take the money there, and women will never see a penny of your grant."

Pleased that his instincts aligned with mine, I licked my spoon, not planning to leave a morsel of dessert behind. "I appreciate your honesty and am glad we see things the same way. But at this very moment, what I appreciate most is the lovely dinner." I hesitated, "and our new friendship.

Let me sleep on the grant some more."

Chapter Thirty-Seven

The following week I began working at Dr. Boro's office, referred to locally as the Lower East Side Clinic. I was assigned to female patients, most in their last trimester of pregnancy, practically all visiting the Clinic for their first pregnancy check-up. Marta, who would later assist with their home deliveries, stood at my side as she translated back and forth between my English and their Yiddish and Russian.

Clinic began with the usual complaints, nerve pain in the legs, fatigue, and indigestion. By mid-morning, I was back in my old routine, reassuring the new mothers-to-be and commiserating with the experienced, who knew what lay ahead. But towards noon, I examined Yetta, a short, heavy-set Russian woman who set off alarm bells in my head. She was new to the Clinic and appeared close to term. Yetta waddled into the exam room, breathing heavily, her face sweating even though it was the mid-winter. She spoke practically no English, and if it weren't for hand signals, my limited Yiddish, and Marta's translations, I never would have made it through the visit.

"How far along are you? Is this your first?" I spoke calmly, helping her onto the exam table, gently squeezing her swollen hands and ankles.

Marta translated. "This is her third, and she's not sure how many months along but thinks she's near the end."

I examined her belly and listened to the baby's heart. "She's certainly near term, but the baby's positioned quite high and large. Her joints are terribly swollen." I turned to look at Yetta while I spoke to Marta. "How old are your other children? Do you have anyone to help you at home?"

The Clinic had recently received the newly invented sphygmomanometer, a blood pressure machine that the hospitals were clamoring about. I listened through my stethoscope. "This can't be right. The reading is far too high." I rechecked it and then again, a third time. Ready to discard the contraption, I took a long look at Yetta's red face and swollen extremities, and I knew the machine was right. "Marta, she can't go home. We must get her blood pressure under control."

Marta spoke back and forth with Yetta, finally sharing the conversation with me. "She lives with her mother-in-law, has an eighteen-month-old and a three-year-old. They're in the waiting room. I didn't tell Yetta she can't go home."

Ben wasn't exaggerating when he described the harrowing plight of the women in the Lower East Side. Uptown, under normal circumstances, a patient like Yetta would be directly admitted, placed on bed rest with a strict diet to reduce her swelling and blood pressure. I knew if Yetta continued her pregnancy unchecked, she might not live to raise her children. "How old is she?"

Yetta recognized my questions attempting to answer directly, showing two fingers, then one. "Two, one," she enunciated, slowly pursing her lips.

"Twenty-one?" Marta confirmed with Yetta in Yiddish.

She needed a hospital. But where? I was sure she couldn't afford Beth Israel, where I had no inside contacts to help. As much as I hated the thought, I'd have to send her to Bellevue, the charity hospital.

"Marta, please bring her mother-in-law to the exam room."

Moments later, a middle-aged-women carrying a screaming eighteen-month-old and struggling to hold the other child's hand arrived in the exam room. The baby smelled sour, his diaper hours beyond needing a change. I helped Yetta sit upright on the exam table, and she took her baby.

With Marta translating, I learned it would be impossible to keep Yetta off her feet at home. On a typical day, she watched five children, her two and her sister-in-law's three, all under five years old. Yetta's typical diet consisted of bread, cheese, and salted potatoes—not advisable for a woman in her fragile condition.

282

"We must admit Yetta to a hospital for the remainder of her pregnancy. I'll call Bellevue and see if they can find a bed for her."

"Oh no, no." the mother-in-law shook her head vigorously. "No can pay."

I placed my hand on her forearm. "I understand. Hold tight. Let's see what I can do. Yetta's condition is dangerous, and my first concern is that she and the new baby stay healthy. Marta, please explain while I make the arrangements. I don't want her leaving the Clinic or going home."

I slipped into Dr. Boro's office and lifted the telephone from its cradle, asking the operator to connect me to the switchboard at Bellevue.

An operator answered on the twelfth ring.

"Hello, this is Dr. Isaacson at the Lower East Side Clinic. I need to admit a pregnant woman with dangerously high blood pressure. Can you find a bed for her?"

"Please hold, doctor."

I waited ten minutes, afraid at any moment, the line would disconnect. Eventually, the operator returned. "I'm sorry, you'll need to find a bed elsewhere. Maternity is full to the gills, mostly Jews. For heaven's sake, where'd they all come from? And none speak English." Click. The line was dead.

Furious, I dialed Mount Sinai. *Would Dr. Lehr put his money where his mouth is?*

Dring, dring. "How may I assist you?"

"Please connect me with Dr. Lehr. Dr. Isaacson calling."

Seconds later, he answered. I could envision the curls of smoke rising from his pipe as he sat at the other end, curious to hear me. "Delighted to hear from you, Dr. Isaacson."

"Good morning, doctor. I'll get straight to the point." I proceeded to fill him in on my work at the Clinic, Yetta's condition, and what she needed in the way of more sophisticated care.

Silence, then voices rumbled in the background. While I waited for Dr. Lehr's response, I spun around and saw Ben standing in the doorway listening, arms crossed, lips in a tight line, and eyebrows raised as if to say, *we need the grant money here, not there.*

I spoke into the receiver, "Dr. Lehr. Are you still there?"

"I'm sorry. My secretary interrupted me with another emergency. By all means, send her. We'll dispatch an ambulance and make the medical and financial arrangements. I'll put a call out to the floor to ensure they have a bed for her. Can you tell me her full name?"

I shared the vital information, eager to return to my patient. "Excellent. I'm grateful."

Dr. Lehr asked, "Is there anything else you need?"

"Yes, my medical staff privileges. I want to check on Yetta tomorrow."

Another silence, then he answered, "I'll see what I can do."

I replaced the telephone in its cradle and turned to Ben, smiling as if to say, *I told you they'd help us.*

* * *

By mid-afternoon, the waiting room had thinned. I finally had a moment for lunch and to get off my feet. The ambulance coach had come and gone, taking Yetta to Mount Sinai. I sat in Dr. Boro's office, unwrapping the chicken sandwich Tillie had prepared for me that morning.

Marta drifted into the room, handing me a fresh cup of tea. "I'm relieved to know Yetta's tucked into a hospital bed. Within a year, women like her will go straight to the Jewish Maternity Hospital. She's quite far from her family all the way uptown."

I took a bite of the sandwich. "True, but she'll get good care at Mount Sinai. They know how to handle her condition." I set my sandwich on the plate. "I wish we saw her sooner. It's so much easier to nip problems like Yetta's early on."

It didn't take long. If I'd had any doubts about my new mission, in less than one day, I was reminded once again how crucial the grant was, that there were thousands of women just like Yetta needing better care. It was not about me, my career, or reputation. I had been given my one chance in a lifetime to truly make a difference for many, and I would rise to the challenge. While deep in my thoughts, Ben entered the office, waving a newspaper.

"Hannah, did you see the paper today?" He held it in front of my face.

Surprised at his urgency, I swallowed my tea. "Not yet. What happened?"

"Your friend, Mrs. Sanger, was interviewed at a rally uptown."

The hairs on my arm stood on end. *Oh no, what did Margaret say to the press?*

"She claimed she secured a one-hundred-fifty-thousand-dollar grant from Governor Higgins to improve the health of New York City women." Then, he paused, "Why didn't you tell me it was so much?"

I looked straight into his eyes, waiting for him to finish, my fury at Margaret building by the second. *What has she done?*

"I had no clue what a staggering fortune you have at your disposal. For God's sake, Hannah. It's enough to pay for the whole maternity hospital."

I raised my voice. "Right now, it's not a certainty. Everyone wants to build a new hospital. You already know about Bellevue. I will not use the whole amount for bricks and mortar. That will never save lives!"

Chapter Thirty-Eight

The following morning, I called Margaret. "Any chance you're free this week for tea? We need to talk."

"I'll be downtown Thursday afternoon. Can we meet at four? Would you be comfortable meeting at the Astoria tearoom? I was going to suggest the Waldorf but was afraid it might be too close for comfort." She paused. "How are you?"

I quickly flipped through my appointment diary. "I'm fine, Margaret." I wanted to discuss the newspaper story in person and could never confide in Margaret about the terrifying nightmares disrupting my sleep. Margaret was anything but faint-hearted. A few weeks at Blackwell wouldn't put a nick in her composure. "Four at the Astoria works. It's a touch awkward, but I can't stay away from those two hotels forever. And a part of me would like to have a few choice words with Mr. Tschirky."

"Splendid. I can't wait to hear how you're doing," said Margaret.

"I need your thoughts on my grant options." I paused. "I'm going to invite Ina too. Wherever I go, I'd like her to join me. She's been so loyal."

I told her the hotel didn't matter, but on Thursday afternoon, the sight of that city block with the Waldorf and Astoria Hotels connected by Peacock Alley sent me into a tailspin. *Buck up and get on with it.* I had enemies all over the city, most still unconvinced of my innocence. Tillie's cautionary words when I was in college came to mind, *A reputation lost is not easy to regain.*

I selected my grey tweed suit that morning, planning to go unnoticed in a sea of smartly dressed women. I couldn't imagine what words I'd use if I ran into Mr. Tschirky. Hopefully, he wouldn't venture out of the Waldorf, where he maintained his main office. *Stop making an opera out of your life, Hannah. You'll come up with the right words if you need them.*

We were well into February, and the deadline loomed. The Governor's office mailed a letter scheduling a March 15th appointment to discuss the proposal, stipulating that he expected a copy on his desk two weeks beforehand. I hoped Margaret could help me think of a convincing argument to keep the money out of Bellevue's coffers.

The horses pulled my coach under the block-long columned entrance, heralding the elegant Astoria, no expensive detail spared. Workmen were busy clearing a soupy brown mixture of horse manure and snow from the marble platform, preparing for the rush of teatime patrons.

I was fifteen minutes early, giving myself enough time to select a private table. I pulled my brim down to conceal my face as I entered the marble lobby, practically bumping into Ina, who was studying a life-size sculpture.

She pulled me into a hug. "This hotel is glorious, just like the Metropolitan Museum. I can't wait to see the tearoom. I heard it turns into the main restaurant at night."

Ina's buoyant exuberance lightened my mood. She dressed simply, but the stylish red feather in her hat matched her chilled rosy cheeks, drawing attention to her lovely face.

"Let's get a table and wait for Margaret there," I suggested.

We paused before the Benzoni statue in the center of the lobby, the one Ina had admired. It depicted an ancient family's flight from Pompeii. The marble couple, full of youth and vitality, shielded themselves from falling debris, the mother clutching her infant to her breast, the husband's face filled with fear, the exact dread I felt every time I thought of Blackwell's Island. I inhaled deeply, reminding myself of the purpose of today's meeting. For Ina, the statue was a reminder of her family's escape from oppression.

"We need to make New York a safe home for people coming here," I mused.

Ina stood staring. "You do, Doctor. You help so many." She gazed thoughtfully at the sculpture. "Isn't the marble luminous? Is that the right word?"

My heart melted, knowing Ina's family had fled persecution. For me, *many* now meant *every* woman in the city. "Luminous is the perfect word." I took her hand. "Please call me Hannah. You're my friend."

Like its sister, The Waldorf, The Astoria used its main dining room for tea in the late afternoon. Ina gawked at the ornate crystal chandeliers suspended from the ceiling and laughed giddily. "Someday, when hell freezes over, I'll have one of those in my mansion."

I answered. "I promise, by the time you can afford it, you'll want something different."

"I suppose." Her eyes danced about the room, unconvinced.

I understood. She wanted to package the opulence and take it home. "Enjoy it. The hotel is like a museum of the elite. And the patrons are a living, breathing part of the exhibit."

Margaret joined us at our table at four sharp. We stood, hugging and kissing, a noisy trio. Nearby, guests turned, regarding us with disapproval. All eyes were drawn to Margaret's very swollen belly as she strolled in, holding her head high with a mocking reminder that pregnancy was part of womanhood.

The maître d' viewed Margaret scornfully.

Her face reddened with annoyance. "Did you see the way those ladies were looking at me? It's because I'm pregnant. I've no intention of hiding indoors as if I were ashamed." She straightened her frock over her belly. "I hope my water breaks and gives them a proper shock!"

"Don't be silly, Margaret. Let's sit down and enjoy our tea," I said calmly.

Ina's eyes danced about the dining room in a state of wonder. "It's not exactly the hospital cafeteria." She held her spoon to the light.

Margaret tugged Ina's arm down. "What in God's name are you doing? The waiter will think you're pinching their silverware!"

"Ladies." I was anxious to capture their attention. "I'm struggling to make a decision, and time is slipping by."

Margaret, caught between her amusement at Ina and my serious tone, nodded. "Have you made a choice? There're scores of little clinics and hospitals in the city. You have an enviable problem."

"I know, I know, but I have a serious issue with Bellevue, and I need your sharp wits."

The waiter approached our table, balancing a sterling tea service, setting it gently on a cloth-covered side table, and inconspicuously arranged our table.

Standing beside us, he announced in an unobtrusive voice, "Please allow the tea to steep. I'll return shortly to pour."

"Did you see that? The waiter's wearing gloves." Ina examined her starched white tea gloves. "Mine are new; see the tiny pearls sewn in?"

"Ina, they're lovely," I said as if placating a child. After all, she was a newcomer to this world.

Margaret focused her attention on me. "I know about Mount Sinai and Dr. Kahn downtown, but what happened with Bellevue?" She rolled her eyes. "You aren't seriously thinking of joining them. I was planning on seeing you back at Sinai. I'll need you there when I deliver in a month." She patted her swollen belly.

I took a deep breath and summarized the careening turn of events at Bellevue with Roger, including his expulsion from Johns Hopkins. "And that's not the half of it." My voice was tight with anger.

"What do you mean?" Margaret asked, feigning innocence.

I leaned into her face, whispering loudly. "If Bellevue wasn't enough of a problem, your statement to the press has muddled things for me at the other hospitals. I wanted to split up the money while having them each think they were getting it all. Now they'll be fighting like cocks in a pen for the full amount."

Margaret's shrugged her shoulders. "Oh, that statement. You know how the press is. They never tell the whole truth. But, I'll admit, I shouldn't have taken their bait."

"What bait?" I asked with a sinking feeling. What else could have happened?

Margaret huffed. "The wretched reporter was the worst sort of misogynist, holier than thou – you know the sort." She wagged her finger at Ina and me. "Women should stay at home changing diapers and ironing the sheets."

I snapped. "It's no excuse. It's not your grant to speak about. Don't discuss it publicly again without checking with me first."

"Not my grant? I'm the only reason we have it. And for the record, it belongs to every woman in this city. You're only leading the process." She exclaimed with indignation.

I sat back and took a deep breath, thinking about her words. "I suppose that's true, but how can I lead the process if you throw boulders in my way?"

Margaret's gaze shifted from the table to my eyes. "You have a point. How about we call a truce, and I promise not to yap anymore."

I nodded. I'd no desire to argue, but I didn't completely trust her apology and would watch Margaret closely until things with the Governor were tied up in a neat bow.

Ina cleared her throat.

"What is it, Ina?" I asked.

"Now that you settled that, how about you tell us a little more about this Dr. Kahn at the Clinic. He sounds interesting, and I don't mean medically."

"Ina, I invited you here to help with my grant problem, not to fix my romantic life. Please stick to the subject." I scolded gently.

Margaret cocked her head to one side, for once looking relieved to have the spotlight taken off her. "Is he your next Prince Charming?"

They both giggled, tittering loudly enough to annoy the women sitting at the table beside us. One was wearing a black felt hat embellished with aqua and crimson peacock feathers. The other, an emerald green that matched the velvet piping on her tweed suit. Their feathers were so long they crisscrossed when they turned to us, knocking both hats askew.

"Oh please, you two." My face flushed, more amused by the battle of the feathers than my friends' curiosity.

Sitting in our plush satin chairs, we watched as the waiter returned to pour tea and arrange a stunning three-tiered sandwich tray of intricate delicacies. On the lowest tray were assorted sandwiches, their crusts removed—egg salad, cucumbers and watercress, and salmon. The middle tier held warm scones wrapped in starched white napkins, their buttery aroma filling the air. Finally, the top level was decorated with dainty confections—tiny orange tarts, slices of Battenberg cake with its signature strawberry and lemon square checkerboard design, and assorted chocolates.

Ina's eyes popped. "Do rich people eat this way every day?"

Margaret and I laughed, enjoying her delight.

"Perhaps the Queen," Margaret replied, striking a haughty profile.

"Ina, there are a few etiquette rules to keep in mind. Tea begins with the savory on the bottom, and we work our way up to the sweets together," I said. "Just like a three-course meal."

Margaret added. "Then there are the Queen's tea rules. Never pick up your saucer, and no pinkies sticking out. The handle always stays pointed to the right."

Ina smiled, starstruck, her eyes agog. "It's too fine to disturb. Thank you so much for inviting me."

"I don't know about you, but I'm hungry," Margaret said, carefully selecting a salmon finger sandwich with silver tongs, then taking a bite. "These days, I'm hungry all the time." She held her un-corseted front.

I ate the salmon as well. "Delicious. I love the creme fraiche. So decadent."

"Hannah, are you attracted to Dr. Kahn?" Ina persisted.

"I can't believe you remembered his name, especially with all of this lovely food sitting in front of you." I laughed, pointing at the trays. "To put the topic to rest, I'm not sure. Right now, my top concern is the grant and finalizing the paperwork."

"What's keeping you from returning to Mount Sinai?" Margaret asked.

I tsked. "Two things. I was insulted by their knee-jerk reaction, firing me for damaging their reputation rather than coming to my defense. Losing my job was crushing. A week later, when they learned about the grant, Dr. Lehr met me for lunch prepared with a full apology. He's the reason I may still have a job there. I'll find out soon enough." I sighed, recalling. "Earlier this week, I sent one of my patients up that way—a test of their commitment. They've treated her like a Russian princess and restored my hospital privileges, at least temporarily."

Margaret considered my remark. "What would happen if this Dr. Lehr left? Would they keep their promise?"

She had a point. "Perhaps not. I'll make sure we have an ironclad agreement before I present any plan in Albany."

Ina asked, "What's the second reason?"

I caught her eyes, appreciating her help keeping the conversation on track. "I also just learned they don't admit Eastern European Jews to their medical school. It's disgraceful! I had no idea when I worked there." I set my sandwich down, my annoyance creeping back. "Now that I shared the options, what do you think I should do?"

Margaret dabbed her lips with her napkin. "Hannah, how should I know? Ask me anything about suffragettes, and I can give you an answer, but not hospitals. What I do know is that you're forgetting everything you've learned. Take off your boxing gloves, for cryin' out loud, and give them a real fight!"

"What are you talking about?" I squinted at her, growing more annoyed by the second.

"Think about Mrs. Garrett and Mrs. Thomas. You wouldn't be a doctor today if not for them using their wealth to force a change at Johns Hopkins. Getting women into the medical school took guts. You've got lots of clout now that you're holding the purse strings. Start using it!"

I chewed my tea sandwich, contemplating Margaret's words, watching my friends chatter about the delicious food, artwork, and finally, the subject they loved the most, the Suffragist Movement.

"I can taste success. We're not far away." Margaret claimed.

We stuffed ourselves silly. I handed several bills to the waiter. "Please prepare a pastry box from the tray."

When he returned, I placed the box in Ina's eager hands. "To share with your family."

Ina beamed. "They'll be thrilled!"

"Ina, there's one thing I didn't mention," I said. "It's part of the reason I invited you today. You're going places, and I'd like to help you get there."

Chapter Thirty-Nine

I prepared a quick cup of tea and dressed in my warmest outerwear. It was five freezing blocks to East Broadway, the location of the Jewish Maternity Hospital. The day before at the Clinic, Ben Kahn invited me to see the building site before the groundbreaking and discuss some of the building details over lunch.

The sidewalk was coated with slippery patches of ice. I stepped cautiously, trudging down Clinton Street to East Broadway. Perusing the neighborhood, I noticed most of the old tenements hadn't changed, and I knew they were still crammed with large families. It wasn't only Jews. Italians, Poles, and other Eastern European refugees entered the ports in droves each month. As one family vacated a tenement apartment, another replaced them, anxious to get their new start. The cycle hadn't changed since before Tillie moved to the tenements in the 1880s. The immigrants' needs were dire, their health just one among many. The schools and Settlement Houses were painfully under-resourced, everyone trying to learn English and find employment. How could I justify placing the grant uptown at Mount Sinai when there was so much struggle down here?

I spotted his brown scarf whipping about in the distance like a flag in the cold breeze. Ben waved, his delight sending off sparks a block away. A thrill danced through me, one I hadn't felt in a long time. Something powerful drew me to him. Was it our shared profession? His lack of pretense, his intelligence, or those emotionally transparent eyes?

He approached, taking deep strides. "Good morning, Hannah. Cold enough for you?"

I nodded, smiling back.

"I love the bite of a nippy morning. It sharpens my senses." His lips twisted mischievously.

I couldn't figure out how to respond, so I kept to our meeting purpose, pointing to the red stakes in the ground. "It looks like they've marked out the building site. Any idea what they knocked down?"

"Something dilapidated to be sure." He reached for my hand. "Step carefully. The ground is full of holes. You best hold onto me."

I threaded my arm tightly through his. His warmth radiated through my coat. I luxuriated in the contact, inhaling his spicy aftershave. I wondered how I hadn't felt an attraction to Ben before when we were both at Mount Sinai. Then I reminded myself that he'd been married at the time. The ring he once wore on his finger would have created distance between us—as it should.

We walked around the staked foundation, then crossed the street to a restaurant. Seated in a warm corner, I removed my coat and settled in.

A waitress approached. "Ready to order?"

"Hot tea," we answered in unison.

The waitress laughed.

I resisted the temptation to flirt with Ben, forcing myself to stay on track, firing questions at him. "Ben, how much will the hospital cost? Have you seen their budget? Where will the money come from?" I stirred honey into my tea.

He appeared amused by my business-like manner. "One question at a time. Everything about this venture is community sponsored. The goal is to complete the hospital on a $100,000 construction budget. The main synagogue, Bialystocker, has already raised half in pledges and cash. There are other shuls involved in the fundraising too, and some have raised as much as $500 from individual wealthy congregants. Poorer families have donated as little as a quarter a week, but it adds up. Everyone wants to own a brick. As you can imagine, raising half before breaking ground is unheard of."

The collective effort by the community was exactly what I hoped to hear.

"That's astonishing. Any chance I can review their plans?"

Ben looked at me eagerly. "How about I arrange a meeting with you and the founder, so you have all your answers? Are we getting the full amount?"

I considered. "I haven't decided. A meeting sounds like the right next step. I need to learn more and see the architectural plans."

Ben cleared his throat. "Why so coy?"

I laughed invitingly, unable to stop myself from flirting. "Will you still be interested in me if I use some of the money elsewhere?" I was surprised by my confidence.

"Oh, you think that's what it's all about, eh?" Ben answered with a broad smile. "I'll have you know when Dr. Boro mentioned you might visit the Clinic before I knew a thing about the grant, I wanted to meet you." He blushed deeply, his cheeks matching his hair. "Am I foolish—showing my cards?"

The swell of infatuation was irresistible. I couldn't keep myself from falling into his web. I hadn't expected unabashed honesty. Ben was so frank about his feelings, so willing to take a risk with heartbreak. "You were a surprise for me too. I barely remembered you from when Tillie was in the hospital years back. Just the red hair." I laughed lightly. "And years later, I was in my own world at Mount Sinai." How had I not noticed him back then? Right now, he was all I could see.

"What do you say, Dr. Isaacson? Should we give courtship a try?" His eyes met mine with such hope and vulnerability I wanted to reach across the table and kiss him.

But I held back, my inner voice warning, *not yet, Hannah. There's too much at stake.* "You didn't answer my question. Would you still feel this way if I didn't use all the grant money downtown?" I asked.

"I'd be surprised and disappointed, but it wouldn't change my question." He pulled his chair away from the table. His sweet smile never left his face. "But, if it makes you feel better, we'll hold off until you've made your final decision. Then we'll be able to meet and get to know one another without the shadow of the grant looming over us."

Chapter Forty

I sat in Healy's Cafe, where we last met, waiting for Dr. Lehr. He strolled in moments after me.

"Young lady, we have to stop meeting like this," he joked as I stood smiling back at him. We shook hands. "I'm delighted you called."

The same waitress we had two weeks earlier approached our table with a coffee pot. "Breakfast with your daughter again this morning?"

Dr. Lehr laughed, amused. "I wish. A colleague. Unfortunately, I only have sons. They'll probably make themselves scarce when I'm a doddering old man, but I love them just the same."

Enjoying the banter, I ordered a small bowl of soup. I knew a full meal would distract me.

Once the waitress left, Dr. Lehr became more serious. "As I said, I was hoping you'd ask to meet again. I'm excited to hear your thoughts." He paused, "and I'm pleased that our shared patient is doing well."

I pulled a folder from my satchel and handed it to Dr. Lehr to review.

He skimmed it quickly, nodding, his eyebrows darting up and down.

I had located a small building near Mount Sinai through Tillie and Abe's real estate connections. It was perfect for expanded maternity and pediatric clinics, an education center for families, and a full-time social worker. The brand-new social work profession was the brainchild of a Columbia University professor, and I wanted to use the best-trained professionals in the city. The social worker would support the patients—interviewing, building access to other non-hospital agencies for housing, food, and jobs. I'd also drafted a dozen or so projects for the Ladies Hospital Auxiliary to undertake once the effort began.

"My word, this is excellent. You haven't overlooked anything except the bottom line. I read that you received quite a fortune." He asked tactfully. "Do you have a total budget for our project?"

I set my cup in the saucer and exhaled, ignoring his last question. Now, the tricky part. "Dr. Lehr, my last breakfast with you completely changed my decision. But I have a few conditions, or this," I pointed to the folder, "can't happen."

He frowned; his previous lightness gone. "You know I have limited control over the hospital."

"I realize that." I treaded carefully. "The first condition concerns the medical school and staff. Correct me if I'm mistaken, but I believe that *is* your responsibility." What if Ben was wrong about the admission policy?

Dr. Lehr nodded, scrutinizing me. "Go on."

"Since we met last, I discovered that there's an unwritten policy of sorts. Is it true the medical school limits admissions to only Jewish students of German heritage? That, as a rule, Eastern European Jews are excluded from admission and medical staff posts? I want to be sure it's not an unfortunate rumor before we continue."

Dr. Lehr squirmed uncomfortably in his seat. "It's complicated."

"Initially, I had no idea until another colleague set me straight." I sat still as a statue. "Honestly, knowing your story, I'm surprised you've allowed it to continue."

Dr. Lehr cleared his throat. "As I just said, it's a complex issue."

Undeterred, I pressed. "I can't make sense of it, and to my way of thinking, it's discrimination of the worst sort. There's nothing more distasteful than a minority group creating its own pecking order." I felt my face burning with discomfort. "I'm ashamed of myself for never having noticed."

Dr. Lehr opened his hands before him. "Let me explain. The practice started in the last century when the original Jewish merchants made their money in New York. Every one of those families was German, and they viewed their own, as you call it, as other German Jews. For the most part, they settled on the Upper East Side near the hospital. They never recognized the others, particularly the Russians, as part of their world."

"But they are, and the policy poses a serious problem for me," I replied. "If you follow the papers, almost every Jewish immigrant landing in New York is from the eastern countries, Russia being only one. Only a handful of German Jews are immigrating these days. So, who exactly does this unwritten rule benefit? Does the hospital only care for German Jews in need? And if they find it in their hearts to extend themselves to treat Eastern European Jews and those individuals later become successful equals, God forbid, what will they do then? Block them from the medical profession like the Germans did to our parents' generation in Europe?" My passion was getting ahead of me. "Not on my, or the taxpayer's, dime."

"Settle down, doctor. Let's talk about this more after I take your condition back to the Medical School Board to discuss." He released a breath. "Is there anything else?"

I closed the folder. "Yes. I'd like an official position as head of this maternity program and one for my secretary, Ina Klein. My plan is to practice obstetrics and eventually train Miss Klein to take over the management of the grant. I'll set her salary commensurate with any man taking on the same duties."

Dr. Lehr sat quietly. "I can make that recommendation to the hospital administration, but I don't have control over hospital employee salaries. That's out of my hands."

Annoyed, I said, "I must disclose that although she's as fair as me, she is Romanian. I hope that's not going to be a problem too."

Dr. Lehr looked at the table. "The restrictions appear quite foolish when it comes down to it." He met my eyes. "I'll take on the bigger admissions issue and discuss the other with administration. You're right; it's time we address it." His thick brows bunched over his nose. "I'll contact you later in the week with reassurances."

I smiled, relieved to have my largest issue addressed, and hoped to shift the conversation to neutral territory with my new friend.

"By the way, you never shared the budget," Dr. Lehr said.

"Yes, I'm still working on that part. And I forgot to mention the final condition. With all the wealth uptown, as a show of good faith, I expect Mount Sinai Hospital to match what I bring to the table from the State." I offered a friendly smile. "It would be Mount Sinai's greatest act of charity in a very long time."

* * *

I walked under the center arch of three tall, matching doors, each topped with a window. Inside, my footsteps echoed as they struck the stone floor. The Orthodox synagogue was far more ornate than my old shul by the farm or the one near the Settlement House. Most were constructed of wood, in lofts or small buildings, and had deteriorated over the years. This building was built to last. Light streamed through the stained-glass windows creating an otherworldly atmosphere, for reaching inward into one's spirituality,

The Bialystoker Synagogue, one of the oldest in southern New York City, was the leading sponsor of the Jewish Maternity Hospital. Tillie, who had read about the shul in the *Jewish Daily Forward,* informed me that the building was previously owned by a Methodist Church, and later purchased by the new Polish Jewish emigrants in the Lower East Side. The congregation had experience raising money for large causes, including the shul's recent restoration, and now the rabbis and their following had ventured into the hospital business to answer the crying need for local medical care.

Rabbi Gerlenter, an older man with a scraggly grey beard, skullcap, and side locks, stood in the sanctuary waiting for me. "Dr. Isaacson?" His voice rebounded off the stone walls and floor.

"Yes. Thank you for meeting with me." I approached, nodding my head in greeting. Although my upbringing was non-observant compared to most Jews in this part of the city, I knew the Orthodox had strict rules for day-to-day life. Physical contact between unrelated men and women was forbidden. "Can we sit and talk?"

"Please follow me." The rabbi said in a thick Polish accent, leading me through a heavy door behind the *bema,* the altar, into his chambers.

We sat at the cleared end of a sturdy table. The other end held a stack of long paper rolls, presumably building plans for the hospital. Although the dark furniture reminded me of Mount Sinai's hospital's board room, heavy with discussions of formal topics, this room was used for the study of the Talmud and Torah as well as meetings with congregants to discuss day-to-day matters, disputes over property, and issues involving family—marriages, births, and deaths. The Orthodox derived their rules of living in modesty and order through the interpretive studies of the holy scripture.

The cumulative effect was powerful, even for a nonobservant Jewish woman like me. I sat quietly, considering the scope of our discussion. If I maneuvered carefully, the outcome could benefit so many.

The rabbi studied me carefully. "And how can I help you today, Doctor?"

I raised my eyes to his, acknowledging his authority. "I have an important proposition, but I'd like to share a little about my background and reason for asking to meet you today."

"Go on," he answered in Yiddish.

Realizing he might not be comfortable with English, I asked, "If you prefer, I know a little Yiddish."

The rabbi smiled, revealing a row of chipped brown teeth. "For a shiksa-looking Jew, you're full of surprises. My English is good enough. Where did you learn Yiddish?"

I proceeded to share a brief version of my life, starting with my earliest days on Papa's farm, growing up in the Lower East Side, my schooling, all the way through my recent ordeal at Blackwell's. "In exchange for the hardship of false imprisonment, the Governor granted a large sum for me to invest in women's medical services. The deadline for my proposal is approaching. They're expecting it in a few weeks."

The rabbi's old eyes gleamed. "You must be a fine *hondler* to have bargained for a large grant."

I laughed. "Actually, I didn't secure it. My friends did. But it's up to me to oversee the funds, putting them into projects that will make a difference for women. We'll discuss the budget later."

"What do you have in mind?" the rabbi asked cautiously, stroking his beard.

I pulled a folder for the Jewish Maternity Hospital from my satchel and set it on the table. "Rabbi, I would like to support the hospital building project. I have enough at my disposal to help in a limited way with construction, but most of the funds would be used for a midwifery school and important new services for women in the Lower East Side, such as mother and infant nutrition and home safety." I opened the folder and pulled a detailed list of the proposal I'd drafted, handing it to him.

He rested wire spectacles on his thin nose and reviewed the document. "Yes, I see. Interesting." His eyes scanned down the page. Finally, he set the papers on the table and folded his hands across his chest. He glanced from the document to me. "What do you expect in return?"

I tapped my fingers lightly at the edge of the table. "My greatest concern would be if your hospital building construction goes over budget, as most do, I will not permit you to tap into the grant portion set aside for education and health care programs. Those programs are central to the project. So, I request a seat on your hospital Board to safeguard appropriation of the grant."

The rabbi studied the tabletop a few moments, then lifted his penetrating eyes to mine. "That's not possible. We will not allow women on our Board. However, you'll be pleased to know that we've considered medical matters by assigning two seats to male physicians."

A thread of irritation laced into my voice. "Rabbi, with all due respect, you must realize that an all-male Board can not properly make decisions on behalf of an all-female hospital, even with male physicians assuming seats."

The rabbi pinched his lips, squinting his distrustful eyes. "What are your other conditions?"

I sat back in the oak chair, finding it impossible to get comfortable. Giving money away wasn't going to be easy. "I have two other conditions. First, I'd like to join the medical staff."

His face relaxed. "That should not be a problem. And?"

I watched him closely, knowing this last requirement would be a problem for him. "The hospital cares for any pregnant woman in need, no matter her race or religion."

The rabbi sprung from his seat, hands still gripping the edge of the table, and stormed, "Absolutely not. We'll never let goyim in! They chased us out of our homes. We left our families behind in their graves because of those barbarians." He caught his breath, lowering himself into his chair. "Besides, the Sisterhood is only raising funds for members of the congregation and newcomers from Poland. The Christians already have their own hospitals." He waved his hands in the air. "All those saints' names."

I sat as tall as I could stretch and nodded. "I understand that it's a sensitive issue. But Rabbi, the grant must be applied without regard to religion or race. The money comes from New York taxpayers. So, the condition is not negotiable."

The rabbi sank deeper in his chair, grinding his teeth. "For a little woman, you have a lot of chutzpah."

It wasn't the first time I'd been underestimated. Pleased to feel the balance tip in my favor, I took a deep breath before attempting to smooth things over. I came prepared for his objection. "Rabbi, you certainly know Deuteronomy 26 far better than I, *how* we are to give to the foreigner as well as to our own people in need. In my synagogue growing up, my rabbi taught us when the Almighty was helping the Jewish people escape bondage in Egypt, he was also showing us that the wonder of human kindness can happen anywhere and at any time. This is such a case of kindness for the other downtrodden."

He sat stunned, wide-eyed, staring at me.

"Rabbi, think about how many women will benefit. It's a tremendous mitzvah to connect open-hearted charity with your shul. Besides, as a practical matter, you know full well this kind of money won't come our way again."

He nodded reluctantly. "You're a sly one. I'll speak to the temple elders. Can we meet again next week, and I'll let you know our decision?"

"Yes, but I'll need a final answer at that time. As I said, the deadline is drawing near."

Chapter Forty-One

The next two weeks slipped by. Meetings with Dr. Lehr and Rabbi Gerlenter peppered my date book. Back and forth, we reworked the proposals, debating the fine points, reneging, making concessions as we hammered out the details, finally securing signed agreements. I barely had enough time to finish the grant paperwork on schedule. Neither man knew the other existed, both assuming they might be the sole recipient of the grant. I'd planned it that way, not sharing their totals, but splitting the grant roughly in half, not wanting to complicate matters further. Both were determined men who would be angling for the full amount. I thought it wise not to share the budget and to let each assume he already had the total.

Although Ben and I were not socializing, we constantly circled each other at the Clinic, finding reasons to discuss our patients, the Jewish Maternity Hospital, seeking every opportunity to get close. I found his calm presence intoxicating and relished the moments I was near him. Although I remained at a comfortable arm's length, he came to me every night in my dreams, holding me in his arms, professing his love.

In due course, Dr. Lehr agreed to most of my terms, including changing the admissions "unwritten" standards to one of Jewish equality. He never elaborated on how much political blood was let for that concession, but life in New York City had changed considerably since the mid-1800s when the Seligmans and their crowd ruled. Presently, the city's eastern Jews were gaining visibility, making a fortune in textiles and garments. They were the hospital benefactors of the future. The administrators were no fools and

303

wanted to keep the new rich in their good graces.

"What about the other conditions?" I asked pointedly.

He cleared his throat. "We've already granted temporary privileges contingent on your ongoing excellent performance. They will be elevated to full privileges within six months. You will also be given a title for the grant oversight."

Although still not what I'd requested, I could live with that compromise. "And my assistant, Ina Klein?"

Dr. Lehr blinked his eyes, appearing unsure how to craft his message. "Your request is unusual. As a matter of fact, the first we've had of the sort. The fundamental problem is that she has not completed high school, and there's a limit to her pay scale without the certificate."

Annoyed, I answered. "This is the dilemma talented immigrants face. She's singlehandedly supporting her family and has just mastered the language. How do you expect her to also attend school?"

Dr. Lehr looked into my eyes. "I'll tell you what. We'll give her the title and a modest raise for the time being. Once she fulfills the requirements, we'll adjust her wage. But she must take the test within a year." He raised his brows. "Can you live with that?"

I sighed. "I suppose. I find it discouraging to think about how many generations it will take to assimilate."

Dr. Lehr nodded in understanding. Attempting to reassure me. "Dr. Isaacson, you're simply going to have to trust the hospital. And besides, I promise to back you up."

Trust was difficult for me. It would also take years if ever, to repair my ability to place faith in strangers. I sighed deeply. "I understand." It would have to suffice for now.

* * *

Rabbi Gerlenter posed a unique challenge. His objections stemmed from his interpretation of the Talmud and Torah, ancient rules involving proximity and authority of men over women in business matters. He remained steadfast on the issue of Board seats.

Immensely irritated by the hurdles Rabbi created, I considered new negotiating strategies. In my sleep, dreams of hospitals and rabbis squeezed out nightmares of the Warden, sending her to the depths of Hell, where she belonged. The morning of my final negotiation with Rabbi Gerlenter, I awoke with a fresh idea.

We hashed it out in his chamber. "Rabbi, I'm comfortable with Dr. Boro on the Board for now. But we need a plan if he steps down—for any reason."

He grunted.

"I would like to select Dr. Boro's replacement, of course, with another male physician. I will choose him with an eye for safeguarding the spirit of the grant."

He rocked his upper body, finally answering in a raspy voice. "Perhaps that will take us through this impasse."

"And," I interjected, "We establish a separate committee of women to oversee the grant projects—half from the shul and the others from the community.

After a pause, the rabbi stood. "I agree in principle but insist the Sisterhood of the shul select the women for the committee, all of them."

An alarm went off in my head. Was he trying to form a puppet committee? We were so close to an agreement. How could I keep his trust while protecting the funds?

"I have a thought, Rabbi," I said softly. "Since I am bringing half of the money to the table, could we both interview each candidate the Sisterhood recommends, then meet to discuss their qualifications? If we both agree, the woman is accepted. If not, they recommend more prospects."

He stared at me.

I couldn't read his expression but knew he needed to believe he'd out-maneuvered me. Just like Dr. Adams in Baltimore, all over again.

He bowed his head. "It's a deal. Young lady, you're a shrewd negotiator."

"Thank you. Now I need to convince the Governor."

"Godspeed," he said as I walked from the synagogue.

* * *

It was such a vast sum of money that I was deeply concerned Governor Hughes wouldn't approve anything I presented. Not only must the grant be well-crafted and thorough but represent the health needs of all women in New York City. I knew in my belly, with Bellevue at my heels, that I'd have to fight hard for my plan.

Selecting two Jewish hospitals was daring. Hughes, a devout Baptist, had no first-hand knowledge of the injustices abroad driving families to our shores. Besides, there was a growing outcry in the city against the number of immigrants pouring in. I worried he might bend to the conservatives who demanded the ports be shut. It dominated the newspaper headlines: *Two Thousand a Day! Who will Pay?* The cost of public services was accelerating at an alarming rate and many established New Yorkers blamed the rise in taxes, disease, and crime on the immigrants—typhus on the Irish, tuberculosis on the Jews.

Although I wholeheartedly supported Margaret's mission to overturn Comstock and legalize blocking devices, I chose to concentrate on the issue of untrained midwives, hoping in the short term, it would reduce the casualties from abortions in unskilled hands. Almost everyone in the city was accustomed to midwives delivering babies and I would keep the discussion with the Governor on childbirth, knowing that women who received the unspoken other service would naturally benefit from the training. In the end, that kept my nose clean and met my larger goal, protecting women.

Governor Hughes was a stalwart Republican and had taken an unusual stand on child labor, protecting children in the factories. It was impossible to predict his stance on other social issues. I must make a compelling case that every dollar would be spent on behalf of all women, no matter their religion or race. So, when I wrote that portion of the grant, I elaborated on the extreme pockets of need across all ethnic populations and how the grant would be spread among them.

In the meanwhile, Dr. Holloway was needling me with a steady stream of correspondence outlining Bellevue's construction plans, schedule, and when they'd draw upon funds. His arrogance fueled my determination. I would wage a fight he'd never forget for the women of New York. Gargoyles be damned!

* * *

With limited access to newspapers at Blackwell's, I'd completely missed out on the drama surrounding the vicious Hughes-Hearst gubernatorial election. In prepping me for my meeting, Margaret couldn't wait to fill me in, of course, colored with her personal slant. "If that swine, Hearst, had won New York, I'd be living in Pennsylvania now. He used his newspapers to spread filthy slander every opportunity he had. Governor Hughes may not be perfect, but at least he's got character."

The two of us had met again for tea, and true to form, Margaret got ahead of herself. "I simply can't wait to have the Governor's ear. Do you think we can manage some time to discuss the Comstock Laws?"

I'd been dreading this moment. "Margaret, you know I wouldn't have a meeting in Albany if not for you." I began nervously adjusting my gloves. "But I don't think you should attend."

Her face reddened as if I'd slapped her cheek. "Why on earth would you leave me behind? You said it. You wouldn't have this opportunity if not for me."

"That's right, Margaret. You had the upper hand with Governor Higgins because he knew his son was guilty. But Governor Hughes has a clean slate. I'm worried if we approach him the wrong way, he might send us packing. This is our big chance to have a stake in the future. Who wants to go back to the dark ages? As I told you, Bellevue already expects the full grant for their construction."

She dropped back in her chair, silent, then met my eyes. "He'd better not. I'll raise Hell and give the muckrakers something to write about if he tries anything slippery."

I was amused at how quickly she switched her opinion of Hearst as it suited her cause. "I know you will. I couldn't ask for a more loyal friend. But I'm in knots over the meeting and want to use a soft touch, win him over with the merits of this plan."

She eyed me ruefully. "But I've been the brains behind your strategy."

I scoffed. "Margaret, you were the first to admit you knew little about the hospital business. Besides, it's too long a trip to take exactly when your baby's due. What are you so worried about missing?"

She drew her lips tightly together, pouting. "I need the introduction. We have bigger fish to fry in this state! All these unplanned, unwanted children—every day!"

I knew then that I was right. She would not contain herself. I sat quietly, watching her relax, her face melting. Relieved to see her calm down, I continued, "Margaret, I'm proposing we attach a midwifery program to the Maternity Hospital. That will help reduce inept midwives performing abortions. I promise once I get his commitment, I'll go to the mats with you over Comstock. I wholeheartedly agree the time is long overdue for women to have a voice in planning their families. But this first meeting isn't the right time."

A sly smile crept across her lips. "I'll hold you to it, Hannah. You know I will."

Chapter Forty-Two

Mrs. Garrett, Tillie, and I met on the station platform in Grand Central Station. At the advice of her physician, Mrs. Thomas had remained at home in Baltimore, feeling under the weather, afraid of catching pneumonia.

The winter would not let up. Even though it was March, snow fell as if it were late January. Albany was, at best, a six-hour train ride north of the city. The ride was long, a half-day following the Hudson River north, through the valley on the eastern slope of the Catskill Mountain range, ominously nicknamed the snow belt.

Tightening our scarves around our necks, we stood in a knot, shielding ourselves from the cold wind blowing across the open terminal. Behind us, light poured onto the station platform through the tall windows built high along the outer walls, but the bright light did little to heat the open area. A chestnut vendor warmed his hands over toasting nuts, their sweet aroma filling the air. Nearby a paperboy, barely more than ten, was hawking the morning news. "Read all about it…."

It was crucial that Mrs. Garrett and Tillie accompany me. Both had met with Governor Higgins in December and were witnesses to his promises. Sadly, Higgins had passed away weeks after leaving office, and I couldn't shake my concern that Governor Hughes would refuse to honor the grant. According to Dr. Holloway, the grant was already promised to Bellevue. I prayed he wasn't right.

Mrs. Garrett was my ace, the only one of us who knew both governors socially. Although she was a steady, sharp negotiator, what truly set her apart was her ability to bridge the social gap. Those years of society balls and vacationing on steamers with one another's families forged an inside bond of trust that Tillie and I could never approach. I was confident my decision to leave Margaret behind was correct. I would have been up nights worrying about her unpredictability and tendency to veer off track.

Tillie hugged herself tightly, hopping up and down. "I wish the train would get here. I can feel the cold coming off the pavement right up my skirt."

I laced my arm under Mrs. Garrett's, helping to steady her. Age was catching up. She never went anywhere without her cane and was often out of breath.

"Thank you again for coming with us. I hope it's not too much of a strain. It will be just a few minutes before the train pulls in. The marquee says it's on time."

She waved my words into the air. "I wouldn't have missed it for the world. At my age, I grab all the excitement I can get."

Right on schedule, the train, barely visible down the tracks, blew its horn as it moved slowly into the station. The engine was coated in icicles and snow, a life-sized Lionel holiday window display.

Mrs. Garrett pointed at the dusting of snow on the train cars. "Oh dear, it's started falling already. I hope they've kept the tracks cleared."

I felt a twinge of panic, regretting I hadn't pushed harder to leave New York a day or two earlier. A travel delay could jeopardize everything. A heavy snowstorm might leave us stranded midway to Albany for days. What if the mountain snow worsened and we missed our appointment? Would the Governor use that as an excuse to refuse the grant? But Tillie and Mrs. Garrett insisted on leaving this morning, calling me a worry-wart.

We boarded the first-class section, settling into our seats. The train moved slowly at first, then picked up speed as it traveled away from the congested city, the rhythmic rocking easing me, my eyes already heavy. It had been so long since I'd been away from the strident city noise and commotion. The wooded countryside, quaint farmhouses with cows grazing in their snow-patched pastures, flickered past the window. The chugging of the train was the only sound for miles.

I sunk into the soft fabric covering the heavily cushioned first-class benches, drawing the matching curtains closed. Even the chatter between Tillie and Mrs. Garrett couldn't keep me awake. I'd been working every night until the early morning hours. Drifting, now more tired than worried, I closed my eyes for a few moments of rest, knowing I must be fresh to make the presentation come alive.

I felt a tapping on my shoulder. The train slowed as we pulled into a station. I peeked through the drapes and saw the Poughkeepsie station sign.

Tillie leaned over me. "Hannah, you've been sleeping for hours. How about we head into the dining room for lunch? They'll stop serving soon."

I rubbed my eyes. I could have slept all day. "How's the weather? Any more snow?"

"So far, so good." Mrs. Garrett answered. "But all this excitement has given me quite an appetite."

I rolled my shoulders back in a deep stretch. "I'll meet you both in the dining car. I'm going to refresh in the lady's restroom."

Moments later, standing in the dining car entryway, I marveled at my dear friend and sister, both extraordinary women, chatting away as if they'd known each other all their lives. Raised under opposite life circumstances, Mrs. Garrett with great wealth, while Tillie was a success story from the Lower East Side. Their loyalty, together with their dedication to the disadvantaged, had forged an unshakable bond. I took strength from their enthusiasm for our mission, pushing away the anxiety that had bedeviled me ever since I learned that the Governor might not be inclined to honor the grant.

The next hour was spent enjoying a splendid lunch and postcard-worthy view from our table in the narrow car. It had been years since I'd traveled by train. The menu was extensive, matching selections with any reputable city restaurant, everything from sandwiches to roasted meats and fish. "I think I'll order something hot to warm up," I said, perusing it.

Tillie glanced at the wall clock. "What do you say we order wine? By the time we arrive in Albany, it may be late for a big dinner."

Mrs. Garrett agreed. "Grand idea! You're right; it's almost one-thirty."

I'd never known an occasion when Mrs. Garrett didn't welcome fine food and drink.

The waiter appeared moments later with a cold bottle of Rosé, and we placed our order.

Halfway through my chowder, I asked Mrs. Garrett, "Any suggestions for tomorrow? Have you ever spoken to Governor Hughes alone?"

Mrs. Garrett finished chewing her veal and studied me thoughtfully. "Yes, I have. He's a shy, polite man, blushes easily around women. When you discuss medical matters, avoid naming female parts. Just use broad terms. He's smart enough to get the picture." She took a bite of her buttered Parker House roll.

Again, I was right about leaving Margaret home. She threw around anatomical terms, medical, and slang with ease, as if they were part of a normal everyday vocabulary.

I shared my nagging concern. "I'm worried the Governor will send us on our way because I picked Mount Sinai and the Jewish Maternity Hospital instead of Bellevue. After all, Bellevue is the city's largest public hospital."

Tillie chimed in. "It's their fault, Hannah. The city leaders let Bellevue decay, and now it's as spine-chilling as Blackwell's. Besides, he's had the proposal for two weeks, and if he wasn't taking it seriously, he would have cancelled our meeting."

Mrs. Garrett's brows furrowed. "Bellevue has become that dilapidated? Shame on the city."

Mrs. Garrett lifted her goblet in a silent toast. "Hannah dear, your instincts are excellent. Relax and be yourself. He'll see your passion and know you won't waste a cent of taxpayer money. Trust me, he has much more serious issues to attend."

Tillie nodded. "I read 1907 will break all records for immigration. Thousands of people are entering Ellis Island every month. The island's hospital is always packed." She pointed to my satchel. "These programs will take a load off the Governor."

Mrs. Garrett cleared her throat, sipping from her water glass. "My Lord, where will everyone live and find jobs? And their children will need schools. The Governor has an impossible task ahead of him."

I nodded my head, brows knit, deep in thought. "That's over seven hundred thousand a year! Obviously, not all stay in the city, but it's staggering, and too many arrive physically vulnerable and poor."

Mrs. Garrett set her fork down. "My point exactly. This project is a drop in the bucket compared to his other concerns. He'll be happy to have you take childbirth off his plate."

My shoulders relaxed.

"Oh dear," Tillie pointed at the puffy snowflakes falling from the sky. "I hope we're not heading into a storm."

The three of us picked at our dessert while the train trudged through the snow squall. I knew my instinct to leave early was right, but Tillie and Mrs. Garrett told me my reasons were rubbish, coming from my nerves. They seemed to forget that I was in for the fight of my life and could have done without the weather concerns.

Under better circumstances, I would have relished the opportunity to find a small cozy hotel in Albany with a roaring fire and luxuriate in the beautiful winter scenery, crafting my strategy. My thoughts were finally set adrift as we sat in the dining car, enjoying the gentle rocking of the train and each other's company.

Since leaving the city, we had traveled through small towns with original native names, Ramapo, Ossining, Croton, Mamaroneck, given to them by tribes of people, more alike than different, who were driven out in a few hundred years. I mused, is that what we're witnessing in Europe? So many Jews, every day, escaping harsh treatment in the homes where they've lived for generations. Imagine how powerful they'd be if they stood together.

A strong jolt. My goblet flew off the table, splashing wine on my dress. "Oh, no! What now?"

Passengers in the dining car scrambled, straightening their plates, collecting their purses, wraps, and other items from the floor. The wait staff swept through the car handing out extra table napkins, apologizing for the disruption, running to the kitchen to retrieve new wine bottles, drinks, and aperitifs.

A deep voice shouted from the front of the dining car. An overweight man wearing the tightest waistcoat I'd ever seen, its buttons straining to keep the fabric closed about him, shouted. "What's going on? I demand an answer."

The waitstaff shrugged sheepishly. We waited, watching the snow fall around us. After fifteen minutes, there was still no answer.

The impatient man, his face beet red with anger, stood abruptly. "No one knows anything around here. I'm going to find out what the hell happened." He disappeared through the connecting doorway, storming off in the direction of the engine car.

We waited for his return. Moments crawled by.

Finally, Mrs. Garrett broke the silence. "I've learned over the years to enjoy the splendor before me before it is gone. Life passes far too fast." She pointed to the wine. "I suggest we enjoy this lovely bottle while we wait for news and thank our lucky stars we still have heat."

Tillie agreed. "You're right. We'll find out soon enough."

How could they stay so calm? It was all I could do was sit and wait, praying the snow would stop. I began picking at my nails.

"Stop that, Hannah. You'll make yourself bleed," Tillie whispered in my ear.

I continued fretting, watching the snow fall heavier by the second, feeling a growing dread.

Moments later, a young conductor, barely more than a boy, passed through the dining car. I signaled to him. "Sir, any news about the delay? And the weather ahead? Do you expect the train to arrive in Albany this evening?"

We held our breaths.

The conductor straightened the lid of his cap, lifting his beardless chin with an air of authority. "From time to time, a cow wanders from the pasture and gets too close to the train. It seems the engineer couldn't stop in time. Poor beast."

We imagined the carnage. Dead animals were a common sight on New

York's streets. But the thought of an animal struck by a train was a gruesome picture, indeed.

The conductor steadied himself on the back of my seat. "The tracks have been cleared, and we should resume our trip momentarily. But we hear the storm is coming in strong from the south. Our engineer plans to pick up speed and outrun it, so hold onto your hats."

Chapter Forty-Three

"One can truly appreciate the magnificence of these mansions when they stand alone, without the city crowding them in," Mrs. Garrett remarked as we stood in the freshly cleared driveway. "This feels more like Baltimore."

The Governor's mansion was indeed breathtaking, adorned with a pyramid-roofed tower, a flow of turrets, curves, and finished with a simple wrap-around porch—formal, yet familiar. Although constructed from the ordinary red brick indigenous to the region, the ornate architecture captured the Italian Renaissance style. Cleverly, the architect finished the job by painting the trim white, offsetting the majesty of the tower, lending a countrified appearance characteristic of the many farming communities scattered throughout upstate New York.

"I can't imagine what it cost to furnish a home this size," said Tillie, always the practical one.

"A fortune!" Mrs. Garrett laughed loudly. The mood shifted from Tillie and my star-struck reactions to one of an enjoyable late winter outing.

The large front double doors opened, and two dark-skinned footmen wearing formal matching suits with overcoats appeared at the entranceway. "Name and business, please?" the taller of the two asked in an official voice, a puff of steam exiting his mouth.

Mrs. Garrett spoke first. "Please tell the Governor that Mrs. Garrett and her associates have arrived for our ten o'clock appointment. May we come in from the cold?"

The shorter servant directed us into the mansion. "Of course, madams.

Please enter and wait in the foyer."

The three of us stood, unsure what to do, as the men disappeared. Moments passed, our coats and boots dripping, forming puddles on the floor. I spotted a chair in the adjacent hallway. "Mrs. Garrett, come with me." Holding the crook of her arm, I led her to the chair. "Why don't you rest while we wait? You'll be more comfortable." I helped seat her in the armchair and handed the newspaper on the adjacent credenza to her.

Mrs. Garrett, flustered, whispered loudly, "Thank you, dear. I expected a much grander greeting. My family's known his for years. What in tarnation is wrong with this generation? Have they completely forgotten their manners?"

I barely heard her as I read the headline at the bottom of the front page. "Ladies, will you look at this!" I turned the paper around to show them the story. A smile crawled across my face. "Finland passed the women's right to vote, the first country in Europe to ratify."

Tillie clapped her hand enthusiastically. "Stupendous! It's the beginning of a new day for women around the world!"

"We must not be far behind," echoed Mrs. Garrett, bolstered by the good news.

Although the glory of Finland's accomplishment filled me with optimism and had successfully distracted Mrs. Garrett, I was acutely aware of the minutes ticking by. I wondered if the Governor was home. And would Mrs. Garrett make a scene if he wasn't? I pulled Tillie aside. "What will we do if he isn't here? I hadn't considered the possibility."

Tillie shot me an anxious glance. "I don't know. Let's ask when the men return."

We walked from the foyer into the hallway to distract Mrs. Garrett. "Are you comfortable, Mrs. Garrett? Tillie asked.

"Yes, thank you. What would I do without you girls? Where is everyone?"

Tillie looked patiently in Mrs. Garrett's eyes. "I think we're worrying needlessly. My guess is they're not terribly punctual. Let's give them a few more minutes."

Close to a half hour passed before a petite older woman rushed toward us, out of breath. She wore a tidy grey hounds tooth suit and circular tortoiseshell glasses. The footmen were at her heels. "Mrs. Garrett, I apologize for leaving you waiting such a long time. We have been expecting you. Let us take your coats."

Mrs. Garrett huffed. "I thought you'd forgotten about our engagement with the Governor. We've traveled quite a way to keep this appointment."

I cast a reassuring look at the woman.

"Again, my greatest apology. I'm Miss O'Hara, the Executive Housekeeper. I'm afraid our butler has taken ill, and things are not quite in their usual order this morning."

Visibly relieved after the explanation, Mrs. Garrett nodded. "I see, dear."

For all Mrs. Garrett's fine breeding, I was acutely aware of her tendency to be abrasive when upset. Both Tillie and I relaxed, seeing her slip back into her customary polite self.

"Thank you for understanding," Miss O'Hara said in her thick brogue. "The gentlemen will take your things, and I'll escort you to the Governor's private office. Do you prefer tea or coffee this morning?"

Mrs. Garrett leaned into my ear. "Now, that's more like it."

I hoped Miss O'Hara hadn't heard. If she did, she had the good manners not to show it. Mrs. Garrett, now getting on in her years, was unaware of how loud her whispers were. I prayed she would stay on script.

The Governor's chamber was close to the main entrance, a short walk down a hallway lined with paintings of former governors and shadow boxes of relics acknowledging the tribes who originally inhabited the state. We were led into a large room with seating arranged around an oversized dark wood coffee table. Long plush couches sat on either side with a high-backed chair on each end. All were upholstered in deep reds, blues, and greens with coordinated tapestry drapes. The coffee table held exotic marble and metal ashtrays from the Governor's extensive travels. The history of the building and portraits reminded me of the hospital Board Room, but on a far grander scale. I felt intimidated remembering the poor treatment I received at Mount Sinai. Would the Governor also be dismissive? What on earth had Margaret gotten me into?

Tillie settled in beside me and reached for my hand, speaking in a soft voice. "If only Mama and Papa could see us now, visiting the Governor in the state capital. It's unbelievable, Hannah." Mrs. Garrett sat at my other side.

"Don't be too star-struck, girls," quipped Mrs. Garrett. "They all put their trousers on one leg at a time. Just like the rest of us." A long butler's bar, laden with decanters and cut-glass crystal, extended across the interior wall. She turned, facing the drinks. "Perhaps we can skip the tea and drink with the men today."

From the first, Mrs. Garrett had dispelled every myth I ever had about the gilded upper class. A tall, sturdy woman, she displayed no pretense of daintiness or delicate fashion, always enjoying substantial topics of discussion, as much as any man. Manners were called upon as they suited the occasion. Mrs. Garrett relied heavily on her best friend, Mrs. Thomas, to navigate touchier, finer matters requiring greater discretion. Since her younger years, when she'd challenged Johns Hopkin's admissions requirements, Mrs. Garrett had grown bold, exuding a joyful confidence.

The Governor's morning coat was slung over the back of his desk chair. A moment of relief passed through me; he was home. While we waited, a servant entered the room with a tray of tea, hot scones, and clotted cream. In my excitement that morning, I only had coffee. The aroma of baked butter and sugar made my mouth water. I seized the opportunity to help myself to a scone while reviewing my plan for the umpteenth time. "I was thinking of opening with an introduction to the proposal."

Mrs. Garrett waved her hand to stop me. "No, no, Hannah, out of respect for the Governor's position, you must let him lead. He's had ample time to review the material you've sent and will have questions. And, if he hasn't, you can be sure his secretary will join the meeting fully prepared. Let them take the lead."

Just as she uttered her last word, the office door flew open. Governor Hughes and a second, younger gentleman breezed in. Although the Governor was average in height, his oversized persona filled the room. He stood erect, wearing a dignified buff wool waistcoat. In contrast to his fastidious clothing, he sported an unruly beard, mustache, and brows so full of low-set curls over his piercing blue eyes that he reminded me of an Airedale Terrier.

Governor Hughes smiled broadly, stepping quickly to help Mrs. Garrett, who was struggling to lift herself from the couch. "Thank you for your patience. On behalf of Pop, who sends his best regards, please allow me to welcome you with a hug. It has been far too long since our families have seen each other."

The meeting had barely begun, and he already had Mrs. Garrett eating out of his hand. I'd never seen her blush so deeply. Would she buck up if I needed her help?

Still holding his left arm around Mrs. Garrett's shoulder, he reached to shake Tillie's hand. "You must be Dr. Isaacson."

"No sir, I'm her sister, Mrs. Levine," she said, shaking his hand.

He stepped in front of me, cordially nodding his head. "Then you must be Dr. Isaacson. Welcome to my home."

"It's a pleasure to meet you, Governor," I said, reaching to shake hands.

"You are very young for such a highly accomplished woman." He was full of flattery.

"I'm afraid I'm not quite as young as you imagine." I had a fleeting concern he'd think my short stature meant I was too small for the job.

Gesturing to the couches, he continued, "Allow me to introduce Secretary Brewster. He'll be assisting me with the grant."

We shook hands with Mr. Brewster. When he came to me, I detected a subtle smirk. My blood simmered. I couldn't let this conniver win.

In the meantime, the Governor was making polite conversation with Mrs. Garrett.

"I'm pleased you sidestepped the nasty weather on your way up."

Mrs. Garrett replied, "The train hit a beast, a dairy cow, and the weather chased us the entire way. But we made it." One would think she'd traveled through a blizzard in a horse-drawn cart.

Governor Hughes moved to his chair at the end of the coffee table, the largest in the room. Mr. Brewster opened his meeting folder on the table

320

before him and then walked to his place opposite the Governor.

The Governor continued, "I'm relieved you arrived in time. That's more than I can claim." He pulled a page from the folder. "Now, let's discuss your proposal. I had an opportunity to review the material with my staff this past week and am very impressed. You thoroughly covered all the requirements of the grant. It's abundantly clear you have a deep knowledge of the health issues plaguing our great city."

Finding myself confused by his flattery, I answered cautiously, "Thank you, Governor."

He glanced again at the papers in his hand and then directly at me. "I understand this incredible sum was placed specifically in your care. An apology of sorts from Governor Higgins, God rest his soul, for the unfortunate actions taken against you by the state and prison."

I sat in silence. The Governor was no one's fool.

"I must ask you frankly, what makes you qualified to take on this responsibility? What is your experience? And how did you arrive at this solution?" He sat back, waiting for me to respond.

I straightened my posture, relieved I'd anticipated his first question, well prepared for my presentation. "I'm glad you asked, Governor. As a child of immigrants, I was raised in the Lower East Side in a tiny apartment during my first few years. I've seen practically every aspect of poverty as well as the hard work and determination needed to rise from it." I drew another deep breath, speaking deliberately. "As a physician, I've seen the terrible toll overcrowded tenements and poor nutrition has on the body. Under those unfortunate conditions, diseases like tuberculosis and typhus run wild, spreading like wildfire from one to the next until reaching epidemic proportions."

The Governor nodded vigorously. We all knew about disease. No one, including the rich, was spared.

I paused, thinking how best to phrase my next point. "I spent two months in the Blackwell's Workhouse overseeing their Clinic and have witnessed first-hand the way incarceration destroys the body, leaving craters in the soul. One can hardly blame the prisoners for succumbing to our lowest animal instinct, the fight to survive."

The Governor, rapt, nodded, "Fascinating. Please continue."

"I was lucky. Like me, many children lose their mothers when they are young, but not all have devoted families left behind to raise them. As we all know, there's no substitute for a mother's love." I glanced at Tillie. "As lucky as I was to have my sister, she was but fourteen when our blessed mother passed, barely a child herself."

He nodded slowly, dropping his eyes to his lap. "God bless you both."

"Anyone who knows my sister, Mrs. Levine, could attest to her extraordinary qualities. She was determined to raise me with a mother's love, to help me reach my fullest potential, educationally and otherwise. Most children are forced to depend on the goodwill of churches and synagogues as well as our limited public funds." I paused, letting my point sink in.

"Yes, indeed," he replied softly. "Often put to work in the factories while still small, when they should be better protected and attending school. I plan to address that issue further during my term in office."

Although impressed with his social mindedness, I refused to let myself be distracted by his personal projects. "At the time my parents sailed from Germany in 1866, they were one of a few thousand who came to New York through Castle Garden each year. They all came seeking a better, fairer life for themselves and their families. I am certain you know the details better than me." I glanced at Mr. Brewster, who appeared distracted, examining his notes. "I read we're expecting close to two thousand people *a day* entering New York through Ellis Island. That's three quarter-million in a single year."

"Yes, we have been tracking the numbers each week, wondering how the European countries can mistreat their citizens in such a disgraceful manner." The Governor followed my glance at Mr. Brewster.

Mrs. Garrett commented, "Indeed, they have treated their people abominably."

Taking the conversation back, I continued, "Of course, we know many leave New York for points west, building our prairies, but for those who stay, few have a vocation, an education, or access to doctors. And only a small fraction speaks English." I took a slow breath. "I wish I could solve all their problems with this grant. I can't. What I can give you is my guarantee that every nickel will be used to improve the health of our city's women. I'll ensure they get the care they need and have safe births. We want New York's mothers to be healthy enough to raise strong, worthy citizens."

A wave of excitement ran through me. I'd made my case exactly as I'd planned. The content of the grant was the detail, but my words were my vision. It boiled down to the passion I planned to bring to the project and the assurance I would fight to achieve my goals. *Please, please be enough to persuade him.*

I looked from the Governor to Tillie and then to Mrs. Garrett. Everyone but Mr. Brewster was smiling. Finally, I turned my eyes back to the Governor.

"That's what I hoped to hear." He flipped through his notes. "Will you be hiring others to get these plans up and running?"

"Yes, as a matter of fact, there's a deep well of talent at Mount Sinai ready to support the development downtown of the Jewish Maternity Hospital," I said confidently. "Dr. Lehr, whom I believe you met recently, has agreed to consult on the project."

This time his lips were set in a tight line. "Dr. Isaacson, one issue still troubles me. On the face of it, these taxpayer dollars appear to be channeled to the Jewish population. Have you considered the rest of the city in your plan? I would have expected you to select Bellevue Hospital to capture a large net of New Yorkers."

I opened my folder, once again consulting my notes, trying to control my annoyance. My answer was carefully measured. "Governor Hughes, there is no doubt that for centuries, Bellevue, more than any institute in New York, has steadfastly served the most vulnerable. It's an icon. But the buildings are old, many rat-infested, and in sore need of renovation."

I took a deep breath and continued, driving into the storm. "As you well know, Bellevue's current building project has been erratic, with a highly extravagant and controversial budget. It's likely to take years to sort it out. From the numbers reported in the paper, it would be near impossible to move forward without diverting the entire grant for demolition and rebuilding. Of course, that would defeat the purpose of the funds, improving medical care for women, an accomplishment attainable during your term only if you keep the grant separate from Bellevue's construction costs."

"I see." Governor Hughes shifted his eyes to Mr. Brewster. A silent message passed between them.

Mr. Brewster was not so quick to give up. "Dr. Isaacson, please don't be naïve; Bellevue is the safety net between dying on the street and saving lives. True, the building is in disrepair, but the grant will go a long way in helping modernize it."

I felt my face redden with anger. I thought of poor Yetta, one of those women he described who was refused admission to Bellevue. And they employed doctors such as Roger Holloway, who had a documented history of assaulting women. Besides, the monstrosity of the hospital project had reached epic proportions in overdesign and building expenses. I reached for Tillie's hand, determined more than ever to convince him without dredging up the worst smut. "Perhaps my sister can share a story from her childhood that helps illustrate my point."

Tillie relived the days in 1879, when at fourteen, she and our parents traveled from our farm north of Central Park in a horse and cart, all the way downtown to Bellevue for care. "None of us had ever been there, and the sheer size was overwhelming. We were swept into the confusion, hurried from one department to another, only to wait for hours to be seen. All the while, I needed to help my parents translate their German to English. Some nurses scorned us for our tattered, soiled clothing. What did they expect? We'd ridden for miles through the city dust to get downtown."

Tillie drew a deep breath. "There are parts I wish I could forget. Finally, Mama was given a bed in the ward and prepared for surgery with little explanation about what to expect, certainly no warning of the dangers ahead. Our Mama made it through the operation but developed a terrible, unsightly infection immediately afterward. I remained by her side until she died. I'll never forget those awful days."

I took her hand and squeezed it gently, handing her Mama's torn lace handkerchief.

Glancing at it, we both knew Mama was right there with us in this very room.

The Governor sat silently, his unkempt brows drawn together. "My deepest condolences. I apologize for making you relive your sadness. Just last week, our Reverend discussed empathy in his sermon, 'Walk a Mile in their Shoes.' It must have been heartbreaking for you and your father. For your entire family."

Tillie nodded, wiping off a tear rolling down her cheek.

Mrs. Garrett cleared her throat. "Completely understandable, son. You have an enormous job and can't be expected to fix everything all at once."

He nodded, shifting his attention to his notes. "Perhaps we can set Bellevue aside for the moment. Let's return to the proposal. Dr. Isaacson, if the grant was used as you propose, how will it reach beyond the city's Jewish women?"

I reminded myself, *keep it simple.* "Let's consider the city by north and south. In the north, there are several large, sophisticated hospitals, such as Columbia and Mount Sinai, offering the finest services, rivaling the best hospitals in the world, caring for the wealthy and poor alike. For example, Mount Sinai, where I've worked the past few years, admits whoever seeks services and includes clinics for those unable to pay, funded through philanthropy. I personally know the doctors and staff, and they share my deep commitment."

Mr. Brewster twisted in his chair. Something more was coming.

I continued. "Additionally, under the terms of the grant, they've agreed to create a so-called pathway for complex patients living in southern New York. When necessary, patients requiring more sophisticated care would be sent by ambulance to Mount Sinai. As a matter of fact, we had our first transfer recently."

"Go on," said the Governor, sitting erect, fully engaged, hands clasped on his lap.

I pulled a contract from the folder. "The Jewish Maternity Hospital is responding to a critical situation in the southern city, for *all* immigrant populations settling there. As you well know, there are many immigrants from Italy and Eastern European countries who are not Jewish. It will be a strictly maternity-use hospital, and I've received a signed agreement from their Board members assuring the hospital will admit patients without regard to race or ethnicity." I handed the agreement to Mr. Brewster to review.

He barely scanned the document and handed it back to me.

I added, "The addition of trained midwives and a social worker to help with home deliveries, nutritional counseling, and directing patients to other medical and non-medical services will round out the offerings."

Mr. Brewster scoffed, "Young lady, as I said before, that is precisely what Bellevue provides today."

I'd had enough. "That is not true. A few weeks ago, I called Bellevue requesting a bed for a pregnant woman in critical condition. She was refused. Officials at Bellevue were prepared to leave her to die on the street, so I sent her uptown to Sinai, a private Jewish hospital."

Mr. Brewster proceeded as if he hadn't heard a word. "What about the name?" He asked.

I looked at him. "I don't follow you."

"If you changed it to New York Maternity Hospital, perhaps it wouldn't sound so ... Jewish."

They wouldn't be laboring this issue if the hospitals had Christian names. I'd known the name might cause a problem and thought about asking Rabbi Gerlenter to change it. But he had been so oppositional through the negotiations that I worried he'd have apoplexy if I returned asking for a name change. I had to push back harder.

Everyone sat silently, waiting for my answer.

I breathed evenly, slowing my galloping heart. "That's true, and on the face of it, a name change might make the hospital more inviting for non-Jews. But it would discredit the very community, most of whom are poor, who funded over fifty percent of the construction by donating nickels and dimes. It was originally their project, and they agreed to open the doors to everyone in exchange for further support from this grant." I paused, knowing my anger was accelerating, getting the better of me. "Specifically, non-Jews needing care. Stripping the name of its trusted founders would be considered an enormous insult." *Stop talking, Hannah!* Even Margaret, with her flippant tongue, would never go this far. I looked at Tillie, whose eyes were fixed on her lap.

Mrs. Garrett cut in. "Now, now. I'm sure Mr. Brewster understands your reasoning. How about we get the conversation back on track? Dr. Isaacson has studied women's hospitals all over this country and Europe and has drawn from others' experiences to assemble the finest, most modern programs for care."

Mr. Brewster interrupted smugly, looking directly at the Governor. "She could have found her answers at Bellevue—no need to hunt all over the globe."

Mrs. Garrett drew a slow, loud inhale through her teeth. I knew she was steaming mad—both at the rude interruption and at Mr. Brewster's arrogance. "Is it you, Mr. Brewster, who has an inside connection at Bellevue? With a Dr. Holloway?"

Mr. Brewster, unmoored by her directness, twisted his face into a grimace, his last attempt to hold ground. "The esteemed Holloway family are distant relatives tracing back to the Mayflower."

Mrs. Garrett leaned into my ear whispering, "Probably came over in the ship's hull, in chains."

I stifled my smile.

She then stretched her head high, her chin pointed upward. "Indeed, I understand that is the same Dr. Holloway we expelled from Johns Hopkins for assaulting women. I tried to warn Bellevue when they contacted me, a trusted Hopkins Trustee, for a recommendation. But Bellevue ignored me. Was it because I am a woman? I wonder." She asked, tilting her head to the side, eyes glinting of caution.

The Governor glared at Mr. Brewster. "Why wasn't I informed?"

Mr. Brewster stood, looking at the floor, trembling.

The Governor's anger mounted. "Don't ever, and I mean ever, pull something like this behind my back again. My office will be run by the book!" He paused, "And, set up a meeting with that President of Bellevue right away. Tell him to bring a new building budget, shaving one hundred and fifty thousand off the top."

Mr. Brewster lifted his pitiful eyes at Governor Hughes. "Yes, sir. Please excuse me." He scurried through the door, like the rat he was.

Governor Hughes exhaled deeply. "Please accept my apologies. Bellevue is delusional if they think they'll turn that city hospital into a palace." He then collected himself, facing the three of us. "Dr. Isaacson, is there any other hospital offering this broad range of women's services in New York City? Do you have anything else to add?"

I nodded at Mrs. Garrett, immeasurably grateful for her intervention. "No, sir. Once we are well on our way, I will write about the concept and submit a manuscript to *The Lancet*, one of the most widely read medical journals. A new version of care."

His eyes met mine, and I knew. I'd been tested. He would trust me with my projects. I felt it in my bones. Once again, Mrs. Garrett had come to my rescue.

The Governor cleared his throat loudly. "In order to address any concerns around the 'open doors' as you call it, we will require quarterly reports detailing the patients receiving care through the grant. This includes religions and ethnicities. I will be watching those numbers carefully myself."

I nodded. "Yes, I understand. Seeing these are taxpayer dollars."

The Governor sat quietly for several moments reviewing the top sheet in his folder, checking that all points had been discussed. "Well then, I am proud and pleased to move forward with your grant. You drive a tough bargain and have the right sensibility to get the job done. To effectively work with Albany, you can't take much guff."

A rush of excitement charged from my hair to my toes—the thrill of victory. Remaining in my seat took every ounce of discipline I had. I grabbed Tillie and Mrs. Garrett's hands, squeezing them tightly.

Mrs. Garrett eyed the butler's bar. "Congratulations! Perhaps a celebration is in order?"

"Yes indeed." The Governor nodded at the footman standing by the door.

CHAPTER FORTY-THREE

"Please pour a round of brandy."

Chapter Forty-Four

I t was late in the evening when we returned to Tillie's apartment. I was filled with jubilation, far too excited for sleep. I wrestled with whether it was too late to make telephone calls.

"Oh, Hannah, go ahead! They're all chomping at the bit to hear how things turned out," Tillie laughed gleefully. She picked up a letter on the sideboard. "I wonder who this is from? It looks like a telegraph."

"Open it. Abe must have left it for you before he went to bed."

Tillie's face broke into a grin as she read the telegram aloud. "It's from Margaret." She tore it open and read.

I wanted you to be the first to know of the birth of our precious daughter. Your partner knocked me out cold after I fussed about dragging you home from Albany for my delivery. I suppose you were right about me going. All is well. Looking forward to your visit tomorrow. Margaret

I couldn't wait to see her. She was my biggest supporter, and without Margaret's insistence from the start to secure the grant, there would have been no meeting in Albany, or reinstatement at Mount Sinai. Despite her impulsive nature, she was a true warrior and now had a new infant disciple.

But right then, I wanted to share the news with Ben, eager to hear his reaction, his excited voice. Ben was always in my thoughts, our time together replaying in my mind. Limiting social contact with him the past few weeks, making sure the relationship didn't taint my proposal, had been brutal. I could not deny my attraction, despite my hesitancy to fall in love again, especially so soon after the fiasco with Joseph. Ben's openness and humility, his gentle way with patients, and even his unruly hair drew me in with an irresistible pull.

An older man answered Ben's house telephone. "Hello."

"I'm so sorry to disturb you, sir. My name is Dr. Isaacson. I was hoping Dr. Kahn was awake and had a moment to speak." I answered.

"Tell me your name again. Are you aware of the time, young lady?" he asked in a brusque tone.

"Hannah Isaacson. I'm terribly sorry. If you prefer, I can call back tomorrow." My anticipation quickly deflated.

"Hannah, you say." A pause, "Ah, you're the one he's been pining over. He'll have a fit if I don't call him to the telephone."

Pining? I stifled my rising excitement.

Moments later, I heard his tenor voice pepper me with questions. "Are you all right? Did you make it there? I read there were snowstorms on your way north. I was so worried."

I smiled, my heart pounding with excitement. "I'm better than all right. I have so much to tell you. We had a grand time, and both proposals were approved!" But my joy came from the fact that he'd worried about me, not the grant money.

"Both? You wrote two?"

"Can we meet tomorrow? I want to tell you everything." I held my breath.

A huff. "Did my Pop really say, 'pining'?"

In the background, I could hear his father's teasing laughter.

"That devil, he just had to embarrass me! See what I mean? What I told you about my parents? He's making my life miserable."

Ben slammed down the telephone. The line went dead. I waited. Ten minutes crept by. Certainly, enough time for him to call back. Nothing.

"What did he say?" Tillie asked.

A growing dread crept through me. Was his anger at being teased so uncontrollable that he couldn't get past it and talk to me? Closing my eyes, I could see the red flag waving in front of me, warning me of danger. Was this just another impossible romance? My heart dropped into my stomach as I walked from the foyer into the parlor, slumping into the Queen Anne chair, restlessly shifting to try and find a comfortable spot. "Not this again. I'll never find someone right for me."

"What happened?" she persisted, following at my heels.

I faced Tillie. "He hung up! Can you believe it? What kind of person does that?" My anger grew.

"Hannah, there must be some sort of explanation. Why don't you call him back?"

"And talk to his nasty father again? First Joseph's sister, now I fall for a man who can't handle his anger? Can't handle someone joking about him? What's wrong with me?"

I jumped out of the Queen Anne chair and grabbed my coat and hat. "I don't need this now. I'm taking a walk to shake it off. I've just promised our Governor I'd handle a ridiculous amount of responsibility. I can't be wallowing in self-pity in that horrid chair."

As I charged out the door, I heard Tillie calling, "Wait, Hannah, it's freezing out. Let's talk about it."

I was done talking. I'd no more tolerance for male antics. Why did I always let men pick me? I should be picking them. Maybe then I would find someone better suited. Someone who valued me as I deserved. But my heart plummeted as I thought of letting Ben go. I buttoned my coat as I ran to the steps, thinking wildly, knowing love had seized me in its tortuous grip.

Was he threatened by my success? Was he angry I split the grant money without telling him? My God, couldn't he handle a little razzing from his father? When would I learn to pay attention to the small clues? Roger, with his dangerous duplicity, and Joseph, the narcissist, had both shown me their flaws. In my haste to feel wanted and loved, I'd refused to see the truth. Would I ever get things right with men?

Too impatient to wait for the elevator, I scrambled down the steps, wrapping my scarf tightly, pulling on my gloves, craving a cold slap in the face to snap me out of my mood. I opened the heavy outer door stepping onto the icy pavement, ready to walk off my angst.

The night was still. Plump snowflakes dropped from the heavens, cleaning the sky of its dirt and grime, preparing for a fresh new day. Filling my chest with the bracing air, I stood still, transported to medical school in Baltimore, departing the hospital after a grueling day with Dr. Adams. I recognized the great distance I'd traveled, appreciating the fortitude I'd found within myself to push forward. When all felt lost, I had been buttressed by courageous women, Mrs. Garrett, Mrs. Thomas, Margaret, Tillie, and Ina, all willing to help each other. As for me, I should be counting my blessings, not obsessing over lost romances. I must be adult enough to accept my circumstances.

A faint shout in the distance startled me. "Hannah, wait up!"

I froze, listening to his feet chomping through the snow, first a walk, then a run, sounding like our locomotive that afternoon taking to the open fields. My heart pounded.

I twisted to face him. "You just hung up on me. I thought…"

He grabbed me into his arms. "No, no. My God, Hannah. I'm so proud of you. I couldn't wait another moment. I dropped the telephone and ran out of my house."

I broke, my emotions engulfing me. "I thought…."

He cut off my words. "It's been unbearable waiting. I never believed I'd find my soul again until I met you. I want to be right by your side, helping. If you'll allow me to."

I wiped away icy tears with my glove, reassured. "I could barely wait to call. You were the first person I wanted to tell—about my amazing day."

Ben pulled off his glove, gently lifting my chin, meeting my eyes with breathless intensity. "I want to hear every word. But first, you must know I'm head over heels. I don't want to lose another moment." He leaned down to kiss me, filling my heart.

I knew this time I had it right.

A Note from the Author

The art of historical fiction requires a seamless amalgamation of fact and fiction, so the reader is accurately transported to the time and place of the story. In the interest of clarity, the following character names and personas were built from fact: The Johns Hopkins trustees, Mrs. Garrett and Mrs. Thomson, the New York State governors: Governor Higgins and Governor Hughes, and Mrs. Margaret Sanger in her early adult years of women's advocacy.

The following characters were rooted but fictionalized for the purpose of the novel: Tillie Levine, based on my great-grandmother, Mathilda (Tillie) Loeb, and Judy Simon, loosely based on the unflappable Lillian D. Wald, founder of the Henry Street Settlement house.

The remaining characters were born in my imagination and bear no resemblance to anyone in my past.

To the best of my research, the worlds, political climate, and medicine of Baltimore and New York City were rooted in fact.

The following non-fiction books were both helpful in building the setting and story, but revealed many lesser-known, spellbinding facts:

- **Our Crowd**, Stephen Birmingham
- **The Excellent Doctor Blackwell**, Julia Bond
- **The Pocket, A Hidden History of Women's Lives**, Barbara Burman and Ariane Fennetaux
- **The Bowery, the Strange History of New York's Oldest Street**, Stephen Pau DeVillo
- **Suffrage, Women's Long Battle for the Vote**, Ellen Carol Dubois
- **Victorian and Edwardian Fashion, A Photographic Survey**, Alison

Gernsheim

- **Damnation Island, Poor, Sick, Mad and Criminal in 19th Century New York**, Stacy Horn
- **My Notorious Life** (fiction), Kate Manning
- **From Midwives to Medicine, The Birth of American Gynecology**, Deborah Kuhn McGregor
- **The Doctors Blackwell**, Janice P. Nimura
- **Bellevue, Three Centuries of Medicine and Mayhem at America's Most Storied Hospital**, David Oshinskyospital, DHosHosp
- **When Abortion was a Crime, Women, Medicine, and Law in the United States, 1867-1973**, Leslie J. Reagan
- **The Gospel of Germs, Men, Women, and the Microbe in American Life**, Nancy Tomes
- **The Women's Suffrage Movement**, Sally Roesch Wagner

Acknowledgements

With great humility, I extend my gratitude to those whose love, friendship, and thoughtful feedback helped me turn an idea, and a life-long commitment to women's rights, into a polished work of historical fiction.

Much support came from strangers: research staff in the New York Historical Society, the New York Public Library, the Tenement Museum, and many bookstores where I met knowledgeable women whose names I failed to note at the time but who had an excitement and thirst to stretch beyond my simple request. They helped me find lost addresses on historical maps of the 1800s when many New York City homes were still simple wooden structures. They enlightened me with rare books and magazines of those lost days. Most precious were their family stories of immigration and assimilation in the United States. Stories waiting to be told. They helped me add texture and depth to my setting and characters.

My profound thanks to the medical workers: physicians, physician assistants, and nurses in my family and professional life who helped fact-check and imagine the experience of injury and illness before contemporary medicine - the vaccines, treatments, and medications we now take for granted. My specific appreciation to Drs. Joseph Ramieri, MD ObGyn; John Halperin, MD Neurology; Ben Taylor MD, Surgery, and Steven Papish MD, Oncology. And an endless thank you to my trusty, tireless trio of exceptional daughters: Laura Johnson, PA; Laura Taylor, RN; and Caroline Hodge, PA, who generously shared hours reading, commenting, and exploring plot options.

In the Hands of Women and its prequel, *Threadbare* (due May 2024), would still be dreams in my head and a pile of notes on my desk if not for my husband David's encouragement and the layers of professional writers and readers who helped me hone my craft. Special thanks to Michelle Cameron at the Writer's Circle in New Jersey, my personal writing partners and friends: Ananya Holland and Marlene May, who will stun the writing world with their work in the years ahead, and my Book Club and personal friends: Patti Bleicher, Renee Polay, Peggy Barnett, Carla Errico, Laurie Kalb, Lisa Ozer, Ilene Rosenbaum, Sandy Sachs, Debbie Spicehandler, and Amy Pollak.

Thank you, Harriette Sackler, at Level Best Books, who believed my story should be told and would resonate with a sizable reading audience. In today's publishing world, writers face enormous challenges in bringing their voices to the world. So many wonderful books can't find their way into the market.

The last expression of gratitude is the trickiest to express. I had every reason to relinquish hope in May 2009 when I received an incurable cancer diagnosis. But with the rapid advances in treatment over the past decade, a team of superbly talented physicians, the loving support of my husband, family, and friends, and last, an unshakable belief in the power of hope, I was able to fulfill my life-long dream of writing.

About the Author

A terrifying diagnosis, a genetic defect, and a lifelong fascination with the history of medicine led Jane Rubin to put pen to paper. After an ovarian cancer diagnosis in 2009, Jane, then a healthcare executive, poured her energy into raising research dollars for ovarian cancer and learning more about her familial roots. Her research led her to her great-grandmother, Mathilda (Tillie), who arrived in New York City in 1866, at sixteen married a man twelve years her senior, and later died of 'a woman's disease.' Then the trail ran cold. Jane was left imagining Tillie's life, her fight with terminal disease, and circumstances surrounding her death. With limited facts, she was determined to give Mathilda an exciting fictional life of her own.

Her research of the history of New York City, its ultra-conservative reproductive laws, and the state of medicine during that era has culminated in a suspenseful, fast-paced, two-book historical series. Her engaging characters are confronted with the shifting role of midwives, dangers of pregnancy, the infamous Blackwell's Workhouse, and the perilous road to financial success.

Jane's other publications include an essay memoir, Almost a Princess,

My Life as a Two-Time Cancer Survivor (2009 Next Generation Indie Book Finalist), and multiple articles in the Coping with Cancer periodical. She writes a monthly blog, The Space Between, reflecting on her post-health care career and writing journey. It is available through her website, JaneLoebRubin.com.

Jane lives with her husband, David an attorney, in Northern New Jersey. Between them, they have five adult children and seven precious grandchildren.

SOCIAL MEDIA HANDLES:
   FB: https://www.facebook.com/janeloebrubinauthor
   Instagram: https://www.instagram.com/janeloebrubin
   LinkedIn: Jane Loeb Taylor Rubin, Jane Loeb Taylor Rubin@LoebRubin

AUTHOR WEBSITE:
   https://www.janeloebrubin.com

Also by Jane Loeb Rubin

Almost a Princess, My Life as a Two-Time Cancer Survivor

Printed in the USA
CPSIA information can be obtained
at www.ICGtesting.com
LVHW091041040624
782219LV00004B/55